CAGE

THE NEW BRADFORDS

TIA LOUISE

This book is a work of fiction. Names, characters, places, and incidents are products of the author's imagination or are used fictitiously. Any resemblance to actual events or locales or persons, living or dead, is entirely coincidental.

PLAYLIST

"Wrong" - Waylon Jennings
"I'm Gonna Getcha Good" - Shania Twain
"Feed Jake" - Pirates of the Mississippi
"Constellations" - Jade LeMac
"Me & My Dog" - boygenius, et al.
"Always Been You" - Jessie Murph
"Jealous Guy" - John Lennon
"Magnolia Wind" - Larry Dean, Mia Dixon
"The Hustle" - Van McCoy
"We Are The Champions" - Queen
"Another One Bites the Dust" - Queen

Scan to Listen

THE BRADFORD FAMILY

Arthur Sage Bradford & Lucille (née Knox)

Jack & Allie

Zane & Rachel

Garrett & Liv

Dylan & Logan

Hendrix & Raven

Edward Wells
Sage Bradford

Hayden "Haddy"
Bradford

Gina "Gigi" Bradford

Austin Sinclair
Kimmie Joy Bradford
Knox Bradford

Maverick Murphy

1
___

GINA

"Doesn't the team already have a fundraiser?" My hand is on the back of my award-winning, white standard poodle, and I slide the clippers methodically over his haunch, around the base of his tail, trimming his fur smooth to the skin.

I'm grooming him in the continental style, which is a favorite among judges of the official American Kennel Club dog shows, and I'm at the trickiest part of the process—the matching pom poms on each of his hipbones.

Spanky is an old pro when it comes to all of this. He was bred to be a winner, and so far, he's unbeatable in the "non-sporting group," which is totally inaccurate as Poodles were originally bred to retrieve water fowl.

Still, winning this competition will put him on track for the national dog show in Pennsylvania, where he has a strong chance at landing Best in Show for the first time ever. The thought makes me zippy with excitement.

After years of working with breeders, training champion

dogs, and even judging local shows, it's about time I had a Best in Show winner.

I don't think people think less of Spanky or me because we've never won the coveted top prize, but it would strengthen their opinions.

"They have a family skate night, and the welcome back parade..." My cousin Haddy, who's like a sister to me, leans against the ceramic-tile counter in my grooming studio, counting on her fingers as she watches me work.

We converted the she-shed behind our two-story bungalow in Los Feliz into my workspace after we moved here.

Our third roommate and cousin Maverick didn't care. He's a star hockey player with the LA Champions, and once hockey season begins, we're lucky to see him at all outside the arena.

"None of those are fundraisers," Haddy continues.

I take a break from concentrating on Spanky's butt to put my hand on my hip and straighten my back. Being a champion dog groomer is a lot harder than it looks. It's precise and careful and occasionally back-breaking work.

"Hand me those small scissors, Hads."

Haddy pushes off the wall and goes to my cabinet of supplies to fetch the sharp, surgical-steel grooming scissors.

"They're all community outreach, but the owners want something to raise money for the children's hospital." She hands me the scissors and returns to her spot. "It's great publicity, and it dovetails nicely with their hockey clinic for kids."

Squinting one eye, I look up at her from where I'm bent over, trimming a stray curl. "Sounds like they're getting a little help from a publicity pro."

Haddy grew up a pageant girl and along with her wins

came appearances at every fundraiser in LA. Big or small, she'd be there smiling and waving in an evening gown and tiara.

She earned a *lot* of scholarship money doing it, which she used to pay for her master's degree in aerobiology. People are always so surprised that she can be so pretty and also be a scientist.

Now she's a mom and engaged to Mav's teammate Gavin Knight. She left her pageant days behind, and it looks like now she's get her sights set on team publicist.

By contrast, I am deep in the world of dogs, and the most hockey I do is attending Mav's games every Thursday they're in town.

"Gav asked for my help brainstorming ideas." Her eyes are sparkling, and I can tell she's already got one. "This is where you come into it."

"And I thought you were out here because you missed me."

As an engagement present, Gavin bought the house across the street, and my favorite cousin moved in with him. Still, she's over here almost all the time.

"I do miss you!" She pretends to be defensive, but the truth is, she's in heaven playing house with her new baby girl and her hot hockey fiancé.

I'm planning their Halloween wedding, and I'm contemplating an Alice in Wonderland theme, since they're doing everything backwards.

Haddy has not approved that suggestion.

"I know." I stand, putting a hand on my hip as I pass the scissors back to her. "Tell me how I come into a hockey team's fundraiser. I'm dying to know."

Her smile gets bigger, and she's practically bouncing on her toes. "Hockey Hunks and Hounds!"

My brows rise, and I tilt my head to the side before returning to Spanky's butt. "And that means…"

"It's a calendar featuring members of the team with their dogs… or with foster dogs."

"That's really a cute idea."

"Right?" Her voice hits a note that makes Spanky pull to the side and stamp his feet excitedly.

"Keep it down. I've got to shape his pom poms, and I can't do it if he's jumping around."

"Sorry." She lowers her voice, and I pet Spanky for a few seconds to get him calm again.

"Almost done, buddy." I thread my fingers through his freshly styled top knot.

Haddy exhales a quiet laugh. "He looks like he's wearing a fur coat. I mean, of course he is, but it looks like something you'd buy at a store."

Nodding, I'm pretty proud of my work on this one. "It's the most popular show clip for Poodles, and we're going for the gold this year, aren't we Spanks?"

I'm using my soothing doggy-voice, and he starts stamping again, doing his best to lick my face. His harness is secured to the side of the grooming tub by a short leash.

"Let's finish up now, boy!" I kiss his shaved nose, and he settles down quickly.

I've had Spanky since he was a puppy, and he's well trained. Except for being a notorious towel thief, which I blame on us. We always laughed when he did it as a puppy, so now he thinks it's a game.

He's still a good boy.

"He looks amazing," Haddy says softly. "You're so good at this."

"Years of practice." I lift the clippers off the shelf,

inhaling a calming breath before I start on the most important part. "Give me a minute so I can finish."

She hesitates as I begin. Once I've made the initial pass, she quietly asks, "Do you think you can help us find some good dogs for the calendar?"

"They're all good dogs." My voice is level as I concentrate on the length of the hip pom.

"We can debate that later." She laughs, and I know she's thinking about the foster dog who barfed on her bed anytime she left her door open.

Mav later told me the dog also furiously humped my favorite throw pillow whenever he got the chance. Naturally, I punched his shoulder for not telling me sooner and bought a replacement cover on the spot.

"That poor dog had a nervous condition... and possibly a UTI. It didn't make him bad."

Haddy makes a snorting noise of dissent before continuing. "Anyway, Gav is putting together a list of players. We just need dogs to go with them."

"I'm sure I can help you." Straightening again, I inspect my work. "How does that look?"

Haddy walks around to where I'm standing to study Spanky's behind. She knows all about competitions and judges, and I trust her opinion as much as my own.

She tilts her head to the side, squinting. "I think that one's a little high on the outside. See there?"

Sure enough, the left side extends a bit too far into Spanky's flank. "Yep. Thanks, Hads."

"No problem!" She returns to her spot, and I step forward, ready to fix the line.

"How many do you need?" I'm leaning closer, laser focused.

"Well, Mav is with Spanky and Gav has Patsy..."

Patsy is her cinnamon teacup poodle, whose real name is Princess Petunia. She was our foster dog after the *unfortunate* one, and my cousin fell instantly in love with her—so much that she sat on the floor in her bedroom and cried when we had to give her back.

Then, after a few weeks, the owner returned the pup to us. She said Princess Petunia was as depressed about leaving my cousin as Haddy was about giving her back.

"So they don't have to be hounds?" I pause to glance up at her. "I mean, it's hilarious to think of six-foot-two, two-hundred-pound Gavin Knight holding the smallest dog on the planet, but Peepee is *not* a hound."

Everyone but Haddy calls Princess Petunia "Peepee."

"Is that a deal breaker?" Her brow furrows. "The only player so far with a hound is Owen."

My insides squeeze at the mention of his name.

Owen Stone is the newest member of the Champions, a forward who moved up from the minor leagues at the end of last season.

He's older than most of the other guys, but he still has that killer, hockey-player bod. He also has shaggy dark hair, a square jaw, and blue eyes that make my stomach dip...

Not that I'm looking for a love connection *at all*.

I learned the hard way that Frenchie from the classic, blockbuster movie-musical *Grease* is right: "The only man a girl can depend on is her daddy."

My dad, Garrett Bradford, happens to be the best dad in the whole wide world, and it'll take a lot for me to get back on the romance merry-go-round after Baxter the love-bomber ghosted me and broke my heart. Talk about amoebas on fleas on rats.

Owen Stone might make my insides ignite, but I am not getting involved with a hockey player, not even a soft-spoken single dad from small-town South Carolina... who has a gorgeous bloodhound and a killer smile.

He's our temporary roommate while he looks for his own place to live, which means he's occupying Gavin's old room. It's down the hall from mine, and I am keeping things strictly platonic during what I expect will be a very brief stay.

"I'm sure only professional dog people will notice they're not all hounds, but I can probably find actual hounds for the rest of the players if you want to stay true to the name."

Stepping forward, I do my calming breaths before getting ready to start on Spanky's last pom pom. Once this is done, he'll be ready to win the show.

"That would be perfect!" Haddy's voice rises a bit, but Spanky doesn't dance in place.

I only pause a moment before starting the final puff ball.

I'm lost in thought, distracted by intrusive thoughts of Owen Stone's take-no-prisoners blue eyes, the way his full lips press together over straight white teeth when he smiles, that ridiculously cute dimple in his cheek...

I don't even notice our surroundings have changed.

Loud noises approach from the outside. It's a mixture of male shouts and a dog baying. The door to my studio flies open just as I'm bringing the clippers around the top of Spanky's hipbone.

A loud *Rooo!* echoes in the crisp tile room just before a massive, copper-colored dog bounds straight into my workspace.

"Oh!" Haddy cries. "Ladybird, NO!"

Spanky lifts his front legs, ready to jump and play just as Owen's bloodhound does the same, and the clippers in my hand go flying across the back of my show dog's rear like a lawn mower.

"Noooo!" I fall back on my butt, as Ladybird bounds over to jump on me.

I'm covered in big, slobbery dog-body. The clippers land with a smack in the back corner of the grooming area, still buzzing.

"Ladybird!" A deep, male voice cuts through the chaos, and two massive male bodies rush into my tiny workspace.

"Gigi!" Maverick is at my side, holding my arm while Owen pulls his oversized hound by the collar off me. "Are you okay?"

Sitting up, I look down at my apron, which now has large, wet patches all over it.

"I'm okay." I shake my head, holding Mav's arm as he helps me stand.

Haddy is across the room, collecting the clippers and turning them off. "I don't think they're broken," she says.

My chest is tight, and I'm afraid to look at Spanky. He's jumping around as much as he can with the short leash holding him in place, and the two dogs rise on their back legs, brushing their noses together with their mouths open in a typical big-dog greeting.

Owen hasn't been here a week, but our dogs are already inseparable.

"Oh, no..." Haddy's tone is mournful.

I don't want to look. I know what I'm going to see.

Forcing a swallow, I quietly ask, "How bad is it?"

My green eyes meet my cousin's bright blue ones, and as much as I love dogs, as much as they're all good dogs, her dismay tests my resolve.

Mav is still holding my arm as we step forward to where Haddy is standing with her hands over her mouth.

"You buzzed his butt," Mav observes drily.

Sure enough, the two pom poms, the hallmark of the

continental style, are destroyed. The one I was working on is shaved in half, and the one I had just finished has a very neat, two-inch wide path cut clear through the middle.

"Oh, nooo!" My hands are on my cheeks.

"Get down, Ladybird," Owen orders. "You know better than to bolt like that. I'm sorry, Gina. I don't know what got into her."

He's standing there, biceps flexing as he pulls his bloodhound away with all his strength. Spanky's tongue is out, and it looks very much like he's smiling. He has no idea the damage that's been done to his award-winning derriere.

"It's ruined." The words slip from my lips on a soft wail.

My body is weak, and I see the Best in Show prize slipping away like a sheet of paper out the window, into the air, down the street, and... *gone.*

Even if his pom poms could grow back in time, it won't matter if we don't win this weekend. And if we don't win the LA regional competition, there's no way we're going to Pennsylvania.

"What is it?" Owen frowns, walking over to where the three of us are standing. "Are you hurt?"

Maverick's arms are crossed, and one of his hands is fisted in front of his mouth. I know my golden-retriever cousin is doing his best not to laugh. If I didn't care so much, it probably would be funny. Maybe one day it will be. What's the formula? *Tragedy plus time equals comedy?*

Haddy's hand is on my back making slow circles. Her eyes are round and empathetic.

"Oh, shit." Owen puts a hand on top of his head. "It's not supposed to look like that, is it."

It's not a question, and all I can do is shake my head. "No, it's not."

"Is there anything I can do?" At least our handsome new roommate has manners.

"Not unless you can grow dog fur in three days." My tone is flat, and I'm doing my best not to cry.

"It's okay, though, right Geeg?" Mav puts a large hand on my shoulder. "There'll be another dog show in a few months, and Spanky can show 'em who's the prissiest poodle in town at that one!"

My head moves in a combination of nods and shakes. Yes, there will be another dog show, but no, it won't be in time for us to enter the national competition.

That bird has flown... or been shaved?

"I'm sorry, honey." Haddy's hand is now on my shoulder, and I'm pretty sure I'm still in shock. "I wish I could do something."

Mav frowns, still in problem-solving mode. "Can't you just shave them off? Not every poodle has puff balls on their butts."

I walk over to unfasten Spanky's harnass from the leash. His perfectly combed top knot is now sticky and matted with bloodhound drool, and I can tell my good boy is dying to run around in the grass with his new doggie bestie.

Sure enough, the second he's free, the two of them bolt out the door into our small yard.

"I've never been able to train her." Owen's tone is all apologies.

I nod. It's true.

"Bloodhounds are notoriously hard to train," I say quietly. "They're guided by their noses."

Ladybird's nose brought her straight to her new friend.

"If there's anything I can do..." he continues.

Shaking my head, I take the clippers from Haddy. "Don't worry about it."

"Could you try a different one?" Haddy goes to the poster of grooming styles on my wall. "What about this... *Bolero* style?"

"It's supposed to look like he's wearing pants, and his legs are completely bare." My head aches, and I'm trying to recalibrate my thoughts. "It's okay, I'll see if there's something else I can do."

"I hope you won't hold it against Ladybird. She's really a good dog." Owen holds out his hand, and I look up into his pretty blue eyes.

I manage to give him a reluctant smile. "Nobody deserves to be judged by one mistake."

"I agree." He returns my smile, and it feels like a sign, not that I believe in things like that.

I stopped believing in signs and fairy tales and Prince Charming rushing in to save the day when seven dates led to one hot night followed by me being dropped like a hot potato.

The best way to protect my heart is to keep it safe in its doggy cage, and that is exactly what I'm going to do.

2

———————

OWEN

My stomach twists, and I grind my jaw. My half-sister Heather has always taken after my stepmom Britt's side of the family more than my dad's.

She believes she inherited psychic powers from her tarot-reading maternal grandmother Gwen, and before I moved from South Carolina, she had a dream where a woman with a dog was waiting for me in the mist like something out of *Wuthering Heights*.

Needless to say, I gave that the ole side-eye.

I do not believe in psychic dreams, and I'm certainly not basing a relationship on one.

I guess after my wife died, I adopted my dad's disdain for mysticism and fairytales. Where was all that magic when she needed it?

Still, I know it's no use arguing with them. They have an answer for everything.

OWEN

Lots of ladies have dogs in LA.

HEATHER

You'll know her when you meet her. She's the one who'll heal your heart, and who knows? You might heal hers as well!

OWEN

I'm not staking my future and Maddie's on some ghostly dream girl.

HEATHER

You never know, Froot Loop.

I chuckle at my dad's old nickname for me from when I was a kid. Before I got "too cool" for it.

OWEN

My favorite food for the first five years of my life!

HEATHER

So I've heard.

OWEN

How's my little girl?

HEATHER

Adorable as always. Missing her daddy and Ladybird.

OWEN

We miss her. Tell her I'm looking at houses tomorrow. As soon as I find one, I'll send for you.

HEATHER

We're packed and ready!

The moon is out, and the sky is filled with stars. It's a beautiful, early-October night, and I'm sitting on the back porch of the bungalow with Gina, Haddy, and Gavin, while Maverick grills up our dinner.

They have a pretty place here with large twinkle lights strung from the tin roof over the wooden platform. The table is black wrought iron with matching chairs, and a side table holds all the plates, napkins, and utensils.

Ladybird is lying at my feet like a sphynx across from Spanky, who's doing the same, and I think my exuberant bloodhound's grooming fiasco has been forgiven. At least, I hope it has.

Gina sits across from me nursing a glass of iced tea and not glaring daggers at us—or crying, like I was afraid she might do earlier when we crashed into her workspace.

We're not staying here long, and I don't want to leave a bad taste in anyone's mouth, especially not hers.

The truth is Gina Bradford hits me right in my weakness.

For starters, she's tall. She's slim, but athletic, and she has long, strawberry-blonde hair and bright green eyes. I don't know when I got a taste for gingers, but her particular shade of rose-gold really does it for me.

She's quick to laugh, and her lips are always shiny and pink—and she smells like cherries. It's the craziest thing. I never thought I had a favorite scent, but the last few days

I've been here, I keep catching whiffs. It makes me want to pull her close and bury my face in her neck.

Which is completely inappropriate and creepy. I hardly know the woman.

She loves dogs.

Not only that, she knows everything about them. Maverick told me she majored in cynology in college, which means she has a degree in dog breeds and behaviors. I didn't even know that was a field of study.

Naturally, I have said none of this to my sister, or she'd be off to the races.

Gina is smart, beautiful, funny, feisty, a scientist, and I haven't had this much trouble *not* thinking about a woman since Angie died seven years ago.

Seven years. Has it been that long? I guess it has, since Maddie started second grade in September. I remember all of it so clearly...

We were so happy, so ready to start our family when we found out she was pregnant. She didn't have a hard pregnancy. In fact, she was glowing and nesting the entire time. I'd just taken up hockey, and she encouraged me to pursue it.

She'd be there at all the games wearing my jersey, growing bigger and bigger with our little girl inside her, and I thought this was my life. I thought it was only going to be rainbows and sunshine from here on out.

Even when it was time, we had no idea the risk was there, lurking like a dark shadow, waiting to destroy it all.

Cardiomyopathy. The doctors said later it was a preexisting condition she probably never even knew about. Her body had never been under the stress of pregnancy, labor, and delivery.

All that planning, all that nesting. She'd prepared everything, and in that one night, it was all over. She gave us Maddie, and then she gave her life.

I'll never forget standing beside her coffin in the rain. A shiny mahogany box sitting on brass rails holding all my dreams for the future, for a family. I tried to be strong, but it broke me.

Dad was at my side, his hand on my shoulder. Britt was there as well, holding my infant daughter.

Heather put her small hand in mine, leaning her head on my arm and openly crying. She was only fourteen, and it was the first time she'd lost a close family member.

I'd lost my own mother when I was a little boy. I barely remember her now, but at least I have flashes of things, scents and colors, and I have pictures of her holding me.

Maddie has none of that. She'll never know her mom or how much she loved her. She'll never know how much it cost to give her life.

Rubbing my fingers over my eyes, I push against these dark memories. They're still so vivid in my mind, and for so long, I've used them as a shield.

The years roll slowly past, and it's still hard to believe sometimes. Maybe it always will be. I don't know.

What I do know is I have to do all I can to keep us safe. No matter how pretty Gina Bradford might be, I can't risk Maddie's heart. Or mine.

"You should train her to use a crate." Gina cuts through my musings, leaning over to scrub her fingers in Ladybird's thick hide.

My dog perks up at her affection, lifting her nose and thumping her tail against the wooden patio.

Gavin Knight, my other teammate, sits beside me with his infant daughter asleep on his chest. I smile in spite of myself, remembering how I did the same with Maddie when she was a baby.

It was just the two of us, and I'd read all the books about skin-to-skin contact and bonding. I'd hold her every chance I got, doing my best to keep her happy and secure in my arms.

"Can you crate train a grown dog?" Their cousin Haddy walks out to join us, carrying bowls of sour cream and salsa.

She places them on the serving table along with soft tortillas and lettuce.

Maverick opens the grill, and the delicious scent of spiced meat fills the air. He's making grilled chicken with habanero black beans, and Gavin warned me our teammate has a flair for spicy food.

Gavin and Haddy lived here before they got engaged, had a baby, and moved into the house across the street. Still, they're here most of the time.

"You can definitely crate train her," Gigi replies. "It might even go quicker since she's older. Unless she had a negative experience with crates?"

She turns her green eyes on me, and for a second, I'm caught off guard.

They sparkle with interest, and they remind me of my stepmom Britt's green eyes. Britt was always loving and encouraging to me, and Gina's sweet gaze strangely makes me feel at home.

Clearing my throat of those thoughts, I reach down to pat the top of Ladybird's head. She and Spanky are facing each other with their tongues hanging out, almost like they're smiling at each other.

"I don't know about crate training," I answer slowly. "Isn't that like putting her in a cage?"

"It doesn't have to be," Gigi says. "Spanky prefers a wire

crate because it's bigger, and he has more room to stretch out. Plastic kennels have more of a den feel, but they're also smaller."

"I don't know if I like the idea of caging Ladybird." I do my best to keep my tone easy, not confrontational. "It seems... cruel."

"That's a very common misconception." Gigi's eyebrows rise as she nods, and I get the feeling she's had this conversation before. "But studies show crate training is very beneficial in helping dogs cope with stress. It gives them a place to go if they're afraid, and if she has to have medical treatments she'll be prepared."

"So a cage is a good thing?" I give her a teasing wink, and her mouth falls open.

She blinks at me a moment, almost like she lost her train of thought, then she clears her throat, shaking her head.

"Yes, actually." She shifts in her seat. "Think of it like a crib for babies, or her own room if she were a child."

"Maddie does like to go to her room and play." I muse.

"Lucy loves her crib," Gavin adds, his large hand practically covering his little girl's entire body.

"You can put a memory-foam cushion and Ladybird's favorite things in it," Gina continues. "And it can be her safe space."

"Patsy has slept in a kennel since we got her," Haddy adds. "It keeps her safe from Maverick."

"Hey!" her cousin calls from where he's working at the grill. "Just standing here making your dinner... And that only happened one time."

"Once was enough," Haddy snarks.

"You wouldn't have even known about it if I hadn't told you," he argues.

My brow furrows, and I look from him to her and back

again. "Is somebody going to tell me what happened? The suspense is killing me."

"Maverick thought he sat on Peepee." Gavin snorts, causing his little girl to stir. "One of Spanky's chew toys was on the couch, and when he flopped on it, it let out a loud squeak."

"I almost shat my pants!" Maverick yells over his shoulder.

Gigi presses her lips together hard, her eyes wide as she fights laughter. I bite the inside of my cheek because Haddy's eyes are narrowed on all of us.

Sitting forward, it's my turn to clear my throat.

"Those chew toys can make you hurt yourself," I say, trying to help my new friend. "I stepped on one in the dark the other night, and I nearly broke my neck."

"Well, anyway, it's just a suggestion." Gigi's voice is warm, and she smiles sweetly as she redirects the subject. "With the transition and moving, it might ease any anxiety."

I look down, thinking my dog couldn't be any less anxious if she tried. She's a big baby, and if she doesn't like something, she's pretty good at letting me know.

Maverick announces the food's ready, and as he spoons the grilled chicken onto a platter, we line up to fix our plates. Haddy takes baby Lucy from her fiancé and steps into the house to feed her. I hope she's not leaving on my account, but Gavin assures me she prefers the quiet when she's nursing.

"I've never met anyone who knew so much about dogs," I say as Gina and I return to our seats at the table.

"It's my life's work." Gigi rolls her soft taco, folding the base like a pro.

"What got you interested in them?"

"She was born because of a dog," Maverick says, taking Haddy's empty chair as he quickly rolls up a soft taco.

"What?" I laugh, looking at Gigi, who's shaking her head as she finishes her bite.

"It's an old family joke." Her green eyes roll. "Mom was overdue with me, so she went for a walk, hoping it would help her go into labor."

Maverick jumps in, taking up the story. "A lady was in the park with a dog, and Aunt Liv says as soon as the dog started barking, her water broke."

I can't help a laugh. "You wanted to see the dog?"

"I don't think that's true, but maybe?" A smile lifts the corners of her mouth. "I've always loved dogs. They're noble, they protect us and help us hunt. Studying them is fascinating."

"I believe you." My voice is low, and Gigi's chin dips.

The faintest pink shade warms her cheeks, and I decide one beer is enough for me tonight. I'm having thoughts I don't want to have about her.

Haddy breezes back, cutting through the momentary tension. "It's better if I feed her before I eat all the spicy food."

She hands the baby to Gavin, who has just finished. "Come here, Lulu," he grins, holding up his little daughter to make eye contact.

Her head wobbles as she smiles, blowing bubbles.

"Three months old?" I ask, remembering when Maddie did these things.

"Almost four." Gavin rests her on his chest, placing a large hand on the back of her head.

I nod. "That's when it all starts happening."

"Yep," he grins, kissing her little temple. "The eye contact, the smiles…"

He's a big guy, but I can tell he's completely wrapped around his daughter's tiny finger. I guess I am, too.

I think of Maddie blinking her big brown eyes at me and making little coos and baby noises.

"Do you miss your daughter?" Haddy asks, and I glance over at her with a smile.

"Yeah. We're never apart for long." I push my chair back to stand. "Speaking of, I'd better get to bed so I can get an early start with the realtor tomorrow."

Ladybird stands as soon as I do, and so does Spanky. The two lift their front legs and then take off down the wooden steps into the backyard, yelping and chasing each other.

"It's a good thing Patsy's not here." Haddy takes her seat. "I'm afraid she'd get trampled."

"Spanky looks out for her," Gina argues. "I'm not sure if Ladybird would, though. She's not used to her."

"She's always been gentle with Madison," I note. "But you're right. She's not used to small dogs."

Gigi looks up at me. "That's a pretty name. Is it after someone in your family?"

Shaking my head, I look down, exhaling a laugh. "My late wife loved that old mermaid movie *Splash*. So I guess you could say my daughter's named after Darryl Hannah."

"I loved that movie!" Haddy lets out a muffled cry around her bite of soft taco.

Gigi leans closer to my side, surrounding me in the mouthwatering scent of cherries. "I'm pretty sure Haddy's seen every movie ever made. Her mom's a total movie buff."

"Only the good ones," Haddy says.

I grin at the four of them. The way they go back and forth, lightly arguing, always bantering, reminds me of my family back in Eureka. We're all close, able to finish each others' sentences and always have each other's backs.

The dogs are jumping around when Ladybird suddenly catches a scent and dashes away. Gigi's white dog is hot on her trail.

"Spanky's trim doesn't look too bad from here," I observe, hoping we're past that mishap. "I've never been into poodles, but he's a good-looking dog."

"He was bred to be a show dog, but I worked with the breeder to be sure it was done ethically." She seems worried, as if I'd expect anything less. "Poodles were bred to be retrievers, but they love to learn tricks and entertain. It makes them perfect for showing."

"I can see that." I cross my arms, watching the two follow each other around the yard. "Why is he named Spanky? Isn't that one of the little rascals?"

"He is a rascal." Her nose wrinkles. "But I give all the dogs nicknames. His full name is Spank My Bottom. It's a show thing. You know."

I don't really know, but I go with it.

Maverick walks up beside us, holding a beer and watching the dogs play. "They've really taken to each other." His blue eyes flicker to mine, then his cousin's. "It's almost like they know something we don't."

Gigi narrows her eyes at him. "Like what?"

"I don't know, but from all you've told me, dogs are smarter than people sometimes." He nudges her with his elbow.

"They're certainly more trustworthy." Turning on her heel, she heads back to collect the dirty dishes.

The tone in her voice leads me to believe she's encountered some untrustworthy humans, and I'm surprised by the burn of anger in my chest at the thought of someone hurting her.

"Hey, Owen, we've got plenty of room if you'd like to bring your daughter here now." Maverick walks with me to the table again. "How old is she?"

"Seven." I pick up my plate to help. "Thanks for the offer. Hopefully, I'll find something tomorrow that I can get into quickly."

Maverick takes the plate from my hand, ignoring my protests. "Still, it takes time to get into a new house. She could stay in Haddy's old room."

Hesitating, I know he's right. "I appreciate the offer. I'd better head up now."

Mav calls to his cousin, "Gigi, show him how Spanky uses his crate!"

Our eyes meet, and she seems a little flustered. I call Ladybird and go to the door leading inside.

"It's okay. You can show me tomorrow." Again, our smiles meet, and my lungs tighten.

I'm definitely tired, so I don't waste time before heading upstairs. I want to be finished in the bathroom and in my own bed with the door closed before she appears.

3

GINA

"What do you think about this?" I turn the iPad so my cousin can see the pictures of a wedding at the Inn of the Seventh Ray in Topanga.

Haddy has baby Lucy on her shoulder as she bounces in place, and I walk over to trade my littlest cousin for the iPad.

"Look at those and tell me if you think that's magical or what?"

We didn't really discuss it after she and Gavin got engaged last spring, but after their "honeymoon" last month in Japan, I figured I'd take the reins on planning their wedding before the guys start back with hockey season.

Haddy's voice goes high. "It looks like an Ewok village!"

Lucy scrubs her baby face against my neck, and my nose wrinkles. "Is that a good thing?" I hug her closer, doing my best to keep her soothed. "I thought we decided Ewoks were the worst."

"They really should've gone with Wookies instead of

Ewoks, but you know how it is." She shakes her dark head. "The artist's mind."

"Actually, I have no idea." Now I'm bouncing Lucy on my shoulder, patting her baby back. "I'm a scientist. I leave the art to Uncle Jack and Knox."

"What art is Knox doing?"

"Kimmie didn't tell you? He's writing poetry just like his dad."

"*Knox* is writing poetry?" I'm pretty sure I see hearts floating around her eyes. "What are we going to do with these guys?"

Our uncle Jack, the oldest of the "Bradford Boys," surprised everyone when we discovered he wrote short poems, observations and thoughts jotted in a small, leather-bound notebook he kept in his back pocket.

The only thing that surprised me more was hearing his quarterback youngest son Knox kept a similar notebook. Apparently he took it out at his high school girlfriend's birthday party and read a short poem for her that stole everyones' hearts.

His school-librarian mom, our aunt Allie, said it was as good as anything by William Carlos Williams or Wallace Stevens. It's possible she's biased, but I don't know. Uncle Jack is pretty good...

"So the men in our families are artists, and the women are scientists?" My eyebrow arches.

"They're also football players," Haddy counters.

"And hockey players... and cowboys."

"And your dad is a sheriff, which reminds me of someone else we know... Someone new." Haddy pauses, her blue eyes circling playfully. "Who could it be?"

She taps her finger against her chin, but I'm not having it.

"Hayden Lucille Bradford." My voice is firm. "Stop it right now. I am not getting involved with Owen Stone."

"Why not?" she whines. "He's gorgeous, and y'all have so much in common!"

My stomach tightens, but I put a firm hand on it. "Like what?"

"Well, for starters, you both have sheriff dads."

"You already said that."

She leans against the bar, crossing her arms. "You both have moms who are serious-minded career women. Your mom's a lawyer, and didn't Owen say his mom's a forensic photographer?"

"I think his mom died." My voice is quiet. "A lot like his late wife."

"It sounded to me like that was a long time ago."

"Can't be more than seven years."

"Which is a long time." Haddy's eyebrow arches.

I can't get over my conspiratorial cousin. "I'm not rushing in on a man with a dead wife and a seven-year-old daughter!"

"And an adorable bloodhound!"

"Who destroyed Spanky's chance at Best in Show this year."

Haddy's nose wrinkles. "Did you really have your heart set on it? I mean, I know it's a big deal, but there are sooo many competitions all the time."

Leaning against the bar, I hug Lucy closer. "I don't know. I guess I thought it would be nice for Spanky to be top dog for once."

Haddy rubs my arm. "I'm pretty sure Spanky thinks he's top dog all the time. He can't help it. We raised him that way, the stinker."

My nose wrinkles, and I put my head on her shoulder.

"We did spoil him pretty rotten as a puppy." Then with a flick of my wrist, I redirect us back to the topic at hand. "Do you like this place for your wedding? If you do, I'll try my best to get you on their schedule this month."

"I love it. Let's do it!"

A smile breaks across my face, and I give the baby a squeeze. "I'll call them. It's probably going to take a little bribery, but I'll do what I can."

"Do you think it'll make a difference that Gavin's a Champion?"

"It might... I'll definitely mention it. And Mav's his best man."

"I think his brother's his best man." She wrinkles her nose.

"I'll pretend I made a mistake. If we even get that far. They might laugh me off the phone."

We're hovering over my iPad when the front door opens, and Owen walks in looking dejected.

He's so tall, and the way his dark brow lowers over his blue eyes makes my throat dry. I want to rush over and put my hand on his shoulder, ask him what's wrong, and offer to help.

Silly response.

"Hey, Owen!" Haddy straightens, frowning. "You okay?"

He seems to snap out of it when he sees us. "Oh, yeah. All good." He clears his throat, and I'm pretty sure he's not. "Just finished up with the realtor. It's a lot."

She walks over to him. "You should try to find something in this neighborhood. We'd love to have you close by. At least I know Spanky would."

My cousin laughs, but I do my best to find a way to leave the room. I don't like these jittery feelings he puts in my stomach, and I'm not getting involved in his house hunt. I've got a wedding to plan, and a calendar to fill with hounds in addition to my regular job.

That's enough for one person.

"Come look." Haddy grabs his hand.

Curiosity outweighs my resolve to remain neutral, and I follow them into the living room to where Spanky is curled up in his crate sleeping.

"See how happy he is?" Haddy looks from Owen to me. "I didn't want you to think we were being cruel to Spanky the towel thief."

"Towel thief?"

"Gigi didn't tell you?" Her voice rises. "Spanky will steal your towel right off you if you're not careful."

"Shit, good to know." He chuckles, and I'm glad to see him smile instead of frown. He has such a nice smile.

He steps closer, and as I blink up to him, something falls into my eye.

"Oh!" Waving at Haddy, I quickly pass her the baby. "Something's in my eye!"

"Let me help you." Owen steps closer as tears flood my vision.

He touches my chin gently, and as he leans closer, I'm surrounded by the clean, masculine scent of cedar and soap.

"Look up if you can." His voice is low.

"I'll try..." I whisper, forcing my lids to part as I look in the direction of my eyebrows.

"I don't see anything." His thumb lightly slides across the top of my cheek, under my eye, and the pain starts to ease.

His hands are so large, cupping my cheek. My heart beats faster at how close his lips are to mine.

"Does this help?" Haddy turns her phone light on right in my eye.

Again, I yelp as more tears come. They actually seem to do the trick, though. Whatever it is moves to the side of my eye, and relief replaces the pain.

"Here..." Owen lightly touches the corner of my eye, then lowers his hand in front of me. "Eyelash."

I hold his arm as I look down, and sure enough, a black lash sits on the tip of his finger. Looking up again, our eyes meet, and he smiles. Blue eyes, white teeth, square jaw... it's a shock of energy through my core, and I wobble, my grip on his forearm tightening.

Now I'm concerned hearts are floating around *my* eyes.

"Silly eyelash," I manage to say, doing my best to grab the reins on my racing heart.

"Want to make a wish?" The way he says it makes me bite my lip.

Shaking my head, I force myself to step away from the gorgeous man with the warm hands and gentle touch. My pulse beats between my thighs, and my mind is racing through all the other places his hands might go.

"You're really good at that." Haddy's voice has a tone I don't like. It's very, *I told you so*, and I know she's plotting how she can matchmake us.

"Comes with being a dad, I guess." Owen takes a step away from me as he turns to where Spanky is on his feet, coming out of his crate. "So, ah, about this cage, I guess it's the word I don't care for."

"Yeah." I redirect my thoughts as well, away from the warmth of this massive man holding me in his arms, touching my cheek, looking deep into my eyes. "I guess it does have negative connotations."

Haddy's standing between us, bouncing her baby on her shoulder with a smug grin on her lips. "It doesn't have to.

There's Nick Cage, and umm... *The Birdcage* is a great old movie!"

Owen takes another step away, putting his hands in his back pockets. "When I played baseball as a kid, we always liked to get in the batting cage."

"You played baseball?" My head tilts to the side. "What made you switch to hockey?"

He shrugs those lovely, broad shoulders. "I'm better at it?"

"Is that a question?" Haddy asks with a laugh.

"I guess not anymore." Owen smiles, and that dimple appears beneath his dark scruff.

"I expect you're very good if the Champions called you up." Haddy starts for the door. "I've got to get this little girl to her crib. It's naptime."

With that, she leaves me alone in the living room with Owen Stone and his magic hands.

My jaw drops, and I don't know what to say at first, blinking up at him with a laugh. "She knows how to make an exit. But she's right. The Champions only recruit the very best... hence the name."

"Right." He nods as Ladybird bounds down the stairs to where we're standing. "I should take her out."

"Yeah... Spanky needs to go for a walk, too." I take his harness and leash off the hook. "Want to go together?"

"Let me run up and grab her leash." He jogs up the stairs, and I bend down to suit up my dog.

As soon as he's back and Ladybird's set, we head out the door with both our dogs trotting beside each other like they've been doing it all their lives.

We're quiet starting out, listening to the sounds of our shoes padding the pavement, kids playing in the yards, the occasional car passing.

Our neighborhood is full of families, and the sidewalks and green spaces make it very dog-friendly. The streets are lined with flowering shrubs and sweet olive trees. It's a little haven inside this giant metropolis.

I glance up at Owen, quietly observing the area, and despite my resolution, I can't help wanting to know everything about him.

"What's it like in Eureka? I love that name. It sounds like a discovery."

He looks down, giving me a brief smile. "It's just a little town near the coast. My whole family lives there. They're part of the founding families."

"On both sides?"

"Well, my dad and stepmom's side. My stepmom Britt was an only child, but my dad has three brothers, which means lots of uncles and aunts and cousins..."

"Sounds like my life in Newhope." Warmth fills my chest when I think of my dad and all his brothers, my aunt Dylan, and growing up with all my family there.

"That's what Mav said." He looks up to where Ladybird is following Spanky into a vacant, grassy lot.

"This is a good place to let them run." I bend down to unhook Spanky's leash. "If she'll stay with us?"

He unhooks Ladybird's as well. "She will."

The dogs take off running, and I chew my lip. "I imagine it was nice to have your family around... being alone with your daughter, I mean. My uncle Jack was a single dad, too."

He nods, watching the dogs. "They gave us a lot of love and support. They helped me get through the dark days, and I always had someone to help with Maddie. But Eureka is like that. It's a small town where people band together, lifting each other up in good times and bad."

"In that case, it's exactly like Newhope." I want to reach out and give his arm a squeeze, but I don't.

"I don't want Maddie to lose that." His brow furrows, and his jaw clenches attractively. "Moving is hard, and I want to be sure she has all the love and attention I did growing up... despite my career."

"How long have you played hockey?" He's clearly older than most of the guys on the team, and he doesn't have the typical, young-player cocky attitude, which is a nice plus, in my opinion.

"I played around before Maddie was born, but after Angie died, I got really serious, mostly as a way to distract my mind." He looks down with a wince. "I would put Maddie to bed, and it would be so quiet in the house... Hockey gave me a way to forget the pain of what I'd lost. I started making good money, and I felt alive again. I had something."

He's talking more than he ever has, and I'm hanging on his every word.

"My teammates were like brothers to me, and when I was flying on the ice, chasing the puck, I could forget about everything except winning." He looks out at the horizon a moment, then with a blink, he seems to remember I'm here. Clearing his throat, he looks down and concludes quickly. "That's when my little sister moved in to help me. She still does."

"You must be very close." I study his handsome face.

He nods, exhaling a chuckle. "She's a lot younger than me, and I'm sure she's ready for me to retire so she can do her own thing. I'd actually planned to retire at the end of last year."

"But you didn't." Without realizing, I've drifted closer to him.

"I finally got my chance to play in the league." He looks down, almost like he's apologizing. "I had to take it. It's a big pay jump, and well... it's the NHL."

"I get that." I think of how I felt about Spanky this year. "When you've been doing something so long, it's natural to want to go for the big prize. It's like Best in Show."

"Is that the top of the dog world?" He glances over at me.

"Yeah, it's the top prize. Spanky's been competing for years, but he's never won it."

"What do you have to do to get it?"

"There are certain qualifying competitions, like the one this weekend. If you win one, you can apply to compete."

His brow falls. "That's why you were grooming him..." With a wince, he looks out at Ladybird, who's bounding around the yard now. "Is there another one you can do?"

"We can do it next year." I do my best to give him a reassuring smile. "We've got plenty of time."

"I'm really sorry, Gina..."

"No, no." I wave him away. "Let's head back. These guys are done."

I can tell he's not ready to let the grooming disaster go, but he relents. I call Spanky, and Ladybird follows, running back to us. We clip the leashes on, and with that, we head back to our little bungalow. The two dogs lead us home the same way they led us here, like they've decided this is how it's supposed to be.

Shaking that silly thought away, I recall his expression when he arrived this afternoon. "Tell me about house-hunting. From the look on your face, it didn't seem like it went well."

"I dunno." He shrugs. "We looked at a lot of really beautiful houses. They're all interesting to look at, but none of them feels like home. They're all so much concrete."

"They build them that way because of the wildfires." I think about what he must be used to in coastal South Carolina. "When we moved here from Newhope, it took a minute to find something that reminded me of home. Luckily, Haddy grew up here, so she knew I'd like this area."

He looks up at the trees. "I'm thinking about taking her advice and seeing if we can find something here. I like the trees, and it's such a big change. I don't want Maddie to feel like I've moved her to a different planet."

"I hope we get to meet her."

He looks over at me, and a light breeze slips through the dark hair around his temples, pushing it across his forehead. My fingers itch with wanting to reach up and slide it out of his eyes, but he does it instead, pushing his long hair away from his face.

We're back at the house, when my phone buzzes, and I jump out of my daydream to check the text.

HADDY

Have you kissed him yet???

My cheeks flame at her words, and I'm about to shove the device into my pocket when another text appears.

HADDY

Stop wasting time... Oh, and ask him about
the calendar. Mav said he has to be in it.

"You okay?" A teasing note is in his voice, and I look up, quickly turning the screen to my chest.

"It's just Haddy... Did the guys tell you about the calendar fundraiser they're doing?"

"Something about hockey and hounds?" He exhales a sharp whistle through his teeth, and Ladybird immediately heads in our direction as he starts for the door.

My jaw drops, and I point at him. "I've always wanted to do that."

"I can teach you. It's how I trained her back home."

Spanky is right behind us, and we walk into the house, trying to remember what we were talking about when he turned into the sexy dog whistler.

"The calendar!" I say loudly, and he frowns. "Sorry, I was just... Haddy wants me to ask you if you'll be in it with Lady-bird. So far, she's the only actual hound they have. Spanky and Peepee are the other two dogs."

He holds the door, smiling down at me. "Looks like you have nine more to go."

"You'll do it?" My voice rises, and he grins.

"Sure, why not?"

"Haddy's going to be so happy! Of course, that means you'll have to spend a lot of time with me. Or at least, Lady-bird will."

"That doesn't sound too bad." My lungs tighten at the way he says it. "Just tell us where and when, and we'll be there."

4

OWEN

"Gav and I have a Tic-Tac-Goal play we've been using for a few years, but we need to switch it up. That's where you come in."

We're only a few weeks away from the start of the season, and we've started practicing all day, every day, getting ready. I'm learning the names of my teammates, most importantly Donovan Price, the team captain.

Price is a giant of a guy, a redhead who pretty much keeps to himself. He's not as showy as Mav, who I knew before I got here was the star of the team and the best right winger in the league.

Gav is a defenseman, but he's great at putting pressure on the offense and stealing the puck. He's the fastest skater I've seen, faster than me, which gives him an advantage. Going in for a pinch, he has to move fast and make no mistakes.

Saxon, or Sax, is the other D-man who covers for him. He also covers Price as left-winger when our captain needs a break. I'm doing my best to skate hard, learn fast, and keep my eye on the puck.

"What do you want me to do?" I look over at Gav, who's circling around, coming up the back of the net.

"In the past when he'd do this, he'd send it straight to me, and I'd slap it into the goal." As if on cue, Gav does just that, and I watch Mav send the puck straight into the net so fast, it's a black blur. "The other teams have been studying us, so we decided to add one more step. Tic-Tac-*Tac*-Goal. You're the second Tac."

"Okay…" My brow furrows behind my mask, and I'm not sure I'm following. "Let's give it a go."

"It starts like this." Maverick skates to the center, and Gavin goes to the line, where he'd be if he were defending.

They spring into action. Gav takes the puck and shoots it across the ice to Mav, who races down the center in the direction of the net.

Akers, our goalie, gets into position like he's going to keep them from scoring, and Mav sends it across to John Hancock, yep, that's really his name, while Gav flies around behind the net.

"Stone, you're up!" Mav yells, and Hancock sends it to me, as I skate closer to the goal.

Catching it with my stick, I keep going, not sure if I should try to score or pass it.

Maverick gives the order. "Now to Gav!"

With a quick slap, I shoot it to my teammate, who has just come around the back corner of the net. My stomach drops when the puck clips the edge of the goal and starts to wobble, taking flight.

Gavin scoops it out of the air so fast, then sends it over to Mav, who slaps it straight past Akers into the goal.

Shouts of approval fill the stadium, and we glide into a huddle, slapping each other on the shoulders.

"Not bad for a first timer!" Gav grins, grabbing the top of my pad and giving me a shake. "The Cliffs won't know where to look."

Sax slaps me on the back, and we continue practicing different plays, passing, and then do a short scrimmage. They're all good guys, even the young ones, chief of which includes Maverick. He's cocky, the resident beautician, but he's friendly and more than ready to help me get up to speed.

Donovan sets a steady tone as team captain, and his pep talks are level but inspiring. He's the oldest next to me, but I'm not pulling any kind of age rank. These guys are helping me achieve a level I didn't think I'd see in my career.

Hell, last year they went all the way to Edmonton to face off against the Slicks, historically the greatest team in the league.

I don't know how many years of play I have left, but maybe we'll win the cup before I'm done. Then maybe I can retire and go back to being a small-town sheriff like my dad.

"We need a nickname for you, Stone." Gav is on the couch with his baby daughter on his chest.

Dinner is finished, and Haddy let me help wash the dishes this evening. I noticed Gigi gave her a side-eye before she ran upstairs saying she had to upload some paperwork before a deadline.

Haddy gave her a return side-eye and told her it would be waiting when she finished washing the dishes.

The two of them went back and forth a few more times,

and I started to get the impression it had something to do with washing dishes with *me*, when Maverick impatiently said he'd help me wash up, which made Haddy relent and do it instead.

Now the kitchen is clean, and I'm standing in the living room behind the sofa watching as the cousins debate which scary movie to watch.

"When I played for the Stingers, they called me Sly," I answer our big defenseman, who is now making goo-goo eyes at his daughter.

"Like 'and the family Stone'?" Haddy jumps around to face me from where she's sitting beside him.

"I guess that's where it came from." I shrug. "It's also because I'm pretty good at slipping the puck past the goal line."

"Yeah, you are!" Maverick shouts from where he's swirling his hand in a large, round fishbowl filled with slips of paper. The giant, flatscreen television is open to the Halloween collection on one of the streaming services. "You should've seen him working with Gav on our new T-T-*T*-G."

He emphasizes the third *T*, and Gigi frowns at him. "What's that?"

"You'll see it when we face off against the Cliffs in two weeks." Her cousin waggles his eyebrows at her.

I've learned the Colorado Cliffs are the Champions' biggest rival, with us alternating wins every season. The guys are eager to beat them every time this year, and I like being part of our best players' strategy.

"I think if you don't find a house by next week, you should bring your little girl here." Haddy shifts into her fiancé's side, holding the smallest dog I've ever seen. "It's so clear you miss her, it hurts my heart."

"I don't know." I look down. "I do miss her, but I'd have

to bring Heather out as well. I think all those house guests might strain your hospitality."

"Nonsense!" Haddy cries. "It would only be for a little while, and Gav and I left two rooms vacant upstairs."

"What does your sister do, Owen?" Gigi turns her pretty green eyes on me, and I remember touching her face, sliding the eyelash off her high cheekbone.

Even struggling with a stray eyelash, she's so pretty, and she smells really good. Her full lips are glossy, and I wonder if she tastes like cherries...

If I *kiss* her.

Her *mouth*. Kiss her *mouth*. *Fuck*.

Clearing my throat, I push those intrusive thoughts away and try to remember what she even asked me.

"Ah... Heather?" I frown, trying to think. "She did hair for a while. Then she said it made her back hurt, so she's been working at her grandmother's tarot studio for a few months now. She thinks she's a psychic."

Internally rolling my eyes, I remember her insistence on her dream.

"What!" Haddy and Gigi cry at the same time, and they hop out of their seats, diving excitedly onto the sofa in front of where I stand.

"She's a psychic?" Haddy asks, holding Peepee against her chest.

The little dog seems confused and shivers with either excitement or fear.

"Your grandmother has a tarot studio?" Gigi asks, blinking up at me. "Do you have psychic powers, too?"

"No, Gwen's not my biological grandmother, but she's always treated me like family." I don't get into the way she also drives my dad absolutely nuts with all her premonitions and vibrations and interfering with his cases.

"Now you really have to get them out here." Haddy stands and walks back to sit beside her husband. "I can't wait to have her do a reading for me."

"*Halloween H2O!*" Maverick cries, holding up a slip of paper. "Joseph Gordon Levitt is a hockey player, and he has the best death."

"Skate to the face," Gav chuckles. "It's got my vote!"

"Yass..." Mav widens his eyes maniacally.

"You've got my vote," Haddy says. "I love all the *Halloween* films, even *Season of the Witch*."

"Weirdo," Mav teases, and she pushes his leg with her foot.

I walk to the stairs, giving them a wave. "I'd better head up."

"Not a scary movie fan?" Haddy leans her head back to look up at me.

"Nah, I've got to call home and shower." I nod to the guys. "Good practice today. I'm beat."

"Don't worry, old man," Mav calls. "We'll have you in shape in no time."

"Old man..." I huff a laugh.

I'm only thirty-five, but he's got me. I'll be sore tomorrow.

Walking up the stairs slowly, I take out my phone.

OWEN

Is Maddie still awake? I keep forgetting the time difference out here, Sorry.

HEATHER

It's Friday! We're all at Gran's watching Hocus Pocus with Mom and the aunties.

My dad's mom started the tradition of keeping the kids at her house on Friday nights when I was a boy.

Then, when Maddie was old enough, she started it up again.

OWEN

Will she want to talk to me instead of watching the Sanderson Sisters?

HEATHER

Of course she will. Hold pls...

Our text turns into a phone call, and my sister's face appears on the screen.

"Hey there, big brother. You're not looking too bad for being on the other side of the continent." She gives me a wink.

"It took me a minute, but I'm on West Coast time now." I continue into my bedroom, where Ladybird is curled on her large, round cedar-chip-filled cushion.

It's been her bed since she was a puppy, and even though it makes all my stuff smell like cedar chips, it reminds us of home.

"Where's my baby girl?"

"Here I am, Daddy!" The sweet voice yells at me through the phone before her face appears on the screen.

Her happy brown eyes, round cheeks, and long blonde hair is a punch of joy straight to my chest. I sit down, smiling back at her.

"Hey, Shortcake, are you taking good care of your aunt Heather?"

"Yes!" She nods her head fast. "We're watching *Hocus Pocus*, but I don't like this part. It's where Max gets struck by lightning."

My lips twist. "Are you going to have trouble sleeping tonight?"

"No, Daddy!" She rolls her eyes, shaking her head. "I'm

seven now. I'm not scared of the Sanderson Sisters. Besides, Grammy Gwen said Bandit can stay at our house tonight."

Bandit is the newest black cat to take up residence at my step-grandmother's house.

"Well, if anyone can keep witches away, it would be Bandit."

"Cats don't keep witches away!" she cries.

"But I thought in the movie—"

"That's Thackery, Daddy. He's trying to be reunited with his sister." She says the words with the disappointment only a second grader could muster.

"I guess I'll have to watch it again. How's school going?"

"It's okay." She shrugs. "Aunt Cass said I could go and read books in the third-grade class now if I want."

"She did?" My aunt Cass teaches at the only elementary school in Eureka. "Why would she say that?"

"Because I already read all the books in the second-grade class!" Like it's so obvious.

"Okay..." I realize I might need to have a chat with our aunt when we move Maddie out here. "I guess that's a good thing?"

"Oh, yes, the third-grade books are thicker, and they have Junie B. Jones. Second-grade books are for babies."

Squealing noises come from behind her, and she looks over her shoulder fast before turning to me again. She squirms in the chair, and I'm pretty good at knowing when she's done talking.

"Do you want to go back and finish the movie with your aunts?"

She makes a cute, worried face. "I can talk to you some more."

"It's okay, baby. I just wanted to see your face and tell you I love you."

"I love you, too, Daddy!" She leans forward as if she'll kiss me through the camera, then drops back onto her butt again.

"Tell Ladybird goodnight..." I turn the phone, so she can see our dog on her bed.

"Goodnight, Ladybird!" Maddie yells in her small voice, which makes Ladybird emit a loud *Rooo!* Which makes us both laugh.

"Maybe you and Aunt Heather can come here in a few weeks. Would you like that?" She nods her head so fast, I'm worried she'll get a whiplash. "Okay, then. Give Aunt Heather the phone and go finish the movie."

"I love you, Daddy!" she yells again, blowing me a kiss before shoving the phone at my sister.

"Love you, too."

And with that, she's gone.

Heather's face appears, her nose curling with her smile. "She might not sleep tonight."

"Or you'll have a bed partner," I chuckle. "How much candy has she had?"

"Aunt Cass made Rice Krispie Treats shaped like witches and black cats. She's had about three of them."

"Jeez, sis!" Air hisses through my teeth. "Give her some milk or something."

"I've got it under control."

"All right, well, have fun, and I'll keep you posted about coming here."

"We're basically packed. Just say the word, and we can hop on a plane."

"I'll go ahead and get tickets for two weeks out. I should have found something by then."

She nods, and I agree to email her the details. Tossing the phone onto my bed, I bend over to give Ladybird a pat on the head. I took her out after dinner, so she should be set for the night.

I'm actually surprised she's up here with me rather than down in the crate with Spanky, which she's started doing over the last few days.

"You heard us talking about cages, didn't you?" She lifts her big head, blinking up at me slowly. I walk over and take a knee, cupping her face in both my hands and giving her a good scratch. "Trying to make me look bad? I've got some Shania Twain with your name on it."

She lifts her head fast, giving me a slobbery "kiss" right across the mouth. It only makes me laugh. I grew up with my stepmom's bloodhound Edward, so I'm used to the drool.

"Time for me to get cleaned up," I say, pulling my shirt over my head and tossing it onto the bed.

Walking out into the hall, I hear the sounds of squeals and loud music coming from downstairs. Mav lets out an "Aw!" and Haddy shout-laughs, "That's so gross!"

"Don't get in the dumbwaiter!" Gigi cries. "Don't do it... Don't... Nooo!"

My lips twist into a grin, and I picture Gina hiding behind that large pillow as she watches the silly slasher film.

Stepping into the bathroom, I push the door closed, turning on the water with her pretty face on my mind. The room fills with steam as the water heats up, and I step into the spray, pulling the curtain closed.

It doesn't take long to wash my hair, my face, my body. My muscles are tired from all the skating we did today, and I take a moment to let the pounding water massage my shoulders.

Thoughts of Gigi's soft lips drift through my head, and I wonder again what it would be like to cover them with mine. I wonder if she would sigh when I kissed her or if she would moan. Maybe she would be quiet. Would she kiss me back?

I picture sliding my hands down her slim waist, maybe cupping her small breasts, sliding my thumbs back and forth across her hardened nipples. I'd nibble the base of her chin, tracing a line along her jaw to her ear.

While I pulled the soft shell between my teeth, I'd slide my fingers around and down her lower back, over her ass to the space between her legs. Maybe I'd give her a lift as I pressed her against the wall and devoured her...

My cock has risen to full mast, and I cover it with my fist, tugging slowly as tentacles of pleasure climb my thighs. Fuck, I need to get out of this shower, go to my room and deal with this fucking boner.

Shutting the water off quickly, I look around for the towel I left on the sink. With a quick dusting over my shoulders and feet, I fling it around my waist and grab a handful of tissues.

I pull the door open and step out into the hall, ready to head to my bedroom. I've only taken a few steps when I realize two things: I'm not alone in the hallway, and a streak of white is bolting straight at me.

"Owen?" Gigi's soft voice has just said my name when the towel is ripped off my waist so fast, it's like a magician whipping a tablecloth off a set table.

"Oh... what?" I'm too stunned to react.

"Oh my God!" Gigi's voice rises, then changes, growing deeper. "Oh... my."

In the semi-dark hall, lit only by the glow from her bedroom and the bathroom behind me, I stand, completely naked.

That asshole Spanky is in the doorway to my bedroom

with the towel in his mouth, wagging his tail. I swear to God, he's smiling.

Gigi's wide green eyes travel from my face, down my shoulders, to my bare stomach, to where they linger on my fully erect cock.

I'm momentarily frozen, but her full lips are parted. Her expression is somewhere between surprise and curiosity.

Gigi's mouth closes, but her eyes don't lift from where she's inspecting my manhood. Then she licks her lips, and I swear my dick gets harder.

Something wicked rises in my stomach, and I don't cover myself. Instead, I duck my head to capture her fixed gaze.

"See something you like?" I sound as cocky as my young teammates, and she audibly gulps.

I don't know where that came from, and she spins away quickly, muttering a *sorry* before scurrying downstairs again. Shaking my head, I can't help a chuckle as I walk to my room.

I'm not a kid anymore, but it's been a minute since I've had that kind of unabashed appreciation from a beautiful woman. So, *sorry not sorry*?

Snatching the towel from that naughty dog's mouth, I close the door.

5

———————

GINA

Owen Stone's cock is incredible.

His entire body is a work of art.

I'd just jogged up the stairs to grab a sweater, and of course Spanky was hot on my trail, thinking we were playing a game. Naturally when he saw Owen with that towel around his waist, he did what he always does.

It all happened so fast, I couldn't even warn him. One second, I was standing at the top of the stairs feeling a chill, the next, my entire body flooded with heat as a six-foot-two naked Adonis was unveiled in front of me.

From his broad shoulders lined with muscles, to his rounded biceps, to the cut of his six-pack torso, to the two lines forming a V down to his fully erect penis.

An audible gulp came from my throat. I couldn't tear my eyes away. Then he stopped my heart when he asked me if I liked it.

His tone was different than it has ever been. It was cocky and teasing, and it did crazy things to my insides. It made me feel like I was on a roller coaster going over the first big hill.

Excitement raced from my stomach to my throat, but I couldn't say, *"Yes, sir!"* I *very much* liked what I saw... *Owen Stone's naked body is gorgeous.*

Instead, all I could do was mutter a quick sorry and dash down the stairs again. I figured I'd use a quilt or one of Mav's hoodies to get warm. Although, after that encounter, I was pretty sure I wouldn't be cold again all week.

What had he been doing in the shower... and could I watch next time? My cheeks burned hot at the thought.

Now I'm in the Champions' locker room with Haddy facing the entire team and going through the names for the fundraising calendar.

The guys are gearing up, getting ready for practice. Half of them seem amused by the idea; the other half aren't really interested.

Gav and Mav have already headed out to the ice. They have their dates and dogs. It's the rest of the "models" we have to coordinate, so we're here, facing a gang of super tall, super-hot, super impatient men.

"As you know, management wants to do something fun to benefit the children's hospital," Haddy starts, confident as usual. "After careful consideration, looking at market performance, a calendar seems like the easiest way to do it."

A rumble of affirmation is the only response.

"The theme is 'Hockey Hunks and Hounds,' and I have a list of names..." she continues. "We only have twelve spots, so as much as we'd like to use everyone, we just don't have enough room."

Haddy's brow furrows as she reads off the selections, and it reminds me of my dad breaking the bad news to teenage boys at high school football camp. Clearly, it's a gene, because none of them seem angry or offended at not being chosen.

The list includes several guys we know, who've been to the house for Halloween parties or Friendsgiving events, Donovan Price, Saxon Walsh, and Aiden Akers. The rest I'm meeting for the first time.

"My cousin Gina here is our animal coordinator. She has hounds picked out for each of you, but if you have a dog you'd like to use, please let us know. We prefer actual relationships to arranged pairs."

With that, she steps to the side with the guys whose names we called to make notes of their pet-ownership status on her roster. I'm left facing the remaining calendar boys, which includes Owen Stone.

I purposely avoided him after our flashing moment in the hall. I wasn't sure how my nerves would react to seeing him again after that naked encounter.

Today, he stands in front of me, fully clothed, with a grin on his face like we share a secret. "I guess you know I have my own hound."

"Yes..." Clearing my throat, I nod, not making eye contact. "We can go ahead and schedule your photo shoot as soon as you're ready. With the season starting so soon, we're hoping to get all the photos taken before games begin."

"Tell me the place and time, and I'll be there, Cherry."

"Cherry?" My nose wrinkles, and I squint up at him, this time making eye contact.

"You always smell like cherries."

"Oh..." I exhale a laugh. "My mom's favorite color is red, and cherries sort of became her thing. I guess it reminds me of her. My dad calls her that sometimes..."

My voice trails off at the implication.

"I like it." His voice is low, and it's clear things have shifted between us.

Whereas before, we gave each other space, not blurring the lines or being overly friendly, now he's standing close, almost touching.

I'm not sure I like this new development. It makes my ears hot and my insides tingly.

"Does tomorrow afternoon work for you?" Taking out the roster, I show him my notes. "I've got Maverick set for this afternoon, and Gavin is tomorrow morning."

"Of course." He grins, and my chest tightens. "What do you need me to do?"

"Just be at the house." I scrub my fingers over my forehead, focusing my thoughts on the job. "It'll be easier for Ladybird if she's in a familiar place."

"Sounds good. What should I wear?"

"Oh, um... Haddy didn't tell you?" Looking around, I spy my cousin making notes with the other players. "Just, ah, your skating shorts... no pants."

His brow arches, and a naughty gleam flickers in his eyes. "No shirt?"

To my horror, my cheeks burn red. I quickly blink away, fanning myself with the roster I'm holding. When I realize what I'm doing, I stop immediately and shove the papers under my arm.

"It's all part of the 'hunks' theme of the calendar, you know." I wave my hand, adding under my breath, "It was Haddy's idea."

"Don't worry, Cherry, I'm not offended." He's still teasing me, and it's almost worse. "I get it. Ladies like topless men. It's the same with guys."

Straightening my shoulders, I force myself to stop acting

like an embarrassed amateur. This is not my first rodeo, and I was recruited for my professionalism and dog expertise.

Lifting my chin, I decide two can play at this game. "You're saying *men* like topless men as well?"

His lips part with a full, pearly white smile. "I guess some do."

He says it with that same swagger he had while naked, only this time, he couples it with a wink. I'm pretty sure I burst into flames on the spot.

"Well, I'd better get going. Have to get Spanky ready for Mav."

With that, I turn and walk straight into the round, metal trash can sitting beside the door. It bangs loudly then starts to spin, rolling around and nearly falling before Owen and I both jump forward to catch it.

I want to die.

"I didn't see that there." I point at the metal canister, putting my hand on the door as I push through it.

So much for professionalism.

Owen's lips press, and I can tell he's fighting a laugh. Turning on my heel, I walk with purpose to the exit.

"THAT RYAN GUY'S PRETTY COOL." Maverick flops onto the couch after treating us all to a habanero mac and cheese dinner with Cajun cornbread.

The kitchen is clean, and we're trying to decide what "family movie" to watch tonight, since we're closing in on our final weeks of being together every week.

In the past, when hockey season started, Maverick would be gone all the time, Haddy would be in graduate school, and I'd be completely absorbed in the world of dog show judging, dog training, dog grooming...

A few things have changed since last year: Haddy graduated and had a baby, and I've backed off on judging dog shows after the last time our house was toilet-papered.

The rest has remained the same. Gav and Mav are gearing up to play nonstop, which seriously shifts our social calendar.

"I didn't think I could fit Spanky on my shoulder," Mav continues. "But the way he did the thing with the prop... it was pretty cool! Wait til you see it."

"You had Spanky on your shoulder?" My eyebrows rise.

Ryan Grantham is the premiere dog photographer in the city. I'd had to leave my cousins with him this afternoon so I could head back and file the paperwork for the Greater Los Angeles dog show, which is the last one that might put Spanky in the running for the best in show competition.

It's probably too late, but I know Ryan so well, I knew they were in good hands.

He started out briefly as my assistant dog handler, which is why I was able to get him to work with us on this calendar on such short notice. Otherwise, he would be completely out of reach.

Ryan works all the "Meet the Breed" events, and he photographs the winners of all the state competitions. He's also a rising star in Hollywood, making a name for himself taking pictures of celebrities and their dogs for local media as well as national campaigns.

"You are going to die at how good these photos look." Haddy plops down on the sofa beside me. "Mav and Spanky are supermodels."

"You don't have to convince me." I shake my head. "I

knew from the start Ryan wouldn't be my assistant for long. He has a great eye."

"He wants to include Lucy in the pictures with Gavin and Patsy tomorrow."

"Ohhh…" I'm immediately swoony, but Haddy looks worried. "Is that okay?"

Her nose wrinkles, and she tilts her head to the side. "I don't know. What do you think? We've done our best to keep her out of the media, but this is for a good cause… She's just so little."

Chewing my lip, I don't know the right answer. "Talk to your mom. They had you when your dad was a football superstar. See what they think. If it were me, I'd do it, but you know how I feel about dogs."

"I do." She boops my nose. "If there's a dog involved, it can only be a good thing."

"Oh, come on, I'm not that out of touch." I lean my head on her shoulder. "Ask Ryan to do both, and when we see what he does, you can decide how you feel. Yes?"

"My best friend's name is Ryan." Owen's deep voice sends a charge through my stomach, making me jump. "It's funny how things like that make you trust a fellow."

Tilting my head, I look up at our newest house guest. "He's not my best friend, but I can vouch for him. He's a really great guy."

"I like your idea of seeing the proofs before deciding." Haddy nods. "You're the animal coordinator for a reason!"

"We're in this together after all." I cover her hand with mine as Maverick cues up *Saw*.

"Seriously, Mav?" My nose wrinkles. "You know I don't like all that gore."

"Gina Grace Bradford." Maverick takes on a playfully

superior tone. "The original *Saw* movie is often considered the best of the franchise for the way it focuses on suspense and psychological tension rather than graphic violence."

I squint at him. "Did you just read that on the Internet?"

Haddy snorts, skipping over to the door. "I've got to get home, but I'll leave you two to sort this one out."

"Owen?" Mav looks over at his handsome new teammate.

"I've got to call my daughter. You forget they're on Eastern time."

"Some family movie night this is," he grumbles. "You'll be sorry when I'm on the ice four nights a week."

Haddy dances back to him, leaning down to kiss the top of his head. "I'll have a movie night with you tomorrow. Pick something fun. Not *Saw*."

I tell them goodnight as I climb the stairs. I've had a nonstop day, and it's going to be another nonstop tomorrow. I hesitate, making sure Owen is securely in his bedroom before I slip across the hall to take a quick shower, wash my face, and brush my teeth.

Spanky is in his crate downstairs, but I never take a chance with that dog in the house. I'm wrapped in my waffle robe as I skip across the hall into my bedroom.

The walls are covered with framed pictures of Spanky winning Best in Breed and first place in the nonsporting category.

On my bedside table is a picture of my two cousins and me at a Champions game. It was before Gavin moved here, so Haddy and I are in our Number 74 *Murphy* jerseys for Maverick.

A few other players are behind him, and they're all so tall and fit. Owen Stone's naked body skates across my brain, and I cuddle deeper beneath my blankets. I think about his shaggy dark hair, square jaw, blue eyes... rounded shoulders, broad chest, lined torso... all the way down to his...

I hear the bathroom door close, and I hesitate, listening. The shower switches on, and I'm flooded with images of Owen Stone's naked body.

I've never been like this about a man before, but he's so mature and focused. He's calm and serious, and the low tone of his voice sends tickles through my insides.

He's older but not too much, and the idea of him being a single dad, slipping upstairs every evening so he can call his little girl, being so committed to taking care of her, being there for her...

The fact he has a body like that is the most delicious icing on the cake. My stomach has been zipping with electricity since that night, and I've got to get some relief.

It's quiet as I reach over to my bedside table to take my battery-operated boyfriend "Bob" from where he's hidden. Then sliding further under my blankets, I close my eyes listening to the sound of the shower spray, imagining the rivulets of water running down that perfectly sculpted body.

The quiet vibrations touch gently against my inner thigh as I bring it higher to the apex of my thighs. With my eyes closed, I imagine his large hands following the same trail, sliding up my legs.

His lips are so full, and his whiskers are so close around his cheeks, I can only imagine what they would feel like touching my most sensitive skin.

Circling my clit with the massager, my lower belly starts to tremble. I exhale a soft *Oh...* as I picture my hands spanning his firm chest, moving lower, over the ridges and lines.

I imagine holding him, pulling him closer, rolling him

onto his back and throwing a leg across his waist, lining our bodies up so that... *OH!*

My orgasm breaks like a sneeze, and I clasp my hand over my mouth to keep from moaning too loudly. My legs shake, and I do my best to calm my breathing. I've lost track of the sound of the shower, and I realize the bathroom is quiet.

Waiting several seconds until I'm sure he's no longer across the hall, I slip out of the bed and peek out into the dark hallway.

His door is partially closed, but I can hear his deep voice talking on the phone with what I assume is his daughter. I hesitate a moment, listening to how sweetly he speaks to her. He's such a good man.

Then I dash across the hall into the bathroom to clean up quickly. I'm only gone a moment. I'm just washing my hands when I hear the sound of nails clicking on wood floors, and a large dog body rushes down the hall.

"What?" I open the door just in time to see Ladybird emerging from my bedroom with Bob clutched between her teeth. "No—Ladybird!" I hiss, running out into the hall in only my sleep shirt to try and catch her.

She's too fast for me, and before I can stop her, she's bursting through Owen's door, hopping onto his bed and wagging her tail, my hot pink vibrator clutched in her jaws.

"Yeah, that's Ladybird," Owen laughs, looking at the screen on his phone. "I'd better go and take care of her. Night, Shortcake."

"No!" Both my hands fly to my burning cheeks as he disconnects the call.

The world shifts into slow motion as he lowers his hand, looking from the dog to me and the dog again. "What is that, LB? Do you have a... *vibrator?*"

Ignoring the fact I'm only in a thin T-shirt, I zip across his room, snatch the device from Ladybird, then run away again.

His deep laughter follows me to my room, hitting me right in my still-simmering core.

6

———

OWEN

"I think Ladybird needs a bath and a trim before her shoot." I'm standing in the kitchen holding a bowl of cereal when Gina enters, the hood of her hoodie over her head.

She quickly retrieves her mug and turns her back as she pours a cup of coffee. I swallow the laugh at the base of my throat.

The sight of her cute little ass peeking out from beneath that short T-shirt as she fled from my room last night, vibrator in hand, is burned into my brain. It's like one of those old peep-show images—just enough. A little curve of flesh, a little bounce, and I want more.

I'm low-key obsessed with this cherry-scented, ginger-haired firecracker who sleeps mere feet away from me every night thinking about God-knows-who while she uses that thing to make herself come.

Hell, the thought of her twisting in her sheets, eyes

closed, lip-biting, legs shaking, had me tugging one out before I went to sleep last night.

Clearing my throat and those lusty thoughts, I continue. "I'd be willing to do it myself if you don't mind me using your space."

Her shoulders drop, and she turns to face me, hoodie still on her head. "It would be quicker if I did it. I know where everything is, and I'm the animal coordinator after all."

"Let me help you. Ladybird always likes to shake as soon as you've got her all good and soaped up."

"Use warm water and distract her with treats."

"That works?" My voice rises, and she nods, still not meeting my eyes. "And here I thought a wet dog shaking water all over you was one of those universal truths."

"It can be, but usually it's stress-related." She takes a step back, almost like she's going to run away. "Using a handheld sprayer also helps."

"Hey..." I set the bowl beside the sink, holding out my hand. "I'm sorry about last night. You ran away so fast, I couldn't—"

"No." She shakes her head, eyes squeezed closed. "Please don't."

"I was just going to say I hope she didn't break your—"

"She didn't." Her green eyes flash, and she's fucking adorably embarrassed. "Let's just drop it, okay?"

"Okay," I say, nodding. "I guess we're even now."

She's quiet for a moment, then her nose wrinkles and she looks up at me. "Are we? I mean, I saw you naked. You only know I have a *personal massager*."

"Ah, yes. A *massager*." I nod, crossing my arms. "I did, however, see your bare ass under that T-shirt. It's cute, and I have a great imagination. Maybe Spanky will do me a solid and let me see the rest of you one of these nights."

"My dog would never betray me like that." She lifts her chin in a cute, superior way. "And I will never give him the chance."

Laughter ripples from my throat, and a big smile breaks across her face as she blinks up at me. She reaches up and pushes the hoodie off her head, then takes a long sip of coffee before setting it on the counter.

"Meet you in the grooming station in five."

"I'll bring the dog treats."

"See how holding the warm water close to her skin is more soothing?" Gigi moves the sprayer in slow circles over Ladybird's coat.

My dog is secured to the side of the tub by a short leash attached to her collar, but it won't be enough to stop her from covering us in dog water if she decides to shake.

"I mean, it's possible she could still get us," Gigi continues. "But that's what the treats are for."

"Got 'em." I pull a plastic baggie from my pocket on cue. "I've got jerky, milk bones, and at your suggestion, apple slices, which I still think is weird."

"Dogs like apples," she argues, keeping her tone low and steady. "Peanut butter is another really good distraction."

"Oh, yeah." I exhale a chuckle, wondering why I didn't think of that. "Ready for the soap?"

"Yes... here." She rises slowly, keeping the sprayer close to Ladybird's coat. "I'll let you take over with the scrubber. Just move it in slow circles, soothing, not stressful."

"I don't think I've ever treated her with such kid gloves

before." I carry the small bucket with the plastic scrubber to where the dog is standing.

"And you've gotten pelted with grimy dog water every time, I bet." Gigi laughs, but somehow, on the way up, she gets tangled in the sprayer hose. "Oh!"

A little yelp rips from her throat as she spins, heading straight for the tiles. I drop the bucket, sending soapy water flying into the air, and lunge forward, pulling her quickly into my arms.

Her hands grip my shoulders, and I look down at her face so close to mine. Her body is soft and warm, and she's breathing fast, her full lips parted. Our eyes meet, a flash of heat shoots through my stomach.

I should let her go, but I can't seem to force my arms to relax. I want to go on holding her this way. I want to dip my chin and cover her mouth with mine. I want to slide my tongue with hers, curl it together, nibble her lips...

Which are now parted. Her breasts rise and fall rapidly with her breath, and her pink tongue slips out to touch her bottom lip. Is it possible she feels the same way?

What would happen if I did it? The thought presses against my temples just as Ladybird lifts her head and lets out a low "Yowl!" before turning her head and shaking her entire body as hard as she can.

"Oh, Ladybird, no!" Gigi cries, pushing out of my arms and holding both hands over her face.

Dog water flies all over us, and I hold up a hand as I laugh. "So much for soothing!"

"It's because I fell." She steps over to grab a towel off a nearby shelf. "Here..."

She presses one end to her face, and I use the other, cleaning myself as best as I can. "Looks like I'll need a shower before the shoot as well."

"Go on up." She shakes her head. "I'll finish up with her, and we'll be ready when you are."

"You sure?" I hesitate a moment, still thinking about how good she felt in my arms. "I can help you. I don't need a lot of time..."

"Go on." She waves her hands at me. "Ryan will be here any minute, and you need to be ready."

I back slowly out of the room as she returns to scrubbing my dog. It's strange how my stomach pulls as I leave her. I don't know how in such a short time she's made me only want to stay.

"Let's try a few here with the poppies," Ryan says, stopping near the wooden fence. "I think the red and orange will work well with her coloring."

He guides Ladybird between the two overgrown California poppy bushes in the backyard, and Gigi sniffs. "Now I'm glad I didn't bug Maverick too much about cutting those back," she teases.

"Do you need them cut back?" I glance over at her.

I'm still wearing my T-shirt as I help coax Ladybird into the different positions Ryan wants. It seems to help keep the tension in check.

Still, the mountain of awkwardness between us is enough for a comedy sketch. First, you have me in the hall pitching a major tent before being completely disrobed by Spanky. Then we had Ladybird retrieving her vibrator and bringing it straight to me.

"You do not have to help me with yard work," Gina replies. "I'll take care of it... sometime."

"I don't mind helping. I'm staying here rent-free, after

all."

"Honestly, I think Mav was going to hire somebody to do it." She steps back, surveying the overgrown bushes. "Knowing our luck, we'd kill it, and I really like having flowers in the yard."

"Ready, Owen?" Ryan calls from where he has Ladybird sitting with her nose in the air. "You can just take a knee beside her. Try to keep her from lying down."

Reaching behind my neck, I pull the shirt over my head. It leaves my hair a mess, but I notice Gigi's eyes widen before she blinks away.

I do as I'm told, taking a knee beside my dog and palming a treat so she stays alert.

Ryan holds a small device with a white sensor near the two of us before backing away and adjusting the lens. He looks through the camera, then pops up frowning.

"Gina, would you straighten Owen's hair?" He goes behind the camera again.

She skips over in front of me, and our eyes meet. This time, she blinks quickly, biting her bottom lip as she traces her fingers through the hair over my eyebrows, sliding it to the side.

"Like that?" Her voice is high, a little breathless.

It makes me wonder if she knows how damn tempting she is.

Ryan leans to the side, still frowning. "See that piece over his left eye?"

She turns again, meeting my gaze. She's still biting her lip as she reaches up, threading her fingers in my hair. The movement is slower than before, a little more deliberate.

"Yes?" She looks over her shoulder at Ryan.

"Perfect. Now get out of the way."

The two of them exchange a laugh, some teasing words, and the shutter on Ryan's camera clicks rapidly.

"Nice... Good energy, Owen." He moves to get a different angle, and the shutter clicks so fast. "Lower your brow like you're thinking about your next slap shot."

I'm not good at dissociating, but I do my best to follow his instructions. Thinking about my next slap shot while I'm kneeling beside my dog makes me want to roll my eyes, but I'm sure that's not the look he's after.

"Yes..." he calls from behind the camera. "Clench your jaw like that."

My eyes flicker to Gina, to see what her response is to all of this. She has both hands clasped in front of her nose, and her expression reminds me a lot of the way she looked at me when Spanky snatched my towel. It's hot, and I have to put that memory out of my head before I get a rise in my shorts.

"Let's try one more pose." Ryan turns a knob on the back of his camera. "Come over here by the tree... Do you think she'd stand on her hind legs for you?"

"I think I can get her to..." I've just started to answer when a white streak zooms past me.

Ladybird jumps into the air, letting out one of her long, happy *Rooos*. She's off chasing Spanky around the yard. The two of them jump and play as the three of us humans stand back watching with our hands on our hips.

"Those dogs sure are happy together," Ryan muses.

Gina and I exchange a look before quickly calling our animals. She lets out a crisp, "Spanky, heel!" While I blow a short whistle through my teeth.

On cue, the two dogs stop playing and return to where we're standing. Gigi drops to one knee, holding Spanky by the collar, while I stand, ready to lead Ladybird to the tree where Ryan originally wanted us.

"Hold on just a second." Ryan holds up a hand for me to wait where Gigi is kneeling. "Just stand right there for a second."

I do as I'm told, and the shutter clicks several times before his smiling face reappears from behind the camera. "That's a fun one."

We return to my shoot, and it only takes a little longer before we're wrapping it up.

"I'll send you all the proofs tonight, once I've finished touching them up." Ryan stands beside Gina rolling the film. "You two have great chemistry here. It's funny how the dogs know they should be together as much as the owners do."

"Oh, no..." Gina's eyes widen, and she holds up her hand. "We're not together."

"You're not?" Ryan's brow furrows, and he gives me a disappointed glance. "Why not? You go really well together."

"I...I just..." Gigi fumbles for words, so I jump in to rescue her.

"I just moved here from South Carolina a little over a week ago." I cup a hand under Ladybirds muzzle. "I'm only staying until I can find my own place. We hardly know each other."

"Huh." Ryan drops the camera into his bag and pulls it over his shoulder. "Well, you could've fooled me. You seem as natural together as your dogs. Either way, I'll send you the proofs tonight, Geeg. Let me know the details on the other guys. I need to wrap this up by Monday."

"I will." She calls a thank you after him, and we're left in the backyard, me with no shirt and her with a handful of dog paraphernalia.

"He's always had a vivid imagination." She bites her lip, looking up at me.

"I don't know." I shrug. "I guess after all we've been through, we are pretty comfortable around each other."

"All we've been through." Her eyes squeeze, and she shakes her head. "He has no idea."

"Good thing we're keeping it strictly professional." Even as I say the words, I don't like how they feel on my tongue.

I don't like the pit they put in my stomach. I especially don't like the flash of disappointment that flickers across her face. It's gone in a blink, but I saw it.

"Yes," she nods, collecting all her things and starting for her small studio. "Good thing."

She says the words so quietly, I wonder if I've misread the entire situation. At the same time, how else could I have read it?

I need to get my daughter here as soon as possible. I need to refocus my thoughts and remember why I'm doing this. I'm not here for romance. I'm here to play the best damn hockey I can and be a good dad. Nothing more.

7

———

GINA

"Oh my gosh, look at this one!" Haddy calls from where she and Mav are huddled over my iPad Pro screen on the table.

Dinner plates are cleaned, the kitchen is cleaned, and Gavin is on the couch cuddling Lucy as always. The guys have started practicing every day, and hockey season is bearing down on us.

I'm feeling the pressure of honoring my commitment to this calendar on top of organizing a last-minute wedding in two weeks, combined with maintaining my dog duties.

Even though I've backed off most of the local judging, I'm still committed to judging the Discover dog show in Hidden Springs this weekend.

At least it's far enough away that any disgruntled dog owners won't follow me home to egg the house or fling toilet paper in the trees or put stink bombs in the mailbox.

Walking over to the table, I see they're looking at the pictures of Gav cradling Peepee on one shoulder and Lucy on the other. With his shirt off, biceps bulging, it is possibly the money shot.

"Ryan is so good at this," I comment, noticing the way the lighting enhances the lines of Gavin's muscles as well as the perfectly contented face of his daughter.

"Lucy is the cutest baby." Mav states it as a fact, which it is. "She's already photogenic, and she can't even hold her head up."

"She inherited it from her mother... and her grand-mother... and her great-grandmother..." I tease.

"That's quite a legacy," Owen says.

Haddy shakes her head, waving at him. "It's very fraught."

"I want to see," Gavin calls from the couch.

"Do you ever put her down?" I tease, laughing.

"Hockey season is about to start," he replies. "I don't want her to forget me when I'm gone all the time."

Haddy and I exchange a melting look, and she walks over to the couch, leaning down to kiss her fiancé's forehead.

"That little girl is not going to forget her big teddy bear." She looks down at the sleeping infant in his arms. "I'll be lucky if she doesn't cry every time you're out of town."

"You'll just have to come with me."

Haddy's brows rise, and she shrugs. "I don't see why not. I don't have school commitments anymore."

I don't ask out loud what my cousin is doing now that she's finished her master's degree. For so long, she was the science girlie, studying the transmission of viruses through the air.

Then she met Gav, got pregnant, and went on her honey-moon to Japan, where she met her counterpart in studying

Kawasaki disease. Since they got back, she hasn't mentioned what's next.

Of course, it's only been a few months—and I'm still thinking she might be the Champions' newest PR director.

"I know what you mean," Owen says quietly, and I notice his stance shift. "I used to feel the same way about Maddie, until Heather started helping me."

"I can't imagine how you must miss her." Haddy's voice is warm.

He changed out of his practice clothes, and now he's in jeans and the gray T-shirt he had on this morning when we were in the yard taking photos.

The one he pulled over his head in one sweep, leaving his dark hair in a sexy mess. I'm pretty sure Ryan was applying pressure to the situation when he asked me to fix it.

He knew I was dying to thread my fingers through that thick mop. I can attest it's as silky as it looks, and his body is as gorgeous as I remembered.

The entire photo shoot, my neck was hot and my mouth dry. His biceps bulged, and the muscles in his stomach flexed, his thighs stretched his shorts... the scent of cedar and soap drifted around him in a tantalizing blend.

His skin is smooth, but his chest is dusted with coarse hair because he's mature. He's a man. It makes me shiver thinking of pressing my bare skin to his.

"I like this group shot of the four of you," Mav calls from where he's still swiping through the proofs. "You're not trying to steal Spanky from me, are you, Sly?"

"He isn't." I walk to the table, giving his arm a playful nudge. "That photo of Spanky over your shoulder is price- less. I'm pretty sure he's smiling."

"Can a dog be cocky?" Haddy asks from where she's sitting beside her fiancé on the couch.

"I don't know, but Spanky is definitely Mav's spirit animal."

"Speaking of spirit animals, look at those two." Mav nods to where Ladybird is lying inside Spanky's crate with my dog right beside her.

"Our two rascals." Crossing my arms, I shake my head. "We should call Ladybird Darla."

"She's such a gorgeous dog," Haddy says, walking over to pet them in the crate. "Have you ever thought of showing her, Owen?"

He rubs a hand over his chin. "Wouldn't she have to be registered or have papers or something like that?"

"Not always." I walk over to where Ladybird is watching all of us with perfect doggy posture. "Some shows judge solely on physical characteristics, and she has good ones."

"I don't think she'd cooperate."

"You're very photogenic yourself." Haddy's eyebrow arches as she swipes her finger across the iPad screen. "These are very good pictures of you two."

We walk over to study the pictures of Owen giving sultry looks at something behind the camera. Prickly heat climbs up the back of my neck when I remember where I was standing as the pictures were being taken. He was looking at me.

Maybe *this* is the money shot after all...

"I love the way you're looking at each other in this group shot." Haddy smiles at me. "You can feel the chemistry through the screen."

Clearing my throat, I take my iPad from them. "Unless you have preferences, I'll head up and pick the best ones to send for the calendar."

"I like them all." Mav walks over to flop on the couch, scooping up the remote. "Spanky's my partner in crime."

I have no idea what that means, but I look over to where Owen is standing at the foot of the stairs watching us.

"Owen?" My voice is soft. "Did you have a preference for pictures? We have the ones of you kneeling, but also the ones of you standing."

"I do like that one," Haddy says. "You have very nice hands for a hockey player."

Owen actually seems a little embarrassed by the compliment, which only makes him hotter.

"I'll let you decide," he says, starting up the stairs. "You're the experts here."

It's quiet when he leaves the room. None of my cousins say a word, and I can feel three sets of eyes boring into me. I can also feel the weight of what none of them are saying. It's clear as day in the pictures, but neither Owen nor I seem ready to acknowledge it.

"Well, I'm heading upstairs," I finally say, ready to get out of the pressure cooker.

"Have a good night, Gigi." Haddy's tone is pointed.

"I always had good luck on that floor," Gavin adds, doing his best not to laugh.

Maverick is the only one not giving me a hard time, and I can only guess it's because his eyes are glued to his phone.

I ignore Gav and Haddy's innuendo, jogging up the stairs just in time to bump into Owen at the top. He's fully clothed, leaving the bathroom, but he stops when he sees me.

"Hey..." he says quietly. "I had a really good time today. Your friend's really good at his job."

"Yeah, he has an amazing eye."

We hesitate, struggling with all the unspoken words about what everyone could see in the pictures.

"Talking about photogenic, I thought you were really pretty in those pictures today." His full lips press into a smile, and he melts me with that sexy blue gaze.

"Thank you," I manage to say, blinking up at him.

Leaning forward, he puts a hand on the doorjamb above me. "I really enjoyed our walk the other day. I like talking to you."

I lift my chin, getting closer to him. "I like talking to you, too."

We're blinking at each other, and that invisible pull is drawing us closer. *Chemistry* is definitely the word for it. It sparkles in the air around us. The only problem is what to do with it.

"I'm no good at relationships right now." His voice is low, husky. "I've got my daughter and the new season starting. It doesn't leave much time for anything else."

My chest sinks, but he's being honest. I appreciate honesty after my last... whatever it was.

"I know all about hockey players and hockey season," I say.

"I'm not boyfriend material." He seems to be struggling with the words.

My jaw tightens, and I don't know why this makes me angry. "I'm sure you're not. Why else would you decide I'm interested in you and then get mad about it?"

"I'm not mad." His voice rises.

"Then why are you shouting?"

"I'm not shouting!"

The click of doggy nails precedes Ladybird bounding to where we are, plowing straight into me, and knocking me into his arms. *Again.*

I fall against his hard chest with a little *oof!* And of

course, his strong arms go around me, holding me close as he gazes into my face.

We're both breathing fast, but I won't fall for a man who plays games. Not again.

"What are you doing?" I try to push away.

"I really want to kiss you right now," he growls, flexing his fingers against my skin and sending currents of lust through my veins.

Jerking my chin, I meet his eyes head-on. "What's stopping you?"

The muscle in his jaw moves attractively, momentarily hypnotizing me. He flexes his fingers on my arms once more before releasing his hold and stepping back.

Looking down, he shoves both hands in his hair, pushing it back before stepping away with one word. *"Everything."*

8

———

OWEN

Gina Grace Bradford is wearing me down.

I'm pretty sure she isn't trying to, but being so close to her, sharing a bathroom, catching her scent everywhere I turn... I only want to press her against the wall and kiss her until neither of us can see straight.

I almost did it last night, but I stopped myself.

What I said to her was the truth. I'm not boyfriend material. Hell, I'm probably too old to even be called a *boyfriend* anymore.

I'm a single dad, a widower. It's my job to put Maddie to bed at night and be sure she's comfortable and secure and not afraid of the dark or monsters in the closet.

I read bedtime stories. I'm asleep by ten.

None of this is appealing to a woman as full of life as Gigi is. Not to mention she's beautiful, and she could probably have any man she wants. Why would she want someone broken like me?

"Head in the game, Sly!" Gav gives me a shove as he glides by on the ice. "We're going to practice T3G again."

We've done all the warmups and drills, now it's time for our scrimmage.

"I'm ready," I lie.

I wasn't paying attention to a damn thing just now. The only thing on my mind was shimmering gold hair with deep red highlights, how I'd love to thread my fingers in those silky locks, pull her head back, cover her mouth...

"Stone!" Donovan's voice cuts through the noise. "Let's do this!"

Nodding, I focus my eyes on the small, black disc, skating hard to the side of the net, where Hancock sends it to me. Gav rounds the net, and I pass it to him, then he slaps it in for the goal just as fast.

T-T-T-G. Time to win.

I'VE JUST FINISHED SHOWERING and returned to the locker room when Mav holds up his phone.

"Dangit." He looks over to Gavin. "Gigi's car broke down in Hidden Creek. Can you pick her up? I've got a photo shoot in twenty minutes."

"I'm going with Haddy to Lucy's doctor's appointment." He winces. "She's getting her first shots today. Haddy will kill me if I'm not there. Can't she get an Uber?"

"She's got all her dog stuff with her."

My throat is tight, and the thought of Gina on the side of the road with a broken car has me on my feet before I can even consider if this is a bad idea. "I'll go."

They both turn to me, but Mav doesn't hesitate. "Thanks, Owen. I'll text you the details. She's got roadside assistance headed her way, but she's out there alone, the sun's going down..."

That extra bit of news has me jerking my jeans over my hips and snatching a shirt out of my cubby. "Tell her I'm on my way."

I grab my duffel bag, and I'm walking so fast for the exit, I'm practically jogging. I'm just hopping into my old Ford step-side truck, thinking I have no idea where Hidden Creek is or how to get there, when my phone lights up with the address.

This old truck was my mom's that my aunt Cass helped her maintain through the years. Aunt Cass knows all about cars, and she claims it will last forever if we take care of it properly. I would never contradict her, but it's possible the LA freeway might be its match.

Either way, I've got a bit of a drive ahead of me, according to my GPS. Hidden Creek is pretty far north of LA. It's not even in the city limits.

I make good time going, but looking across the freeway at the line of cars moving the opposite direction has me worried. It's backed up for miles.

I'm wondering if we can find an alternate route when the voice comes through the speakers telling me my turn is 800 feet away.

I exit the freeway, and it's only a short drive before I see Gina leaning against her silver Nissan on the side of the road staring at her phone.

She looks so different in a long black blazer, black dress pants, and a white silk shirt. She's wearing black boots, and her hair is smoothed into a sleek ponytail. She looks very professional. It's hot.

When she sees me pulling up, she pushes off the side of the car and walks over. "What happened to Mav and Gav?"

I can't tell if she's teasing as I hop out, slamming the door behind me. "Maverick had a photo shoot, and Gav is at Lucy's doctor's appointment."

"Oh, right." She nods. "Haddy is so worried. It's her first round of shots."

"I hated those visits." I walk over to where her car is stalled on the shoulder. "What happened?"

"I don't know. I stopped for the red light, and when it was time to go, it just died. A guy helped me push it onto the shoulder."

Opening the door, I slide into the driver's side to try giving it a start. I press the button, but nothing happens. It only makes the noise like it's trying.

"It doesn't sound like the battery or alternator." I lean forward, trying again. "It might be the fuel pump. Those tend to go out at the worst possible times."

"What's a fuel pump?" Her glossy lips twist, and I'm momentarily distracted, thinking about standing in the hall with her, looking down at those full lips, wanting to kiss her so badly...

And walking away.

"It's the thing that pumps fuel to the engine."

"So my car had a heart attack?"

"It's a good analogy, but it's more like a valve failure."

"What can we do?"

"You can't do anything with a busted fuel pump." Holding out my hand, I gesture to my truck. "I'll give you a ride home, but it'll have to be towed to a repair shop."

She looks down at her phone again. "I called roadside assistance. They're coming to jump my battery, but I think I can change it to a tow."

"See what you can do. I'll get your stuff." I walk to her trunk where she has a large briefcase and a bag filled with colorful ribbons reading *Best in Breed* and first, second, and third place.

"I was able to change it. Should we wait til they get here?" She frowns, looking around over her shoulder.

That makes me chuckle. "I think it'll be safe to leave it. This car isn't going anywhere."

She follows me slowly. "I meant to tell you, I like your truck."

"Thanks, I inherited it from my stepmom. She almost ran over my dad in it on her first day at work."

"What?" she cries, falling back against the white leather seat.

"Brakes went out. Luckily, she wasn't going very fast." I think about the story my parents tell all the time of my stepmom's first day back in Eureka, working with my dad. "She was also blasting Shania Twain music with the windows down, so they heard her coming."

Gina laughs. "You'll have to play some for me when we get back. I've been dying to hear Ladybird howl."

"It's pretty funny." I glance at her with a grin, the tension leaving my chest.

I was worried she was mad at me last night. I'm glad to see she's not.

"I almost didn't recognize you all dressed up like that." I nod at her power suit. "You look like the CEO of Dog World."

That makes her snort. "Dog people take these shows very seriously. We're all expected to look the part."

"I'm not sure what the part is, but you look great." I give her a teasing wink.

"Thanks." Her nose wrinkles as she glances out the window shyly.

When my eyes return to the road, I have to slam on

brakes. All the cars ahead of us have come to a complete stop, and I see flashing blue and red lights stretching far in front of us.

"What the hell?" I look around at cars slowly pulling off onto the shoulder and heading back in the direction we came.

"Let me text Aunt Raven and see if she can help us." Gigi has her phone out, thumbs flying over the screen.

"Who's Aunt Raven?" I glance over at her.

"Haddy's mom is chief meteorologist for KCLA. It's one of the TV stations in town."

Squinting, I look up at the sky. "I don't understand. Are you expecting rain?"

"She's also on the traffic desk. She'll let us know..." A few seconds pass, and Gigi's shoulders drop. "Oh, no."

"What?"

"The bridge up ahead is closed. Aunt Raven says a semi-truck carrying a load of down pillows flipped. Feathers are everywhere, and all southbound lanes are closed for cleanup. That's why everyone's turning around. She says we can drive three hours out of the way, or we have to try and get a room at one of these motor hotels before they're all gone."

She doesn't have to tell me twice. Turning the wheel, I do a hard U-turn on the shoulder and drive quickly to the last exit we passed.

"She said there's a cute little motor lodge just off the road ahead called Delve Inn. Supposedly it has four stars, and visitors call it *quirky*." She frowns. "I'm not sure I like the sound of that."

"Four stars is good, though."

Worried green eyes meet mine. "I hope so."

I follow the road, and sure enough, after a few miles we

spot a long, beige motel off to the right. A neon-lit sign above reads Delve Inn, and it looks like something out of an old movie or on Route 66.

"Quirky is right."

Gina's brow furrows. "It looks like the set of *Psycho*."

"I don't like the look of that." I nod at all the cars crowding the parking lot. "Did she say if there was anything else? *Psycho* or not, we might be lucky to get a room."

"Just be cool." Her voice is low. "I'm prepared to turn on the puppy-dog eyes if I must."

That makes me chuckle, and I pull up to the first cottage, which has a door marked *Office*. We step into a small, pine-scented room with a slim guy dressed in a beige corduroy blazer behind the desk. He's even chewing gum, which is starting to creep me out. *Psycho* is right, and it's freaking October on top of it.

"Hi, there," Gina says brightly. "I'm Gina Bradford, and this is Owen."

"Gina, Owen," the guy nods as he says our names. "I'm Ned, the manager here. Do you need a room?" He blinks from me to Gina before turning to his desktop, lightly hitting his head with his hand. "Of course, you do. Why else would you be here? What I should say is how many nights?"

"Just tonight," Gigi answers. "The bridge is out, so we can't get back to LA."

"Yeah," he laughs softly. "We haven't had this many guests since they built the freeway. I-I wasn't around then, of course" he quickly explains. "It's just what I've heard my mother say."

My hand is on Gigi's upper arm, and I give it a gentle squeeze, pulling her closer so I can whisper in her ear. "We are going to be stabbed to death in our shower."

Her shoulder rises, and she exhales a little noise before

smiling at the skinny Norman-Bates lookalike. "Do you need a credit card?"

"Yes, please, and an ID if you don't mind."

I hand over my credit card, and after taking all our information, Ned leads us down the row of doors to one that's labeled twenty-one.

"Lucky number." He smiles, stopping and turning to us.

"Really?" Gina's eyes are wide. "How so?"

"Twenty-one is when all the fun begins." He pauses a beat, then tilts his head, "At least that's what I've heard."

"You're not twenty-one?" Surprise is in her tone.

"I'm twenty-two actually." That's all the explanation we get. "Here's your key. I know it's old-fashioned to have metal keys, but we like hanging onto some of the old ways."

My hand is still on Gigi's arm, and I squeeze it tighter.

"Thank you, Ned." Her voice is strangled, and as soon as we get inside and close the door, she bursts out laughing. "He's *got* to be doing it on purpose. There's no way he really says those things for real."

"I don't know." I lean closer to the window, sliding the curtain back with my finger and watching him walk back to the office. "All I know is that door's staying locked, and if he invites us for milk and sandwiches, *run.*"

Gigi goes to the picture on the wall and attempts to take it down. "Doesn't move. I guess that's a good thing?"

"I showered after practice, so I'm good for tonight."

"I showered this morning, so I'm good."

Turning, we look around the very plain, very small room. It seems clean, no weird smells, and the air conditioner at the window drones steadily, creating a nice white noise.

"This might be a problem." Gigi nods at the one bed, which is smaller than a queen-size.

I look around the room to see it only has a desk, a chair, an armoire, a tiny sofa... *loveseat?*

"What do you think? Should I sleep on the floor?"

"No way!" She shakes her head frowning. "I can't let you sleep on the floor when you're in this whole situation because of me."

"What are you saying then? Bathtub?"

"Owen." She makes a face like I'm being ridiculous. "We're both adults. We can sleep in the same bed for one night."

She walks over to put her bags in the corner beside the desk, then she slides the long coat off her shoulders and drapes it over the chair. My eyes glide down the length of her ponytail to where it ends between her shoulder blades, drifting lower to her perky butt in those black pants.

I remember the sight of that butt peeking out at me from beneath her shirt the other night, and heat rushes to my pelvis.

"Don't you agree?" She turns to face me, and I clear my throat, walking over to put my wallet and keys on the bedside table.

"Sure." I nod, wanting to agree, while I'm not entirely sure.

C'mon, of course we can. We're adults, not teenagers.

I'm a dad. I can share a bed with an attractive woman for one night and keep my hands to myself. Probably...

That said, she's beautiful, it's been years, and I'm not dead yet.

I give it a solid *maybe.*

"Should I order us some food?" *Good distraction.* I pull out my phone, opening the food delivery app. "Looks like we can get tacos, pizza, gyros..."

"Do they have chicken shawarma? I'd like that and

hummus." She walks over to dig in her bag. "I wish I had something better to wear besides this outfit."

"Hang on." I lift my duffel from where I left it by the door. "I just came from practice, so I've got..." I shove the plastic laundry bag holding my sweaty clothes to the side. "A T-shirt and an extra pair of boxer briefs."

I hold up the maroon underwear and the oversized white tee.

Her eyes light, and she skips over to where I am. "Are they clean?"

"I wouldn't offer if they weren't."

"They're perfect. Thanks!" She swipes them out of my hands and disappears into the bathroom.

I order our food and look around the room. There's no mini-bar or fridge, but at least there's a very basic coffee pot. I hear the bathroom door open, and when I look up, my stomach dips.

Her hair is still in that long ponytail. My T-shirt and shorts hang loose on her slim body, and her face is washed, no frills.

She's the best thing I've seen in a long time.

I can't get over how she makes my old T-shirt and boxer briefs look so good. I can't believe I gave them to her. Now she's like a walking temptation I'm supposed to share a bed with and not touch.

"Food should be here any minute." I try to clear my head, looking around the room to assess our options. "We could share the desk... but there's only one chair. That sofa is really small."

"We could have a picnic on the floor?" She steps into the bathroom again and comes back with a towel that's seen better days. "This can be our blanket."

I take the thin towel from her and spread it over the

carpet. "Here." Holding out a hand, I help her sit, even if she doesn't really need it.

I'm about to sit across from her when a sharp knock at the door makes her yelp. She grips my arm, and I step over to look through the peephole.

"Food's here."

"Oh my gosh," she sighs, putting a hand on her chest. "I thought it was Ned with a knife."

I open the door and grab the paper bag, then I lock us in again, double-checking in case the young manager decides to come back dressed as Mother.

We ordered the same thing, only I got steak instead of chicken. Coke for me, iced tea for Gina, and we're digging in like it's our first meal of the day.

All the skating I did this afternoon has me ravenous, and for a few minutes, we quietly wolf down our food. When I finally come up for air, she's leaning against the bed, touching her lips with a paper napkin.

I straighten, doing the same. "How'd the dog show go?"

"Same as always." She takes a sip of tea. "I walk around the dogs, lift their ears, check their teeth, check their nuts."

I almost shoot Coke through my nose. "Their nuts?"

"They have to be fully intact." She nods, and I glance at her hands, which she holds up, turning side to side. "Don't worry, I washed them."

"Who was the winner?"

"An Afghan Borzoi named Some Like it Hot Hazel." She stabs a piece of chicken, putting it into her mouth. "I've worked with Haze before, and she deserved it. She's absolutely stunning. Long, golden fur like pure silk. A perfect example of the breed."

She looks up at the window like she's picturing the dog

right now, and I think I wouldn't mind watching Miss Gina Bradford judge a dog show.

"So you've been into dogs your whole life?"

Her nose wrinkles, and she nods. "Pretty much. Were you into hockey all your life?"

"Nah, I didn't even know what hockey was when I was a kid."

We've put our food containers aside, and now I'm leaning beside her against the bed. Gina has her hand on her stomach, looking up at me.

"Oh, that's right! You wanted to be a baseball player."

I shake my head. "When I was a little boy, I wanted to be a sheriff just like my dad." She makes an *aw* sound, and I nod. "I thought my dad was the greatest guy in the world."

"Thought?" Her eyebrow arches.

"Sorry, *think*. He's still the greatest guy in the world. I just meant, that's how it was, just me and him." I tilt the plastic bottle in my hand, remembering those days. "Then my stepmom Britt came along, and she taught me card tricks and magic, and he got really pissed."

"Why?" Her eyes widen.

"After my mom died, he stopped believing in magic... and pretty much anything requiring faith."

Her chin drops, and she circles a piece of grilled chicken in the bowl of hummus. "Is that how you feel?"

Her voice is quiet, and I think about the question.

"Sort of... but in a different way." I scrub my fingers over my forehead, remembering all the times I blamed myself for what happened, for not noticing more. "I'm more in the realm of, you can never be too sure."

"Tell me about it." She sniffs, lifting her chin.

"What happened to you?" Then I realize how the question sounded, and I laugh. "I mean, who shook your faith?"

"I don't know if that's a fair way to say it." She hesitates, looking down at the plate in her lap. "Maybe I misinterpreted the situation, read more into it than was there."

"What did he do?" I realize an edge of anger has entered my tone.

I'm ready to find the dickhead who damaged her trust and... force him to apologize.

"It's kind of embarrassing." She puts her food container in the paper bag, turning away from me.

I reach out to put my hand on her shoulder. "It's okay. I don't judge."

She looks up at me, biting her bottom lip. After a momentary hesitation, she relents.

"When I first moved to LA from Newhope, I tried dating a few guys. They were all nice enough, but it seemed like once we slept together, they were ready to move on."

"Jerks," I mutter.

Her slim brow furrows, and she nods slowly. "So when I started dating Baxter, I decided not to sleep with him right away. Like I thought we should get to know each other better first."

"Sounds smart."

"So I set a number of dates I thought would give us the right amount of time..."

"A number?"

Bending her legs, she leans forward to put her forehead on her knees. "Stop, I realize now how I set myself up for it."

"What was the number?"

"Six."

"Six?" *Wow.* I lean back against the small sofa across from her, sipping my Coke and nodding. "What's so special about that number?"

"I don't know. It felt like a good, round number." She

squirms, and I do my best to maintain my no-judgment vibe.

"Okay…"

"I figured we'd go on a date a week, and if six weeks isn't long enough… I mean, that's almost two months!"

"It is." I nod.

"But he doubled up."

"Doubled?"

"More like tripled," she huffs. "He took me to art openings, outdoor concerts, picnics…"

"Picnics are free."

"Then when we got to six, he was very…" She leans against the bed again, squeezing her hands on the top of her knees. "So I slept with him. And I never heard from him again."

"Hmm…" It's a low growl in my throat, and now I really want to find this guy.

Gina's shoulders rise, and she covers her face with her hands. "I know—I did it to myself, whereas if I'd just put out on the first or second date, I could've saved myself all that time and effort and embarrassment."

"You don't really think that's the right answer, do you?"

She shakes her head, dropping her hands and looking down. "I don't know. Maybe I do? Maybe I'm just not—"

"Hey." Leaning forward, I catch her chin in my thumb and forefinger. "Look at me, Gina."

She stills, blinking those pretty green eyes up at me. The scent of cherries drifts around us, and all I can think of is how again, I want to kiss her so badly.

Only this time, I don't want to stop at her lips.

"You are so much more than you know. Any guy who can't see that is a fucking asshole."

9

———

GINA

Heat flashes in my chest, racing up my neck, all the way to my cheeks.

Owen Stone holds my face with the tips of his fingers, leaning closer so his scent of soap and cedar permeates my brain, and I have never had such a strong attraction to anyone in my life.

"How can you say that?" I laugh softly, doing my best to grab the reins on my racing heart. "We hardly know each other."

"I see you. You take care of everyone at your house, the dogs. You help everyone with their special projects... You're really great Gina."

"Thank you," I say, flustered and looking down.

Tilting my iced tea to the side, I wish it were something stronger. Maybe some purple drink?

"This is such a crazy place." He pushes off the floor, collecting our garbage and carrying it to the small bin.

The muscles in his tight ass flex with every step, and I

remember his bare chest from the photo shoot, broad, lined, scattered with light brown hair. I remember him standing in the hall completely nude, penis erect, and I cross my legs in an attempt to cool these burning feelings for him.

"I wonder if you're right, and he's putting on an act." Owen turns around, and I gulp a breath, hoping he can't tell the way I was ogling him just now.

His blue eyes narrow, and he returns to where I'm sitting.

"Nobody knows who we are here." A hint of mischief is in his voice. "We could put on our own act."

"What do you mean?"

"Two can play his game. We can pretend to be different people as well."

My brow tightens, and I'm intrigued by his suggestion. It sounds like a fun way to pass a night in a creepy, *Psycho* motel.

"Who would we be?"

"Marion Crane would be too obvious." He glances up at the popcorn ceiling. "We could be John and Kendall Grant, but instead of looking for your sister, we could be here on our honeymoon."

My throat tightens, and the heat in my chest is real.

Sliding my ponytail over my shoulder, I decide to embrace the charade. "John is not very good at this," I tease.

A naughty twinkle is in his blue eyes. "Why not?"

"It's our honeymoon, and you brought me to a cheap place like this? With all your money?"

"Maybe I have a fantasy…"

Rising onto my knees, I crawl over to where he's sitting with his back to the loveseat. "What kind of fantasy?"

He shifts closer, placing large hands on the sides of my legs, parting them so I can straddle his lap. My heart beats faster when his hands go beneath the back of the shirt I'm wearing.

"The kind where I saw you broken down on the side of the road and brought you here." His voice is a husky whisper. "I couldn't keep my hands off you any longer, so I had to have you. Just this once..."

My breath hitches, and I allow him to pull me closer. I'm not wearing a bra under his thin, white tee, and my nipples are sharp points piercing the fabric.

"This sounds like a very specific fantasy." I whisper, feeling the erection growing in his jeans through the thin cotton boxers I'm wearing. "Why here?"

He groans deeply. "I couldn't drive any farther without having you."

My mouth waters. I place my hands on his shoulders, rocking my core over the stiff muscle beneath me. He lets out another hiss, placing his forehead against my chest before moving his mouth over my breasts, pulling a tight nipple through the thin fabric.

A groan rises in my throat, and I shove my fingers into his thick hair. It's so soft. I curl them, pulling as I dry-hump his lap. He traces his lips up my neck until our faces are a breath apart.

"Will you let me kiss you now?" he asks, and I lean forward to seal my lips to his.

His hands move up to cup my cheeks. Tilting my face, he deepens the kiss, licking his tongue against mine and pulling my lips with his teeth.

A soft whimper escapes on a breath, and he reaches down to lift me off the floor in a sweep, carrying me to the bed.

I don't ask questions; I don't break the spell. I'm on my

knees on the side of the bed, and he steps back to pull his shirt over his head the way he did at the photo shoot.

His dark hair is a mess on his head, and I exhale a swoon, reaching down to do the same, lifting the shirt over my head.

My hair is still back in a tight ponytail, and when I reach up to undo it, he catches my hand.

"Leave it." It's a rough order, and I obey.

His blue eyes are dark and hungry, and it sends fire roaring through my veins, through my core, all the way to my toes.

"What do we do now?" I whisper.

"Touch me." He steps closer, and I reach out to do what I've wanted to do for so long.

I trace my fingers over the lines of his chest, down to the lines in his stomach, watching as his muscles tense in the wake of my caress.

His breath trembles, and large hands are on my back, pulling me closer, pressing my breasts to his firm body. The warmth, the friction of our skin, makes me ache.

"It's been so long," he whispers as my hands move lower, to the waist of his jeans.

Hesitating, I blink up to meet his eyes, wondering what this will mean and how it will change things.

His hands move down my body, following the curve of my lower back, over the swell of my ass, until his fingers go between my thighs, lifting and pulling me closer.

I gasp, powerless as dark blue eyes hold mine.

The muscle in his square jaw flexes, and he leans closer, his breath a warm whisper against my cheek. "Just this once, I want to kiss every part of you. Will you let me?"

My chin dips, and I nod before he even finishes speaking. "Yes."

Not wasting a moment or even allowing for a chance to reconsider, I unfasten his jeans, pushing them lower so I can slide my palm up and down his hard cock.

Again, his mouth covers mine, and with a groan, our tongues collide. This time, I kiss him back with equal force, curling my tongue with his and chasing his lips with mine.

Breaking away, he bends down to shove his jeans off his feet, straightening so I can have a full view of his glorious physique once more.

Licking my lips, I follow the lines of his muscles, the curl of his fingers.

Blinking up to his eyes, they're hungry, and a naughty thrill races to my core. I lean forward, taking his erection in my hand and curling my tongue around the tip, flickering at the base.

"Fuck…" he groans, threading his fingers in my hair. "Gina…"

"Kendall," I say, blinking my eyes up to his before pulling him deeper into my mouth, to the back of my throat.

Another low groan, and now his eyes are glassy. His lips are tight over his clenched teeth, and I feel his hips make the slightest thrust. He's holding back, and I slide my hands to his waist, around to his ass, pulling him closer, deeper.

He cups my cheeks, whispering a swear. Salt is on my tongue, and he pulls me up with a little pop.

"Stop." He puts a finger on my swollen lips. "I'm too close. I don't want to come down your throat."

Reaching down, he cups my breast with one hand, pinching my nipple lightly with his fingers before kneading my soft flesh. Then he steps forward to pull it into his mouth, tracing it with his teeth.

I arch my back higher, making it easier for him to devour me. My fingers return to his soft hair, and his mouth moves higher, up my chest to my neck. I lean down to kiss the side of his ear, inhaling the clean scent of his shampoo.

Lifting his chin, he covers my mouth with his, giving me a brief kiss before straightening to meet my eyes.

"Get on all fours and face the wall." It's a low order, and I move around to comply.

Facing the opposite wall, I wait as he puts both hands on my hips, pulling his boxer briefs off my body. Cool air swirls around my legs just before his face goes between my thighs, and he drags his tongue up and down my core.

"Oh, shit..." I hiss, my arms bending from the intense rush of pleasure.

He doesn't stop, circling his tongue over my clit persistently, with just the right amount of pressure. My entire body is focused on his movements, and my lips part.

My eyes squint as tendrils of pleasure trace up my legs, growing higher, centering where his mouth covers me. He keeps going, as if he's conjuring that pleasure, drawing it to him like a charm. More circles, more ribbons of pleasure, then he changes to a suck, and I break.

"Oh... Owen..." My voice trembles as my pelvis jerks.

He gives me one more swift pass before leaning up and biting my ass. "John."

My forehead rests on my hands as the waves recede from my body, but he isn't finished. He moves around behind me, and I hear the sound of a condom wrapper. Glancing over my shoulder, his brow is lowered, and his eyes are on his cock.

He moves the tip up and down my slippery entrance, teasing me and coating himself before lining up and meeting my eyes. "Ready?"

I nod, arching my back again as he slowly invades. He's

bigger than any man I've been with, and I exhale a moan as he sinks all the way, leaning down to whisper in my ear.

"You okay?"

My eyes are closed, but again, I'm nodding as he speaks. "Yes..."

With a gentle kiss to the top of my cheekbone, he rises, wrapping my ponytail around his hand and starting to thrust faster.

A primal sound rises from my throat, and I push back, meeting his thrusts and wanting more. I need more. It feels too good. It's wild and passionate and dirty and hot.

He hits a place deep inside me no one has ever found, and I'm desperate for it to keep going, for more.

He pulls my hair tighter, and I rise up, until I'm practically bouncing my ass against his hips. My head falls back, and I moan as the shudders take over my limbs.

He cups my breasts, pressing his mouth to the side of my neck and biting, sucking.

It's a pinch of pain mixed with pleasure, and my hands cover his as I continue to ride. He grows thicker. His grip on my body tenses, and he holds. His stomach shudders at my back, and he lets out a moan so loud, I come more.

I feel him jerking deep inside, and I rise onto my knees to drop again, giving him another thrust, drawing another, shuddering moan.

Strong arms wrap around my waist, and he holds my back against his chest, his cheek presses to my shoulder. We're breathing hard, and a bead of sweat rolls between our bodies.

I wrap my arms over his, and it's as if we're melting into one, the most intense bond forging. With my eyes closed, I imagine us fitting together like puzzle pieces...

It's too much to think... even for a fantasy, so I shake it away, loosening my hold and starting to rise.

He reaches between us to dispose of the condom. He goes into the bathroom, and I hear the sound of water running. Removing the bedspread, I lie on my side on the white sheets. It's not the greatest hotel, but at least the sheets are clean and don't feel like sandpaper.

The water stops, and when he returns, he's holding a washcloth as if he'll hand it to me. Instead, his eyes slide down my still-naked form in a way that has my body heating up again.

"Did I say just once?" A grin lifts the side of his mouth.

My eyebrow arches, and I return his bad-boy grin. "I think you did, but maybe I misunderstood?"

"What I meant was one night." He sits on the bed, reaching out to put his thumb on my chin. "How does that sound?"

Puckering my lips, I nod. "It sounds very sensible. What else are we going to do with this bed all night?"

"Make the most of it." Reaching out, he pulls my body flush against his, causing me to exhale a sigh.

My elbows bend, and I trace my fingers along his rounded shoulders. "We've been alone too long, John. We need to make up for lost time."

He leans his head down to kiss the base of my neck, the top of my shoulder. "You are a very intelligent woman, Kendall. I admire that about you. Now I'm going to fuck you again."

A laugh bursts through my nose, and a butterfly beats wildly in my stomach. "I have no problem with that."

10

———

OWEN

The pale blue glow of dawn warms the edges of the curtains, and I blink at the pebbled ceiling overhead as the world seeps back into focus.

I'm in a cheap motel somewhere north of LA, and my body is completely entwined with the most beautiful woman I know.

I don't want to let her go.

I don't want to move in case she rouses and says what I'm already thinking. *What are we doing here? We can't do this.*

But we made a pact. It was only a fantasy. *Just one night…*

My phone buzzes, and I pick it up to read the text on the screen.

He has no idea. Only, I wouldn't characterize this as a disaster. Far from it.

Lifting my other arm, I quickly tap a reply.

OWEN

> We didn't get feathered, but we did sleep at
> the Bates motel.

MAVERICK

Good thing you showered at the arena.
What's your ETA? Something arrived
for you.

Gina stirs at my movements, rolling off my chest with a soft sigh. My chest squeezes, and I don't want to leave this room, even if it does resemble the set of one of the greatest horror films of all time.

She sits up, and my eyes slide down the elegant column of her back. Her ponytail is gone, and her hair hangs in a strawberry-blonde curtain over her ivory skin.

She lifts the sheet in front of her to cover her perfect breasts, and I reach out to put my hand on her waist.

"Sleep well?" My voice is low, a little husky.

Turning her face, she looks over her shoulder to nod. Her eyes are still closed, but a grin curls her lips. It tightens my stomach, and I want to push my phone away. I want to wrap my arms around her and pull her under me again. *I want another night...*

"I guess we'd better head back," she says, standing and walking to the bathroom.

The door closes, and I lift the device to reply to my friend.

OWEN

> Getting on the road soon.

MAVERICK

Drive safe.

"DADDY!" The little voice breaks from the door of Maverick and Gina's home as soon as I step out of my truck.

It's followed closely by the loud *Rooo!* of Ladybird, loping right behind my flying seven-year-old.

"Maddie!" I drop my duffel bag and scoop her up as soon as she reaches me.

Her little arms are around my neck, and I hug her tiny body tight against my chest. My throat clogs, and damn, my eyes heat. I didn't realize how much I'd missed this little nugget until right this minute. This is the longest we've ever been apart since the day she was born.

"Aunt Heather said you missed me, so we came right away!" She lifts up a stuffed toy zebra, jumping him on my shoulder. "We had to be on an airplane for a long, long time, but Zander played with me the whole way. And they had *Sharkboy and Lavagirl*, and I ate pretzels that tasted like honey, but I didn't like riding in the airplane. It was really bumpy and kept doing this."

She moves her little hand up and down in a wavy motion, and laughter ripples through my chest. I kiss the side of her head, giving her another squeeze before putting her down.

"I'm sorry you had a rough flight," I say. "I sure have missed you, Shortcake."

She bounces over to my dog, giving her a hug. "Ladybird has grown!"

"Has she?" I squint an eye, trying to see it.

"Yes! And I met her friend Spanky, and they like to jump up and put their legs on each other like this..." She bats me with her arms, seeming more like a seal than a dog.

"I've noticed that." I pick up my duffel, following her into the house.

She takes my hand, and Ladybird bounds behind us. Just inside the door, I see my sister Heather standing with her arms crossed and a smirk on her lips.

"Who knew you lived with a dog lady?" Her eyebrow arches.

I don't even respond to that. Instead, I pull her in for a hug, cutting off any psychic delusions.

"Good to see you, sis. What made you decide to come early?"

She still has her arms crossed, but she's full-on smiling now. "I got a text from Haddy Bradford saying you missed your little girl too much, and could we come out to LA now. Of course, I said yes. I figured you were just being sweet not telling me yourself."

"That Haddy," Mav shakes his head, chuckling. "She just had a baby a few months ago, and she's been worried about Owen ever since she found out he's a single dad."

"That's really sweet," Heather says, giving him a smile.

"Are you the lady with all the dogs?" Maddie's voice is loud in the foyer, and my neck tightens when I realize I completely left Gina behind in the truck.

We didn't say much on the drive back from Hidden Creek. The radio played softly, and I rested my hand on the top of her thigh.

She traced her finger over my knuckles, her gaze drifting out the window, and I'm pretty sure we both were a little stunned and unsure what to do or say about what happened.

"Hi, there." Her voice is kind. "Are you Maddie?"

My daughter nods her head in her signature, too-hard way. "I'm Madison Birgitte Stone, and I'm seven years old!"

"You're almost in double digits!" Gina bends her knees, putting herself on my daughter's level. "What do you do for fun, Madison?"

"It's okay, you can call me Maddie." She puts her hand on Gigi's shoulder. "I like to swim and I like to ride my bike and I like to play with Ladybird and Zander and I like to jump on the trampoline at Grannie B's house and I like to get facials where you put cucumbers on your eyes and I like to make pigs in blankets with Daddy..."

"Phew, that's quite a list!" Gigi laughs, and her green eyes dance in a way that hits me unexpectedly hard. "I don't think we can do all of those things, but we can do some of them."

Maddie's brown eyes widen, and she puts both hands on Gina's shoulders, facing her. "Okay!"

"I'd better take my stuff up and shower." I turn to Maverick, not my sister, who is boring holes in me with her eyes.

I don't need psychic powers to know what she's thinking.

"I put the girls in Haddy's old room." Maverick slaps the top of my shoulder. "It's a little tight, but they should be fine for a little while. Haddy offered her guest room if it's too crowded, but I figured that would sort-of defeat the purpose of getting them here."

"You guys are really great." I can't find the words to say how much I mean it.

"How long have you had Zander?" Gina is still chatting with my daughter like they've known each other forever. "He looks like a wise old zebra."

"Oh, he is." Maddie's eyes are wide. "He was my daddy's zebra! Did you know if a horse and a zebra have a baby, it's called a *zorse*?"

"I did not know that." Gina laughs.

"It's true, and a group of zebras is called a dazzle."

Maddie barely takes a breath. "Daddy said he thought they should be called a *zazzle* and Pop said Daddy should've been a zebrologist, but Aunt Cass said that's not a real word."

I pull Heather close before heading upstairs. "Don't let Maddie talk Gina's ear off."

"Looks like they're both right where they want to be." My sister slants her blue eyes up at me, but I'm not getting caught in her dream web.

"I'll be right back."

I'm moving fast as I jog upstairs. I drop my bag in my bedroom, fish out my dirty clothes, and dig around before remembering I gave my backup boxer briefs to Gina last night. Before I yanked them off...

Everything we did last night presses against my temples, but I have to honor our "just one night" agreement, now more than ever.

It was only a few nights ago I was wishing Maddie was here to help me refocus my thinking. Now she *is* here, and I have to start behaving like her father again, not like a single guy.

I'm *not* a single guy. I'm a single *dad*. Big difference.

I shower quickly, washing away all traces of all the different ways I had Gina Bradford on my body. A tinge of regret twists in my stomach, but I can't dwell on it.

Stepping out of the shower, my jaw clenches when I notice a spot on the top of my chest. I can't wash away a hickey.

We were stone-cold sober last night, and we were ravenous for each other. I remember all the places I marked her with my mouth.

My dick rises when I think of all the places she marked me with hers. Looking down, I see another spot on my lower belly, below my navel. I remember her knees beside my ears in a sixty-nine position... Fuck, that was hot.

I scrub the towel over my head and face, doing my best to shove those memories away. I guess it's a good thing we had a marathon night of sex. Now I'm sated for a little while.

Who am I kidding? I'd do it all again tonight if Gina asked me. If I didn't have other commitments, that is. Tonight, I'm back on Dad duty.

I pull on a pair of jeans and a fresh T-shirt, scoop up my bag of sweaty clothes, and head down the stairs just in time to hear Shania Twain say, "Let's go." It's followed by the strains of a guitar, and Ladybird immediately joins in, howling at the top of her lungs.

Maddie starts to sing the lyrics to "I'm Gonna Getcha Good" along with Shania, and Ladybird almost sounds like she's trying (and failing) to hit the notes as well.

My eyes go like a laser to Gina, who is on the couch with her hands clasped in front of her face laughing. Maverick stands behind the couch, laughing as well.

Spanky dances around in front of his friend, lifting his front feet off the floor and seeming confused by all the howling.

Heather stands beside the fireplace with Haddy, who must've walked over while I was in the shower, and the two of them are fawning over Baby Lucy.

I pause on the stairs to take in the scene. They're all so happy together. They fit... the same way Gina's body fit with mine. Something moves in my chest, but I rub my palm over my forehead. Clearly, I'm letting the psychic mess with my mind.

These are all likeable people. Of course, they get along. It doesn't mean matrimony.

The song ends, and my daughter hops off the couch to hug Ladybird.

"You have a beautiful voice, LB!" she cries, and our dog responds with a firm lick across her face, which makes her fall back laughing.

Gina gives her a warm look before going to where my sister is standing with her cousin.

"Owen told us you're a tarot reader," Haddy says, blue eyes wide. "You've got to read Gina's cards!"

"Okay..." I don't like the conspiratorial tone in my sister's voice. "I'd really like that."

Gina breaks in. "What we've *got* to do is finalize these wedding details, Haddy. We're running out of time."

"Sounds like I got here just in time," Heather teases. "You want that reading now?"

"Let's put a pin in that," Gina says, then she explains how she tried to get a venue booked, but they wouldn't budge on their schedule.

"Why don't we just do it in Newhope?" Maverick calls from where he's standing behind the couch. "You can do it on the bluff where your parents got married... sorry, where they renewed their vows."

My sister frowns, looking at her new friends, and Haddy quickly explains. "They got married here in LA at the Justice of the Peace. Then they went back and did it again with the family. That's actually not a bad idea, Mav... Do you think we could?"

Gina looks like she just swallowed a goldfish. "You're trying to kill me."

Haddy's brows rise, but she grabs her cousin's arm. "Clint can help us... and all the aunts will pitch in. You know they'd love it."

"Who's Clint?" Heather asks, blinking from one to the other.

"He's our uncle Craig's husband, and one of the best wedding planners on the Eastern shore," Haddy explains.

"What about Gavin's family?" Gina's voice is strained.

"Newhope is closer than LA," Haddy says. "Just see what Aunt Dylan says."

"It sounds like you've already decided." Gina takes out her phone. "We've got to call them now and see what they say."

The three women take off into the other room, and I'm left with my daughter, Mav, and the dogs. I walk down the last two steps, intending to carry my sweaty clothes to the laundry room, when he stops me.

"So..." He stands straighter, lowering his brow and inhaling as if to broaden his chest. "You spent the night with my cousin? Where did you sleep?"

"I... uh..." I'm surprised by his question and this sudden change in demeanor. "I offered to sleep in the bathtub."

I'm not ready to tell him Gina flat-out rejected that idea, so instead we spent the night replicating every pose in the Kama Sutra.

He holds his frown for a moment longer, then he breaks, punching me in the shoulder. "I'm just messing with you. You're a good guy, Owen. I think it's cool you're into Gigi."

"Oh, I wouldn't say..." I don't know how to finish that sentence.

I *am* into Gina, but I don't think starting a relationship in the face of my situation is the best idea.

"You're not into Gina?" Mav's brow lowers again, and his voice turns sinister. "What's wrong with my cousin?"

"Nothing!" I answer fast, and again he laughs, punching my arm.

"Dude, you really gotta lighten up. Anyone would think I'm hitting a nerve."

He has no idea.

"Did you hear Ladybird sing, Daddy?" Maddie skips over to where I'm standing, holding up her little arms for me to lift her.

"I did." I lean down to kiss the top of her blonde head. "Let me put these clothes on to wash. Come with me."

I head for the laundry room, which is right off the kitchen... which means I have to enter the space where the three women are intensely discussing wedding plans with what sounds like even more women on FaceTime.

"Of course, we can make it happen!" A voice on Gigi's iPad cries. "How much time do we have?"

Haddy and Gigi exchange a look, then Gigi answers. "Less than a week."

"I love a challenge." A smiling face appears on the large screen, and I'm caught for a moment by the strawberry blonde hair, upturned nose.

I'm sure it's Gina's mother.

"Owen!" Heather calls from where she's right in the middle of the planning. "Can we go to Newhope for the wedding? Please?"

"I want to go to a wedding! Please, Daddy?" Maddie stands beside me with her little hand in the pocket of my jeans, and I'm holding the load of dirty laundry, with all the women looking at me expectantly.

No pressure or anything.

"Are we even invited?" I ask.

The room erupts into female voices.

"Of course, you are," Haddy cries. "We can put you in Miss Gina's guest house. She's the wonderful old lady Gigi's named for... Bonus, she's very spiritual."

Haddy elbows my sister, who gives me big puppy-dog eyes.

I shrug, not really having a choice. "Sounds great. When do we leave?"

"Wednesday." Gigi's voice is neutral, and I notice she seems to be avoiding my eyes.

She turns to the counter, and I get the distinct sense she's angry with me.

I'm so confused. Why would she be angry?

"If it's okay with the coaches," I add. "But even if I can't go, I don't see why Heather and Maddie can't be there."

"Oh, you have to go!" Haddy walks over to me. "Gavin will be so disappointed if you're not there."

I'm not sure that's true, but I comply. "I'll do what I can."

"Yay!" Haddy bounces, giving me a little hug before returning to the group.

They're back to planning, but I hesitate a moment, watching Gigi as she swipes her finger across the screen of her iPad. She turns her back to me, so no smiles or bashful glances.

Something has changed, and maybe I should be glad she's letting me off the hook after last night.

Guess what? I'm not.

GINA

Maverick and Gavin booked a small plane to take the wedding party to Newhope, and the entire flight I sat in the back with my iPad on my knees, pretending to work on wedding plans while avoiding the group at the front of the plane.

Or one person in particular at the front of the plane.

Owen sat near the cage containing both our dogs with his daughter standing between his legs, hugging a stuffed zebra as she happily chatted with Heather and Haddy like one of the girls.

She's the cutest thing with her big brown eyes and lively personality. She's smart and quick, and she reminds me of my oldest cousin Kimmie Joy at that age. Growing up, Kim was always with the adults, unlike us "littles."

He glanced back at me a few times, and my chest squeezed every time I felt his eyes on me. I only slid lower in the seat, adjusting my headphones.

I don't know why I'm letting him get to me this way. It's

not like I expected him to make a big deal out of us spending the night together. We said just once, right?

But we didn't just *spend the night together*. I'm pretty sure we set records. We did things that are illegal in some states.

We didn't talk much the following morning. We got dressed, collected our things, and left the Delve Inn, and in the light of day, I felt intensely that we were *not* John and Kendall Grant. What we did that night was very real, even if we said it was only a fantasy. Could he do that? Could I?

His warm hand on my thigh driving back made me think it might be more, but the way he bounded out of the truck, slamming the door without even looking back...

It was like Baxter the love-bomber, the major-league ghoster, all over again. I'd let my guard down, he got what he wanted, then he left without even looking back.

"You're here!" Mom runs to me as soon as we step out of the rented black SUV, pulling me into her arms and squeezing me so tight. "Oh, I've missed you. Let me look at you."

Straightening her arms, she holds me out, and my nose wrinkles. "We just saw each other in June."

"That was four months ago, Gina Grace!"

"I need to let the dogs out."

As if on cue, Mav emerges from the driver's side of the vehicle, singing, "Who let the dogs out?"

He dances over to lift my mom off her feet and twirl her around.

It only makes her slap his arms playfully. "Maverick Murphy, you'd better get to your mamma's house before she skins us both."

"I'm going, Aunt Liv!" Mav kisses her cheek before heading back to the waiting car.

Haddy is in the backseat making out with Gavin before she collects all of Lucy's things.

I open the back of the car so we can let Spanky and Ladybird out of their shared crate. It was the only way we could get Ladybird on the plane, and Owen insisted we couldn't leave her, even with the assurance I had friends who would come over and walk them and take care of them.

Both dogs leap out of the vehicle and start to run and jump with each other. Owen, Heather, and Maddie are in their own SUV headed to Miss Gina's guesthouse a little farther north of downtown.

"Just be sure they don't get into Mee-Maw's prized chickens." Mom takes my arm as we walk slowly toward the house. "You know how she is about those birds."

After I moved to LA, my parents sold our old house and added about two-thousand square feet to my grandmother's little cottage near the bay. Dad said they were going to have to move in with her eventually, so it just made sense.

My grandmother was on cloud nine, because she's always loved my dad. Everybody loves my dad, the six-foot-four former star-NFL-player turned sheriff of Newhope.

"Is that my Gigi?" The screen door slams, and I take off running to jump on his back, hugging him around the neck. "Aw—I think you've gotten heavier!" he teases.

Laughing, I squeeze him tighter. "If I'm getting heavy, you're getting old!"

"Sassy." He shakes his head, poking my ribs. "Just like your mamma."

I jump down, wrapping my arms around his waist as we walk to the house. Much like Gavin and Lucy, he was my first big teddy bear, and he has a special place in my heart. He's also overprotective as hell, which kind of makes me want to tell him about Baxter.

Maybe Dad could stuff him in a dumpster, which is right where he belongs. Owen, on the other hand...

"So we're marrying off our first baby this weekend." He shakes his head. "Who knew Haddy would be the one breaking the seal, after all the fuss her dad made about marriage and babies and poop."

"I think he said the same thing, Uncle Grizz!" Haddy walks up beside us, holding a sleeping Lucy on her shoulder.

"Oh, let me have that little sweet potato." Mom takes the baby, and Haddy takes my hand.

"Is this the same fella who showed up at Christmas last year?" Dad squints an eye at her, and she nods rapidly, reminding me a bit of Maddie.

"He sure is." My cousin beams, and it makes me laugh. "Gavin Knight."

We're at the house, and Dad straightens, expanding his chest the way Mav likes to do when he's acting tough. "I remember that guy. Where is he anyway?"

"He just left with Mav to spend the night at Aunt Dylan's house," I explain. "They're trying to be traditional, of all things."

"They have a baby?" Dad asks, and I nod. "And they went on their honeymoon to Japan last month?" I nod again. "And now they want to be traditional?"

"Just go with it Pop." I slap his shoulder, and he chuckles.

We continue into the large house, and I go straight to where my grandmother and mom are swooning over Lucy. Haddy carries our luggage to the foot of the stairs before joining us.

"She looks just like you did as a baby, Hads." Mom reaches out to hold my cousin's hand. "I'm so happy y'all decided to have the wedding here. Now we can all be together."

"That's what I wanted." Haddy puts her head on my mom's shoulder. "Growing up in LA, I looked forward to our visits here so much. It just seemed right."

"You could've told me that sooner," I grumble, not really mad.

Having the wedding in Newhope makes everything so much easier. For starters, I have an additional five people helping me, my four aunts and Clint, who's an actual, *professional* wedding planner.

"I don't know why you all have to rush back on Saturday," Dad grumbles, and I reach out to hold his hand.

"The guys have to play, and I've got dog shows. But we'll be back at Christmas."

"Let's get you ladies some dinner." Mee-Maw hops off the couch, heading for the kitchen. "It's ten here, but I know it's only seven for you. I've got shrimp and grits warming on the stove."

Haddy and I are both on our feet when she says the word *grits*, heading for the kitchen.

Dinner consumed... *inhaled*?, Lucy fed, everyone showered, Haddy and I decide to share one of the guest rooms upstairs.

I'm just snuggling under the blankets when my phone buzzes with a text that stops my heart.

OWEN

Hey, just checking on Ladybird.

I force my tight lungs to breathe, thankful he can't see how flustered I am. My hands tremble as I reply.

GINA

She's in the cage with Spanky, happy as
can be.

OWEN

Thank you for helping with her. I really
appreciate it.

GINA

Glad to do it.

Gray dots appear on the screen, floating, floating...

I wait, watching, wondering what in the world he might say and if it might be anything along the lines of, *I miss you.*

The dots disappear, and my throat aches. Seconds pass, and nothing happens. My stomach knots. *I will not cry... I will not cry...*

Then my phone lights up again, and I almost squeal.

KIM

We've got to do a better job with this
cousins' chat. I didn't even know y'all were
coming home until today!

I swallow the thickness in my throat, pushing those feelings away. This is a happy time, and I won't let some guy ruin it. Even if I did agree to play his game.

GINA

I didn't know we were coming until two
days ago.

KIM

Y'all should've told me two days ago. Just
because I'm teaching all the time doesn't
mean I get left out of the loop.

HADDY

I'm sorry, KJ! I didn't realize how much I wanted to get married here until I did.

MAV

What does that even mean?

KNOX

Girl logic. Don't question it. Just go with it.

HADDY

That feels rude...

SAGE

The stables are free if y'all want to be sure it doesn't rain.

GINA

It's not going to rain! I won't allow it.

SAGE

Just putting it out there.

MAV

You said pudding.

KNOX

He said putting it out.

KIM

Can we not be middle schoolers? How can I help, Gigi?

GINA

Clint is taking the lead on wedding prep, but we have two dogs and two little girls.

KIM

Two?

HADDY

Gav's new teammate Owen Stone is here
with his sister Heather and his adorable
daughter Maddie... Also, Heather does tarot
readings.

KIM

What! Where and when can we do one???

HADDY

I know, right? They're staying in Miss Gina's
guesthouse, so tomorrow.

I peek my head out from under the blankets.

"Hads!" I'm not sure why I'm whispering. "Shouldn't we check with Heather before we drop the entire clan on her head demanding tarot readings?"

"She'll love it!" Haddy whispers back. "But you're right. We should warn her."

HADDY

Don't tell the aunts until we make sure it's
okay with Heather.

KIM

My lips are sealed. See you all tomorrow!
This is more fun than Marry-Fuck-Kill!

MAV

I've always wanted to play that game.

KNOX

Me, too...

SAGE

I'm afraid I'd get killed.

KIM

Girls only!

GINA

What she said.

HADDY

I don't make the rules (sad-face emoji)

SAGE

Sounds like we're crashing.

KIM

You really will get killed!

MAV

Mom would let us play. It's the dads who can't.

HADDY

We're starting our own tradition. Tarot bachelorette!

GINA

That sounds dangerous.

KIM

Danger's my middle name, Baby!

"IT'S BEEN SO LONG since I've had a tarot reading!" Miss Gina's blind eyes gaze into the twilight sky.

We're sitting under her back porch at a wrought-iron table under glowing yellow twinkle lights as the sun sets.

It's the evening before the wedding, and incredibly, we managed to pull everything together in a day. It's not so incredible if you take into account Clint's connections and reputation in the area. He was able to pull strings all over the place, hitting the LA Champions hockey team angle hard.

This evening, he has all the guys at a haberdashery in

Sterling being fitted for their suits. Baby Lucy is with Aunt Raven and all the moms and aunts back at Cooters & Shooters, and I expect she'll be thoroughly spoiled next time we see her.

The girls and I are all at Miss Gina's having a magical bachelorette party.

A butler brings out a tray of crystal tumblers filled with a deep purple liquid, and I lean into the table, whispering, "Is purple drink still purple drink if it's served in Waterford crystal?"

"I wouldn't know! I've never had anything in crystal," Heather whispers back. "But we had the most divine breakfast, and I adore the guest cottage. I feel like a princess."

We all take our tumblers and sip the perfectly blended cocktail made of purple Kool-Aid and Everclear... or whatever Miss Gina has that approaches 190-proof grain alcohol.

"Back in my day, everyone was doing seances," the kind old lady continues. "They were so much fun!"

"Did you ever see dead people, Miss Gina?" Maddie is obsessed with our hostess and her fairytale-like castle and flowy clothes.

We were all obsessed with her as little kids, playing with her annual springtime litter of kittens, swimming in her Olympic-sized lapis-blue swimming pool, running all over the grounds of her Italian-style mansion on the bluffs of Sterling Bay, riding in her elevator.

We grew up thinking she was our real great-grandmother. Imagine our shock when we found out she was only a lonely blind lady our Aunt Dylan had befriended back when she sold Girl Scout cookies.

Uncle Zane would drive her over, and the two became thick as thieves. They got even closer after our real grandparents died, and now she takes care of all of us like we're her actual family. I'm even named after her.

"I never saw any dead people." Miss G's brow furrows as if she's thinking hard. "I do remember the table rising off the ground once. My father said it was all sleight of hand. 'A bunch of hooey!' he said."

She imitates a man's voice in a way that makes her laugh. Her white-gray hair is styled in a bob that curls under her ears, and in the warmer months she wears flowy linen outfits. In the colder ones, she wears flannel.

"I'd love to do a seance," Heather's eyes are wide. "I don't think I could do one, but maybe my grandmother Gwen could."

"I'd love to meet her." Miss Gina reaches across the table in Heather's direction.

Owen's sister reaches out and squeezes her hand. "She would adore you."

"I want to play with the pretty cards!" Maddie jumps up and down beside her aunt, causing Ladybird to rise from where she'd been lying and let out a loud *Rooo!*

Spanky is on his feet at the sound, wagging his tail and walking around the chairs, concerned.

"It sounds like the dogs want to play, too!" Miss Gina claps her slender hands.

"Your dad said we have to wait until you're older," Heather tells her niece, provoking the fiercest pouty face.

"Daddy never lets me do fun things!" She crosses her arms hard.

"Here, come stand by me while she reads mine." Miss Gina reaches for the little girl, pulling her into her side. "I can't see the pictures, so you can describe them to me."

That does the trick. Maddie perks up, nodding rapidly. "I'm good at describing stuff."

"I bet you are." Miss G pats her back, and we all walk over to watch.

"I'll do a simple, three-card spread." Heather takes out the deck of purple cards with gold-foiled illustrations. "What is your intention?"

"My goodness..." The old woman leans back in her chair, putting a hand on her chest. "I have no idea. I don't need anything. I've done all I want to do... I guess, what should I focus on now?"

That makes me smile, and I sit on the side of her chair, wrapping my arm around her shoulders.

"My sweet Gina." She pats my hand. "I remember holding you as a newborn."

"Let's see..." Heather places three cards face down on the table, then one by one, she turns them over. "First, in the past position, we have the Queen of Pentacles."

"She looks just like you!" Maddie cries. "It's a woman sitting in a pretty chair in flowy robes with flowers all around her."

"I like the sound of that..." Miss Gina smiles, nodding. "What does it mean?"

"It's in the upright position, so it means financial security... you've always been a reliable, nurturing person."

"I'm convinced!" Kim takes the chair beside Heather to watch. "I can't think of a better way to describe Miss G."

"Next, in the present position, is the Four of Cups..."

"It's a guy sitting under a tree, and a little cloud is handing him a cup," Maddie whispers.

We all lean forward, curious. "It's reversed," Heather says, "Which means you need to get out more and engage in society."

"I'll do it!" Miss Gina slaps her leg, laughing. "I was just thinking the other day I've been cooped up too much lately, especially now that you all are getting older."

"I'll bring you to Cooters & Shooters with me on Thursday." Kim puts her hand on the lady's back. "And we can go to the football games on Fridays. *The Nutcracker* is coming up..."

"It's getting better already!" Miss Gina smiles.

"Finally, for the future, we have the Star in the upright position, which is a wonderful thing." Heather smiles, lifting her blue eyes. "It means renewal, hope... You're going to leave a legacy."

"It's a pretty lady in a dress dipping her toe in a puddle with stars all around," Maddie tells her.

"Isn't that wonderful?" Miss Gina turns her head as if she's looking at the group of us. "I hope all of this comes true. Thank you, Heather."

"My pleasure. I love a good reading." Heather slides the cards together, shuffling them and looking up at us. "Who's next?"

"Not me." Haddy holds up both hands. "I've got everything I want, and I'm not taking a chance following that perfect reading."

"Gina?"

"I'm good!" I shake my head, snorting a laugh. "I don't need to know what next great disappointment lies in my future. I'll take it as it comes."

"Seriously?" Kim cries. "What a bunch of party poopers! It's the whole reason we're out here. I'll go next."

She pulls up a chair, and Heather scoots around to be across from her. "What's your intention?"

"I guess I'll follow Miss Gina's lead. What's next?"

"Let's do this." Heather grins. "I'll do a past, present, future read again."

She shuffles the cards slowly, then slides them over for Kimmie to cut.

Our oldest cousin only taps them with her knuckle. "Miss Gina didn't cut."

"I'm no role model," the old lady teases.

"If you're not, then nobody is," Kimmie replies just as fast.

"Here we go..."

Like before, Heather places three cards face down in front of our cousin. She turns the first card over to reveal an older boy bending down to hand a little girl a bouquet of flowers.

"The Six of Cups..." Heather says. "It's in the upright position, which symbolizes nostalgia, and safety in the past. You're holding onto something very tightly from your childhood."

Kim blinks wide brown eyes up at me, and I don't know why it makes me nervous. Heather's hand moves to the next card, and she turns it over to show a blindfolded woman holding two long swords.

"The Two of Swords, also in the upright position." Heather's brow furrows. "It can mean you'll face a difficult decision because of hidden information... Or you're in a period of indecision, where you're carefully weighing your options. Either way, look inside yourself and trust your intuition."

"Okay..." Kimmie's voice is quiet, and I can't tell if this is making sense to her.

I'm completely baffled.

"And finally..." Heather turns over a card showing a naked woman dancing with the sun shining over her head. "Oh, yay! Even though the sun is reversed, that only means there's a delay. Soon the clouds will break, and you'll find the joy you're seeking."

Heather is smiling big, blinking across at her, but Kim's expression is still.

I reach over and put my hand on her arm. "Was that *not* what you wanted to hear?"

She blinks out of it at once, smiling up at me. "Sorry, no, that was fun. Clear as mud, but a lot to think about!"

My nose wrinkles, but Heather is happy.

"What a relief! I hate when I get bad cards for people. I do my best to guide them to the light, but sometimes there's just no way out of it."

"That settles it," Haddy laughs. "We're stopping there. No point in tempting fate."

"Oh, stop being a baby," Kimmie prods. "Just pull one card, and see what happens. They can do that, can't they, Heather?"

Our new friend squints at us. "I don't usually do single card pulls, but we can try it for fun."

She gathers the cards again, giving them a shuffle before holding the deck out to Haddy first, who pulls a card, then it's my turn.

I study the ornate deck with its beautiful drawings and shimmering accents. I know it's only a deck of cards, ink on paper, nothing more. Still, my chest is tight. With trembling fingers, I reach out and pull a card from the center.

"Haddy can go first," Heather says. "Let's see it."

Haddy turns the card over, and it's two men holding cups under what looks like the medical symbol of snakes on a staff.

"Two of Cups!" Heather's voice is high, and she exhales a laugh. "This is good for marriage. It signifies an emotional connection, a partnership. Both parties are equally valued.

It transforms any previous conflict into a commitment built on mutual trust."

"It's so true..." Haddy's blue eyes mist. "We did have conflict in the beginning, but I trust Gavin now as much as any of you, my family."

I quickly grab a tissue from the snack cart. "Don't cry! It's perfect."

She sniffs, taking the napkin and dabbing her eyes. "It is perfect."

Now I'm *really* nervous. "You're batting three for three. Can we possibly get a straight line of good readings?"

Heather meets my gaze. "Let me see your card, and I won't tell you if we don't. We'll just put it back in the deck."

"Deal," I say, handing the stiff card to her.

She turns it over, and her brows tighten. My stomach dips when I see a man standing confused in what looks like a cage of tall sticks.

"It's bad..." I start, but Heather holds up her hand.

"No, it's a message. The Nine of Wands is about resilience. You've been hurt, but you're close to a victory." She looks up, sliding her fingers over her eyes. "Grandma Gwen said once this card is courage wrapped in exhaustion. Move slow, be cautious, but let hope walk beside your fear."

My stomach tightens, and I swallow the lump in my throat.

Heather doesn't know anything about my past, so it's impossible she made this up to fit me. Our eyes hold, and she smiles, studying my face.

"Does that mean something to you?" she asks.

I start to tell her it does, when all at once, Kim's, Haddy's, and my phone all light up. Kim's makes a sound like bells, but Haddy's and mine only buzz.

Miss Gina holds up her hands. "My goodness! What's happening?"

"It's a text from Maverick," Kim says, before bursting into laughter. "Oh, no! Your dads are giving Gavin the traditional bachelor-party lap dance!"

"What does that mean?" Heather's eyes widen, and we all crowd around our phones to see the video.

"I want to see!" Maddie bounces on her toes, but Heather touches her shoulder.

"When you're older."

"This is one of those times I wish I wasn't an old blind lady," Miss Gina grouses, and Maddie walks over to lean on the side of the old woman's legs.

"Don't worry, Miss Gigi," she says. "I never get to do the fun stuff either."

"Madison Stone, you get to do all kinds of fun stuff," Heather fusses. "Just not everything."

Haddy puts a hand over her mouth, laughing as Gavin is seated in a chair, his hands tied behind his back with a satin ribbon. The music changes, and our dads and Uncle Craig dance out in black satin hot pants and blond wigs.

Uncle Hendrix dances right in front of Gav, turning to touch his toes and smile up at him through his legs. It only lasts a moment before Uncle Craig drapes a white feather boa around his neck and starts pulling it back and forth quickly.

Gavin sneezes, and Haddy snorts through her hand. "Poor Gavin! This is so wrong."

Gavin's dad yells a loud *Gesundheit!* from somewhere in the crowd.

Haddy's future husband shakes his head. "No help there."

Kim slaps her hand on Haddy's shoulder. "I hope he realizes he's officially in the group." The dancing continues. "Welcome to the family, Gavin Knight!"

12

———

OWEN

Newhope is a lot like Eureka, only without all the kooky magicians and mediums... all of whom are related to me.

Still, it's been a long time since I laughed so hard in one weekend. I can't get over how well everyone gets along, down to the dogs. I'm chalking it up to the happy vibes around the wedding and not my sister's premonitions and pointed looks.

It's been a nonstop whirlwind of activity since we stepped off the small plane Mav and Gav chartered for Newhope. Again, I offered to pitch in, but they waved me away. I'm not sure when I'll stop being a guest and start being one of the team.

Gigi is still avoiding me, and it's making me itchy and uncomfortable being here with her family, even as a guest.

I wanted to talk to her on the flight, but she stayed in the back of the plane the entire time with her headphones on, claiming she was working on wedding prep.

Every time I'd glance back, her brows were furrowed over her pretty green eyes, her full lips were pursed, and her fingers twisted in the side of her hair. It sent an unwelcome longing through my stomach, remembering threading my fingers in her hair, pressing my thumb against her bottom lip as I pulled it down to kiss her.

Then, as soon as we landed, the women were swept away in one direction while the men, including me, were swept in another.

I didn't expect to be in Gavin's wedding party, but he insisted. Considering all I have to do is wear the clothes they give me, stand where I'm told, and have all the free food and drinks I want, I could hardly say no.

Heather, Maddie, and I are also staying in a luxurious guest cottage on the grounds of an Italian-style estate overlooking the waters of Sterling Bay. It's freaking gorgeous and complete with a welcome basket and continental breakfast, which has my daughter utterly delighted.

She doesn't get to eat donuts every day for breakfast at home, but it's a special occasion, I guess.

Our host is a sweet old blind lady, who took my hand as soon as we arrived, smiled up at me, and said I felt like family to her.

It was more magic and premonitions and things I don't buy into, but it was a kind gesture. I simply patted her hand and thanked her for her hospitality.

The next morning, I was whisked away to take care of all the guy stuff, which included fittings and a bachelor party with all of Haddy and Gavin's male relatives.

I thought the Stone family was big. This is like a mob scene.

Heather and Maddie are thrilled to be spending time with the female Bradfords, and except for baby Lucy, my daughter is the only "little" here, which means she's the designated flower girl.

Haddy has no idea how happy this makes my daughter, and I want to let her know how much I appreciate it. Moving her away from our family in Eureka for the first time in her life has put me on edge.

She's only ever known our small town, surrounded by people who all know her and love her. Los Angeles is going to be a big adjustment, even with Heather and me there.

It's made it difficult for me to think past her comfort and mental well-being.

Falling in with the Bradfords has been a help I never expected. Someone said it's because Maverick is just like his mom. I don't know what that means, but at least my daughter has a safe place to land.

Hell, I really need to find a house in the neighborhood when we get back—for her as well as Ladybird. She and Spanky are clearly doggy-soulmates. Who are currently back in their cage at Miss Gina's mansion, happy as peas in a pod.

The rest of us are congregated around a large pier with a flower-covered arch, filmy curtains, and a small audience of mostly family.

"You ready?" Mav's cousin Knox walks up and pats my back. "Last-minute change. You're walking with Gina."

Energy surges in my chest, and I frown up at him. "I thought Gina was walking with..."

"Austin can't make it, so Maverick is helping as an usher. I'm walking with Kim, and you're taking Gina. Everything else is the same."

"Okay." I nod, thinking it's a little more than just a last-minute change.

Last night, Gina still wasn't looking at me, which was

quite a feat, considering we had a whole rehearsal and a dinner to get through. I tried to go to her after we'd finished eating at their family restaurant, but she'd slipped out the back door.

My brow lowers, and I wonder if my sister had anything to do with this rearrangement. Maverick and Gigi walked together at the rehearsal, and they were saving a spot for their older cousin Austin, who I've never met.

He's Kim's step-brother, her stepmom Allie's son from a previous marriage. I've only heard them talk about him briefly like some kind of celebrity-unicorn.

He's also a star NFL quarterback, so it's possible he is some kind of elusive creature. I know once hockey season starts, we're all MIA for nine months.

"That's your cue!" Knox gives me a push, and I realize the string quartet has begun playing.

Stepping out from behind the curtains, my breath catches when I see her waiting there. Her strawberry-blonde hair lifts in the soft breeze, and the skirt of her dusty rose dress ripples.

Her green eyes widen when she sees me, and she takes a hesitating step back. That's when a hand appears from behind the curtain and pushes her forward.

"Oh!" Her lips form a circle as she stumbles to me, and I step forward to catch her.

"You okay?" My voice is low, and she feels so good in my arms.

Her sweet cherry scent surrounds me, and all I can think about is how many times I kissed those lips, how she moaned my name in ecstasy, thrusting...

I've got to stop.

"I'm fine." Her soft voice is firm, and she straightens, cutting a look in the direction from where she was pushed.

"That's our cue," I say, giving her a confident smile.

She inhales deeply then puts her hand on the outside of my forearm. It's the most platonic touch, almost like she's concerned I have a contagious illness. I hate it.

We walk slowly down the aisle, and the warmth of her body burns like fire at my side.

I reach over and cover her slim hand with mine, pulling it into the crook of my arm. She takes a sharp breath, but I don't let her pull away. I want to hold her hand.

At the front, center, I give it a little squeeze before letting her go. She turns away and doesn't respond, going to the end of the line.

The rest of the bridal party follows us, until at last, it's Haddy's turn.

The music changes, and the audience stands. We strain our eyes to see her walking down the aisle with one hand in her dad's arm, and her baby girl Lucy cradled in her other.

She and the baby are both wearing glittering white dresses, and the candles and the setting sun cast it all in a dreamy glow.

When they reach the front, Gavin steps down to kiss his daughter before they hand her off to Haddy's mom. Holding hands, they walk up the steps to the minister and begin all the rituals of the wedding ceremony.

My mind drifts over these past few days. I met all the men in this family this weekend, and they are *characters*. Gavin's dad is former military and just like his son, only with lighter hair.

Haddy's dad is the youngest of four football-playing brothers, which makes him loud and outgoing. Their favorite story is how he wore a snorkel mask to change Haddy's poopie diapers... Trust me. I understood completely.

Baby girls might be sugar and spice and all that, but their dirty diapers stink to high heaven.

Gigi's oldest uncle, Jack, was a single dad for a long time, which gave us an immediate connection. I stood back with him and his brother Zane, watching as poor Gavin got a lap dance from Haddy's dad, Gigi's dad, and their uncle Craig.

It left me concerned they might *all* be crazy... which would fit in very well back home in Eureka. No judgment.

Now, listening as they say their vows, I do my best to distract my mind from my own wedding. It's a painful knot in my throat when I remember that guy, and all the dreams and hopes and fairytale ideas he had. How young he was.

I've been to therapy, and I don't want to let the brokenness and guilt creep into my heart again. I've dealt with those wounds.

Still, watching this couple I know, these kind people with so much love and anticipation in their eyes, I wonder how much you can trust anything.

Dropping my chin, I look down at my feet as I do my best to maintain an open mind and heart. I have to for my daughter's sake.

"I promise to love, honor, and protect you as long as I live," Gavin says, holding Haddy's hand. "You've made my dreams come true, and it's with you, Princess, a woman I thought was so far out of my reach... I solemnly swear, I'd give my life for my girls' happiness."

Haddy's bottom lip quivers, and when she blinks, two big tears hit her cheeks.

"Oh, Gavin," she sniffs, breaking into a sputtering laugh. "How do you always know how to steal my heart? I had all these beautiful words planned, but all I can think to say is I love you so much. I'm so happy I was wrong about you."

That makes everyone break into chuckles. Their love is

so pure. Perhaps it can crack the protective walls around my heart.

The minister says all the stuff about rings and all that, and I sneak a glance at Gigi standing at the end of the row of bridesmaids.

She's smiling, her pretty eyes misty, but she seems a little melancholy. I know she's happy for her cousin and Gav. I've seen them together enough to know they all love each other.

Still, something's wrong, and I've got to find out what.

The preacher tells them to kiss, and Gavin pulls his wife into his arms, dipping her backwards and holding her close to his chest. They straighten, and Haddy's foot rises. Everyone cheers and whistles, and they turn to be presented to us.

Gavin throws out his arms and yells, "Time to party!"

Mav jumps into the aisle and leads the charge up the concrete path along the bay that leads to the large restaurant with the tin roof and the big sign overhead reading *Cooters & Shooters.*

"Can I go to the party, too, Daddy?" Maddie has my hand, jerking it up and down. "Can I?"

Heather walks up from where she was seated beside our hostess. "Of course you can! You'll hang out with Miss Gina and me."

"What about Ladybird?" Maddie puts a hand on her hip.

"Ladybird and Spanky are snug in their crate together at the house," Heather tells her. "We'll see them tomorrow, now come with me."

My daughter skips along with the crowd headed for the restaurant, where the reception will be held, but I catch my sister's arm.

"I can take care of her tonight if you want to..." I shrug,

looking at the number of single guys in the group. "Meet someone."

"Owen Stone, do you really think I'd hook up with someone so far from anywhere I plan to live? That sounds like a recipe for disaster."

"I don't know. I thought maybe you wanted to have some fun."

"I'll have plenty of fun. I'd rather you get out there and have some fun yourself. Stop thinking about all your responsibilities all the time and let your hair down for once."

"You might say I let my hair down by taking the offer to move to LA. Uprooting you, Maddie…"

"Stop." She puts a hand on my chest. "Playing in the NHL, getting a huge pay increase, these are not irresponsible decisions. I'd say they're very strategic ones. Which is why tonight, you're going to stop thinking strategy and start thinking smut."

My eyebrows shoot up. "What does that mean?"

"It means I expect you to find a certain dog lady and get it on, doggy style."

"I'm out of here." I hold up both hands as she claps gleefully. "If only to get away from my baby sister discussing my sex life."

"You're not a prude, and I'm not a baby. Now go find her."

Shaking my head, I act like I disapprove. The truth is, I appreciate my sister giving me the chance to find Gina, not to hook up with her but to find out why she's been treating me like a leper.

Champagne and purple drinks are flowing. Music blasts through the dining hall of Cooters & Shooters. All the tables have been moved to the perimeter, and couples are dirty dancing while Gina's dad, Haddy's dad, and their "uncle" Craig shake their butts on top of the bar.

It's like a freakin Mardi Gras in here, but I can't find Gina. I've gone from one end of the large dining room to the other, and unless she sees me coming and runs away, she's not here.

"There you are!" Maverick grabs my shoulder, pulling me close. "Why aren't you dancing? It's a wild night."

He's a bit tipsy, so I take a chance asking, "Have you seen Gina?"

I hope he's had enough alcohol that it won't make a difference I'm specifically asking about his cousin, our roommate.

I'm wrong.

"I knew it!" He laughs, placing both hands on my shoulders and giving me a good shake. "I'm going to be living alone in that bungalow before it's all over." His head tilts, and his expression changes. "I'm not sure I like that. I don't want to live alone."

"No, no, you've got the wrong idea. I just... ahh..." What the fuck could it be if not that? "The dogs!" I practically shout the words. Clearing my throat, I do my best to play it cool. "I need to ask her something about the dogs."

"Well, she's your girl." Mav leans close, patting me hard on the chest. "Gigi knows everything about dogs. She's probably better with dogs than she is with people."

Placing my own hands gently on his shoulders, I hold his eyes. "I'm aware. Where is she?"

His brow lowers, his blue eyes slide to the side, then he shakes his head, laughing. "How the fuck would I know?"

I manage to hide my frustration. "I'm going to find her."

I'm about to push through the crowd again, when he pulls me back. "You know, the path along the bay leads to her parents' house. I wouldn't put it past her to cut out early. She's like that sometimes."

My brow relaxes, and I nod at him. "Thanks, man."

I head straight for the back door, cutting through the playground, and hopping over the low fence that separates it from the sandy shore below.

Jogging up to the sidewalk, I squint into the darkness, holding a hand up against the tin street lamps. Maybe she came this way. Maybe it's wishful thinking. I don't even know what I'm doing.

When we had our night, we agreed it was just once. What is this obsession I have over knowing her moods? She could be unhappy about a million different things. It doesn't have to be me.

Fuck it. I have to know why she's unhappy. I don't care what it means. I've reached the end of my patience, and I won't rest until I talk to her.

My chest relaxes, and I exhale deeply when I see her slender form ahead, walking slowly in the direction of her parents' house. I start to jog, and the closer I get, I pick up on little things.

First, she's walking really slowly, shaking her head and kicking her feet. She lifts her hand repeatedly, wiping her cheeks... *Is she crying?* Why the hell would she be crying? And how can I fix whatever it is to make her stop?

Slowing down, I take a less aggressive pace, but still with enough speed to catch up with her. I glide up beside her, and when she notices me, she does a little jump.

"Owen!" It's a sharp gasp. "What are you doing here?"

"You left early." My hands are in the pockets of my dress pants, and I shrug. "I guess I was wondering why you wouldn't stay for cake."

She only glances at me briefly, then her eyes are on her feet again. "It's all so beautiful. I'm so happy for them."

Her voice cracks on the words, and she quickly wipes her cheek again. It's like a knife stab in my chest, and I reach out to catch her arm and stop her.

"Why are you crying?"

She doesn't meet my eyes, which I hate. I hate it a lot.

"It's a wedding..." She tries to force a smile. "You're supposed to cry at weddings."

"I don't think those are tears of joy." Dipping my head, I try to meet her eyes. "What's really going on, Gina?"

Her arm bends, and she slides out of my grip. "Purple drink is still purple drink, even if it's in fancy glasses."

"I don't know what that means." I want to hold her hand.

"It means I'm probably a little drunk. I'm probably just in my feelings, and it has nothing to do with anything else."

"I don't believe you." Lifting my hand, I cup her cheek, forcing her to look at me. "You're not drunk, Gina."

The moonlight bathes her face in silver, and she blinks wide green eyes up at me. It's like a hand reaching down my throat and grabbing my lungs in a fist.

So many things I want to say, but all of them feel wrong. I want her so badly. Who the fuck believed I could only have her once? What kind of bullshit was that?

Yet, it was the agreement we made. What can I promise her? What can I give her besides my broken, guarded self? She deserves better than that.

"At least let me walk you home."

"You don't have to." She shakes her head, waving her hand. "Newhope is literally the safest place in the world. Go back and celebrate with Gavin and Maverick. Y'all are teammates now. Make some memories."

A knot aches in my throat, but I don't care. Despite

everything inside me telling me this won't work, I step forward, tracing my finger along the line of her cheek, moving her hair behind her shoulder.

"I can't do that." My voice is quiet. "I can't have fun when I know you're crying."

She shakes her head, wrapping her fingers around my wrist and moving my hand away from her face, her hair. "I can't hear that from you now. Not after..."

Her voice breaks off, and my chest aches. "Because of what happened?"

"Because you never really know people. You said it yourself."

Fuck, that hurts. "I didn't mean..."

"Please, Owen." Her gorgeous green eyes meet mine, tears lingering in them. "I can't do this again."

"Again?"

"I've been down this road, and I'm the one always left behind with a broken heart." She puts up a hand, shaking her head. "I'll be okay. Just give me a minute. It was a one-time thing. We agreed, John and Kendall."

"Right. John and Kendall." My voice is quiet, and I'm pretty sure I can't do this either.

I knew with every fiber of my being to stay away from her, to let her live her life in peace, but I crossed a line I can't uncross.

The right thing to do would be to respect her wishes, to go back to Maddie and Heather, to do what I always do, be the best dad, provider, protector.

But what the fuck is the point of anything if I can't protect this woman with the tears in her beautiful eyes who made me feel more alive than I have in seven years?

Stepping closer, I gently touch her hand. "I'm sorry, Gina."

She nods, lifting the hand I touched to swipe a fresh tear off her cheek. "I know."

With that she turns, and holding the skirt of her dress, she runs to the house, leaving me aching and raw. This thing between us, this connection, has pulled my heart from my chest, but I don't have a leg to stand on.

I created this mess. But I think finding a way to fix it is worth the effort.

Maybe it's the first sprout of hope, like a tiny seedling pushing through the cold, ravaged ground of what used to be my heart. Maybe it's this weekend, and the love of this massive gathering of family and friends giving me courage.

Maybe you never really know anybody, but looking around, I know her.

13

GINA

"It's Thursday night—you know what that means!" Haddy is in my bedroom dressed in Gavin's jersey with Lucy in a carrier wearing a onesie with the number 5 under *Daddy* on the front and a tiny purple ribbon in her newborn hair. "Baby's first hockey game!"

"She's adorable." I bend down to lift her little booty-clad feet. "Aren't you adorable? Yes, you are!"

Her blue eyes are wide, and she blows bubbles at me while she scrubs her little heels against the carrier.

I'm dressed in my black leggings and white turtleneck and my usual Champions jersey with Maverick's name over the number 74 on the back.

Since we returned from Newhope, I've done my best to get back to normal, which means focusing on dog business.

Haddy pulled me in to approve the final proof of the "Hockey Hunks and Hounds" calendar, and I defiantly ignored the burn in my stomach at the sight of Owen shirtless on one knee with Ladybird. Even if it did look like he was staring directly at me through the pages.

"Have you seen the wedding photos?" Haddy stands in front of my armoire mirror applying lip gloss while I tie my hair up in a scrunchy so the *Murphy* on my back is visible.

"You got them already?"

"Clint sent me an email with the link. I'll forward it to you. It has the best picture of you and Owen walking down the aisle."

My eyes slide to hers in the mirror, and I don't miss the sly glint there. It verifies what I already suspected.

"You did that on purpose, didn't you?" I put my hand on my hip and turn to face her.

"What?" She blinks wide blue eyes, but I'm not fooled.

"You switched me from Mav to Owen so I'd have to walk down the aisle with him."

"I didn't have a choice! Austin bailed at the last minute, which was very uncool of him. I'm tempted to send his gift back. But I really want that espresso machine..."

"Sage would've made more sense as an usher. He's younger."

"But Mav isn't *hope walking beside you when you're afraid.*" She gives me a little wink, referencing my tarot card.

I tug her ponytail. "That was uncool, Hads. Owen is not interested in starting a romance with me. He's made it very clear."

"To who?" Her brow furrows. "From where we're all standing, there's nothing but burning chemistry between you two. His daughter adores you, his dog loves yours, his sister practically predicted you'd be together."

She grabs Lucy's carrier, and we head down the stairs.

"That tarot reading was so vague it could've meant anything. How do you know it wasn't about Spanky winning

Best in Show? Doing my job without any major awards takes a lot of courage."

"Oh, pooh." She waves her hand at me when we reach the bottom. "Every single person in LA dog-world knows you're the leading expert on all things dog."

"That sentence doesn't even make sense." I shake my head, shoving my phone into my pocket. "That's not how we talk about the circuit."

"Well, it's the truth. You're constantly getting called to train dogs, certify breeds, walk dogs, judge dog shows. Nobody cares that Spanky hasn't won Best in Show."

"Like the movie?" Heather skips in from the kitchen to join us. "I love that movie! It's so funny?"

"What movie?" Maddie bounces on her toes beside her aunt.

They're both dressed in matching black leggings, turtlenecks, and Number 13 Champions jerseys. Heather's has *Stone* on the back, but Maddie's has *Daddy* as well. Maddie's hair is also in pigtails with confetti hair ties of purple, white, and black, the Champions' official colors.

"I want to watch the doggy movie!" She takes my hand.

"Oh... well..." My nose wrinkles, and I glance at Heather.

She's very no-nonsense. "It's a movie for grown-ups, Mads. We'll find another dog movie for you to watch."

"I like *Isle of Dogs*." I bend down to her level. "Have you seen that one?"

Maddie shakes her head, causing her ponytails to fly around her face, and I give her a little squeeze before straightening. "We'll watch that one together."

Her hand is still in mine as we head out to pile into Gavin's Rover. Lucy's carrier is snapped into her carseat base, and we're off.

The guys are on the ice when we arrive, stretching,

warming up, and skating around the rink. Music blasts from the Jumbotron, and they toss Champions-logo pucks to the fans crowding around the plexiglass dividers.

My eyes immediately go to Owen gliding up to Maverick. They speak briefly before circling apart, and he turns, looking directly to where we're standing at our seats near center ice.

"Daddy!" Maddie jumps up and down waving Zander the zebra, and that handsome smile curls his lips... and my toes. "Daddy, Daddy!"

He flies up close to the glass where we're sitting and blows her a little kiss. She pretends to catch it, and his smile turns into a handsome laugh. *Dammit.*

Then his blue eyes meet mine, and he gives me a wink. It's a flash all the way to my toes, and of course, Haddy sees it.

"That was *cute.*" She pushes her elbow into my side, and I feel my cheeks burning.

"He's a really great dad."

"I bet he's really great at other things, too."

She has no idea how great.

Gavin skates up to the glass sending kisses to Haddy, who lifts baby Lucy out of her carrier for him to see. She waves her little arm, and he laughs, waving as he skates backwards to the guys.

"Not sure how much of this she even understands." Haddy quickly wraps her in her blanket again, stowing her in her carrier with a small pair of noise-cancelling headphones on her head.

"Still, it's adorable."

Maddie is on her knees beside the baby, lifting her little arm and saying, "Go, Champions!"

The Jumbotron buzzes, and their signature mix of

Queen songs "We Are the Champions" and "Another One Bites the Dust" plays loudly as fans blow air horns.

We watch the pictures of the guys in their uniforms and helmets flash by one by one on the screen, and everyone yells loudest for Mav and Gav, who established their reputation last season as the dynamic duo.

The Colorado Cliffs glide out, and a player circles straight around to Mav, bodychecking him into the boards.

"What the fuu...dge?" I yell, realizing just in time we have a seven-year-old with us now, not that it makes a difference.

We're surrounded by infuriated fans dropping F-bombs, and the guys cluster around, ready to fight. The guy who did it throws his gloves on the ice, and the Champions' Number 8 skates to the center of the rink.

"Who is that?" Heather leans close, grabbing Haddy's arm.

"Chris Schultz," Haddy answers, pointing to the guys. "He's the enforcer. Price is the captain. Akers is the goalie..."

I duck my head, wondering if I should put my hand over Maddie's eyes as the guys start punching each other repeatedly. The linemen circle watching them, but not interfering.

"Fight! Fight! Fight!" Maddie yells, and I look over at Heather, confused.

"Is this okay?" I mouth to her, and she grins, nodding.

I bend down to her level. "You're not scared?"

"Oh, no." She shakes her head, frowning at me. "Fighting is part of hockey culture. It's what they do."

My eyebrow arches. "Who told you that?"

"My daddy." Maddie lifts her chin, confident in her knowledge. "It's part of the game, but you only fight on the ice. *Never* off."

I mean, she's not wrong.

"You're really smart." I pat her back. "And so grown up! Only very mature people understand that."

"I read third-grade books." She blinks her big brown eyes at me.

It makes me grin. "I can tell."

The two big guys beat each other around the head for a few minutes, a jersey is ripped, but it's not too bloody. Then they each skate to their respective penalty boxes to do their time, and the game begins as if nothing happened.

The Cliffs are our biggest rival, and they play hard. We watch the guys skating back and forth on the ice at top speeds, slamming into the boards, stealing the puck. Hancock's stick is broken, and Price tosses him a new one.

Each team gets close to scoring, but the goalies aren't letting anything past them. Akers catches a puck in his mitt and tosses it to the referee, and Mav skates forward for the face-off.

We jump up and down, holding each other's hands as he sends the puck "unexpectedly" to Gavin, who slings it to Hancock while Owen skates right up the middle. It's the *Tic-Tac-Tac-Goal* combination, and we know where this is going.

Hancock passes to Owen, confusing the Cliffs who were already closing in. Owen shoots it to Gav as he comes around from behind the net. A pass to Mav, and with a slap, it's a goal.

The crowd goes crazy, and the Jumbotron blasts their score song. We all jump up and down together, cheering for the guys. Fans near us blast air horns, but Baby Lucy sleeps through it all with her ears covered.

I'm breathless as I lean into Haddy. "When did they start with the air horns?"

I notice they're all striped purple, white, and black with the Champions' logo on the front.

"I thought it would be a fun thing for the fans. We came up with a logo sketch, and the gift shop stocked them."

"This was your idea?"

She shrugs, and my eyebrows shoot up. "I'm getting four for the next game!"

"Okay!" She laughs, checking her baby girl before returning her gaze to the rink. "I can't believe she's sleeping through this."

"I can't believe she's sleeping at all without Gavin holding her."

My bestie-cousin gives me a hug. "Why is this so much more fun than football?"

"Because they're ridiculously fast on those skates?" My nose wrinkles. "Because they wear those suits, and they're all tall and hot?"

Haddy gives me a naughty grin. "Because they can fight!"

I throw my arms around her, laughing. "It's true!"

The Champions manage to hold off the Cliffs through the final period. Smaller fights break out as the gameplay intensifies, but neither team manages to score again.

It doesn't matter, because the boys win, and the fans are stomping and cheering and blasting their horns.

"Halloween is on a Saturday this year." Mav hangs over the back of the couch studying his phone. "It's the same day we play Anaheim again."

"I remember that game last year," Gav groans from where he sits holding Lucy.

"You played like shit." Mav shoves his broad shoulder. "I was ready to punch you in the face."

"Haddy wasn't speaking to me."

"Never let girl drama interfere with your game." Mav points from his cousin-in-law to our new housemate.

"Playing helped me forget all my drama." Owen's deep voice is measured.

"I can't wait for you to have some girl drama." Haddy has Princess Petunia in her arms, so she bumps Mav with her hip. "What's the deal, anyway?"

"Easy on the solar plexus." Mav takes the teacup poodle from her. "I have a strict rule about dating. Hockey is my number one love, and if that's okay with the ladies, we can have some fun. But hockey is my life."

"That sounds eerily familiar," I say from where I'm sitting on the floor, brushing Spanky. "What was up with that Cliffs' player punching you in the face?"

"Phew, talk about drama." Mav straightens, shaking his head. "He's been carrying a grudge since we collided last season. Moron. It was a loose puck!"

Maddie is right at my side walking Zander across Ladybird's back. "There's this girl on YouTube, and she won a ribbon for walking a dog in a show!"

"You're right. Her name is Caitlyn Mellor." I slide the brush over Spanky's shoulders. "She's only four years old."

"Could I walk Ladybird like that?" She puts Zander on Ladybird's head like a hat.

The large bloodhound only blinks, turning her big head to look at the little girl.

"Sure, you could." I smile, setting the brush aside and glancing up at Owen.

He's been quietly observant since our conversation on the beach. He gives me space, but I feel him waiting. It vibrates in the air.

As for me, I've put my feelings for him in a box with a tight lid on top in the back of a tall closet in my mind. He wants to be a good dad. He doesn't want a relationship. Done.

It helps that they've been gone so much playing, but on nights like this when we're all at home, I have difficulty keeping that box in its place.

His gaze is a hot laser on my skin.

"I'll teach you to walk LB if your dad doesn't mind," I clarify.

"I don't mind." The affection in his low voice tingles in my stomach. "You might have your work cut out for you, though. I've never been able to train that dog."

"She comes when you whistle," Maddie argues.

"That's true." He gives her a warm smile.

My stomach is all squishy in the middle... Because he's so sweet to her. That's all.

"I'll teach her." Maddie is determined. "I'll walk her like that little girl and her dog."

"I'd like to see Peepee run in one of those obstacle courses," Mav calls from where he's holding Haddy's pooch.

"It's called an agility challenge," I tell him.

"Those dogs can move!" He glides Peepee through the air like she's flying. "What do you say, Peep? Think you can beat those fancy dogs?"

"Don't swing her around like that, she'll barf." Haddy takes her from Mav, cuddling the tiny canine against her chest. "She's already a fancy dog."

"She's so cuuuute," Maddie runs over to pet the tiny poodle.

"So about Halloween," Mav brings us back to the beginning. "We're playing that day, but we'll be done and back in time to party. Hell, we'll be ready to party. We're gonna whup Anaheim's ass!"

"*Maav...*" Haddy gives him the wide-eyes, tilting her head at the little girl beside her.

"What'd I say?" He looks from her to Owen.

"It's okay, she hears worse stuff at the games." Owen leans down to pet Ladybird, and his arm is magnetically close to mine.

I clear my throat and stand, walking over to where my cousins are behind the couch. "What's the theme this year?"

"There's not really a theme..." Mav starts.

"Oh, please, all of you were in Star Wars outfits last year. I was the only one left out."

"Can we do a mermaid theme?" Maddie bounces on her toes. "I love *The Little Mermaid*! You can be Ariel!"

"I don't care for the *theme* of that movie," Owen grumbles from where he sits.

"*Daddy!*" Maddie stomps over and gets right between his legs, putting her hands on his shoulders. "You already told me it's a cartoon, and I should never trade anything valuable just to be with a stinky boy!"

"Even if he is a prince." Her dad looks her straight in the eyes.

She only lifts her chin. "I still like Ariel."

Haddy and I are doing our best not to laugh or smile or even look at them.

"How does Ladybird feel about Ariel's singing?" Mav asks.

"She loves it." Maddie walks over to hug the dog. "She tries to sing with her."

"This I gotta see." Mav looks at Owen. "We can have a non-problematic undersea party. I'll be Captain Jack Sparrow."

"He's not problematic?" My eyes narrow.

The door opens, and Heather stumbles into the living room holding a large box. "This was on the front step. I think it's the calendars."

"The calendars!" Haddy jumps to take the box, carrying it to the table, and we all crowd around to look. "Grab the box cutter."

"Here." Mav reaches between us and pulls the top open.

We all grab a glossy booklet and open it to the middle.

"Mr. June." Mav holds it up. "Centerfold, baby. Check us out, Spanks!"

Spanky stands, wagging his tail with his tongue out.

Gavin is Mr. May, holding baby Lucy in his arm and Peepee in his hand.

"It came out so well," Haddy sighs. "Ryan did such a great job."

Owen is Mr. July, and I swallow the desert in my throat when I see his level gaze, brow lowered over shimmering blue eyes. A hint of a smile lifts his full lips, and a dusting of whiskers covers his square jaw, square chin... *swoon.*

"Why aren't you wearing a shirt, Daddy?" Maddie frowns, turning the pages. "None of them are."

"Okay... it's time to start dinner." Mav puts his copy under his arm. "Who's up for Mexican street corn, black beans, and hot chicken?"

Five loud, enthusiastic *Mes* answer, but Owen holds up his hand. "Can we get one not hot chicken for Maddie?"

"Only for Maddie, the shirt police." Mav gives her little head a scrub with his palm before heading to the kitchen.

"I'm not a police!" She waves his hand away, smoothing her hair.

"I'll take these to the house and come right back." Haddy picks up the box.

Gavin stands, shifting Lucy to his shoulder. "I gotta take this little lady home for a fresh diaper. Somebody laid a rotten egg."

"Haddy can do it." Mav pauses at the door. "Come have a beer with Owen and me."

"Oh!" Haddy's blue eyes widen. "Ahh... no."

Gavin hesitates then quickly laughs. "It'll only take a minute. She's got this big ole box to carry."

"Right—this box!" Haddy says it too loudly, and my spidey senses are on high alert.

"What's going on?" I step closer to where my cousin is standing. "You're acting weird."

"I am not!"

"Oh, yeah, you are." Mav hustles over to where she's standing, flanking her other side. "What are you hiding?"

Haddy's shoulders straighten, and she lifts her chin. "I'm not hiding anything, and I don't appreciate this grilling."

I'm about to call it off, assuming they're going home for a quickie, and we're being uncool.

But Mav points his finger. "You can't change a poopy diaper!"

"I... I don't know what you mean! Of course, I can."

We all pause. My eyes go from Haddy with the red face to squirmy, stinky Baby Lucy to Gavin biting the inside of his cheek.

"Oh my gosh, you can't!" I shout before breaking into laughter. "You're just like your dad, and you were trying to hide it from us!"

"It's not fair–something happened!" Haddy cries. "It's like her poops changed, and now they smell so *bad*!"

"That's true." Owen nods, pressing his lips together sympathetically. "It's like one month, there's not much smell, then the next... *whoa*."

"Right?" Haddy's voice is high, and she points at Owen as if for backup. "Owen knows!"

My phone is in my hand, and my thumbs are flying. "I can't wait to share this with the cousins."

"NO!" Haddy jumps over to grab my phone. "Do *not* share this with anybody. I'm working on it. For now, Gavin is helping me."

"Do you need to borrow a snorkel mask?" I snatch my phone back from her. "Your dad has one."

"Oh, Haddy." Mav shakes his head, giving her a disappointed look.

We're all giggling when my phone lights up in my hand. My stomach drops, and I almost toss it onto the couch when I read the screen.

BAXTER

Hey Genie-girl. How's my favorite
dogstress?

"Gina?" Haddy steps forward to hold my arm. "Are you okay?"

Heather steps up, reaching for my free hand. "You look like you've seen a ghost."

"What is it?" Owen is at my side, putting his large hand on my back.

"It's..." I hold out the phone to Haddy, and her face instantly reddens with anger.

"What the... *hay*?" She edits her response, taking my phone. "You didn't block him?"

"Block who?" Heather looks between us, and Owen's brow lowers.

"I didn't even think about it." My voice is quiet. "He ghosted me. Why would I need to block him?"

"Because he's a rat..." Haddy steps closer, lowering her

voice, "B-A-S-T-A-R-D. Now block him this instant."

"What's a bastard?" Maddie frowns up at us, and Haddy hiccups a breath.

"Whaaat?" My cousin's voice hits a weird pitch.

I lean forward. "She's seven, Haddy, she knows how to spell."

"It's a grown-up word for a bad person," Haddy says, petting her head and giving me the eye.

I shake my head. "Does blocking him make it seem like he hurt me? I don't want to give him the satisfaction."

"He did hurt you. Give it to me. I'll block him for you."

"Who is *he*?" Owen's voice is growly impatience.

"Baxter Babbit." Haddy reads the screen. "He's as idiotic as his name. Nobody calls you *Genie*, and what's a *dogstress*?"

"He always thought he was funny."

"He's a..." more low murmuring, "*dickhead* who broke Gigi's heart and treated her like garbage."

"I wouldn't say he broke my heart." I try to laugh, but it sounds weird. "He did treat me pretty bad, though."

"He's the guy you told me about." I glance up to see Owen's jaw is tight. "Where is he? I'd like to block him."

Exhaling another weird-sounding laugh, I take my phone from Haddy. "He's nowhere. Nobody's going to find him, and we're all done talking about it." I make a very dramatic show of tapping my phone screen. "Blocked."

"They always come back." Haddy shakes her head, going to the door. "Jerks."

"I have an idea!" I bend my knees, so I'm on Maddie's level. "Why don't we take Ladybird out back and see what we can teach her before dinner? Want to?"

"Yes!" Maddie yells, tossing her dad's calendar onto the table. "Come on, Ladybird! Let's be fancy!"

Straightening, I look from Owen to his sister. He's clearly still angry, but Heather's eyebrow is arched like she just collected some valuable information.

I'm wobbly from the shock, but I manage to play it off. I think. "Let's see if we can make Ladybird fancy!"

14

OWEN

Maverick stops me in the kitchen with a beer. He's standing in front of the sink shaking a container of chicken breasts in hot sauce.

"Can you get over my cousin?" He laughs.

"No, I can't." My brow is down, and I'm seething.

How dare that fuckface text Gina out of the blue? She tried to hide it, but the shock was clear on her face. Her cheeks flushed, and she actually looked ashamed. As if she has anything to be ashamed of.

I'm going to find that guy, grab him by the neck, and... *block* him. With my fist.

"Whoa, who burned your biscuits?" Mav holds up a hand laughing, and I realize he wasn't in the room for the text.

"Sorry." I try to shake off the rage and take a cooling sip of beer. "What were you talking about?"

"I was talking about Haddy not changing poopy diapers. The real question is what were *you* talking about?"

"It's nothing. Just some guy texting Gina."

Mav's brow furrows. "A guy texted Gina..." He nods slowly. "And that bothers you."

It's not a question, and I realize I've shown my hand. "It's not like that... It's because—"

"Because I was right at the wedding!" He laughs, slapping my shoulder. "And you tried to play it off. I knew there was something going on there."

"It was a text from Baxter."

"The asshole?" Mav sets the container down hard. "He'd better not be sniffing around here again. I'll punch him right in the nose."

"I'll help you."

Mav nods, grabbing my shoulder. "You're a good man, Sly. Have you seen the wedding pictures of you and Gina?"

"No..." I think about walking with her down that aisle, how beautiful she was, how she tried to pull away from me. How I found her crying. How she ran...

"They're really good. I'll send you the link."

A *Roooo!* from the backyard breaks the tension, and I nod at my friend. "Thanks, now let me see what these ladies are doing."

I step out onto the back porch to see Gina walking with Spanky. She walks like a supermodel, the leash in one hand and the other extended like a ballerina.

She's dressed in long, navy track pants and a short, white crop top that shows off her flat stomach in a sexy, casual way. Hell, everything she does is sexy to me.

Spanky clearly knows what he's doing. His head is high, and he trots, lifting his legs like one of those show horses.

Maddie stands beside Ladybird. She's wearing black leggings and a purple T-shirt that reads *K-Pop Demon*

Hunters, and her blonde hair is twisted up in little space buns on the top of her head.

She's not a model, but I'd give her a ribbon for cutest handler. So what if I'm biased.

She watches Gina with all her might. Her little brow is tight over her brown eyes, and she lifts Ladybird's leash in the air, doing her best to mimic Gina's form.

Our droopy dog doesn't budge.

"Come on, Ladybird!" She gives the leash a few tugs until finally the big bloodhound stands, then lifts her front legs and puts them on Maddie's shoulders. "Oh, Ladybird... No!"

Maddie staggers back, and the dog lands on the ground again.

"She can't jump on the judge or she'll be disqualified," Heather calls. "I learned that from *Best in Show*."

"Maybe I should start off with Ladybird," Gigi returns to where my daughter stands with her hands on her hips beside the big dog. "You can get the feel of walking with Spanky. He's done it so much, he doesn't even need a handler."

"Okay!" Maddie skips over and takes Spanky's leash. "Like this?"

"That's right," Gina calls. "Now walk him around the backyard like Caitlyn does."

Maddie takes off marching beside Spanky, and the two women stand back watching.

"That's really good, Maddie!" Gina calls to her. "I think you've got it!"

"Now we just have to teach LB!" Maddie calls back, skipping with Spanky.

The white dog jumps beside her, and the women laugh.

They're quiet for a moment, and I'm about to walk up and join them when Heather speaks.

"I've been thinking about your reading." Her tone is tentative. "When I've done them in the past, they're usually about romantic relationships."

"You've done that reading before?"

"Not that one exactly. It's more about the feelings, the vibes. It's all the same." My sister tilts her head. "What's making you cautious with love?"

"I don't know." She shrugs, exhaling a huff. "Dumb Baxter, I guess."

"The guy who texted? What did he do?"

I know this story, and I'm not looking to hear it again. Still, I want to know more about this reading my sister mentioned, and what it has to do with Gigi and love.

"Six dates is a lot," my sister says.

"Yeah." The dejection in Gina's voice makes my jaw clench. "He said he wanted to be my doggy boy."

"What does that even mean?" Heather's tone is disgusted.

"I don't know. He was always making references I didn't get."

"He sounds weird."

"He didn't seem weird to me," Gigi sighs. "I thought he was kind of dorky, but in a cute way. He was just the last in a line of jerks... Or I don't know, maybe I'm just bad at sex. I don't seem to have what it takes to keep them coming back for more."

I'm about to break through the hedge at that. Gigi is *not* bad at sex, but my sister's reply stops me.

"No man is nicer than the one who hasn't slept with you yet."

"Tell me about it." Gigi laughs softly, but it doesn't sound happy. "I just want to matter to someone. I want to love so hard it burns, you know? I want a guy who'll bring me flowers just because he's thinking about me."

"Not because he cheated and feels guilty."

"Right. Oh, wait... Did that happen to you?"

"Actually, no." Heather sounds as wistful as Gina. "It's just a cliche. I've been too busy helping with this little lady to date much."

"Owen said something about that. Like you're ready for him to retire."

"He said that?" My sister laughs. "Well, next time he tells you something like that, tell him not to worry. I've read my cards, and I'm right where I'm supposed to be."

"He'll be glad to hear it."

She's right, I am glad.

"Don't forget to have hope," my sister tells her. "Remember you're close to a victory."

I hear them moving this way, so I walk back to the porch. I turn her words over in my mind, burning... flowers... I wonder what my sister means. If Gina's close to a victory, I want to be a part of it. I want to be part of all of it.

When I enter the kitchen, Gavin is back. He's holding a beer, and Mav is turning the chicken breasts over in the air fryer.

"Almost ready," Mav says. "Is Haddy on her way?"

"Yeah, she just took a minute to feed Lucy." Gav leans against the counter.

"How'd the diaper change go?" Mav snorts. "Somebody's got to tell Uncle Hen that Super P is a chip off the ole block."

"She's going to get mad if you call her that." A warning is in Gav's tone.

"What's Super P?" I grin, looking from one to the other.

"Don't you *dare*, Maverick Murphy!" Haddy enters the

kitchen with the baby on her shoulder, patting her little back. "You're really pushing it tonight."

Both guys straighten, and Maverick returns quickly to flipping the chicken.

"You know they make this balm," I jump in to change the subject slightly. "I think it's called Stink Stick, actually, and it comes in scents like coffee and mint. You put it on your upper lip, and it blocks the odor."

"Thanks, Owen." Haddy gives my arm a gentle touch. "My uncle Jack said something about that. I was hoping things would go back to how they were before."

Looking down, I shake my head. "I hate to break it to you, but those days are over. And when she starts on solid food, well..."

"I'll see if I can track down one of those stink sticks." Haddy nods, catching my drift.

"On that note," Mav straightens. "Who's ready to eat?"

"LADYBIRD DOESN'T WALK FANCY." Maddie's bottom lip pouts as she sits on the edge of the sofa beside Gina. "She kind of flaps."

My daughter flails her arms in a way that looks very much like our klutzy bloodhound.

We finished dinner, cleaned the kitchen and wandered into the living room. Gavin sits in an armchair holding his little daughter with Haddy sitting on the arm. Gina and my daughter are watching clips of dog shows on Gina's large iPad, while Heather cycles through movies on the streaming service.

"She'll learn." Gina rubs her hand on my daughter's back.

It makes me think of home and a real family with a mother for my little girl... What would that be like?

"*My Dog Skip*?" Heather asks, and Gina gives her a thumbs up.

"No dogs are harmed in the making of that film," she says, teasing.

"How does that song go?" Mav walks in, giving Haddy a bump. "'God loves a terrier'? Sing it, Hads."

Haddy immediately launches into the song with a perfectly pure singing voice. My eyebrows rise, and I sit a little straighter. She's only two lines in when Ladybird straightens her front legs and sits up, dropping her head back and letting out a long howl.

Mav falls back laughing, and Haddy jumps off the side of Gavin's chair to kneel in front of our bloodhound as she continues.

"Get your phone!" Gina waves at Maverick. "Take a video!"

Haddy keeps singing, putting her arm around Ladybird's back as my dog continues to howl, hitting different notes for different lengths of time.

Haddy breaks, falling forward as she laughs. "It's like she's trying to sing along!"

"That's what I said!" Maddie runs over to sit beside them, hugging our dog. "It's okay, Ladybird. You don't have to be fancy. You can be a singer!"

"I was thinking about being a pet psychic." Heather turns to Gina. "What do you think? Know anybody who'd be interested in something like that?"

"Really?" Gina's nose wrinkles. "I kind of... don't think that's real."

She puts her hands over her eyes like she's hiding, and it's all too cute.

"Who cares?" Mav cries. "I bet we could find folks who'd be interested. LA is woo-woo like that. Post it on social media and see what happens."

"I think I will," Heather laughs, standing. "Come on, Mads. Let's get cleaned up and watch a movie in bed."

My daughter jumps to her feet before skipping to me and throwing her little body against mine in a hug. "We can read a bedtime story tomorrow night, okay, Daddy?"

"Okay, baby." I give her a tight squeeze. "I love you."

"I love you, too!" Then she stops and gives Gina a hug. "I love you, Miss Gina!"

"Aw, thank you!" Gina hugs her back. "I love you, too!"

My daughter continues making her way around the room, telling everyone goodnight, but Gina's response simmers in my chest.

It stays in my mind as we continue visiting a little while longer. I watch her, and it's like the air around her glows. She smiles, and the room brightens. Her hands move as she tells a story, and it's like she's conjuring magic.

Clearly, I'm falling asleep from nonstop hockey.

Gav is the first to call it. "I don't know about you guys, but I'm beat."

He shifts his sleeping daughter to his shoulder and stands, and Haddy walks over to hug Gina. "I'll touch base with you tomorrow about calendar distribution."

"Calendar distribution?" Gina frowns.

"I just mean putting a few in your studio for people to buy. Don't get all wiggy."

"I'm not wiggy." Gina snorts as they head out the door for their house.

"Night, guys. Don't be too loud." Mav gives us a wave before disappearing into his first-floor master suite.

That leaves Gina and me alone, facing each other. She

blinks up at me briefly, giving me a cautious smile, which I hate. I don't want her to be guarded around me.

In my very best, nonthreatening tone, I ask, "Do you need to shower? I can wait."

"I won't be long." She walks to the stairs, hesitating at the bottom. "Thanks."

"No problem." I lean against the back of the couch, watching as she jogs to the second floor in those track pants.

I think about her shapely legs, and tracing my lips up her inner thighs. Heat moves below my belt, and I wonder what she might say if I suggested we try again.

Before I can think myself out of it, I take out my phone. My thumbs fly quickly over the screen, and I hit *send*.

My chest is tight, and fever is in my brow. *What the hell did I just do?* Rubbing my hand over my stomach, I exhale a chuckle. I don't know, but I'm not sorry.

15

―――

GINA

Owen Stone was like a ball of fire at my back all evening.

He sat in that chair behind me in those loose, faded jeans and dark gray T-shirt that could barely contain his broad chest just watching us.

Haddy's comment, Heather's comment, that silly tarot reading, all of these things swirled around in my mind, and it almost made me believe... Until I saw that dumb text from idiot Baxter still on my phone, reminding me just how bad it can be.

Swiping my finger, I deleted it.

Thankfully, I have the dogs. Dogs are so loyal and trustworthy. They're better than people.

A dog would never pretend to love you, then disappear without a word. Dogs work hard to make you proud. They sense when you're sad and put their head on your lap or snuggle beside you.

In a way, they're a lot like little kids.

Maddie is adorable doing her best to train Ladybird, and I don't have the heart to tell her some dogs just aren't cut out to be show dogs. Even when they are, it takes years of training, usually starting from the time they're puppies.

It's possible we could get LB to that point, but I'm concerned Mads needs to grow several inches first.

Stepping out of the shower, I quickly dry my body with the towel, making sure the bathroom door is securely closed. Spanky has been less of a prankster since Ladybird showed up, but he still can't resist snatching a towel.

I open the door carefully, peeking my head out, so I don't run into any of our house guests. Then I dash across the hall into my bedroom and shut the door—again, *securely*.

Lord knows I don't need Ladybird dashing in and stealing my *personal massager* either. Of all the things these dogs have done. Maybe they are conspiring to get us together...

Silly thought.

I've just pulled on my thin, cotton sleep pants and a white tank when my phone lights up on the bed. For a second I freeze. If it's that stupid Baxter again... but I blocked him.

My shoulders relax, and I pick up the device, expecting it to be Haddy trying to pull me into another hockey scheme. My eyes flash when I see the text.

OWEN

John is wondering if Kendall might be available tonight.

I gulp air. My heart beats hard in my chest, and I'm having trouble inhaling. *What is happening today? Is Mercury in retrograde?*

Standing in the center of my room, I read and re-reading

his words, trying to figure out what he means and how to reply. Finally, I just ask.

GINA

Available for what?

OWEN

John would come to her, but it might be less noticeable if she came to him.

My eyes drift to the wall my bedroom shares with Haddy's old room. They're not paper-thin, but I can hear the occasional bark of a dog or cheer of a kid from the movie they're watching.

With trembling fingers, I reach out to open my door. The hall is dark with only the faintest, flickering light coming from beneath the room where Heather and Maddie are staying. I look left, down the hall to the yellow light shining beneath Owen's door.

I take one step in his direction, pulling my own door closed. Another step closer, and his door opens. He stands there, looking straight at me, and my heart jumps to my throat.

He fills the doorway, and the light coming from behind casts him in silhouette, accentuating his broad shoulders, muscled arms, narrow waist, and thick thighs.

Adrenaline surges in my arms and legs. My stomach quivers, but somehow I manage to take another step closer, then another.

His dark hair is messy around his face, and his dark brow is lowered. Still, I can see a naughty grin curling his mouth. His blue eyes are fixed on me like a predator, and it's thrilling and forbidden, and I can't stop myself. I'm drawn to him like a flame. Even if I don't know what this means or if I'm afraid it's a bad decision, I'm making it.

When I reach him, he takes my hand, pulling me inside and shutting the door behind me. My back is to the wooden barrier at once, and his arms are on each side of my face, caging me against his massive body.

We're breathing fast. The energy radiating between us is crazy, and I can see my breasts rising and falling rapidly.

"What do you want?" It's a shaky whisper.

He leans closer, tracing his lips along the line of my jaw. "John is wondering if Kendall might be up for one more night."

Heat floods my veins, and I swallow the thickness in my throat.

My voice is barely audible as I try to understand. "When... Where?"

Lifting my chin, I meet his darkened eyes, and my core clenches. He leans forward so slightly, dipping his nose into my hair and inhaling. My eyes flutter closed.

"Delicious," he murmurs before pressing his lips to the top of my brow.

I melt against them. Reaching out, my fingers grasp the front of his gray shirt, curling in the fabric. He smells like soap and cedar, and as his mouth moves lower, down to my cheek, closer to mine, I want him so much.

When... Tonight.

Where... Right here.

"Can I kiss you?" His voice is low.

"Yes."

A whimper slips from my throat as he consumes me. I'm off my feet, legs wrapped around his waist, and our lips part. Tongues curl together, and I chase his kisses, meeting him in the middle.

His hard cock is pressed to my center, and tilting my waist, I rub my clit up and down the length, heat rising with every stroke. He groans deeply, turning and carrying me to the bed.

He steps back briefly to lock the door, then he returns to where I'm lying, looking down on me with a desire that matches my own.

His chest rises and falls, and he curls his fingers, dragging his nails along my skin as he slides my pajama pants down my legs.

I'm left in only my lacy white underwear and the thin white tank top. He licks his lips, devouring me with his eyes as he unbuttons his jeans.

"Come up here." It's a low order, and I rise onto my knees in front of him.

He hooks his finger and thumb in the straps of my tank, pulling them together in the center of my chest, causing my bare breasts to spill out.

Then he moves his hand higher, circling one hardened nipple with his thumb.

"Fuck, you're gorgeous." With his other hand at my back, he lays me down on the bed, then proceeds to cover them with kisses, sucks, bites.

My fingers stab into his thick hair, and I writhe, moaning as fire singes my veins.

"Owen..." I gasp, not even caring if this is real or pretend.

Everyone keeps telling me to hold onto hope, and I'm about to have a victory. I'll take an orgasm as a victory. Several orgasms, thank you very much.

His mouth moves down the cotton shirt until he reaches the top of my panties. Yanking them off, he buries his face in my bare pussy, his mouth moving fast as I cry out in pleasure.

Just as fast, a pillow covers my face, and I clutch it with

both hands as he circles his tongue rapidly over my clit. My back arches, and my noises are muffled.

Orgasm surges to life in my belly. My hips circle in time with his movements, and my legs start to shake as he drags me closer to that magical cliff with every stroke. Three more passes, and I fly over the edge, stomach jerking, legs quaking, mind erased.

He kisses my lower belly, and stands, and I hear the rip of foil. I'm still buzzing when I toss the pillow aside so I can see his face.

He's focused, feverish, lining up his cock at my entrance. He drags it up and down, coating himself in my orgasm before finding the place and driving it home with one hard thrust.

We both groan loudly, and he bends his arms, lowering his face to the pillow beside me to muffle his own noises. Hearing his desire makes me hotter, and I lift my hips to take him deeper.

He's thrusting fast, scooting me across the bed with every hit. I squirm beneath him, grasping his shirt, pulling it up so I can trace my nails over his luscious body.

Our skin slaps together, and he rises again. I hold his neck, doing my best to ride him as he fucks me hard and fast. A bead of sweat trickles down his cheek, and I lean up to kiss it away, savoring the taste of salt on my tongue.

Again, our mouths collide, chasing and licking, and all at once he holds, groaning deeply as I feel him coming inside me. His dick pulses and his arms circle my waist, pulling me flush against his body.

It's primal and perfect, our bodies melding together. We're still breathing fast, and his large hands smooth my hair back from my face as he kisses my cheek, my eye, then down to my mouth.

Holding his face, I kiss him back. It's less frantic now, more savoring, tasting. We're returning to Earth together, holding onto each other.

"Come here." He takes a second to dispose of the condom, then he lays on the bed beside me, gathering me into his arms.

My cheek is against his chest, and I listen to his heart beating steadily, gradually slowing. I listen to his breath swirling in and out as he traces his fingers along the line of my back.

It's so peaceful, so secure, my eyes start to close.

"You're not bad at sex." His voice is a low vibration against my cheek, and my eyes pop open. "You're actually very good at sex. Ten out of ten."

I lift my head. "You heard that?"

A grin curls his lips. "I was walking out to check on Ladybird's progress, and I overheard you and Heather talking. That Baxter's a dickhead."

"Yes, he is." I nod, resting my head on my hand.

My eyes trace down the line of his shoulder to the swell of his bicep. He lifts his finger, tracing it along the line of my hair and sliding a piece behind my ear.

I blink up to meet his eyes, needing to know. "What are we doing, Owen?"

His lips press, and his brow furrows briefly. "We're having fun. I'm trying to understand why I don't feel guilty being here with you."

"Because of Maddie?"

"Not really. I'm pretty sure my daughter adores you."

"The feeling is mutual." I smile.

He blinks down. "After my wife died, I swore I was done. I'd never build my life around someone again. It hurt too bad to lose it."

"You were grieving."

"It was more than that." His voice is rough. "I wanted to bury that part of me with her. I wanted to shut it off."

We're quiet, and my chest aches. I don't know what to say, so instead, I ask softly. "How did she die?"

He hesitates. The second hand on an old analog clock ticks once, twice...

"Her heart stopped. She had Maddie, and that was it. They couldn't bring her back."

"Oh." My stomach drops, and I sit up, holding the sheet over my body. "Owen, I'm so sorry." I imagine him with a newborn. "You must've been devastated."

"The doctors said it was a pre-existing condition, but it made no sense. She was so alive and ready. They asked me if she'd had weak spells or if she seemed unusually tired. She did, but I thought it was because she was pregnant. Why did I think that?"

By the end, his voice breaks, and I lean forward, gently placing my hand on his cheek. "No... it's a tragic thing. It's not your fault."

"Everyone says that, but it doesn't change how I feel. Only time has helped."

Blinking down, I understand the need for a pseudonym, the need for John and Kendall. It's an escape, permission.

"At first, I lived like a monk, thinking if I devoted myself to her memory, I could make up for letting it happen. Then, I grew angry at her, like I wondered if she hid it from me... Then I hated myself for being angry. Then I decided to block it out."

"That only works for so long." I slide my hand down the length of his arm, threading our fingers at the bottom. "You have to feel it eventually."

"That was my life." He lifts my hand, pressing it to his

lips. "Until now. It's the first time I've felt like I could move on, the first time I've felt strong. I don't know why."

His warm lips trace my knuckles, and my eyes close again. My eyes heat, and I press my lips together. I scoot around in the bed, placing my cheek on his chest again, wrapping my arms around his waist. He's such a good man, a devoted father.

So many feelings for him are in my heart, so many feelings for Maddie. Tonight was incredible, and I can't go back to pretending there's nothing between us. Not after this.

With a deep inhale, I push myself to sitting, looking down on his perfect form twisted in the white linen sheets. "I'd better get back to my room."

He sits up, reaching out to cup my cheek. "Okay."

I turn my face to kiss his palm. "It's more than a fantasy to me."

Our eyes meet, and his are clear now. "I want this."

My stomach twists, but I know the truth. "Me too."

16

———

OWEN

Our game against Anaheim is a shutout, just like Mav predicted, and I'm moving up in the crowd rankings. Fans are starting to recognize me, and I've even spotted a few *Stone* jerseys in the stands, which is a real confidence booster.

I was able to get the puck past their goalie once, but Mav stole the show, scoring a hat trick. The crowd went wild, caps flew onto the ice, and our fans were on their feet stomping and blowing air horns.

Gliding around, laughing and slapping hands with my teammates—it's a feeling I haven't experienced in a long time, a joy I'd forgotten I could have.

My night with Gina was on my mind the whole day. I hated that she couldn't spend the night in my bed so I could kiss her, hold her, make love to her again like we did at the Delve Inn. That night was crazy.

But she was right. It wouldn't be good if Heather or Maddie caught us sleeping together. Not yet.

Before Maverick, Gavin, and I left, we spent the morning helping put up Halloween decorations, mostly stringing lights in the trees and other things that required ladders and height.

Mav was chugging red Mountain Dew and eating red M&Ms. I made the comment that all that red dye couldn't be good for him, and I quickly learned it's his good luck charm. Gavin's is Haddy, which they went round and round about the entire drive.

I didn't even weigh in that mine is blowing a kiss to Maddie. I do it before every game, and if it's one like this, when we're out of town, I blow her a kiss from the window when I tell her goodbye.

Either way, we smoked Anaheim, and we're all in high spirits when we arrive back at the house, showered and in our suits. Trick-or-treating has ended, and the party is in full swing.

"Daddy!" Madison runs to me the minute I walk in the door. "Look at all the candy I got!"

She drags a satin pillowcase over, and I take a knee. Then she drops it onto my leg, and I let out an *oof*. The dang thing must weigh five pounds, but I'm more curious about her costume.

She's in a shimmering white dress with a blue headband around her head and a staff that looks like a triton.

"Who are you, Shortcake?"

"Miss Gina said there are a lot of sea princesses who are smarter than Ariel." She turns around, looking down at her dress. "I'm Salacia, Queen of the Sea."

"That's fancy." I pull her onto my lap. "I bet Salacia wouldn't give away her voice for a stinky boy."

"Oh, no. She's a queen!" She lifts her little chin, and I tweak it with my fingers before kissing her cheek.

"You've made quite a haul here, Sally. Save some for me. I've got to get changed into my costume."

"Who are you going to be?"

"Arr, I'm one of Mr. Maverick's pirate crew." I stand, checking out all the decorations.

Cobwebs hang from the light fixtures, and plastic spiders are on the tables. Purple and orange twinkle lights surround the windows, and outside, fabric bats and ghosts hang from the trees.

"Spooky guacamole!" Haddy exits the kitchen wearing a red sweater and black skirt that hugs her body like a glove along with a black wig with a sausage-like ponytail in the back.

In her hands is a platter with a small jack-o-lantern that has guacamole pouring out of its mouth, surrounded by blue corn chips.

"That looks like barf!" Maddie cries.

"You're gonna love it," Haddy replies, setting the dish on the table then pointing to the kitchen. "Now get your royal tushy to the kitchen, or I'll sell you to one of these pirates."

My daughter takes off running, and I turn to her with my eyebrows raised. "What the...?"

"Gina made her chicken nuggets and tater tots. It's our specialty, and Gigi said she can't eat candy until she has dinner." Haddy crosses her arms, smiling after my daughter. "Luckily, I don't have that problem, but I do need to feed Lucy before everyone gets here."

Mav ducked into his room as soon as we walked in the door, and he staggers out in full Captain Jack Sparrow attire. "Where's my purple drink, wench?"

"Get it yourself!" Haddy flicks her fingers at him. "I've got a baby to feed."

She rushes out the door, and Mav pretend-waddles up to me. "You're a fine fellow. Spare me a quid?"

My eyes narrow. "Fresh out."

"Well, off with you! We don't need any suits at the party."

"Right." I'm still wearing my suit from when we left the arena. "I'll be back."

I take the stairs two at a time, and when I crash into my room, my pirate outfit is on the bed waiting.

I quickly remove my clothes and toss them over the back of the chair. Just as fast, I'm dressed in brown breeches, a white shirt with giant puffy sleeves, and knee-high boots.

I grab the plastic sword off the bed, and I'm about to head down, when I stop and look at my hair. It's shaggy and getting too long. I need a haircut, but it'll work for tonight.

Striding down the hall to Heather's room, I spy a band on her dresser and quickly pull my hair back in a small ponytail.

Being a single dad has a few perks, like knowing how to tie a ponytail for one.

That done, I trudge down the stairs just in time to see Donovan, Saxon, and Akers charging in the front door. We're all dressed as pirates, and as soon as we see each other, we all let out an *Arr!*

Heather starts to laugh, but I almost miss the last step when Gina enters the room, carrying a tray of Jell-O shots with eyeballs in them. Her hands are in front of her, and the top of her shimmering blue-green dress cuts dangerously low on her breasts.

My dick jumps, and the memory of covering them with my mouth floods my mind. I'm momentarily dumbstruck watching her, until I realize eyes are on me. Hustling down the stairs, I step over to where she's just put down the tray.

"Oh!" She yelps when she turns around, bumping into my chest.

Her strawberry hair is straight down her back, and a tiny gold band is on her head like one of those ancient crowns. Iridescent sparkles are at the corners of her eyes, and her lips are a swirly, glossy pinkish-purple color.

She looks like she came straight out of the sea, an old-school siren sent to bewitch me off my ship and take me straight to the bottom of the ocean with her.

"You look like a scurvy bloke." She pokes my chest with her finger, squinting one eye like a pirate. "We'll have you boiled in oil and keel hauled... or whatever."

I'm still trying to remember how to form sentences, but she doesn't seem to notice.

She laughs at her silly words then leans into my chest. "Good thing I'm only a sea nymph." Then she frowns. "What's wrong? Is there guac in my teeth?"

"No..." I shake my head to restart my brain. "You're beautiful. I mean, *really* beautiful. I've never seen anything like you."

Clearly, my brain is taking the slow lane. In the meantime, Gina's cheeks turn a pretty pink color, and she smiles up at me.

"Thank you, kind sir." Rising onto her toes, she kisses my cheek. "Maybe we'll save the keel-hauling for another day."

I'm about to suggest we find a secluded place for me to slip her my keel when Gavin walks in the front door wearing a black sailor shirt with a big red collar.

He's wearing some kind of prosthetics that make his forearms look huge, and he's holding Lucy in a bright red canvas bag. A teeny white sailor's cap is on her head, and I get it.

I point to them. "Popeye, Olive Oyl, and Sweetpea!"

"It's Swee'pea, sailor." He growls, putting a small pipe between his lips. "Get it right."

"Oh, Popeye!" Haddy skips up beside him, bending one knee and kissing his cheek.

Gigi laughs, but I catch her arm, turning her to face me. "I need some help with this."

I gesture to the front of my shirt, which is hanging wide open, and her bottom lip drops. She quickly closes her mouth, fixing her eyes on my shirt.

"Let me see." She lifts the thin strings, and her fingers graze my bare chest as she slowly tries to tie the laces.

Her nose wrinkles, and her cheeks turn even pinker.

"What are you thinking about?" My voice is low.

"Your chest is like a sculpture." She exhales a fluttery laugh. "Why are these laces so hard to tie?"

I reach up to cover her hands with mine. "Leave them. I'm sure a pirate wouldn't care if his shirt wasn't laced properly."

Her eyebrow arches, and she blinks those pretty green eyes up at me. "As someone who knows?"

"A lot of pirates settled in South Carolina."

"I thought your family was so straight and narrow." She tilts her head. "Your father's a sheriff."

"*Your* father's a sheriff, and he dresses in drag and gives lap dances."

Her head ducks forward, and she laughs. "It's true!"

I put my thumb on her chin, lifting her face to mine. "I really want to kiss you right now."

"What would happen if you did?"

"I'm not sure. I've never kissed a magical sea creature before."

"Or have you?" She reaches up to cover my palm with hers, lowering my hand.

Then she turns and walks back to the kitchen, looking over her shoulder. "I'd better check on your daughter."

My eyes slide down the length of her body in that thin, form-fitting dress. It's the grown-up version of the one my daughter is wearing, and I think about Maddie and Gina.

I think about my daughter having a mother for the first time. I need to have a chat with my little girl. Soon.

Heather's voice at my shoulder pulls me back to the present. "See something you like?"

I turn to see my little sister dressed in a pirate wench outfit. It has a black vest-like corset thing that pushes her breasts up in a way I don't like.

Glancing around the room, I notice a few of my teammates checking her out. "Aren't you cold?"

My voice is gruff, and she frowns. "It's not cold in here at all. In fact, it feels pretty perfect."

"You sure are showing a lot of skin."

"You are not about to pull that big-brother shit on me tonight, Owen Stone. Not after all the times I've passed up dates to help you with my adorable niece."

My chest is tight. "You're just putting a lot out there. I don't want to get into a fight tonight."

"Then don't." Her voice is sharp. "It's Halloween, and maybe I feel like a treat."

"Well, hell, why didn't you have a treat in Newhope?"

"I told you why. Things are different here."

"Yeah, they are. These guys are my teammates. I'm with them all the time."

"Who says I'm interested in a hockey player?" Her eyebrow arches. "I'll be lucky if he has all his teeth."

"I have all my teeth."

"Only because Grammy Gwen cast a spell so you wouldn't get hit in the face with a puck."

"She did not."

Heather gives me a look, and I hesitate, thinking. I have had a few close calls in my career. Still, that doesn't mean... *Does it?*

"Well..." I don't know how to respond to this new information. "Just don't date any of my teammates."

"Deal." She sticks out her hand, and I give it a firm shake.

"I guess that means I'm on Maddie duty then?" I do my best to keep the disappointment out of my tone.

With the way Gigi looks tonight, I was thinking John might need to sneak into a bathroom with Kendall.

"Actually, Haddy offered to watch her for us tonight. She said she'd be leaving early anyway because of the baby, and she and Maddie could have a movie night. *Mr. Toad and The Legend of Sleepy Hollow.*"

"Good one."

"And Mads has never seen it, so bonus!"

"Well, have fun tonight. Make good choices."

"I always do." My sister turns to go just as Ryan the photographer walks through the door.

Heather waves and runs over to him, and he gives her a smile I kind of don't like. But at least he isn't a Champion.

A woman with bobbed dark brown hair and a tall guy who looks Russian are also with him. They're dressed as Natasha and Boris, and they all mix in with the crowd dancing in the middle of the living room where the furniture used to be.

Looking around, I realize Spanky's cage is gone, and I didn't see Ladybird in my rush to get changed and get back down here.

I turn to go to the kitchen when I notice Donovan dressed as a pirate, bending down and talking to Gina. He's smiling at her, and she reaches out to grab his arm, giving it a firm shake.

He says something in her ear, and her eyes close. My vision goes red, and I forget about the dogs, my daughter, my sister... everything. *What the fuck?*

Without really thinking about it, I stalk over to where the two of them are standing.

"Hey, Sly," my team captain says. "Or should I say *matey*?"

He's teasing, but I'm grinding my teeth so hard, I might break Gwen's spell.

"You okay, man?" Don's eyebrows lower as he reads my face.

"What's going on over here?" My voice is growly.

"Owen," Gina laughs, her voice noticeably higher. "We're just chatting. I-I've been friends with Donovan for years..."

"Friends. Is this friendly?"

"Yeah." Donovan straightens to his full height, a taunting grin curling his lips. "You got a problem with it?"

I stand straighter as well, not backing down. Donovan is an inch taller than I am, but I don't really give a shit. I'm ready to punch him straight in his crooked nose.

"Maybe I do."

His shoulders drop, and he exhales a laugh. "Owen, bruh. It's not what you think. Trust me."

Gina's eyes are wide, and she puts her hands on both my arms, turning me away from him. "Come with me."

I hold Donovan's pale blue eyes a beat longer before letting Gina drag me into the kitchen. We push through the door, where I see Maddie sitting at the bar with Zander, dancing him back and forth along the granite countertop as she watches *It's the Great Pumpkin, Charlie Brown* on Gina's iPad.

"What were you doing out there?" Her voice is a sharp whisper.

"He was hitting on you."

"Oh my gosh, Owen, he was not!"

"He had his hands on you, and his face was in your hair." Most likely sniffing up all of her sweet cherry scent.

Something like amusement dances in her eyes as she grabs my wrist, dragging me to the back of the kitchen, away from everyone, and into the laundry room, slamming the door.

My brow arches, and I reach for her.

She blocks my hand. "I'm going to tell you something, and you have to swear to me you will never, *ever* repeat it."

"I don't like the sound of that."

"Stop misreading everything and listen to me." Her green eyes flash with impatience, and fuck, bossy Gina is hot.

"Okay." I hold up both hands.

"Donovan is gay."

The small room falls silent, and we blink at each other. The noise of the party seems far away in this small room, behind the closed door. The sound of our breathing is louder, and I wonder if anyone would hear if we...

Then I realize she's waiting for me to say something, which now seems silly. I'm a lot less mad than I was ten seconds ago.

I straighten, looking around the room, my unexpected, jealous rage forgotten. "You're sure about that?"

"Oh my gosh, yes!" She drops her head back, groaning. "All last year, Maverick and Haddy were trying to push us together. He finally just told me, because he said he didn't want me to think he didn't find me attractive or whatever..."

"So he *does* find you attractive?"

She steps forward, putting her hands on my shoulders and smiling. "Yes, he does. In fact, he told me I looked very beautiful tonight."

My jaw clenches, and I might be remembering my rage.

I look over my shoulder in the direction of the party. "Mother..."

She catches my chin, pulling my face back to hers. "He's not bisexual. He's 100 percent gay, and you can't tell anyone."

My eyes narrow. "I would never out him, but if he's so gay and he thinks you're so beautiful..."

"He doesn't know how the guys will react, and he likes being team captain." She steps back, twisting her fingers. "Of course, Mav wouldn't care. We grew up with our uncles Craig and Clint..."

"My aunt Cass's little sister lived with a drag queen before she got married. Auntie Monay still lives in Eureka with her dog Angie Dickinson II."

Gina's eyes widen, and she holds up a finger. "We'll come back to that. The point is, he's not ready to come out, and it's a very personal thing. You can never, *never* tell him I told you, and if he does choose to come out at some point, you'd better be the most surprised member of the team."

Catching her by the waist, I pull her to my chest. "How surprised would you be if I told you John needs to see Kendall right now?"

Her lips press into a smile, and she reaches up to thread her fingers in the short pieces of hair that have escaped my ponytail.

"I do love a guy in a ponytail."

Leaning closer, I kiss the side of her jaw. "How do you feel about pirates?"

"Hmm…" She exhales a noise that registers straight to my cock. "I've never been with a pirate before."

Moving my face above hers, I look down at her soft lips. "I'd be up for a quickie… if you would?"

She rises onto her toes, wrapping her arms around my neck. Our noses slide together, and she nods. "I would."

"Fuck, Gina." I groan. "I might've begged."

A soft laugh slips from her throat as I consume her full lips. We kiss through our smiles, tongues curling, as we pull each other closer.

Her dress is beautiful, and it's all the way to the floor. I can't figure out the best way inside it, until she turns to face the washer.

"Here…" She grabs the skirt, pulling it higher. "Help me."

Oh fuck. My dick is so hard, I'm not about to question this. I slide my large hands up the outside of her thighs, lifting the sparkling garment over her cute, round ass.

My brow collapses, and I grip her soft flesh with my hands, kneading it, spreading it apart with my thumbs.

"I love your ass." I groan.

"Owen…" she moans, and I know, it's supposed to be quick.

I unfasten my pants, letting them fall so my cock is exposed. Sliding my hands up her thighs, I find her clit and begin to circle. She's already so fucking wet.

"Fuck…" I reach down to search my pockets. "I don't have a condom."

"Just pull out," she groans. "Hurry, I need you."

"Gina." My throat aches, and I know this is risky.

I have too many feelings for her, and trusting my animal

brain to know when to stop is asking a lot. But the crack in her voice is more than I can bear.

Grasping my dick, I slide it up and down her dripping core before thrusting balls-deep into her body.

"Fuuuuuuk…" I groan, gripping the shelf for support. "Gina, holy shit, that's good."

My voice is ragged. She's so hot and warm and tight and wet. I'm pretty sure my brain broke, and then she starts rocking her ass against me.

"Fuck me, Owen," she whispers, and I almost blow right there.

Gripping her slim hips, I pull her body against mine, squinting my eyes to keep from coming in two pumps like a fifteen-year-old.

"It's too good…" I groan. "I've gotta stop."

"Don't you dare," she gasps, fucking me with her hips.

"You feel so damn good. I'm gonna come."

"Just a little more." Her hips keep rocking, and I gulp back a yell.

Two more thrusts, and I yank my cock from her luscious body, holding it away from her sparkling dress as I come on the dirty clothes in the open basket.

"Oh, shit…" My legs shake, and I can't believe I had the willpower to pull out. "I'll clean this up."

Gina turns, pulling my face down to hers and kissing me long and hard. I put my hands on each side of her, kissing her back with equal force, equal hunger.

"You didn't finish." Dropping to my knee, I toss her leg over my shoulder and bury my face in her sweet pussy.

"Oh, shit!" She lifts her hips, gripping the back of my head with her hand.

I lick and suck, faster as she rocks her hips against my face.

"Right there... Right there!" She hits a note the dogs probably hear, then breaks into shudders, pulling my hair and moaning.

I kiss the inside of her trembling thigh, straightening on my knees to wrap my arms around her waist. She bends down to hug me, kissing my temple as her fingers comb my hair.

A loud cheer comes from the party, bringing us around, and I stand, straightening my pants and tucking in my shirt. She cleans up with an unstained washcloth then smooths her dress and straightens her hair. I scoop up the dirty clothes and toss them into the machine.

I flip the switch to rinse only. We can worry about sorting and all the rest tomorrow. She starts to exit through the door, but I catch her arm, pulling her to me again.

Looking down, I hold her cheeks in my hands, gazing into her bright eyes. I'm so different now.

I came here a broken man. A man who thought life had nothing left for him. A man who didn't want a second chance, who wanted to bury that part of himself.

Now I have her, this magical creature. Looking into her eyes, I see a family, a mother for my little girl, someone to share my life with.

She steals the breath from my lungs, she makes me irrationally angry at the thought of another man touching her. She makes me irrationally happy...

Tracing my finger along her jaw, I huff a laugh. "I'm sorry."

"For what?" Her pretty brow lines with concern.

"How I acted just now... I didn't know I could feel that way."

"Oh..." Her head tilts, and a teasing glint is in her eyes. "I'll let you make it up to me."

"I will."

"Next time you're blind with jealousy?" Her eyebrow arches.

"If I fuck your brains out every time I'm jealous of you, there won't be anything left."

She places her hands on my face, rising on her tiptoes to kiss me long and slow. "You never have to be jealous, Owen Stone. I'm not going anywhere."

17

GINA

"What if we host a Día De Los Muertos party for foster dogs?" I lean back against the couch cushions, looking over the still-decorated living room. "We can include the shelter, too. Extend the holiday, and do some good."

"I think that's a great idea!" Haddy paces back and forth behind me, bouncing Lucy on her shoulder. "Were any of the calendar hounds fosters? I'll let the team know."

"What's a foster dog?" Maddie flops onto the couch beside me holding Peepee.

"It's a dog that needs a home for a little while." A frown pulls her lips, and I try to explain better. "Like maybe its owner can't keep it anymore or the owner passed away, and the shelter needs to place it with some nice people until they find a permanent home. Peepee was a foster dog."

Maddie looks down at the teacup poodle, stroking it with her finger.

She blinks up at me, wrinkling her nose. "I'm like a foster dog."

Haddy does a spit-take behind me, and I put my arm around Maddie, pulling her close. "No, you're not. You have your daddy and your aunt Heather."

"My mom passed away." Her voice is quiet, and I glance up at Haddy before answering.

"I know, honey." I rub my hand up and down her little arm. "Does that make you feel sad?"

"Not really. I never met her, but my daddy said she was real nice and she loved me a lot. My grammy Britt said her heart grew so big with love for me, she had to go on up to heaven and be an angel watching over me."

My throat aches, and I lean my cheek against her little head. "People who love us that much make the very best angels."

"You're real nice, and I'm staying with you until we find a home." She looks up at me. "I'm a foster dog, too!"

"I mean..."

Haddy jumps in to save me. "Do you think it's a good thing to be a foster dog?"

Maddie's lips twist, and she pauses. Then she smiles, nodding and blinking up at us. "Peepee's cute, and she's your real dog now. Maybe someone nice could be my mom one day, too."

"Know what? I think you *are* a foster dog." Haddy smiles, reaching down to boop Maddie's nose with the tip of her finger. "And I bet one day, you'll have a very nice mom, who'll love you very much."

I'm not sure if this is okay, but at the same time, my heart is so full of affection for this little girl.

I think about all the things Owen and I have said to each

other. They are here temporarily, but what if our situation became permanent?

Things are changing between us, and while it's way too soon to say anything certain, maybe one day... who knows what the future holds?

The door opens, and the guys come bustling in. Gavin immediately takes Lucy out of Haddy's arms. Owen walks over to where Maddie and I are sitting on the sofa, and Mav extends his arms wide.

"Great news!" he announces. "The Schillingers are selling their house."

"What?" Haddy turns to him, pulling one of his arms. "Where are they going?"

"Moving to Malibu, just like all the other old people in this 'hood."

"What does that mean?" I look from my cousin to Owen, who's now sitting on the other side of his daughter wearing a satisfied expression.

"It means, we're going to make them an offer they can't refuse," Mav says. "And the Stones will be our new neighbors a block to the north!"

He's so confident, and I turn to Owen. "Is this what you want to do?"

Even though we love our secluded little neighborhood, it's a bit of a drive to the arena where they practice every single day and where many of their games are held every week.

"I mean, if I were coming here alone, with no attachments or needs, I'd probably look for something closer to downtown." He shrugs. "As it is, I've got a daughter and a sister... and I want to be close to the people I care about."

The warmth in his voice, the way his eyes fix on mine,

puts a knot in my throat. His meaning is clear. If the people he cares about were only Madison and Heather, they could easily move with him downtown, closer to the arena.

"Well, I think that's perfect!" Haddy skips over to hug Owen's shoulders, moving quickly to Maddie's. "We'll be great neighbors, and Lucy can grow up with family close by..."

I don't correct her use of the word *family*. I know they're all lobbying hard for Owen and me to be a couple, but the truth is, you can't hurry love. It's a song, but it's also a fact.

As strong as my feelings are for him, he's dealing with so much on his own. His grief, his feelings about commitment.

The things he shared with me are important, and I would never rush him or me into a decision like that.

"I'm going to call my realtor and see if she can help me get an offer on the table this week." He stands, taking out his phone. "I'll see how quickly we can close, and maybe we can be out of your hair before Thanksgiving."

"You're not really in our hair," I say quietly, glancing up at him.

He looks down at me, and the smile on his face warms my insides. "It'll be good for me to have my own place. For many reasons."

I'm pretty sure I know what those reasons might be, and I hope I'm right. I hope one of them is me.

"I'm a foster dog, Daddy!" Maddie pops up between us, hugging Haddy's dog against her chest.

"What?" He laughs, putting his hand on her shoulder.

"It's like an orphan," Maddie tells him. "But Aunt Haddy said one day, I might have a nice lady to live with me and be a real mom... like she did with Peepee!"

"That's basically what I said..." Haddy chuckles.

"You're much sweeter than a foster dog." I reach out to tweak her chin.

"I'm so lost." Mav shakes his head. "*How* is Maddie like a dog?"

Haddy steps forward, grabbing the reins on the conversation. "We were thinking it would be fun to host a party for the animal shelter. The house is all decorated, and maybe some of the guys might want to adopt their calendar pets!"

"Were those dogs up for adoption?" Owen looks at me.

"A few were from the shelter, but most of them have owners."

"Let's do it!" Mav leans forward onto the couch. "I don't mind foster pets... as long as they're not humping the couch cushions like there's no tomorrow."

"What's humping?" Maddie frowns, and Haddy glares at him.

"It means working real hard," Mav says, giving her the thumbs-up.

"Stop." I push his hands down. "Just... Stop."

Maddie's little brow is still furrowed, and she looks at me.

"It's an adult word that doesn't mean what it used to mean." I slide her hair behind her ear. "Only really, really old people say it now."

"Oh, like Uncle Mav is *old*," she nods slowly, like she gets it.

"Exactly." I cut my eyes up at him. "Really old, like Uncle Mav."

"Dude, I'm not even thirty!" Mav holds out his hands. "That's just mean."

Gav shakes his head, cuddling Lucy. "Let us know what you need for the adoption party. We'll get the guys to come over and help out."

I look around. "I'll text Carla now."

Taking out my phone, I send a quick text to my friend. It doesn't take her long to reply, saying she'll bring every pet they have.

"They'll be here first thing in the morning." I read my phone to the group.

"Text me all the details, and I'll share them with the team," Haddy says.

"On it." I send it to her, then I text the neighborhood news what's happening.

By tomorrow, I expect we'll have a house full of people ready to give a dog a good home.

"AND CLYDE IS NOW OFFICIALLY part of your family." Carla stands to shake the tall hockey player's hand.

He thanks her and leads the small Beagle back to his waiting family. I grin, clasping my hands under my chin as I watch the children excitedly hugging their cute new dog.

"You are so good at matching dogs with their owners." I turn to her, pulling her into a hug. "How do you do it?"

"I'm a pet psychic!" She holds her hands up, waggling her fingers in a jazzy way.

My eyes widen. "You are not..."

"No." Carla deadpans, and we both snort a laugh. "Not that I'm saying it can't be done. I'm not convinced it can't!"

"I don't know." I shake my head. "The jury is still out as far as I'm concerned."

"Want to come and look at the house with me?" Owen's large hand covers mine, and my breath catches.

"Yes..." But I hold up a finger, turning to my friend. "Would you be okay if I disappeared for a few minutes?"

"Of course!" She waves her hands at me, chuckling. "Please go with the handsome, rising hockey star and look at a future home."

"It's not like that," I start to argue, but when I look up at Owen... the way he's looking down at me... I'm not so sure.

We head down the steps to the sidewalk, then past a few houses to the now-empty one on the same side of the street as mine.

"Since the Schillingers have already moved out, we're closing this week." Owen holds the door, and we step into a big, open floorplan with two bedrooms and three full bathrooms on the first floor. "We can start moving in on the fifteenth."

The floors are split brick, and the living room has a gorgeous, vaulted ceiling made of yellow-pine planks. Yellow pine stairs at the back wall lead to the upstairs floor, which has two more bedroom suites.

"Come look at this." Owen clasps my hand, leading me to the master suite on the first floor.

The bedroom is beautiful with pine floors, beige walls, ceiling fans, bronze fixtures. It has a wall of windows looking out over a garden of flowering bushes, but Owen doesn't stop for any of it.

Holding my hand, he leads me to a small door off the side, which opens to a path leading down to a cute little cottage in the backyard.

The door opens, and my breath catches. "It's a she-shed!"

The walls are painted pink, and a flower box is in the window.

"It has electricity and wireless." He steps inside the gingerbread workspace. "It doesn't have plumbing, but we can run a line out here. I don't know how much it costs to have a bathroom installed..."

I stop in the middle of the room, turning to face him. "What are you saying?"

He looks down, rubbing a hand over his chin. "I'm just saying it has a lot of potential."

My lips press into a smile. "I think it does."

18

OWEN

"And here are the keys to your new home." My realtor hands me the fob with the miniature hockey puck on the keychain. "The previous owners thought that would be a fun touch. They are so happy to have sold their home to a single dad who's a Champion and a friend of the Bradfords."

"They're nice folks." I take the keys, slipping them into the pocket of my jeans. "I'm glad they were so easy to work with."

"They got what they wanted here, and now they're moving on to their next chapter, just like you're moving into your next chapter."

It's been a busy three weeks. We had our pod sent from Eureka, and with everyone's help, we spent most of November unloading furniture and moving our things between games and practice.

It all fits perfectly, almost like it was meant to be here, my sister observed. I'm doing my best not to get caught up in her vibes and visions, but I have to be honest, between her and the dogs, they're starting to wear me down.

My realtor wishes us all the best before she leaves, and I walk through the arched doorway into my new chapter. The house is ready to be occupied, and I think about what I want here.

I'm pretty sure it includes someone with bright green eyes, silky rose-gold hair, who smells like cherries. I'm less sure how it will happen or if it can be as quickly as I'd like, but it's the future I see.

"That is a very serious look on your face." My sister walks down from the second floor. "What are you thinking about?"

I look up to her. "We should have a housewarming party."

"When is your next open Friday night?"

I pull out my phone, scrolling through the calendar. "Looks like the end of this week. Is that too soon?"

"Never fear." My sister waves her finger. "I can make it happen."

"Here." I take the keyring from my pocket and give her a key to the house. "Invite everybody. I feel like celebrating."

"Any particular reason?"

"Yeah." I nod, my eye catching on the she-shed in the backyard. "A very particular reason."

Heather bounces over to give me a hug. "Leave it all to me, big brother. I'm so ready for this to happen."

I don't say it out loud, but I am, too.

"IF YOU LOVE DANCING, this is the place for you." Maverick

reads the email invitation my sister sent everyone. "That's what I'm talking about. Break in the new place right!"

When he puts it that way, with that Maverick Murphy gleam in his eye, I start to question my decision to have a big party. Maybe we should've kept it small.

"We're not going to trash the place," I quickly tell him. "We're just going to have dancing."

"The last time I danced was in Newhope at my wedding." Gavin stretches his back against the locker beside me. "The day after I got a lap dance from my father-in-law."

A laugh barks from my throat, and I pat his shoulder as I push to stand. "I'm not going to lie, my family is crazy, but your family gives them a run for their money."

"If we're too crazy, you're too old!" Mav throws up gang signs, and even Gavin breaks.

"So you coming or what?" I look at the two of them.

"Hell, yeah!" Mav clasps my hand, pulling off his sweaty jersey. "I'll dress up and everything."

"We'll be there," Gav says. "We just might have to leave a little early with the baby and all."

"Understood." I'm happy everyone is coming, and they can stay as long as they want.

I'll be with Gina.

Grabbing my bag, I head out to my old truck, tossing it in the back and making the drive home. The guys and I usually carpool to the arena for games and practice, but I've got to pick up Heather's order of food and supplies for the party.

It isn't too much, and I'm back in time to get changed and help set up if needed.

"Finally!" Heather dashes from the kitchen to take the box from my hands. "I need you to grab the ladder and hang these on the tree out front while I get dressed."

She puts a roll of twinkle lights in my hand and rushes into the kitchen.

"Hey, man, need some help?" Ryan walks out of the door my sister just entered.

He's wearing bell-bottom jeans and a wide-collared shirt unbuttoned to his stomach. An ivory horn hangs from a chain around his neck.

"That's some getup." I pass him the roll of lights. "Get started on these while I change clothes."

Tables are set up throughout the downstairs living areas, and all the furniture has been moved to the walls. A disco ball has replaced the fixture on the ceiling fan in the great room, and streamers hang over all the windows.

"It looks like *Eurovision* in here," I say on my way to my bedroom.

"Look at me, Daddy!" Maddie follows me into my room. "I'm a disco dancer!"

She starts spinning in place, and the long white fringe on her sleeves flies out. She doesn't stop until she bounces off the side of my bed and falls onto the rug beside Ladybird.

"Whooooa!" she cries, flapping her arms on the way down.

Thankfully the rug has a pretty thick pad underneath it, but the dog rises and lets out a loud *Rooo!*

She jumps up and hugs Ladybird. "You're okay, LB!"

I squint an eye at her. "How much sugar have you eaten today, Shortcake?"

Since she started at the neighborhood school, I'm pretty sure they've had a party every month. Today was for Thanksgiving, and when she left this morning, she was dressed in all black with a white apron and a little white hat.

"Miss Beanie had Starbursts for everybody and Cissy

had Sprees." She jumps up, flapping her arms so the fringe rises and falls in swirls around her. "And we all had turkeys made of cookies with candy corn tails!"

"That sounds about right." I put my hand on her shoulder, turning her towards the door. "Go ask Aunt Heather to give you a glass of water, and see if Ladybird wants to walk down and see Spanky."

"Okay!" she shouts, running out the door at top speed.

Shaking my head, I notice a pair of bootcut jeans and a silky, maroon shirt with a wide collar waiting for me on the bed with a note from Heather that says *Wear this*.

I showered at the arena after practice to save time, but going by the store has me rushing now. Our guests will start showing up in a little more than an hour.

I step into the pants and pull on the shirt then step in front of the mirror to assess my outfit. Taking out my phone, I send a quick text.

OWEN

When did my party get a disco theme?

It only takes a minute for her to reply.

GINA

Heather had it on all the invitations. Didn't you get one?

OWEN

No, but fool me once.

GINA

It's going to be fun! Just go with it.

OWEN

You're not going to believe the outfit she bought me. I look like Bohemian Rhapsody.

GINA

I look like Roller Girl.

OWEN

That's hot. Are you on skates?

GINA

Too dangerous. I'm on platforms.

OWEN

Nice. Come on now. I need to see you.

GINA

Hmmm… since you put it like that…

OWEN

Meet you out front.

I notice how tight my pants are across the fly as I start for the door and have to make an adjustment.

In the living room, my sister is wearing a gold-satin bell-bottom pantsuit and a long scarf tied around her head. She's carrying a platter of Jell-O shots, only this time they have candy-corn pumpkins in them.

"Nice." I nod at her outfit. "I didn't know we had a theme."

"Every party needs a theme." She smiles, circling her finger around my head. "I like the shaggy hair. It's very disco."

"I need you to cut it." I've been putting off a haircut since Gina said she liked my ponytail almost a month ago.

"But you have such a nice flow," Heather teases, walking past me to put the shots on the table. "You look like a real NHL star."

"Does Maddie know not to eat those?" I point to the Jell-O shots.

"Yes. The ones with pumpkins are for the adults. The

ones with nothing are for her. I gave her one when she came down."

"I told her to drink a glass of water," I groan. "She's had so much sugar, we'll be lucky if she makes it to the party at all."

"Haddy said she can crash in their guest room tonight with Spanky and LB."

Twisting my lips, I nod. "That's not a bad idea."

My sister heads for the kitchen, and I hurry out the front door just in time to see my two former roommates strutting up the sidewalk.

Gina is sexy in an orange and pink minidress with wide, bell sleeves and a deep V-neck. She's wearing white platform shoes, and she has Spanky strutting proudly on a leash at her side. Her long hair hangs straight down her back, and glasses with round pink lenses are perched on her nose.

Maverick makes me laugh in his navy leisure suit and teased-out curly-curly blond wig.

"What's crackin', Jack?" He points finger-guns at me, and he's talking like one of the guys from *Anchorman*.

"You are freakishly authentic." I jog down to meet them. "I don't know about this blond wig, though."

Without thinking or even hesitating, I put my hand around Gina's waist, pulling her to me and kissing the side of her head.

"Right on." Mav's eyebrow arches at my greeting. "I'm going to leave you and see if I can't find my own foxy lady."

He flashes a peace sign and struts into the house. Gina puts her hand on my shoulder, smiling up at me. "I think you look hot."

"I like you in these shoes." I lean forward to pull her lips with mine. "It's easier to kiss you."

A long *Rooo!* comes from behind me and Spanky lifts his

front legs like he's trying to charge. We look over my shoulder to where Ladybird is peering through the slats in the fence around my backyard.

"I think our dogs have missed each other." Gina steps out of my arms to walk Spanky to the gate, quickly unfastening the leash and letting him into the backyard.

"I've been missing you." I lean down to sweep her long hair away and kiss the side of her neck. "These out-of-town games are killing me."

She straightens, putting her arm around my waist and pulling her body against mine. "Me, too."

"It's got me thinking about things." I put my hands on her hips.

"What kind of things?" Her voice lowers, and she studies my mouth.

"Things we should talk about over lunch on Sunday."

"Are you asking me on a date?"

"Yes."

Her pretty green eyes blink up to mine, and when they meet, the pull is as strong as ever. I want to tell her all the things on my mind right now, but the front door opens, and music spills out around us.

"Hey, you two," Heather yells from the entrance. "Get in here! It's a party!"

I look over to where Haddy is standing beside her waving, and I thread our fingers, leading Gina to the house.

The disco ball turns, sending sparkles of light bouncing off the floors, the windows, and the glasses of champagne. My teammates filter in, including Donovan and a guy who isn't on the team.

They're being very casual, but knowing what I know, I wonder if they might be more than friends.

When we got back on the ice after Halloween, I apologized to him for my jealous outburst. He only laughed and told me not to worry about it. I was embarrassed, being the new guy and all, but after a few hours of scrimmage, we were back to normal.

Then we kicked the Seattle Beavers' asses, and all was right with the world.

So far, we're running undefeated, but the season's only getting started. We still have Edmonton to play... and Detroit and Winnipeg and Toronto.

More guests pour into the house as the night wears on, and Gina never leaves my side. A handful of guests do the Hustle, with my daughter right in the middle of them, and we all laugh at how good she is.

She's been running nonstop since she got home from school, but I can see in her eyes, she's on the verge of a crash. I need to get her to bed before she has a meltdown and starts crying. It still happens, even at seven.

Heather is with her friends, which means I'm on Daddy duty, until Haddy walks up to us with Lucy on her shoulder. They're wearing matching mini-dresses in a tiny floral pattern. Haddy has a band around her forehead, and so does a sleeping Lucy.

"We're taking off now," she shouts above the music. "We can take Maddie and the dogs with us if you'd like to party a little longer."

I look down at Gina, and her nose wrinkles adorably. "I hardly ever stay out late."

She's so cute, I turn to Haddy. "If you don't mind, I'd really appreciate it. I think Mads is going to crash pretty hard."

"Don't worry about a thing." Haddy waves her hand. "Glad to help move things along."

Gina narrows her eyes at her cousin, giving her a little

pinch, but Haddy only laughs, patting her baby's back and calling to my daughter.

Maddie staggers over to where we're standing, her stuffed zebra in her arms, and I take a knee. "I think it's time for Spanky and LB to go to bed. Would you go with Aunt Haddy and help her?"

My daughter puts her hands on my shoulders and nods slowly.

"Zander's so tired. He's been dancing *a lot*." Her eyes start to close, and she leans forward, falling on me in a hug.

I can't help a chuckle. "Sure you can walk down the block?"

"I got her." Gavin bends down and scoops her up. "We'll take care of the dancing queen."

"Thanks, man." I hold out my hand for a fist bump.

"No problem. It's good practice."

We say our goodnights, and they leave. Then, I turn to look at my lady. Her glasses are gone, and her eyes are so bright. I want to call it a night myself and take her to my room, but Heather dances up to us.

"Did Maddie go home with the Knights?" she asks, looking all around.

"Yeah, I'll need you to pick her up tomorrow. We're hitting the road early."

"I'll pick her up." Gina puts her hand in the crook of my arm. "We're closer."

"If you don't mind?"

"I don't." Her nose wrinkles, and I notice my sister is holding a crystal bowl of shiny dark chocolates. "What's that?"

"Oh, it's special chocolate Meredith's boyfriend brought from Russia."

"Russian chocolate?" Gina's eyes widen. "They're so pretty. What do they taste like?"

She takes a few squares and pops them into her mouth. Heather's jaw drops, and she holds up a hand. "Wait..."

"I'll try some." I take a few squares as well, popping them into my mouth.

"No!" Heather catches my wrist, but I've already eaten the small squares.

"They taste odd." My nose wrinkles, and I try to make out the flavor. "It's like chocolate, but what is that? Dirt?"

"I think it tastes like..." Gina's brow furrows as well. "You're right. That's definitely dirt. What kind of chocolate is this?"

My sister's face is lined with worry. She doesn't answer right away, instead, she takes a square and eats it.

"Why are you looking at me like that?" I glance at Gina, and her eyes go wide.

"Oh, no..." Gina puts her hands over her mouth. "Was that...?"

Heather presses her lips together, nodding slowly. "I tried to stop you."

"Stop us from what?" I look from one to the other. "What is it?"

"It's psychedelic mushroom chocolate," Heather shouts over the song 'Brick House.' "I was trying to warn you, but you beat me to it."

"How much did I take?" I look at the dish she's holding, feeling queasy.

"It's about a gram and a half per square. How many did you eat?"

"Two." Gina and I both say at the same time.

"That's not so bad." Heather puts the bowl in a drawer

and closes it. "You're going to feel it, though. Maybe you should go to your room until it wears off?"

"How long will that take?"

"Four hours." Her nose wrinkles, and she gives me a resigned smile. "Just go with it. Relax. Don't fight it."

"What's going to happen?" I look around the room of guests all dancing like we're in Studio 54. "Am I going to jump off the roof?"

"It's not acid," Heather laughs. "The lights will be more vivid... colors more colorful. It's a pretty harmless trip, although sometimes people have visions. I'll keep an eye on you."

"How soon does it start?"

"You'll know when it starts. You'll feel really relaxed and happy."

Great. This is just great. "I have to play tomorrow."

"Good news." Heather leans close. "There's no hangover."

Reaching out, I take Gina's hand, pulling her close. "I've never done anything like this before. Should we go to my room?"

"We'd better." Gina has a frustrated expression. "I *have* done this before, and I spent four hours puking my guts up."

"Oh, shit." Heather didn't say that could happen.

I frown, trying to find my sister in the sea of dancers I don't recognize. She's over with Ryan and Meredith and Meredith's tall boyfriend, who supplied the drugs.

Gina wraps her arms around my waist, and we walk away from the music into my bedroom. The lights are on in the bathroom, and as we enter, the music seems to float in the air around us like a visible current.

It curls and drifts in shiny ribbons, looping around my

back and under my arms, lifting me off the floor, higher and higher.

A soft haze fills the space around me, and I'm surrounded by mist or clouds. I've lost track of Gina, and I consider going to find her. I need to make sure she's safe, even if she is more experienced than I am.

I start to search, but my attention is caught by a large rectangular space to my right. It's an open door, and soft golden beams shine through it. I know in my gut it's a portal to another dimension, and apprehension tightens my shoulders.

I don't want to do this. I don't believe in the supernatural. I raise my hands to push it away, but I keep moving closer to the light, or wait... *Is the light moving closer to me?*

"Owen?" A female voice I recognize tightens my throat.

My stomach drops, and tears spill onto my cheeks. Sorry, anxiety, fear all strangle me, but I manage to find my voice.

"Angie?" It's a hoarse whisper.

A petite blonde with big brown eyes so much like my daughter's walks through the doorway to stand in front of me. She's surrounded by golden light, and a peaceful smile is on her face. She seems to be drifting rather than walking.

I swallow again, and this time my voice is clearer, just above a whisper. "How is this happening?"

My hands are still raised, palms out, as if I'll hold the vision back, but as she draws closer, I try to touch her. She's like a hologram.

"Owen." Her voice is soothing.

I slide my fingers through glittering air. "Is this real?"

"I wanted to see you."

My heart beats faster, and it's difficult to inhale. "Why?"

"To tell you I'm at peace."

"You are?"

She nods slowly.

My throat knots, and more tears spill onto my cheeks. "I'm sorry, Angie. I'm so sorry I didn't help you."

Her head tilts to the side, and she blinks slowly. "You helped me."

"Not when you needed it."

All the words I want to say jumble in my head. I think of all the things I've held onto, all the things I wished I could tell her if I ever got the chance.

Slowly, she lifts her hand. "Stop blaming yourself."

"I should've known you were so tired." A heave jerks my chest, and I drop my chin. "I should've known..."

"It doesn't matter now."

"It does matter," I groan. "Maddie will never know you."

She doesn't answer. She only begins to drift away in the shimmering golden light. I think I hear the sound of sparkling water or tinkling glass. It's like high-pitched wind chimes.

Her eyes hold mine, lingering as if she's waiting for me to regain control.

"Maddie knows you," she says gently. "Take care of her. Take care of you, and let me go."

My legs are weak, and I lower to my knees. My entire body is drained, and I put my hands in front of me on the rug, moving all the way down to lie on my side.

The vision expands as if I'm in a movie theater, and she's on an IMAX screen, looking down at me with large, doe-eyes. The light around her grows brighter until I have to squint, then I can't see her anymore. It's blinding white, slowly fading, growing dimmer and dimmer until the room is completely dark.

The house is quiet.

I'm lying on the floor in my bedroom, hidden between

my bed and the wall. I'm alone, flat on my back, staring at the ceiling.

I touch my face. My cheeks are damp, but my chest is calm. I sit up slowly, a little shakily. My mouth is completely dry, and I hold onto the side of the bed to help me stand.

Gina is there, lying in the center with her arms and legs spread wide like a starfish. I reach over to touch her hand, and I can tell she's only sleeping. Leaving her, I go to the door and open it to see the party is over. Everyone's gone, and my sister is lying on the couch also asleep, a crystal ball cuddled to her chest.

19

———

GINA

"She's telling me it's time to come out now." My hands are up, and rainbow lasers shoot all around us from the disco ball. "Her voice is not squeaky like in a cartoon. It's like a regular voice."

"Whose voice?" Heather's blue eyes are wide, and she holds my arm, looking all around the room.

"Can't you see her?" I point to the fluffy white Bichon Frisé sitting on the rug watching us. "She's wagging her tail and telling me it's time to be born."

Heather moves her hands in an arc in front of my face. "You're the lady with the dog."

"I am." I reach up to hold her hand in mine. "I'm the dog lady."

"My sister." Her eyes flutter closed, and she squeezes our hands together. "I dreamed about you. I told him it was you before we even met. I saw you through the mist holding a dog. You will heal him, and he will heal you."

The Bichon Frisé shakes its ears and rises up on its back legs before running down the hall.

"I have to follow this dog. This dog is my spirit animal!" I take off running after it, leaving Heather dancing under the rainbow lasers.

We run upstairs and down, and then we go outside, where I slow to a stop.

Looking up, I see a sky full of stars. They swirl together like that painting by Van Gogh, and I sit down to watch them curl like waves then uncurl and slide apart.

"It's so beautiful," I tell the dog sitting beside me also watching.

Then the stars swirl to form a heart, and I see a man and a little girl. I reach out my hands, and they reach back. The circle is complete, and we're so happy. We dance around the heart holding hands like it's "Ring Around the Rosie."

My eyes close, and I'm stars now, too. I'm light and fizzy, smiling so big as we release hands, all drifting down together.

The next thing I know, a large hand strokes the top of my head, moving my hair off my cheek. My lips are stuck together, and I have the worst cottonmouth.

"You okay?" Owen's voice is soft, and he pats my shoulder gently. "Need a sip of water?"

Nodding, I sit up slowly. My eyes are still closed, but I reach for the water. I'm desperate for it.

"Here," he says. "Let me help you."

Both of my hands clasp the glass, and I manage to pry my lips apart, drinking big gulps. Finally, I can open my eyes, and he's sitting in front of me, watching me with a peculiar grin on his face, like he's seeing me in a new way.

He's never looked at me like this before, and I try to remember what happened last night.

Oh, yeah. *Mushrooms.*

"Feeling better?" he asks, and I nod. "I've got to get on the road, but I wanted to be sure you were okay before I left."

"I'm okay. Are you?"

"Yeah." He huffs a laugh. "A little shook up. I hope you weren't barfing the whole time."

"I wasn't." I lower the glass, looking at the delicious water. "I followed a dog around. I think it was the dog that made my mom go into labor."

He chuckles deeply, and my stomach squeezes.

"How do you know?" His deep voice is so lovely, and I remember holding hands and dancing around the stars with him.

"It told me to come out now." That makes him laugh more, and I squeeze my eyes together before breaking into laughter as well. "Can you believe that was my mushroom trip? Aren't they supposed to be spiritual and help you find answers or whatever?"

"You'll have to ask Heather. She's the expert."

"She was standing under rainbow lasers the last time I saw her."

He reaches up and slides a loose piece of hair behind my ear, still looking at me like I'm something precious and delicate. It makes my skin prickly and my cheeks flush.

"What happened to you?" I ask softly, reaching for his large hand, and holding it in mine.

"I'll tell you about it tomorrow on our date." He lifts my hand, kissing the back of it. "I've got to go now. Mav's waiting for me."

I smile up at him. "Hit the ice and rock it."

"Right." He hesitates, then leans closer and kisses my lips before starting for the door.

My eyes slide from his broad shoulders to his perfectly tight ass, and I exhale a happy sigh before falling back on the bed again.

Staring up at the ceiling, I try to remember everything from last night, chasing the dog up and down the stairs and out into the yard.

The dog part was silly, but the part that warms me most was lying on the grass watching the stars align in patterns that symbolized love and family.

Holding hands with a man and a little girl, forming a circle around a beating heart. The only thing missing was two dogs who knew before we did what was coming.

If mind-altering drugs can be trusted at all, which it's possible they can't, that's a really great dream.

Shaking my head, I climb off the bed and start collecting my things. Dreams or drugs, I have to get Maddie from my cousin's house, and Haddy texted me about some important hockey business we need to discuss.

"How do you feel about *Pucks for Pups*?" Haddy holds up her hands, spreading them like she's unrolling a banner in the air.

My brow furrows. "What is it?"

"The calendar was such a huge hit, we thought it would be fun to do a corresponding dog show!" She loops her arm through mine. "You were the inspiration for it actually."

"In what way?"

"I saw you teaching Maddie how to walk with Lady-bird, and I thought people would pay money to see the guys walking their dogs from the calendar. Maybe they could be shirtless or in tight jeans... Or they can just wear those suits, because..." My cousin's nose crinkles, and she shivers.

"Who are you? Buck Laughlin?"

I'm referencing the inappropriate color commentator in the mockumentary *Best in Show*, of course.

"You know, he had some pretty good ideas." She has her phone out, busily tapping on the screen and ignoring my tease. "A calendar of ladies washing dogs in wet T-shirts would be a big hit with the guys... and some of the ladies, too, I'd wager."

"It's also highly inappropriate and sexist."

"That's the *joke*, Gigi, but you know as well as I do something like that would fly off the shelves. And how is it any more sexist than our calendar?"

Waving my hand, I'm not getting into a discussion of gender-based power dynamics today. I'm still floating on memories of my blissful doggy-family mushroom trip, and I don't want to kill my vibe.

"So you want to have a dog show where the hockey players walk their dogs in either tight jeans or designer suits?"

Her lips pinch, and she gives me a not-so-innocent grin. "The designer suits would be better... and hotter."

"It sounds more like a fashion show."

"Isn't that basically what a dog show is?"

I shake my head. "Not at all. Handlers have a specific way of walking the dogs. It's called *gaiting*, and it's used to evaluate whether the dog conforms to breed standards."

"Can the guys learn to do it?"

"I don't see why not." I shrug. "They just have to practice walking their dog at the correct speed to showcase its natural gait."

"Yay! I'll spread the word and see how many tickets we

can sell." Her thumbs continue flying over her phone screen. "Oh, and could you recruit some judges for us? Hopefully ones who'll work for free? It's for charity."

"Oh, sure. I'm not doing anything."

"Geeegeeeee!" she yells as she walks down the hall to Lucy's room.

I shake my head. She knows I'm going to help her.

I walk over to where Owen's daughter is on the sofa hugging Zander and watching *The Fox & The Hound, Part 2* with Spanky and Ladybird on the rug beside her.

"I loved this movie when I was your age." I lean on the back of the couch near her. "It's not as sad as the first one."

"I like Granny Rose!" Maddie rocks, bopping her feet as the dogs start to sing a country-folk song. "Do you think Ladybird could sing like Copper?"

"Hmm..." I watch the group of cartoon dogs harmonizing. "I think Ladybird has her own special way of singing."

The dogs break into a chant, and Maddie says it with them. "Like a bird in a tree, we're meant to be..."

Haddy returns to the room holding Lucy. She starts singing the song as well in her perfect, pageant voice as she bounces the baby.

Maddie climbs onto her knees. "Can I hold baby Lucy?"

"Let's see." Haddy walks around to sit on the couch, and Maddie scoots closer to her. "Have you ever held a little baby before?"

"No." Maddie's brown eyes are wide, and I walk around to sit on her other side.

"I'll help you then." Haddy turns her five-month-old around, laying her across Maddie's lap. "Put your arm under her head like this, and hold her waist with your arm."

Maddie cuddles the baby, and Lucy blinks up at her.

"She's so cute," Maddie coos. "Hey, baby Lucy, I'm your friend Maddie."

My heart melts, and I put my hand on Maddie's back. "I can tell she likes you already."

"You can?" The little girl's eyebrows shoot up, and she looks up at me. "How can you tell?"

"Well, she's not crying."

Maddie looks down, shaking her head and leaning down. Lucy blinks several times. Her little brow crinkles, and I hold my breath... Then she breaks into a big baby-laugh that shakes her whole body.

"Oh, she really likes you." Haddy smiles, giving Maddie a squeeze. "Let's put her in her bouncy seat, and you can sit in front of her. I bet that will make her laugh even more."

"Okay!" Maddie looks up at her.

My cousin takes the baby and secures her in her blue chair. Maddie hops down in front of her, leaning forward and shaking her head again, and again, Lucy breaks into a full-body laugh, this time adding a loud squeal.

"She likes me!" Maddie looks up at us, and I'm in love.

"Play with her for a minute while I get something from the kitchen." Haddy stands, walking around the couch.

"Look, Lucy! This is Zander the Zebra. He's my best friend next to Ladybird... and Spanky, I guess."

I'm still watching the little girls, when I notice a hissing sound. I look behind me, and my cousin's eyes are wide. She tilts her head in the direction of the kitchen for me to follow, and I lean down to hug Maddie.

"I'll be right back."

She nods, completely absorbed in making Lucy laugh.

As soon as the kitchen door closes, Haddy grabs my arm, blue eyes sparkling. "What happened last night?"

"What do you mean?"

"After we left, did you and Owen..." She does a little wavy hand-motion. "Bow chicka wow-wow?"

"You are such a nerd." I roll my eyes. "Nobody says *bow chicka wow-wow* anymore."

"Shut up! Did you do it?" Haddy grabs my arm again, playfully shaking it.

"We did..." I hesitate as her eyes get wider and wider. "Mushrooms."

Haddy's face and shoulders collapse. "Mushrooms? Is that some kind of sexual enhancer?"

"I don't think so." I pluck a fresh cranberry from a bowl on Haddy's bar. "Last time I did mushrooms I barfed the whole time. Last night I chased an imaginary dog, who I thought was my spirit animal, all over the place. Maybe she was?"

I turn the cranberry in my fingers.

"I'm so confused." Haddy reaches over and takes the berry from me. "Why in the world would you do mushrooms instead of *it*?"

"It was an accident. Heather had this chocolate, and we didn't know it had psychedelic mushrooms in it."

"Gina! That's freaking dangerous. What if you'd OD'd?"

"I agree." I nod, looking up at her. "Instead, we just drifted around for four hours then fell asleep all over the house."

"I'm very disappointed in you. The whole reason I took Maddie was so you two could finally get it on." She walks over to the refrigerator pouting, and I press my lips together thinking of John and Kendall.

"What's that face?" She looks over at me, then she runs back to grab my arm, pulling me around and staring straight into my eyes.

"You're so weird." I try to pull away, but she won't let me.

"You've already done it! Ahh!" She jumps up and down, pulling me into a hug. "I'm so happy! You and Owen are perfect for each other. We've already been over all the reasons, and the tarot, and..."

"Things are moving in a positive direction." I nod, thinking about last night and how he pulled me close, kissing me right in front of Maverick.

I think about this morning, him bringing me water and smiling at me in that way I felt from my stomach all the way to my toes.

"He's nothing like Baxter." Haddy returns to the fridge.

"Ew, don't even say that name." My upper lip curls. "Can you believe that jackass had the nerve to text me?"

"I absolutely can. You're a wonderful person. You're beautiful and smart, and everyone loves you." She returns holding a sparkling water and wraps her arm around my shoulders. "He probably realized it and hasn't stopped kicking himself since."

"I hope somebody's kicking him," I grouse, walking over to the door leading to the living room. "I've got to get the dogs home."

We return to where Maddie is holding Peepee now and walking around the living room like a march.

"Instead of teaching Ladybird to walk fancy, do you think we could teach Peepee?" Maddie runs over to where Haddy and I are standing.

Haddy squints, turning to me. "I don't know. Patsy is more of a hopper than a walker."

"That's what I mean about gaiting." I take a knee, looking at the size of Peep and the size of Mads. "You actually might be a perfect match. Your legs aren't as long as an adult's. It will probably help her."

Maddie gasps, her mouth and eyes forming large circles. "It will? Can I, Aunt Haddy? Can I?"

Haddy looks at me. "If she could walk with her in the charity show, people would love that. Especially since she's Owen's daughter."

"We'll have to get permission from your dad, of course." I watch Maddie cradling Peepee like a baby. "Let's give it a try, Mads. Mind if we borrow Peep for the day?"

"Not at all." Haddy walks with us to the door.

Maddie puts her hand in mine as we cross the street to the house I share with Maverick. I glance down at her, and she's watching the dogs walking side by side as she carries Haddy's smaller one.

Tilting her head, she looks up at me. "I made Lucy laugh."

"You sure did." I give her hand a squeeze.

"And she laughed and laughed. Her whole body was shaking!"

"She's really cute." I nod, stopping to open the front door and taking off the leashes as Spanky and Ladybird bound into the living room.

Maddie follows me, petting Peepee's head. "I think I'll be a good mommy one day."

My throat tightens, and I bend down to give her a hug. "I think you'll be a great mommy. You take good care of your daddy, and you're so sweet to the dogs and Lucy."

She puts her hand on my shoulder, her expression serious. "I think you'll be a good mommy, too."

My lips press into a smile as my nose heats. "You do?"

"Yep." She nods. "You take good care of Spanky and Ladybird and me and everybody!"

"Thank you." I lean forward to hug her. "I hope I never let you down."

OWEN
Just got home. How are you feeling?

IT'S ALMOST MIDNIGHT. I'm in bed reading a spicy romance novel on my Kindle when my phone lights up. Scooping it off the nightstand, a grin splits my cheeks when I see his words.

GINA
All good. Had a fun day teaching Maddie to walk Peepee.

OWEN
Yeah, I had all the videos on my phone when I got to the locker room.

GINA
She's a future dog-show girlie!

OWEN
Sounds like a fun profession. Feel like walking outside?

"What...?" I whisper, hopping out of bed and dashing over to the window.

My chest squeezes when I see him there, bathed in moonlight and gazing up at my window.

Without even replying, I dash out of my bedroom, run down the stairs, and throw open the front door.

"What are you doing here?" I whisper, stepping out onto the porch.

I hadn't even considered what I was wearing, and now I realize I'm in my skimpy sleep shorts and thin white tank. My pussy flutters when I remember all the things he did with this top last time I wore it. It flutters more when his brow lowers, and he walks to the porch steps.

I take a step down, putting my face level with his, and he places his warm hands on my waist.

"I wanted to see you." His voice is low. "Last night didn't exactly go how I'd planned."

"Last night was ridiculous." I slide my hands onto his shoulders. "Although it reaffirmed my love of dogs..."

I don't say *and other things*, since we're still working out what we're doing here.

He wraps his arms around me, pulling me closer. "It reaffirmed some things for me as well."

"Like what?" I tilt my head, holding his gaze.

Lifting his hand, he places it on my cheek, sliding my hair back with his thumb. "Like how good it feels when we're together. How all the tension melts away."

My eyes blink slowly, and we move closer, meeting in a kiss. He pulls at my upper lip with his, and I wrap my arms around his neck, allowing him to open my mouth. Our tongues curl and slip, and I exhale a soft sigh.

His hand moves to my back, pulling my body flush against his, and heat races to my core. His lips move to my jaw, and his beard roughs my neck. My fingers thread in his hair, and I feel the brush of his jeans through my thin, cotton shorts.

He groans softly, and it heats my veins. "I want to carry you inside and spend the night."

"Okay," I gasp, holding his neck and kissing his cheek, his lips.

He kisses me back briefly. "I've got to get home, but I'll be back in the morning for our date. We'll make it an early lunch."

"Breakfast in bed is good," I tease, smiling as I kiss him again.

"There would be very little eating," he laughs softly. "At least of food."

I exhale a *hmm*, thinking of how that would go. He kisses me once more before taking a step back.

"I'll be here at eleven." One more touch, and he walks backwards in the direction of the sidewalk.

I return to the porch, watching him bathed in silver light as he walks away.

20

———

OWEN

"How was your first mushroom trip?" Heather leans on the bar across from me picking brownie-bites from a pint of ice cream labeled *Gingers*. "Was it everything you thought it would be and more?"

"I have never once thought about a mushroom trip." What I do think about is Gina standing on her porch just now, looking like an angel.

"Okay, Bubba, spill it."

My eyes narrow. "I've warned you about that nickname."

"Look, just because I wasn't around when Aunt Pinky called you *Bubba* doesn't make it any less hilarious."

"It's not hilarious. It's annoying."

"Spoken like a true oldest child." She takes another bite of ice cream. "Did you barf?"

She switches topics so fast, it takes me a beat to realize she's back to the mushrooms. "No."

"What happened then?"

I lean back against the counter, crossing my arms. *What happened...*

A lot. It's been on my mind all day. Thankfully, it didn't impact my game play, and we beat San Jose handily. Still, I've been all twisted up inside.

On the one hand, I feel a relief I haven't felt in seven years. On the other, thinking about what it means stirs up feelings of guilt I thought I'd put away.

"Okay, you are taking *way* too long to answer me, so I'm guessing it must've been intense."

My brow furrows, and I decide just to say it. "I saw Angie."

Her eyes widen, and she puts the pint and the spoon on the counter. "You saw *Angie*?"

I nod, and she turns and walks straight to the cabinet over the stove. She opens the doors and takes down the bottle of Stone Cold single-barrel reserve whiskey my uncle Alex gave me when I left Eureka.

It's my late grandfather's old recipe that my uncle cultivated and turned into a world-renowned label. It also turned my family into multi-millionaires.

My sister pours us each a finger and hands me a glass. She lifts hers, and we clink before tossing it back. *Smooth.*

"Now." She takes my arm and leads me to the table. "Tell me everything that happened."

Normally, I would roll my eyes at her theatrics, but in this case, I'm not so sure.

"It was like I was being lifted up, and there was light all around me." I try to remember the details, but some of them are hazy now. "She was there, smiling. She kind of reminded me of that old movie *Wild at Heart* when the Good Witch appears to Sailor."

"Never saw it."

"Well..." I try to think of how to describe it. "She had light all around her, and she seemed to hover in front of me."

"What did she say?"

Bending my elbow, I rub my fingers over my closed eyes trying to remember her exact words, the order of our conversation.

"She told me she was okay. She said she was at peace." Again, those words hit me in the chest hard. Clearing my throat, I push past the emotions. "She told me to let her go and get on with my life."

Heather presses her lips together, nodding slowly. "It was her spirit. She can feel you still holding onto her, and she wants to transition."

"I don't believe in that."

"It doesn't matter if you believe in it or not. It is." Heather reaches across the table, holding my hand. "Why are you afraid?"

My jaw clenches, and I don't like her choice of words. "I'm not afraid."

"Owen." She arches an eyebrow. "You have a beautiful woman falling in love with you. You've been given permission to let go and live. Why are you still hesitating?"

"I'm having a hard time believing it was real and not just what I want to happen." I lean closer, lowering my voice so Maddie doesn't hear. "I was on drugs."

"Mind-expanding drugs. Native Americans have used psilocybin to commune with the spirit world for generations." She leans back in her chair. "It was real."

I study my hands, remembering holding her face, sliding my thumb across her cheek. "When I look at Gina, I feel so strongly like, *it's always been you.* But how can I feel that way? It's like I'm forgetting what came before, how I got Maddie."

Her reply is quiet, thoughtful. "I think you and Angie had something really special. She was my first big sister, and I loved her." Her lips press together, and she continues slowly. "That doesn't mean she was your soul mate. I'm not taking anything away from your relationship, but her path took her away from you."

Pushing out of my chair, I walk over to pour another shot of whiskey. "I don't believe in soul mates. What if your soul mate dies? Then what?"

A touch of impatience enters my sister's tone. "You can be perfectly happy with someone who isn't your soul mate."

"Heather," I groan.

"It's simply a deeper connection when it is. It's spiritual. You can feel it, and I think you're beginning to understand the difference."

My voice is quiet. "The way I feel about Gina... should make me feel guilty."

"Why?" She stands, walking over to take my hand.

"It feels like I wasn't truly in love before."

She blinks up at me, her brow crinkling. "It doesn't have to mean that."

An ache is in my throat, and I look down at my hands, her slim ivory one covering mine. "I always wanted to be a good husband. I want to be a good dad, like we have. Protect and provide."

Reaching up, she wraps her arms around my shoulders. "You were the best husband, Owen." Her face is at my ear, and I pat her arm as she hugs me. "You're the best dad, and you deserve a second chance. Dad had one, and so should you."

MAVERICK

What's this I hear about everybody doing mushrooms at the party?

GAVIN

I went home with my ladies. The only mushrooms I had were on pizza.

OWEN

Hey, group chat!

MAVERICK

We're carpooling, we're all in Haddy's dog show... Now back to the mushrooms. Why didn't I get any?

OWEN

It was an accident. Heather was putting them away, and we thought they were regular chocolate.

MAVERICK

New rule, if anyone has magic mushrooms, they have to share them with the group. Capiche?

GAVIN

Not me. I've got a baby now.

OWEN

I'm happy never doing them again. It was a lot.

MAVERICK

Second rule, if you know someone's doing magic mushrooms, you let me know, and I'll make the decision for myself.

OWEN

I'm pretty sure Ryan and Meredith still have some if you want a square.

MAVERICK

That's what I call a team player. Good
work, Sly.

SHAKING MY HEAD, I put my phone in my pocket, checking
my reflection before heading downstairs. My hair's still too
long, but otherwise, I'm good.

"Did you see me walking Peepee, Daddy?" Maddie
meets me at the bottom of the stairs, holding up her arms,
Zander in hand.

I reach down to lift her onto my waist. "I sure did. You
looked like a real pro out there."

"I'm going to walk with her in the dog show. But only if
you say it's okay. That's what Miss Gina said."

Her eyes are round, and I smile, thinking of Gina
working with her, teaching her to walk that little dog,
supporting my position as Maddie's dad. *A second chance...*

"I think that would be a lot of fun, Shortcake."

"You do?" A huge smile breaks across her face, and she
throws her arms around my neck. "Thank you, Daddy! And
you're going to walk Ladybird!"

My brows furrow, and I put her on her feet again. "I
don't know if that's such a good idea. We've talked
about LB."

"You can do it." She holds my hand, walking with me to
the door. "It just takes practice, and then after a little while it
just clicks into place like a puzzle piece. That's what Miss
Gina said, and it's true."

Stopping at the door, I give her another hug. "If Miss
Gina said so, I'll give it another try. Now I'm meeting her for
lunch. Wish me luck."

My daughter's face scrunches. "Why do you need luck to
eat lunch?"

"I'll tell you later." I tweak her chin and jog out to my truck.

It only takes a minute to drive down the block to our old residence. Gina walks out when she sees me, and she looks so good. She's wearing a navy plaid skirt that shows off her long legs, and a navy sweater that clings to her body in a way that should be sinful.

She skips out to the truck, her long hair shining in the morning sun, and I hop out to open the door for her.

"Such a gentleman." She pauses to kiss my lips before climbing into the cab.

My eyes slide down to the hem of her skirt rising up the curve of that ass, and I fight the urge to touch her there.

"I'm not always a gentleman." I shut the door, jogging around to the other side and climbing in.

She scoots across the seat to lean closer and whisper in my ear. "You're not, and I like it a lot."

I catch her face before she can move away and kiss her. "Good."

It's a short drive to the Alcove, and it's not too crowded when we arrive.

"I love this place!" Gina grabs my hand. "It's like something out of a storybook."

"That's what Maverick told me. He said you have a thing for greenery."

"And this place is historic. You know these are two of the oldest homes in Los Feliz? They date back to the 1800s."

She's so excited, I can't help a chuckle. "As long as the food's good."

"The lemon ricotta pancakes are incredible, and they have great vegan and gluten-free options."

"I'm not either of those."

We follow the hostess to our booth, and Gina orders the

lemon pancakes. I get the short rib Benedict. The waitress brings us both coffees, and when she leaves, our eyes meet.

For a moment I study her face, her soft hair, her pretty green eyes. Her nose is slightly upturned, and she has the faintest sprinkling of freckles across the bridge.

"What was your favorite breakfast food as a kid?" She lifts her coffee cup in both hands, puckering her glossy lips before taking a sip.

"Froot Loops." I exhale a laugh, taking a sip of my own coffee.

"Why is that funny?" Her brow arches.

"My dad would call me Froot Loop when I was a little boy, and it made me so mad." I sit back, remembering last night, Heather calling me Bubba. "I had a real problem with nicknames when I was young."

"To be fair, Froot Loop isn't the greatest nickname." Her nose wrinkles.

"How about you? Any dog-related nicknames in your past?"

She shakes her head. "I've only ever been Gigi, for Gina Grace."

"It's a beautiful name—after the old blind lady I met at the wedding."

"Right. Miss Gina." Her slim finger circles the rim of her cup. "She was always so wise and sweet. She looked out for all of us."

"Like you do now." I reach across the table to cover her hand with mine.

"I don't know." She watches our hands as our fingers entwine. "We all look out for each other, I think. My cousin Kim was the oldest, so she looked out for us first. Then Haddy and I came along, the Bradford twins."

"Twins?" My brow arches as I think about her cousin's

dark hair, olive skin, and sapphire blue eyes. "What's that about?"

"Both of our parents... both sets of parents?" Her green eyes rise to the ceiling, and she shakes her head. "They both got pregnant with us at my aunt Dylan's wedding, so we *should* have the same birthday. But I was a few days overdue, so Haddy's a little older."

"Right... the dog." I can't help a laugh. "I don't think it could possibly be true that a dog caused your mom's labor."

"I don't either, but I *have* always loved dogs." She shrugs, and the server appears with our plates.

Our orders are placed in front of us, and the lady asks if we need anything else. Satisfied we're all set, she leaves us alone again.

The food is delicious. Gigi gives me a bite of her pancake, and I declare her the order winner. My dish is good, but hers is better.

It's not until our plates are cleared, and we're lingering over cups of coffee that I swallow my nerves and get to the point.

"I really like spending time with you, Gina." Our eyes meet, and hers are warm and open. "I'd like to be more than just friends."

Her eyes sparkle, and she leans forward, speaking low. "I think we already are. I don't do the things we do together with friends."

"Right." I slide my hand across the table to hold hers. "I haven't done this in a while. Sorry if I'm rusty."

Her other hand covers mine, and a sweet smile curls her lips. "You're not."

"The thing is..." My brow furrows. "I have to think about Maddie. She's lost so much, I can't let her fall in love with you if it's only for a little while. If we're just temporary."

Gina nods, studying our hands as well. "She's such a fun little girl. We've already gotten so close. I can't imagine not knowing her." Her eyes blink up to mine, and she shrugs. "I want to see how she turns out."

My throat is tight, but I have to say the words. I hate them, but it's important. My fingers slide against hers, and I inhale slowly.

"I'm older than you, Gina." I hesitate. "I don't want you to feel pressured, but I need to know if all of my baggage is too much. If you don't want a ready-made family that's not entirely yours."

Her lips pucker, and she takes a minute, which I appreciate. Her eyes linger on my hands, and when she speaks, her tone is thoughtful.

"I've found that families form in all sorts of ways. Some people are born into them, and others you graft into your tree. Either way, I've always loved my family, real and found."

"Still..." My stomach knots. "I can't bring someone into Maddie's life who might leave again."

"Into Maddie's life?" She blinks up at me, and I know she sees right through me.

It's not about Maddie being hurt, it's about me. I've fallen hard for this woman, and I'm not sure I would ever get over losing her.

"Yeah." My voice is flat. "Maddie."

"Okay," she answers quietly. "What are you saying then?"

"I'm just saying if you need some time, or if you need to think about it, I understand."

"You understand," she repeats.

I'm surprised I can speak for the tightness in my chest. "Yes."

"Well, thanks for not ghosting me at least." She tosses

her napkin onto the table and stands. "Thank you for brunch, and I appreciate you taking the time to explain yourself."

"What?" My brow furrows, and I sit back as she stands, pulling her purse over her shoulder. "What are you doing?"

"It was nice knowing you, Owen Stone." Her lips are tight, and her green eyes flash with anger. "You know what? You really are a *Froot Loop!*"

She turns on her heel and storms to the glass door, pushing it open and walking out.

I sit for a moment, stunned and confused, before digging in my pocket and taking out several twenties and leaving them on the table.

By the time I'm out the door, she's nowhere to be seen. I hop into my truck as I take out my phone, tapping on her contact info and hitting the call button.

It rings and rings and finally goes to voicemail.

"What the fuck?" I shout, hanging up without leaving a message.

I give it a few more minutes before I call again. Again, it rings and rings before going to her voicemail. This time I do leave a short message.

"Call me," is all I say.

I'm driving down the street, looking all over the place for her, then I hit her number again. It rings and rings, and I swear I'm going to throw this phone out the window if it goes to voicemail...

"Stop calling me!" Her voice is loud, and I hear noises around her. "I don't want to talk to you anymore."

"Where are you?" I shout back, straining my eyes along the sidewalks. "This is no place to be walking."

"I'll call a ride share if I need one."

"Tell me where you are right now," I order.

"No!" I hear the tears in her voice, and I'm about to lose it when I spot her red hair shining in the sun before she disappears under the shade of a thick tree.

Accelerating quickly, I cut across the lane of traffic, waving a hand at the car honking loudly at me. Pulling onto the shoulder, I kill the engine, and jump out, running to catch up with her.

She looks back and sees me, and God dangit... she breaks into a run. She's freaking fast, too.

"Stop running!" I yell as I chase her.

"No!" she yells back at me, and I cringe as we pass people turning to watch us.

"If this ends up on social media, you're going to be sorry."

That's the only thing that makes her stop. She's breathing hard when I catch up to her, and I look around, making sure I don't see any phones or cameras out.

It appears we're safe, and I'm thankful I'm not *that* popular yet, even if I'm getting there.

Holding her arm, I make her look at me. "What is going on? Why are you running from me?"

"Because." She pauses to catch her breath. "You're not putting this on me, Owen Stone."

"Putting what on you? What are you talking about? I was trying to share my feelings with you, and you walked out on me."

"You weren't sharing your feelings with me. You were saying if this doesn't work out and Maddie gets hurt, it's all my fault. And that's not fair, and you know it."

Tears are in her green eyes, and it hits me hard. Stepping back, I put my fingers on the bridge of my nose. "That's not what I meant at all."

She's shaking, and a tear falls onto her cheek. It's more

than I can take. Reaching out, I pull her to me, pressing my lips to the side of her head. "Stop crying."

"Don't tell me what to do." She tries to get away, but I hold her tighter, not letting her go.

"Stop fighting and talk to me." It takes a few seconds, but she finally stops struggling.

I step back, still holding her arms, but her lips are tight.

"Please, Gina."

"You're saying I can walk away, and you'll understand. Just like that. No fighting, no trying..."

I can't tell if she's more angry or hurt, and it just proves I'm a goner. Because whichever one it is, it's tearing me up inside.

"No—I meant that I understand if it's too much for you."

She shakes her head, starting to walk again, but I'm right there beside her, keeping pace.

"Why does that make you angry?" I catch her arm, bringing her to a stop.

"I don't want someone who will let me go that easily." Our eyes meet, and her bottom lip wobbles. "I want more than that."

My throat knots, and I pull her to my chest. I know what she wants. I remember every word she said to my sister that evening in the backyard. I also know I'm a chickenshit. This isn't about Maddie getting hurt. It's about me.

"Please don't cry." I smooth my hand down the back of her head. "I'm an idiot. I thought if I told you my fears, you'd understand, and it would make them go away. I wasn't trying to put them on you or blame you or let you go. Hell, Gina, I never want to let you go, and it's fucking killing me. It's fast, and it scares me. And I want this... I want *you*. So much."

Her shoulders jerk with an inhale, and slowly, her head

moves up and down in a nod. I relax my arms, letting her step back to look up at me.

"I want you, too." Her voice is wobbly but sure.

It's everything, and I pull her to me again, covering her mouth with mine.

Then I realize people around us are clapping, and a smile curls our lips. We blink our eyes open, and I cup her cheeks in my hands, sliding my thumbs to wipe away the tears.

I give the crowd a little wave as I pull her into my side, leading her back to my illegally parked truck.

21

———

GINA

"You are looking at the new official PR director for the Los Angeles Champions hockey team!" Haddy enters the house, arm raised, doing her pageant wave.

"What?" I hop up from the couch, where I've been swiping through grooming cuts for Spanky. "Congratulations! And I gotta say, it's about damn time."

"Well, I wasn't entirely sure I wanted to take a full-time job with Lucy so small and nursing, but we were able to reach an agreement where I can bring her with me if I need to or work remotely."

"You've been doing so much free marketing for them, I would imagine they'd give you anything you wanted."

"The location really was the holdup." She walks over to plop beside me on the couch. "It's kind of a haul to get from here to the arena. I'm surprised the guys do it every day."

"Blame it on Mav. He's the one who insisted on living with us."

"And bringing all his teammates with him." She leans her head on my shoulder, looking at the pictures on my screen. "Are you still thinking about that Best in Show prize?"

"Not really." My voice is quiet as I swipe over to pictures of pure breeds.

A noise comes from the crate, and Spanky jumps to his feet. Then he looks all around like he's lost something.

"What's he doing?" Haddy's brow furrows, and she looks at me.

"I think Spanky the towel thief is missing his new lady friend." We watch as he walks over to the steps and looks up to the second floor.

"I've never seen a dog pine for another dog before. They're not even compatible breeds!"

My lips twist, and I think about it. "A blood-poo?"

"Gigi." My cousin makes a barf-face. "That sounds like a medical condition."

I fall to the side, holding my stomach as I laugh-groan. "It sounds like you'd better call 9-1-1, *stat!*"

"You made me throw up in my mouth."

"Hang on..." I type on my iPad quickly. "I've got it—a Bloodhoodle."

My cousin's nose wrinkles. "That's not much better."

"Oh, I like this one... a Poohound!"

"No." She shakes her head. "It sounds like it does nothing but poop. Or search for poop."

"A Snooperdoodle?"

"Yes." She holds up two thumbs. "That's the one. *Snooperdoodle.*"

"The only problem is I'm pretty sure Ladybird's fixed."

"Well, Spanky doesn't need to know that. I'm not even sure he'd be the best daddy doodle."

"How dare you?" I pretend to be offended. "Spanky would be a very attentive daddy doodle!"

"He's a spoiled-rotten rascal, and you know it." She elbows me in the side, as she hops off the sofa. "I'm not saying it's all his fault, but he is a lot like his uncle Mav."

"Uncle Mav likes to praise him when he's being naughty."

"Uncle Mav is going to be one sad camper if he's left in this house all alone. You'd better track down a dog for him before you leave."

"Who said anything about me leaving?" I press my lips against the smile trying to curl them as I return my attention to the screen.

"You know it's true. Now I've got to get back to my own little poo."

"And baby, too!" I call after her.

She waves heading out the door. "See you in a few hours!"

OWEN

Did you get the gift I sent you?

A HUGE SMILE splits my cheeks when I see his words on my phone. My insides have been all zippy and swoony ever since our brunch-turned-fight-turned-make-up slash make-out session in the park.

Yep. That's what it was! In front of God and everybody.

Even though we weren't exactly hiding our feelings before, we're *really* not hiding them now. We haven't said anything to Maddie just yet, but I know it's coming. We're just letting it all unfold naturally.

When the three of them join us for dinner now, I love that Owen will put his hand on my waist and lean down to kiss the side of my cheek. Or he'll put his arm around my shoulders when we're sitting on the couch watching a movie. Or he'll reach up and hold my hand if he's sitting and I'm standing beside him.

It all has me walking around with a goofy grin on my face and a glowy light in my eyes.

GINA

> Do you mean the bag with the purple, white, and black jersey inside with a 13 and the name Stone on the back?

I grin, biting my bottom lip as I watch the gray dots bouncing on the screen.

OWEN

> That's the one.

GINA

> I'm modeling it in the mirror right now.

Holding up my phone, I take a selfie of me wearing Owen's jersey along with my black leggings and white turtleneck and send it to him.

OWEN

> Hot. Can't wait to see you in it tonight… and out of it later.

GINA

> I can make that happen. (sly emoji)
> Although, it's too bad Mav won't have anyone in his jersey.

The guys are on the ice warming up when we arrive a few hours later. Lucy and Maddie are in their *Daddy* jerseys with Gavin and Owen's numbers on the front, and Heather and Haddy are in *Stone* and *Knight*. I'm in my new *Stone* jersey, feeling proud and a little shy.

"Maybe we should get Heather a *Murphy* jersey to wear?" Haddy's lips twist as she surveys our outfits.

Just then a group of four females runs down to the plexiglass divider, jumping up and down and waving... and all wearing *Murphy* jerseys.

"I think Mav's going to be okay," Heather says with a laugh, nodding in their direction.

"Miss Gina is wearing Daddy's jersey tonight!" Maddie stands on the seat in front of us, putting her hand on my shoulder. "Does that mean you like Daddy best of all now?"

My throat tightens, and I cautiously smile. "Is that okay?"

Her little eyes slide left to right, then just as fast, she nods really hard. "I think that's super okay!"

She does a little jump, but I catch her around the waist. "Easy there, want to walk down and get your puck from your dad?"

"Okay!" she shouts.

I straighten, looking up to see Owen skating over to say something to Mav. His long dark hair sticks out from beneath his white helmet, and I hum a sigh watching him maneuver expertly across the ice.

The guys skate away from each other. Owen skates backwards as Mav nods and points, and I don't know why he seems so much sexier to me now. I guess it's because of everything we said. *I want you... so much.*

He turns and looks up at us, and when our eyes meet, my whole body heats right up. I lift my hand to wave, and a big smile breaks across his handsome face. It makes me laugh, and I take his daughter's hand.

We walk down the stands, a little to the right of the quad of girls giggling and waving at my cousin. Owen skates up to where we are, doing a hockey stop and sending an arc of ice against the boards.

Our eyes meet briefly before he looks down at his daughter, holding up the puck.

Maddie holds her hands over her head, jumping up and down, and yelling, "Daddy! Daddy!"

He grins, holding the puck over the top of the plexiglass. I reach up and take it from him. Our fingers brush, and I swear it sparks.

Maddie continues jumping up and down, her blonde hair bouncing around her shoulders as she waves the round, rubber disc at him.

He blows her a kiss, and she pats her hand to her lips over and over again, blowing her own kisses back to him.

They're so adorable, and I think about how long they've been doing this together. I think about being part of this family. I think about making this family a part of my own.

I've always been a daddy's girl. My big, over-the-top dad has always been my most fervent supporter, the most concerned person for my happiness, the biggest defender should I need it.

Owen is all those things for Maddie, and I want to join our hands and be a part of this circle of love like I saw in my vision, sitting in the yard with that silly spirit-dog, watching the stars swirl above us.

Looking up, I notice his eyes are on me, and Owen presses his fingers to his lips before extending them in my direction. My cheeks heat, and I quickly do the same. His chin lifts, and he turns, skating back to the rest of the team.

"We can go to our seats now!" Maddie grabs my hand, walking ahead of me through the stands to where Haddy and Heather are waiting.

Haddy holds Lucy against her chest facing the ice, and the baby seems to understand at least a little of what's going on. Her blue eyes are wide, and she has a big smile on her face as she kicks her squishy baby legs.

We're at our seats, and I turn around to see Gavin at the plexiglass divider, waving at his baby girl. Lucy kicks harder and squeals a laugh.

"Do you think she knows it's him?" I lean forward to follow her gaze down to her dad.

"I'm almost sure she does," Haddy says. "I don't know why else she'd be squealing so much. She's a total daddy's girl."

"She hasn't had much choice in the matter." I wave at Gavin, who's watching his two ladies with the most smitten expression.

My heart squeezes, and I think about the conversation I had with Heather not so long ago, what I want... what I hope to have.

Haddy nudges my arm, nodding in the direction of the ice. "Someone's got his eye on you."

Owen skates across center ice, and sure enough, his eyes are locked on me.

A smile breaks across my face, and I hold up my hand to wave just as the Champions' signature mix of Queen songs begins.

"GAV AND MAV! GAV AND MAV!" The crowd chants around us, and airhorns go off as Mav skates around to slap the puck straight past the goalie's shoulder.

The Jumbotron lights up with *Make Some Noise*, but it's not necessary. The place explodes. Air horns blast all around us, and we're all jumping up and down screaming.

They're facing off against the Atlanta Frost, which is Mav and Gav's old team, and they were keyed up heading into this game. My cousin is on fire as always, but tonight Owen has managed to get two pucks past the goalie as well.

We're down to the final period, the game is tied, and I'm holding my breath as Owen flies across the ice in front of us. He only needs one more goal.

My hands are clutched together in front of my lips, and Maddie stands on the seat right beside me, her little hand on my shoulder.

"Daddy's going to get a hat trick! Go... go... goooo!" she shouts.

We all clasp hands, and I feel the slightest tap on my shoulder. I don't want to tear my eyes away from the ice.

Haddy is beside me. Heather is on the other side of her, and we're all watching, waiting, hoping.

Once again, tapping on my shoulder. Only this time it's more insistent.

Exhaling a soft growl, I let go of Haddy's hand to turn and see who (*TF!*) is bugging me in the third period of the most exciting game we've had all season, with Owen teed up to score a hat trick.

"What is it?" I do my best to gentle my tone as I turn around.

My heart stills in my chest when I see a tallish guy, a little under six-feet, standing in front of me. His light brown hair is cut high and tight, and a pair of horn-rimmed glasses are perched on his nose.

He's slim, dressed in a maroon sweater and jeans, and he has both hands shoved in his pockets.

"Baxter." It's not a question. It's a statement of utter disbelief.

"Hi, Gina." He ducks his head, looking down. "I figured I'd find you here... with Mav playing and all."

I'm not sure whether to be shocked or pissed. "What do you want?"

"You won't answer any of my texts." He has the nerve to give me a look of confusion.

"I blocked you."

"Oh." His chin pulls back as if I'd hit him. "That seems rude."

"Does it?" I can't keep the sarcasm out of my tone. "As rude as sleeping with someone and then completely disappearing without a single word for more than a year?"

His lips press together, and he lifts his chin, looking out at the guys on the ice. He actually makes a pretty decent pensive expression. *Bastard.*

Then his brown eyes return to me. "I need to talk to you. I have something I need to say."

"I'm sorry." I shake my head. "I'm really not interested in what you *need* to say to me. Maybe a year ago I'd have wanted to know, but now... I honestly don't care."

"Please, Gina." His tone is a mixture of firm and pleading, and I try to decide just how annoyed I am right now.

"You've really got some nerve coming here like this and demanding to speak to me."

"Would you just give me five minutes? I think it would help us both."

Haddy turns at my side now, and her face wrinkles with horror. "What are *you* doing here? Can't you take a hint?"

"Hi, Hayden. I just need to talk to Gina for a minute."

My cousin puts a hand on her hip, looking from him to me. "What do you think?"

"Please," he says again, brown eyes fixed on mine. "I'll never bother you again."

"Oh, good grief." I grab his arm, dragging him into the aisle and down the steps to the hallway that leads to the concourse.

He follows me into the narrow space, and I stop, crossing my arms and facing him. "Make it quick."

A loud *Aw!* comes from outside in the stadium, and I look over my shoulder. I want to get back to the game and see if Owen makes his third goal.

"Well, you see..." Baxter looks down, his light-brown hair falling over his eyes. "It's like this, Gina. I'm an addict."

My arms fall to my sides, and curiosity takes the lead over my anger. "An addict?" He nods, but I'm confused. I never saw any signs of... "What kind of addict?"

"Well..." He clears his throat. "I've struggled with narcotics since I was in a car accident two years ago. I thought I'd beaten it when we were together, but an old friend came to visit after that night, and... well..." His voice lowers. "I hadn't."

I momentarily forget about the game, taking a deep inhale. "I'm really sorry to hear about that."

"I went on a binge, and when I came around, I was sleeping in a park in another city. I didn't know where I was." He winces, studying his hands. "That was my rock-bottom, I guess. I knew I had to get myself clean or I might not make it."

Frowning, I scratch my eyebrow trying to figure out the nicest way to say I'm glad he's okay, and I really have moved on. Thanks for letting me know. See ya.

"Well... that's really awful." I give him a sympathetic tone. "I'm glad you told me, I guess, rather than letting me think it was something I did."

"You didn't do anything. You were great. I really enjoyed spending time with you and all the dogs and everything." He shook his head. "I was obsessed."

"You were kind of a love-bomber." I think about all the nonstop dates... which I had thought was about getting in my pants. Maybe it was?

Crossing his arms, he looks down. "Sleeping with you was so good. It was so—"

"That's okay." I cut him off. "We don't have to relive it."

"Right." He nods. "Sorry. Ahh... part of my recovery is to find people I've hurt and try to make amends. It's like step nine? So I was trying to see if there's some way I can make it up to you that doesn't cause harm to you or to anyone else."

My brows rise, and I straighten. "That's not really necessary."

"It would help me a lot if you'd let me do something."

I'm so involved with our conversation, I only barely notice the screams and air-horns going off behind me in the arena. Music plays, and the game has probably ended.

"Honestly, there isn't anything. I mean, how do you make up for a broken heart?"

His eyes widen. "I broke your heart?"

As I think about the words, I think about how my heart has been the more I've gotten to know Owen.

"No," I say, shaking my head. "I only thought you broke my heart. The truth is, I've learned a lot about love in the past few months, and it was really more the confusion and the self-doubt that hurt me. After you ghosted, I mean."

"I ghosted you," he nods, looking down again. "Man, that was a shitty thing to do."

"Yeah." I nod, looking down as well.

I'm not about to let him off the hook for it. It was really shitty, and I felt like shit for a long time.

"It made it hard for me to trust people," I add.

His eyes squeeze shut, and he rubs his fingers over them. "Dang. How do I make amends for that?"

Inhaling deeply, I straighten, considering the question. "You know, just coming here and telling me all of this... it doesn't turn back the clock, but I can let it go now. I don't have to wonder why or what happened anymore. That's amends."

"Is it?" He frowns, looking up at me. "It doesn't feel like enough. Like maybe you should punch me in the face or something."

A laugh breaks from my throat, and I shake my head. "I think that would violate the 'no harm' part of the step."

He huffs a laugh, nodding. "I always wondered what that meant. I guess it means I shouldn't allow you to beat me to death."

"Trust me, I imagined hitting you in the head with a frying pan several times."

"You're a really great girl, Gina." He holds out both hands. "Would a hug be a way to make amends?"

My lips press into a half-smile, and I shrug. "Sure, why not?"

Stepping forward, I put my arms around his waist, and he wraps his arms around my shoulders, pulling me flush against his torso. He squeezes, making silly grunting noises, and I laugh. I try to step back, but he holds me tighter.

"What is this? One of those thirty-second hugs?" I quip, not really wanting to hug him anymore.

My hands move to his waist in more of a pushing back fashion, and he finally relaxes his squeeze. "You always smell so good... like cherries."

The skin on the back of my neck prickles, and I don't like the sound of that. It's too intimate—a lot like the way he's looking at me right now.

"Well, consider us all amended." I pat his shoulder, giving him a parting smile. "Take care, Bax, and I hope you continue to improve."

His brown eyes are warm, but I'm done here. I turn, and when I see the man standing at the entrance to the hall, dressed in full Champions hockey gear, helmet off, brow lowered in anger, my heart drops all the way to my feet.

"Owen... What are you doing here?" My voice is a shaky gasp.

Without a word, he turns and walks straight out of the hall.

22

———————

OWEN

Mav and Gav are on edge tonight. Even if we're playing on our home turf, we're facing off against the Atlanta Frost, their old team. Atlanta knows our dynamic duo better than any of our competitors, and it's clear from the drop, they're itching for an upset.

Guess what? Atlanta doesn't know me.

I'm having a killer night. After starting off right, blowing kisses to my girls, seeing Gina up there in my jersey... Hell, it was better than I even expected it to be.

We were all out on the ice, warming up, talking about what was coming, but my spidey senses were on full alert when the five of them took their places in the stands.

Haddy was there with Gav's baby girl. Heather was there with my little girl. Gina was the only wildcard.

Sure, I'd texted her. I had the selfie of her in the mirror on my phone, but it wasn't until she took off her jacket that I saw the big 13 on her back. She swept her hair up in a ponytail, revealing the name *Stone* across her shoulders, and I broke out into a laugh.

Hell, yeah. My girl is here with my name across her back. Now I've got two good luck charms.

The Jumbotron went off, sirens called, and it was time to play some hockey.

These guys are tough. I skate forward, doing my best to find an open space and anticipate plays. I know all our signature layups from Maverick, but so do the Atlanta guys.

They scrimmaged with Mav & Gav before any of us did, and they're putting the pressure on hard.

Maverick passes the puck to me, and I go around, looking for an opening to pass it back. Seeing none, I decide to do my own signature play. It's something from the minor leagues, where I look like I'm taking the puck back to center ice.

Then at the last second, I switch back, go down on one knee, and give it a slap shot. The puck flies so fast, right over the goalie's shoulder, for the score.

The stadium erupts in cheers and air horns. A group of spectators begins shouting *Sly! Sly! Sly!* and I glide around, feeling pretty good about myself. Looking up in the stands, I see the girls jumping up and down, holding hands and smiling so big it's contagious.

I grin, circling back around to take my place on the ice. Maverick is the lead center, and he makes the signal for our *T3G* play, as Gavin has started calling it.

It's a variation of their old play, but we've been using it a lot. We're counting on these guys having not done their research, which I know is a big risk at this level.

Still, we run it like we've practiced. Mav brings the puck down center ice, passing it over to Hancock midway. Here's where the switch-up occurs. Hancock sends it to me on the other side of the rink instead of to Gavin.

I take it around, seeing Gav clear the net, and passing it fast to him. He slaps it over to Mav, and faster than the eye can register, it's through the goalie's knees for the point.

Again, the stadium erupts. We all skate together, patting each other on the back, and celebrating. It was a great play, but the game isn't over.

The Frost are mad now, and they manage to sneak a puck past Akers. Mav skates right up to the defenseman, and whatever he says results in a body check. The big guy is on Mav, and just like that, we're all in it.

I'm across the ice, slamming my fist down on the shoulder pads of Frost's 72. He's been pissing me off all night, keeping me from the net, bodychecking me into the boards. We all take a minute to punch it out and blow off some steam before the linemen come in and break us all up.

Gliding back to my spot, I look up to see our girls in the stands still holding hands. Their faces are so serious, and even my little Maddie is watching us with so much intensity. I shake my head, looking down. You can't buy that amount of dopamine.

The puck is moving, and we're chasing it down the ice so fast. If I make one more goal, I'll score a hat trick. It'll be my first in the big leagues, and I expect it'll put me right up there with "the dynamic duo" Gav and Mav on the lips of all our adoring fans.

The puck comes down to our side, and we're all following it. I feel Mav moving back, almost like he knows what's on the line for me, and he's giving me space to take it. He's the best guy like that, not trying to steal the spotlight, willing to let us all shine.

The puck hits my stick, and I do a quick curve, passing it

over to Hancock, getting the defenseman off me before I circle around again. A quick glance up at the time, and we're down to seconds.

Seconds to bring us from facing sudden-death overtime to winning this thing. The guys want it. We all want it. The energy of the team, the crowd, the fans, drives me onward.

Hancock sends it back, and I scoop it into my stick. Two steps, and with a hard slap, it hits the edge of the net. My stomach rises to my throat, and I'm not sure.

I hold my breath as it wobbles, as the goalie reaches out, and at the last second...

He misses.

The place explodes in screaming, air horns, stomping. Caps rain down onto the ice, and it's all over. The final buzzer sounds as the Jumbotron lights up with the words *Make Some Noise*—as if this crowd needs it. They're all on their feet.

Our goal song plays, and the guys huddle around me, slapping my back, grabbing my neck, pulling me in for a hug. Lifting my chin, I can't help a laugh when I see everyone dancing to the music and waving their hands.

It's my first big play in the NHL, and I think of the one person I'm so happy is here to see it. The person I want to share it with most. My eyes go to the stands where the girls sit.

Haddy is there bouncing Lucy and waving her little arm. Heather has both of my daughter's hands in hers, and they're dancing side to side. My brow lowers, and I look all around, but I don't see Gina anywhere.

The smile on my face fades a bit.

"Hey, bro, let's do this!" Mav pulls my arm as he skates off the ice in the direction of our locker room.

My heart beats faster, and I start to get worried. Did

something happen to her? She's been at her seat the whole time.

Hopping over the boards to our bench, I quickly remove my skates. I leave my gear by the bench, stepping into the stands, not worrying about the spectators grabbing me and doing their best to slap my pads.

They're all happy, but I'm too distracted by finding her. Music plays, everyone celebrates, but when I enter the short hall leading out to the concourse the sounds fade to silence.

Her back is against the wall in the shadows, and a guy I don't recognize has his arms around her. He's holding her tight against his body, and she appears to be holding him in response.

Anger burns like fire in my throat as I watch him move his nose into her hair, inhaling, and closing his eyes. *What. The Fuck?*

My muscles vibrate with adrenaline, and it takes everything in me not to rush forward, grab him by the neck, and throw him across the hall.

The one thing that stops me from doing it is when Gina steps back, she smiles up at him and exhales a little laugh.

She touches his shoulder, and my insides freeze. My world goes black, and I have to get out of this place. She turns and sees me. She says my name, but I can't answer. The anger in my chest is too strong, and without a word, I turn and leave in the direction I came.

23

GINA

He won't talk to me. My heart hammers in my chest, and I've texted, called... nothing. It's all silent.

I want to be angry at Baxter, but it's not his fault. Tears are in my eyes, and I ache to my bones.

How long had he been there? Had he even heard what we were saying?

I chased after him to try and explain, but he'd scored a hat trick that won the game. He was a superstar, and the excited crowd was a crush around him.

As much as I tried to jump and push through them and scream his name, in their minds, I was simply another adoring fan.

When it was clear I couldn't get to him, I decided to give up, and instead, I'd meet him at his house and explain when he got there. I booked a rideshare and texted Haddy that I was leaving.

As soon as it dropped me off, I ran straight to his house to wait.

I sat on the porch steps in the dark studying my phone, counting the seconds, wondering how long it might possibly take. Eventually, Heather and Maddie pulled into the driveway, climbing out of the vehicle singing the Champions' victory song, but he wasn't with them.

My shoulders fell, and I couldn't stand. I didn't want them to see me this way, so instead I sat in the darkness, watching them enter through the side door. I laid my forehead on my arms as I listened to them laughing and chatting so happily.

I turned my phone over and sent another text.

GINA

Please talk to me. I don't know what you're thinking right now, but it's clear you don't understand…

It's the tenth time I've sent essentially the same message. The status under the blue bubble goes from *delivered* to *read*, and then silent.

Tears coat my cheeks, and I exhale a moan. My thumbs move rapidly, and I text again.

GINA

Please, Owen

It's all the same. No reply.

Pushing against my thighs, I walk slowly down the sidewalk in the dark, back to my house. It's also empty. Of course, Maverick is out celebrating this win. It's a huge night. They beat their old team in a game that was pure fire. I had so much fun watching them. I was so happy.

I take Spanky out in the backyard, waiting as he runs around and uses the bathroom. When he's finished and trots back to me, we return to the house. I check his food and water, then I slowly climb the stairs.

I go through the motions of washing my face, brushing my teeth... I walk across the hall to my bedroom, take off my boots, take off my clothes.

When I take off my new jersey, though, I stop. I hold it in my hands reading the word *Stone* over and over. I remember his chin lifting and I could almost hear his proud laugh all the way up in the stands when he saw me wearing it.

I hug it to my chest, chewing my lip as hurt and angry tears burn in my eyes. Is he actually ghosting me right now? I crawl beneath my blankets, angry and sad. I didn't do anything wrong.

They're leaving in the morning for Tampa. They're going to be gone for three days. I can't live like this for three days, but what can I do? Why won't he let me explain?

Taking out my phone, I send one more text. Then I drop my head against my arm and switch off the light.

"WHAT HAPPENED TO YOU LAST NIGHT?" I'm at Haddy's house.

She's sitting across from me at her kitchen table, nursing Lucy while I stare into my coffee cup.

The guys left this morning, and even though I set an alarm and got up when I heard Maverick moving around downstairs, it was too late.

My plan was to intercept Owen when the guys met up to ride to the airport together, but Maverick told me he left on an earlier flight.

He didn't want to see me.

I didn't say it out loud to my cousin. I only hugged him and made up an excuse for getting up early to see him off—something I never do. Then I went upstairs and crawled into my bed again.

For a half hour, I tossed and turned. Then, I got dressed and walked over to have breakfast with Haddy.

Now I hold my mug in both hands, gazing into the chocolate-brown liquid as if it can help me feel better.

"Did you and Owen have your own little private celebration?" She smiles curiously. "Come to think of it, I didn't see him after the game at all."

My throat closes, and I can't take it anymore. Shaking my head no, I inhale a shuddering breath. "No... We didn't do anything."

I blink down, and tears fall onto my cheeks.

She reaches across the table, covering my hand with hers. "Gigi, what happened? Did that idiot Baxter do something to hurt you?"

A thick lump is in my throat, and all I can see is the anger burning in Owen's blue eyes right before he turned and pushed away from me, into the waiting crowd.

"Owen saw us. He... he saw us, and he was so angry, he left. Now he won't speak to me."

Haddy's brow tightens. "What were you doing?"

"Nothing!" I cry. "Baxter is an addict. He didn't ghost me. He went on a bender and woke up on a park bench in another town. Far away. He has a real problem."

My cousin's lips press into a frown, and she moves the baby around to her other breast. "Well, that's terrible. Did you have any idea?"

I shake my head. "I would never have guessed it... Although, thinking about how he acted in the beginning, how aggressive he was… He was always showing up to take me somewhere. It was a lot."

"It was six," Haddy notes. "You told him six dates, and he wanted to get in your pants."

"True…" I nod. "Either way, he's doing the steps. He came back to make amends."

"How do you make amends for ghosting someone?"

"That's exactly what I said. I told him just knowing was enough, but he actually offered for me to punch him in the nose."

Her face lights up with a smile. "Did you?"

"Of course not. I gave him a hug."

"You have got to stop being so understanding all the time," Haddy groans. "People are not dogs. They're not all good."

"Well, Owen saw us, and he didn't even let me explain."

"Leave it to me. Next time *I'll* punch Baxter in the nose. You don't have to be there."

Shaking my head, I exhale a whine, putting my hands on each side of my face. "I don't care about Baxter. I care about Owen not talking to me."

Haddy's expression softens, and I put my head down on my arm, shoulders shaking.

"Easy, now." Haddy squeezes my hand before putting a squirmy baby Lucy on her shoulder and patting her little back. "It's okay, Lulu. Aunt Gigi is just having a crisis."

"I am…" My stomach is in knots. "I don't know what Owen is thinking. When I saw his face, he was so angry. Then he just walked away."

"Why didn't you go after him?"

"I did! He went straight into that crowd last night, and the harder I pushed to get to him, the more they pulled me away. So I tried to come here and meet him at his house, but he never came home. I've sent text after text... I've called..."

Bending my knees, I put my feet on the chair and wrap my arms around my legs. I hold myself tight as angry sadness twists in my chest.

With my eyes closed, I see so clearly the storm clouds in his pretty blue eyes, the tightness in his square jaw, the clench of his fists. His shaggy brown hair that I love to tangle my fingers in moving away from me, as he pushed straight into the crowd and was pulled further and further away.

He *wanted* to get away from me.

"Hey, now." Haddy is at my side, wrapping her arm around my shoulders. "Don't cry, Gigi. He can't stay gone forever. He bought a house here."

"I'm just so mad... and sad... and I don't want to lose him, Hads." My heart beats hard, and I try to calm my breathing. "We had this whole talk about Maddie and trust and not wanting to start anything unless we were sure... I can't let him treat me this way. At the same time, I can't let him decide I'm too much of a risk."

I put my fists on the side of my head and exhale a frustrated growl.

"Hey, look at me." My cousin shifts around in her chair, putting her hands on my shoulders. "He's not going to decide anything like that. He just needs to cool off. All relationships have bumps, but you're meant to be together. It's in the cards."

I lean my head on her shoulder, exhaling heavily. "It's just all so new and fragile." Lifting my phone off the table, I give it a shake. "And this stupid thing is useless. I'm sick of waiting for it to go off, and it never does. I want to throw it out the window."

"Give it to me." She takes my phone out of my hand. "You need a distraction. Let's go through the charity show and see if we have everything we need. When the guys get back, we'll have to move fast to have it ready before Christmas. They only have so many free days to practice."

I'm not okay, but I let her drag me to her office where she has all the plans pulled up on her computer screens.

24

OWEN

MAV

You can't cut your hair. It's your good luck charm. First San Jose, then the hat trick. Don't change anything.

GAV

Change your underwear. And your socks.

OWEN

I've got to at least get a trim.

MAV

No more than half an inch.

GAV

Is that some rule you just made up?

MAV

Trust the process.

OWEN

There's a process?

GAV

Let Gina do it. She's a good groomer.

OWEN

I'm not a dog.

MAV

That's not what I've heard…

OWEN

What have you heard?

MAV

Not enough, actually. Get on that.

OWEN

I'm getting on the ice.

I shove my phone into my bag not wanting to think about things like good luck charms and haircuts and Gina's fingers in my hair.

I've been tense and angry for two days straight. The last thing I want in my head, messing with my game is what happened.

That game should've been the best night of my life. Gina was in my jersey, I had both my girls blowing kisses. They gave me the lift I needed to make the magic happen.

Sure, I've scored hat tricks before in the minor leagues, but it's a whole different level to do it in the NHL. The defensemen are a lot tougher, and the goalies don't let anything past them. It's a combination of timing, luck, and lightning speed.

Now, when I close my eyes, I see her in that guy's arms. That guy who I've since learned was Baxter the bastard. He broke her heart, and yet, when he reappears, she goes back to him?

This is worse than when I saw her with Donovan, and I

feel worse than I felt that night. I'm too old to be acting like a jealous punk. I'm too old to be fighting these feelings of jealousy. I don't *like* these feelings of jealousy.

I need to step back and think about this. I've been following my heart, my emotions, my sister's visions... and they've led me to the same place I was before, a place I swore I'd never be. Only this time it's worse.

She's been blowing up my phone, but I can't talk to her yet. My emotions are out of control, and I need to get my head straight. I need to talk to my dad.

Coach said I could take an extra day after our last game on Sunday and fly to Eureka. I'll miss a practice, but with the way I've been playing, I've earned a personal day.

I just have to get through this weekend.

Before facing off against Tampa on their home turf, I look up at the camera and blow a kiss to my baby girl. That hasn't changed.

My play also hasn't changed. I've been in this position before, hurting and needing to do whatever it took to numb the pain. I played hard and earned my spot on this team, and I'm not letting anybody down.

Maverick and I work the puck down the ice, trying out a new Figure Z formation we've been practicing. He passes it to me, and I pass it to Hancock, skating to the outside and holding off the defenseman as Mav flies forward for the final pass, which he shoots past the goalie for a score.

We don't have as many fans in this part of the country, but we can still hear our side going wild with air horns and chants.

Again, we're taking it all the way. Thunder's number 52 is coming at me hard, but I'm in no mood to deal with him. Mav sends a pass my way, and before I can grab it with my stick, he slams me into the boards.

Forgetting the play, I grab him by the pads and spin him into the wall, and it's on. The guys are all around us, and fists fly. The linemen allow it for a bit, then 52 and I are each sent to our teams' boxes for a two-minute penalty.

I kick the side of the door when I enter, before sitting on the bench. Anger surges in my veins, and I know it's really about her. All of it is about her.

Every player is that fucking Baxter, and if 52 gets in my way again, I'm likely to draw blood.

While I wait, Mav and Gav do one of their signature plays, intercepted by the Thunder defenseman. The guys are right. Tampa knows every move in our arsenal. It's time to start working on some new plays.

I watch them, strategizing options we can try on in practice. It distracts my mind, and my anger is finally cooling off when it's time for me to get back in the game.

Donovan skates up to me as soon as I'm out, putting his large hand on my shoulder pads. "Leave 52 to me. Focus on scoring. They don't see you coming."

My jaw is tight, but I nod. He's right. I scored a hat trick back home because Atlanta didn't know what to do with me yet. The only thing they do know is 52 throws me off, but our team captain is blocking him now.

Mav skates up to me, speaking in my ear. "Gav's going for the pinch. He'll send it to you this time."

I nod, turning and making eye contact with our defenseman. "I'm ready."

It's a play they usually complete together, but we're all thinking on our feet this game, looking for ways to mix it up.

Gav's play is successful, and he gets the puck to me. I'm moving fast in the direction of our goal when the Thunder defenseman moves in for the block. At the last second, I pass it to Sax, turning and moving away from the guy.

I'm beside the net when I see the puck fly and bounce off the goal. We keep at it, playing faster through each period. Tonight, we only score one point to the Thunder's two. It's another barn burner, but this time Tampa takes home the victory.

We head to Nashville next to play the Terminators. They're a decent team, although not quite on our level. Still, it's a fast, physical match, and we come out with another win.

By the end of the weekend, the team is amped up and closer than ever. We're starting to gel, and I'm finding that sense of home and family I had with my old team in South Carolina.

On my way to the airport, I check in with Maddie. Seeing her little face soothes the ache in my chest, and I remember a time when it was just me and her and Heather and hockey. It was all so simple then. I hadn't complicated my life by falling in love.

"You need to come home soon, Daddy," she says, her brown eyes so serious. "Something's wrong with Miss Gina, and you always make her smile. She needs you."

I can't answer her. I only tell her I'll see her at dinner Monday, and after we disconnect, I get the text I knew would be coming from my sister.

HEATHER

What happened? Gina said nothing's going on, but I'm not dumb. Why are you going to Eureka?

Leaning my head back, I can't answer her either. It's way too complicated, too deep, and too much to get into over text. I simply press my head against the seat and keep it short.

I'm good. I'll explain when I'm home.

Now, sitting on the small passenger plane miles above the earth, I finally read the texts from Gina. Each one is more urgent than the last, and they all say the same thing, *Please talk to me.*

Gazing out the window, I picture her green eyes, her full lips, her pretty smile. I remember holding her in my arms, how good it felt, and the pain in my chest is like a knife pushing through my lungs.

I will talk to her. I will explain, but I have to go home first.

"COME HERE AND GIVE ME A HUG." My stepmom Britt meets me at the door.

Her blonde hair is tied up in a ponytail, and her green eyes sparkle with joy. I bend down to hug her, and she pats my back, making a grunting noise as she squeezes.

"Hey, Mom." I hug her, straightening.

"I can never get over how tall you've gotten. Let me see those teeth." I smile at her, and she squeezes my cheeks. "Perfect. Now where is my sweet grandbaby?"

"In LA with Heather. I'm just making a quick trip. I need to talk to Dad about something."

Grammy Gwen steps up in her flowing caftan and frizzy white hair. Gold bangles are stacked on both arms, and her eyes narrow.

She circles a finger around my face. "Your aura is off. What's wrong?"

Forcing a laugh through the tightness in my chest, I shake my head. "You know I don't believe in all that stuff."

"That doesn't mean it isn't real," she answers, sounding just like my sister.

Heather's a chip off the ole block.

"It's always good to see you, son." Dad steps forward to pull me into a hug. "What brings you all the way over here during hockey season?"

"Do you have time to talk? I need to run something by you."

His dark brow furrows, but he nods. We walk outside, strolling down the street of the old neighborhood I know so well. We pass homes of my relatives and friends, homes I know so well from when I was a boy, running, playing hide-and-seek, fishing with my friends.

We walk past my grandmother's house with the massive live oak tree out front. It's the same yard where I would play with Britt's old bloodhound Edward. Man, I loved that dog. He's the reason I got Ladybird for Maddie.

We continue out to the end of the lane, over a narrow wooden bridge, down a small hill to a wooden fishing pier. It was built out over the marshy grasslands leading out to the ocean.

It's the same old fishing pier where my great-grandfather would take my uncle Alex when he was a boy. The old man was dead long before I was born, but I've heard all the stories about him passing his secret recipe for award-winning bourbon to my dad's younger brother.

My great-grandfather was close to all my uncles, but he had a special relationship with Alex. I imagine it being similar to my relationship with my dad. Some family members just seem to speak your language better than others.

"What's on your mind?" Dad asks when we reach the end of the wooden platform.

He's dressed in his khaki sheriff's uniform, and I consider how different he is from Gina's dad, who is also the sheriff of a small town on the coast.

They both take their jobs seriously, but my dad is quiet, thoughtful, no-nonsense... Which made him falling for my mom with her family of fortune tellers, magicians, and escape artists all the more unexpected—and they've been happily married for more than twenty years.

"Do you remember how it was before you met Mama Britt? When it was just you and me?" I glance up at him.

His brown hair is gray at the temples now, but his shoulders are still broad. We're the same height, but in my mind, he'll always be taller than me, always wiser.

He nods, his brow furrowing over blue eyes just like mine. "It was pretty rough, but Mom helped me a lot. Are you worried about Maddie?"

"No." I shake my head, choosing my words. "I've been thinking about how you used to take me to Sunday School and drop me off, then pick me up after because you didn't believe in that stuff."

"Okay... not what I expected." He winces, putting his hands on his hips. He takes a deep breath, looking out over the marsh. "I was going through a pretty hard time back then, a sort-of dark night of the soul as people call it."

I think about those words, and I think it's exactly where I've been for seven years. A long, long, dark night... I wonder why I've waited so long to have this conversation with him. Everyone talks to my dad when things get tough.

"Miss Priddy had told us how Jesus walked on the water, and I was so scared to ask you about it. Ryan said you'd get mad, but you told me never to keep things from you. You said to come to you, no matter what it was."

A smile softens his features. "That hasn't changed."

I take a step closer to where he's standing, studying the tall grasses mixed with spiky palmettos in the brackish water. The rivers here all lead out to the sea.

Dad and his brothers have worked hard to keep this little town nestled between Kiawah and Hilton Head pristine. So many developers would love to turn it into a high-end tourist destination.

"I asked you if it was magic, but you said it was a story about faith."

"Did I use the word *faith*?" He squints one eye at me.

"You said it was about having faith we could do things we didn't believe we could. Like Peter believed he could walk on the water."

"Right, I remember now," he nods. "Seems like it didn't turn out so well for ole Pete."

"He got scared, and he started to sink." My chest is tight as I remember.

Looking up at the trees, I can still see myself as that little boy riding in the backseat of my dad's truck. He was the smartest person I knew, and after we lost Mom, he became my safety net, my rock. I hung on every word he said, and for every problem, I knew he had the solution.

"You remember that day pretty well," he says. "I hope I gave you a decent explanation."

"You did. You said if I believed I could do something, I had to have faith that I could. Even when it got scary."

Water ripples as it flows around the plants, over rocks. A frog takes this opportunity to sing a long note.

Dad nods, putting a strong hand on my shoulder and

giving it a squeeze. "That's some good advice, even if I did give it to you."

He makes me smile, and I follow him slowly up the pier toward the house. Dad's brothers, my aunts and cousins, my stepmom, and my grandmothers are all gathering to visit, share food, and catch up before I have to leave again.

I don't have much time, and I need to ask him the question that brought me here.

"I've met someone, Dad." He stops, turning to face me as I continue. "She's my teammate's cousin, and the three of us sort-of lived together for about a month. She's really smart and beautiful... and young."

His brow furrows. "How young?"

"Seven years."

"Your mama Britt is seven years younger than I am."

"It's not the age difference that's bothering me... It's me."

This is the part that makes me uncomfortable. I shift on my feet as if I'm trying to find the least painful posture in which to say the words.

"When I lost Angie, I made a vow. I never wanted to give another person the power to hurt me that bad again."

He gives me an understanding nod. "You've found someone who's changed your mind?"

My chest is tight, but I push through it. "I can't date, Dad. I'm too old, and I've got Maddie... It's not fair to her."

"Maddie will be okay." His eyes move between mine. "But it sounds like you're worried about more than your daughter."

"I get really jealous. Before I came here, I saw her hugging her ex-boyfriend, and I... I wanted to kill the guy." Heat is in my chest.

A smile cracks my dad's face. "Don't tell me anything incriminating. I don't want to have to arrest you."

"That's my point. I've never been a jealous guy."

He looks up, thoughtful. "In my experience, jealousy is usually about something else. Something you don't want to say out loud. Do you think you can't trust her?"

"No. I know I can."

His blue eyes pierce right through me, right to the truth. "Then what's that jealousy really about?"

I lift my hands, pressing the heels over my damp eyes. I have to confess the truth. I have to say what's lurking behind these feelings, what's driving me here.

"I'm scared, Dad. I love her. I love her in a way I don't understand, and I'm afraid I'll lose her." My chest seizes, and I confess it all. "I don't know if it's some kind of... PTSD? I only know I can't go through that kind of pain again. I barely survived it the first time, but with Gina... I wouldn't get over it."

He closes the space between us in two easy strides, pulling me into a hug. My shoulder is in his chest, and he places a hand on my back, giving me a few solid pats and a brief squeeze.

My dad. My rock. The one person I've always been safe with, who I can always be vulnerable around. He holds onto me, just like he did the first time I was afraid, when I was just a boy.

"Love is a risk, son." His tone is gentle. "But when you take that risk, you get the most beautiful thing in return."

"How will I know?"

"Ask her to marry you."

My brows shoot up, and I huff a laugh, shaking my head. "It's too soon."

"Is it?" He frowns. "Sounds to me like you know what you want now."

"Yeah, but that doesn't mean she knows."

"Then she'll say no, and you can stop worrying about it."

The pain in my chest breaks, and I rub my hand over my forehead, looking up to exhale a chuckle. "That might be the best small-town advice you've ever given me."

"You're a small-town guy."

"I guess I am."

"Listen to me." He puts a hand on the top of my shoulder. "I've never been more terrified in my life than when I thought I'd lost Britt. That's how you know it's a love that will last. When you can't breathe without the person. When the pain of being apart from them is so great, it drives you to do anything for them."

I want someone to burn...

"What if these feelings are too big for me?"

"They're as big as your heart. Trust your old man, and have faith. You're too young to be alone." He nudges my arm, giving me a teasing wink. "And get that hair cut."

That makes me laugh, and it feels good to let it out. I'm glad I came here. I know what I need to do. "Thanks, Dad."

25

———————

GINA

My gaze is laser focused as I walk slowly down the row of hounds. They all stand at perfect attention, jaws level with the ground, four legs spread in an active stance. In dog-show language, it's called a stack.

Their handlers, dressed in suits or formal dresses, are equally poised and alert.

Haze is here, the Afghan borzoi I've worked with on numerous occasions. Her coat gleams like spun gold in the lights.

Next to her stands a long-haired dachshund with an equally shiny black coat. I recognize him from previous shows, and I can tell they've been training, working hard to level up.

Two Irish wolfhounds jog out next, and their wiry gray coats and bearish gaits make me want to sit down and cuddle with them.

I do not. I am a very serious judge.

Following them is a dog I've never seen before, a whippet, which is similar to the Italian greyhound, but with a better temperament. His handler is also new to me, and he lifts his chin in a superior way.

I give him a tight nod. He has a very good-looking dog who has clearly been well-trained.

"I'd like to see the borzoi, the sloughi, the dachshund..." My chest tightens when I see a gorgeous, rust-colored bloodhound standing with its chin lifted. "The bloodhound and the whippet."

A ripple of approval moves through the crowd, and the five dogs step forward. I walk slowly down the ranks, giving them all a good once-over. I've seen and inspected the first three on several occasions, so I don't spend as much time on them.

I slide my hand over Haze's soft fur, lifting her face and inspecting her eyes. Bright as ever.

The bloodhound is a new one to me, and I have him stand as I run my hands down his sturdy shoulders. He has a good build and nice, excessive folds of skin. A really good specimen.

Next is the whippet, who is a lively little guy. His light gray coat is smooth, and his ears are perky and eager. I do a quick rundown of his legs, I cup his balls briefly, and... wait.

My eyes flicker to his handler, who doesn't make eye contact with me. He keeps his chin level, looking straight ahead, but I notice a twitch in his brow.

"I need a second opinion here." I motion to Lisa, who has just finished judging the miniature breeds.

She walks over to me quickly, and I lean into her ear, whispering. "Plastic."

Her brow rises, and she repeats my inspection, running her hands down the length of the dog's body. She checks his legs, and when she gets to his testicles, she hesitates. Her lips twist into a frown, and she nods slowly, sadly.

Dammit. I agreed to judge this show last-minute because I'd hoped it would cheer me up. I've done nothing but lie on the couch and miss Owen for two days. Not even working with Haddy on the charity show could distract me.

Now this.

I look down at the bright-eyed little fellow, and my heart is heavy. They're all such good dogs, such avid little competitors.

My eyes go to his handler, and I can tell he knows what he did. He thought he'd slip it past me. He thought I wouldn't be experienced enough to notice.

It's probably my pent-up annoyance with the whole Baxter situation and Owen and all of it, but I want to punch him in the nose.

Instead, I remain professional. "I'm sorry, we have to disqualify this dog."

"What?" The man's voice rises, and he has the nerve to act outraged.

"Neuticles are not allowed in American Kennel Club confirmation dog shows." I lift my hand to the side for the officials to escort them from the ring.

"How dare you?" he shouts, but I turn away, going back to the remaining four dogs.

When I was a young judge, things like this would've flustered me for the rest of the day. Today, it simply makes my job that much easier. I can only award four ribbons, and I have the order all set in my mind.

"Take them out by the bloodhound, the dachshund, the sloughi, and the borzoi." The handlers lift the leashes and trot around the large ring, showing off the dogs' perfect gaits. "That's the order, one, two, three, and best of breed."

Applause fills the arena, and I walk over to the judges' table to sign off on the book, making it official. The handlers will take the dogs to the platforms to receive their ribbons and be photographed, but my work here is done.

I give Lisa a wave, and she gives me a wry smile. She has to do another round of judging with the toys, but I'm done for the day. After that last little drama, I am *so* done.

As I make my way to the exit, my eyes land on a little girl sitting with an older woman in the stands, and my chest aches. I think about Maddie.

I'd love to bring her to one of these shows so she can watch and learn. I think of all the things I want to do with her, with both of them. I remember the circle I saw in my vision, holding hands with a sparkling, starry heart in the center.

Walking slowly through the curtained hall leading to the exit, I notice the winner of the miniatures competition. It's a fluffy white Bichon Frisé wearing a bright blue ribbon.

I stop to pet his head. "He's excellent."

"Thank you so much, Miss Bradford." The owner seems nervous, and I forget I'm kind of a celebrity in the dog world. "It's our first blue ribbon."

"It's well-deserved. Miss Brashears is a strict judge."

Pausing for a moment, I look into the dog's big brown eyes, and I remember my spirit animal's message. Even if it was a mushroom trip, my heaviness eases, and I decide to let hope walk beside me the way Heather said.

"He has a good heart. I can always tell."

The dog owner says more words of gratitude, and I give her a wave.

Walking out to my car, I remember the last time I judged a last-minute, out-of-town show. The fuel pump went out on this silly car, and he came to save me.

I think about that night in the hotel room, all the things we said and shared. It gives me an idea for one last thing to try.

"HAVE you been on the couch all weekend?" Mav bustles through the front door, dropping his duffel and carrying his gym bag to the laundry room.

I'm lying on my stomach, watching bad reality television. The kind that makes me feel better about myself. At least I'm not *that* fucked up.

"No!" My tone is defensive. "I went to Haddy's on Friday, and we did a lot of planning for the charity show. She needs you to give her the date of a free Saturday to teach you all how to walk your dogs."

"Pretty sure I know how to walk a dog, Geeg." He passes me on his way from the laundry to his bedroom.

"Then I judged a dog show this afternoon. It was pretty exciting."

"How so?" He takes off his blazer and hangs it in the front closet.

He really is a handsome man, which is funny to think, considering we grew up together. He looks more like his dad every day, which is saying a lot. Tall, dark, and handsome, but with those Bradford blue eyes just like Haddy and Knox. I'm the only one with green eyes like my mom.

"I spotted a fake nut." I do a little cupping motion with my hand.

Mav's brow crinkles in horror. "What the hell does that mean?"

"We had this new dog today, a whippet, and he had a plastic testicle."

"Why would you ever give a dog a plastic nut?"

"The owner clearly thought I wouldn't catch it." I dust off my shoulder, returning to the couch. "Clearly, he didn't know who he was messing with. I had Lisa verify before we ejected him from the competition."

"Dang." Mav disappears into his room for a few minutes before returning in sweat pants and a long-sleeve tee. "That's harsh, Gina."

"I know." My lips twist sadly. "I get so frustrated when owners try shit like that. Dogs have feelings, too, you know, and he was the smartest little hound. I liked him."

"Does this mean our house is going to get TP'd again?" Mav flops onto the couch beside me.

My nose wrinkles, and I look in the direction of the front door. "I hope not."

"Stink bomb in the mailbox?"

"That really hurts Mr. Gibson more than me. We need to set up a Ring camera or something to capture footage. Turn them in to the feds."

"That's not a bad idea." He shifts on the couch beside me. "What're we watching tonight? *Best in Show*?"

"I just watched that with Heather. *Frankenweenie*?"

"Nah, that's a Halloween film. It's after Thanksgiving. By the way, Friendsgiving next Tuesday?"

"I'll check with Haddy. *Turner and Hooch*?"

"Sure."

It might be just the two of us, but putting my head on Mav's shoulder, watching Tom Hanks adjust to life with an oversized mastiff is just the comfort-watch I need.

I sent my last-chance text earlier this afternoon, and I still haven't gotten a reply. Now *I'm* starting to get angry. I think it's time for me to stop crying over men who ghost...

26

———

OWEN

It was on my phone when I got back from spending the afternoon with all my Eureka relatives. Holiday season is upon us, and everyone is in town.

My best friend Ryan stayed with me, filling me in on all the news. He's slowly taking over the job of editor, publisher, reporter, and photographer from his mom at the Eureka *Gazette*.

My cousin Pinky bounced around the group, bossy as ever. Her bright red curls were impossible to miss, even from a distance, and even though we butted heads *all. the. time.* as kids, we grew up to be really close as adults.

My uncles and aunts observed us all with proud amusement, the next generation.

I had to walk over and take a knee by the little dog my

drag-queen "aunt" uses in her act. The previous Angie Dickenson was a miniature pink poodle. Angie Dickenson II is a teacup Yorkie.

"Is it okay if I take a picture of her to send to my... roommate?" It's the wrong word for how important Gina is to me, but I can't call her *my fiancée* just yet.

Hell, she's probably not speaking to *me* now. I have a feeling I'll have to do some serious groveling to make up for my weekend of inner turmoil. My weekend of going off the grid, giving up the fight, and facing the irrevocable truth: I can't live without Gina Bradford.

"Yes, you can, honey." Auntie Monay places a large brown hand on my shoulder. "Thank you for asking. Angie the Second isn't as bold as Angie the Great was."

I take a quick photo with my phone before walking over to my aunt Cass's little sister AJ and her outlaw husband Raif.

"Hey, how's Nikki doing? Is Porkchop still around?" I'm talking about the little girl AJ brought back with her from Branson when she ran away from a "bad situation."

That's all they told us as kids. It all came out in the wash, like everything else did when we were growing up here in Eureka. It's a small town, but it's never been quiet or boring.

"She's so smart." My other "aunt" smiles proudly like she always does when she talks about Nikki. "She's working for the UN doing French-to-English translations. She's just brilliant, and to think..."

She shakes her head, touching the sentimental tears from her eyes, and I give her a hug. "I hope to see her again soon."

They're the wildcards of the family, but they have the biggest hearts.

Dad drives me to the airport after lunch. Our conversation from earlier is on my mind, and when Gina's last text comes through, I make the decision to go for it.

"Did you think about what I told you?" Dad stands beside me at the tiny airport outside of town.

"I haven't stopped thinking about it," I look down, admitting the truth.

"Let me know how it goes." He pulls me in for a hug, and I slap him on the back. "Don't be afraid, son. You got this."

His words give me confidence. "Thanks, Dad."

"I'll probably be home after dinner, but I'll fill you in on everything when I get there." I'm talking on FaceTime with my sister as we taxi into the private airport in LA. "I've missed my girl."

"That sounds positive." Heather is bright-eyed and smiling. "Does that mean things are better now?"

"Let's just say I hope we do some celebrating when I get back. I'll keep you posted."

We disconnect as the flight attendants give me the okay to move around the small cabin. I'm the only one on this cross-country flight. The rest of the team came back yesterday evening.

I was more than willing to fly commercial, but the coach told me after how I've been playing, I'm a star now. That's going to take a little getting used to.

While I'm flying, I text Haddy and Maverick, then I take out my laptop and work on setting up a few additional items.

When I'm finally off the plane, sitting in the black SUV taking me across town to Los Feliz, I actually do start to feel like a star. Don't worry, I won't let it go to my head, but being able to place last-minute special orders and have them delivered exactly when I need them? *That* is a level of fame I can get used to. It also helps to live in the second-largest city in the U.S.

A quick text from Haddy lets me know everything is in place, meaning Gina is at home. I thank the guy for the ride, grab my bag, and take a quick breath before climbing the steps to the cute bungalow I used to call home.

I'm dressed in my suit from after the game, and my too-long hair is back in a small ponytail. Waiting on the porch is the cellophane-wrapped bundle and a small blue box I special ordered.

I put my duffel bag beside the chair and pick them up. I take the pouch out of the box, inspecting the contents briefly. *Perfect.*

Straightening my jacket, I smooth a piece of hair off my face before I tap the door lightly three times and enter.

The television is on, showing highlights from some national dog show. Mav glances over his shoulder and stands, giving me a nod before heading to the kitchen.

"You're going to miss the judging!" Gina calls after him, and her sweet voice hits me right in the chest.

I swallow the emotions thick in my throat and walk to the couch where she's lying, holding the remote.

"Owen!" she gasps, sitting up quickly.

She's dressed in a pink tee with a bunch of dogs on the front and the words *Man's Best Friend*, only it has a *Wo* in script before the *Man*. She's also wearing black PJ pants with white poodles all over them.

Her strawberry hair is up in a ponytail, and her face is washed. The sprinkling of freckles is visible across the bridge of her nose, and she looks so damn good, for a moment, I have trouble remembering all the things I planned to say.

"Gina," I start, but my voice is hoarse.

I clear it, and I'm about to start my prepared statement when her lips tighten into a frown.

She throws the remote onto the couch, cutting me off with a sharp, "No."

Then, she turns on her toe and walks quickly past me to the stairs, running up them without even looking back.

"Wait..." I frown, looking up in the direction she fled.

Mav sticks his head out the door to the kitchen and waves his hand in a scooping-upward motion. "Go get her!"

I look down at the bouquet of roses I'm holding, and I hesitate, waiting for it...

"What...?" Her voice rings out from upstairs. "Who did this?"

None of this is going how I planned it, but hell, when has my life ever followed a plan?

I jog up the stairs to find her standing in the hall with both hands on her head, looking into her bedroom.

I stop on the landing, remembering the night so long ago when I was in this very same spot, watching her in her doorway. I remember how badly I longed for her that night... I think it's only gotten worse... and when our eyes met, she came to me then.

Her arms drop to her sides, and she turns to face me now. "Did you do this?"

"You said you wanted someone to bring you flowers just because he was thinking about you. I haven't stopped thinking about you since Thursday night, so I figured I should give you the same amount of flowers."

I ordered enough white tulips, pink and white roses, and blue hyacinths to fill her bedroom. Haddy and Mav helped me arrange them all. Well, Haddy arranged them. Mav kept Gina distracted while she did it.

And apparently, I owe Haddy "big time," because it took six trips to sneak them all in without raising suspicion. No worries—I'll do whatever she wants if this goes how I plan.

"Well..." She exhales through her lips, sounding almost reluctant. "They're beautiful."

"The lady at the flower shop said those are the flowers that say *I'm sorry*." My eyes haven't left her. "I didn't even know there were specific flowers for that."

I take a cautious step closer, holding out the bouquet of red roses in my hand. "I got these because they mean *I love you*."

She's shaking her head no as her beautiful eyes fill with tears.

"No." Her voice wobbles, and my chest aches. "You can't just show up here and say that to me after ghosting me for three days."

Another step closer, I lift my hand. "Gina..."

"You didn't reply to any of my texts," she continues. "You didn't answer any of my phone calls. You just went on playing hockey, having fun with all your friends while I was hurting."

I'm shaking my head as she speaks. "I was *not* having fun. I was in hell." My tone is level, and I'm doing my best to stay apologetic even as the memory of that guy touching her has heat flooding my veins all over again. "I couldn't talk to you like that. It was all too much."

"It was all very innocent." Her voice is firm. "But you didn't let me explain. You cut me off without a word."

Those tears finally hit her cheeks, and they're like knives to my heart.

"God, Gina..." My voice breaks. "If you could see inside me, if you knew how torn up I was all weekend—"

"I can't see inside you, and I don't know." Her voice rises, but it cracks on the words. "I won't do that again, Owen. I won't be with someone who'll shut me out like that. It hurts too much."

I've taken careful steps closer with every word, and now I'm standing so close, I could touch her. She's not wearing shoes, and even though she's tall, she seems so fragile looking up at me.

Her beautiful green eyes that haunt my dreams are now filled with tears, and my lungs are so tight it's difficult to breathe. Still, I know I'm in the doghouse because of my own behavior, and I deserve it.

Lowering to my knees, I put my hand on her waist. "You have no idea how it hurts to see you cry... Can I hold you?"

"Owen..." Her voice wobbles, and I take it as permission.

I pull her to me, wrapping my arms around her waist and resting my cheek against the soft cotton of her shirt.

"Gina..." I utter the word like a prayer. "I'm not used to feeling this way about anyone. It scared the hell out of me, and when I saw him touching you, holding you..."

Her voice is soft. "I told you not to be jealous."

Lifting my head, I look up into her beautiful eyes, which are blinking fast now. "I love you, Gina Grace, and I'm a jealous motherfucker when it comes to you. I wanted to rip that guy's arms out of their sockets and beat him to death with them." Lowering my chin, I put my forehead against her sternum. "That's why I had to talk to my dad. I knew he'd help me understand how I was feeling... and why."

"You talked to your dad about me?"

Looking up again, my eyes hold hers. "When my mom

died, he went through a lot. He was angry, and he stopped believing…"

"Like you?" She slides her fingers through the sides of my hair, moving the long pieces behind my ears.

"Yes." My breath stills, and I hold her eyes with mine. I have so much to say to her, but I need us to be in a better space. "Would you cut my hair for me?"

Her brow furrows. "Right now?"

"Yeah." I rise, taking her hand. "Would you?"

Moments later, I'm sitting in a chair in her grooming studio, in the middle of the ceramic-tiled space. The last time I was in here, she was showing me how to give Ladybird a soothing bath… Then LB shook dirty dog water all over us.

Gina drapes a cloth around my shoulders, and she takes out a pair of scissors. "How short do you want it?"

"Mav said no more than half an inch, but I need it off my neck."

Nodding slowly, she takes a plastic spray bottle off a nearby table and uses it to wet my hair. Then pulls a regular old black comb from the top of my head down the sides. It's intimate and caring, closer than any words I could say.

"You're good at this." I've watched Heather when she used to be a stylist, and I can tell Gina knows what she's doing. "I thought you only groomed dogs."

"Who said I don't?" Her eyebrow arches.

I huff a laugh, blinking down. "I walked right into that one."

"Look straight ahead now." I lift my eyes, and they lock with hers for a brief second.

She blinks away quickly, but a pretty pink color blooms across her cheeks. I decide to take it as a good sign.

I'm quiet and still as she threads her fingers through my

hair, snipping again and again, not going past her cousin's designated trim limit.

Finally, she gets to a point where she stops. She puts the scissors down, and she stands in front of me, threading her fingers through my damp hair, lifting it and inspecting the layers.

"This will give it a style, and I brought it up so it's not on your neck."

She takes the drape off my shoulders, carrying it to a basket near the back wall. Then she returns to where I'm sitting, watching her.

"Thank you." I look up, wondering if she felt the tone shift as well. "Can I pay you?"

She shakes her head. "Your money's no good here."

Reaching for her waist, I pull her to me, between my legs. "I hope my words are."

"Words are nice, but actions are better."

"I'll do anything for you, Gina. I didn't know I could love like this again until I met you. Only this time, it's a bigger love than I've ever felt before. It scares me, because I know this time I wouldn't get over the loss."

Reaching up, she moves my hair off my cheek. A hint of a smile curls her lips. "Let's walk back to the house. You need to get home and see your little girl."

"I won't sleep tonight unless I know you've forgiven me."

Her eyes blink down, and she takes my hand. "Come on."

We walk slowly back to the house, and when we get to the back porch, she pauses. Our hands are clasped, and I lift her fingers to my lips.

"I love you, Gina."

Her lips tighten, and she nods. "I know."

27

GINA

He exhales a laugh, nodding. "You know."

Then he presses his lips to the back of my fingers again in a way that floods my entire body with heat.

I have no idea how I'm managing to be so strong right now. Everything inside of me wants to give in and say it's okay, it was just a spat, forget about it... He filled my entire freakin room with flowers. And not just any flowers, *I'm sorry* flowers. Who knew I'm sorry flowers were the best flowers? White tulips, roses, and hyacinths?

Lifting my hand, I thread my fingers in the sides of his hair again. I nearly lost it just now cutting his silky hair. His warm breath was on my chest as I leaned forward to lift and snip. His warm cheeks were at my wrists when I pulled it out to trim. I wanted to crawl into his lap and cover his mouth with mine.

It was the sexiest haircut of my life.

Of course, I'm usually grooming dogs, and there's nothing sexy about that.

Cutting Owen's hair was fire. My chest burned, my knees trembled, and it took all my strength not to fall into his arms.

But he hurt me. He walked away without letting me explain. He ignored all my calls and didn't reply to a single one of my texts for three days... While he went to talk to his dad.

About me.

I watch him walk away with his Armani coat over his arm and that duffel bag in his hand. He pauses at the gate, giving me one last smile before stepping through it and heading down the sidewalk to his home, and I melt against the door jamb.

Maddie needs to see her daddy tonight. Heather misses him, I'm sure.

I'll let him think about what he did for a full eight hours, then I'll forgive him first thing in the morning.

I huff a bittersweet laugh, resting my head on the wooden frame, then I close the door and walk slowly to the kitchen.

It's empty, and I return to the living room, wondering what happened to Maverick. Clearly he and Haddy were in on this whole thing. There was no way those flowers got into my bedroom without their help.

"I'll take Spanky out," I call in the direction of Mav's downstairs suite.

He doesn't answer, but I'm not concerned. I walk over to my dog's crate, then I stop when I see it's empty. My brow furrows, and I look in the direction of Mav's bedroom.

"Mav?" I call louder, walking to his door. I knock a few times, growing louder when he doesn't answer. "Maverick?"

He walks out of the bedroom, doing a little dance with his eyes closed while he rubs a towel in his wet hair, and I realize he's wearing earbuds.

"Maverick!" I wave my hands.

"Shit!" he shouts, throwing the towel across the room. Then his brow lowers, and he looks behind me. "Didn't you and Owen make up? I thought you'd be going at it by now."

"He has a daughter, Mav. He went home to see Maddie and Heather."

"So y'all are good?" He walks over, putting an arm around my shoulders.

"We will be."

"I gotta say, that boy did some serious work today to make it up to you."

"He needed to." My lips press into a smile, and I think about my bedroom-flower garden.

Then I remember. "Hey, where's Spanky? I was going to take him for a walk, but he's not in his cage."

"What?" Mav walks from his bedroom into the living room. His voice grows louder, and he looks up, calling, "Spanky?"

Confusion tightens my chest, and I look from him to the empty cage up to my room. "You don't know where he is?"

I run to the stairs, jogging up and running to my bedroom. It's still filled with the gorgeous, fragrant flowers, but there's no sign of my dog.

"Spanky?" I call, ripping the sheets on my bed up and looking under it.

I dash out into the hall again, running into Haddy's old room, which was recently Heather and Maddie's room. It's completely empty.

I run down the hall to the guest room that was also Gavin's, then Owen's bedroom. *Empty.*

My stomach drops like a rock to my feet. I give the bathroom a quick check before running down the stairs again. "Did you find him?"

Mav shakes his head, blue eyes wide. "He's not up there?"

Panic floods my veins, and my hands start to shake. "No... Where is he, Mav?"

My cousin dashes through the door to the kitchen. "Did he follow you outside?"

"I didn't notice..." I was too busy blinking heart-eyes at Owen.

We run into the yard yelling his name. I run along the entire perimeter of the fence surrounding our backyard, calling his name. It's only silence.

"Maverick!" I shriek, and I'm about to collapse when he catches me.

"Hang on... hang on. Let's call Haddy." He takes out his phone, dialing her number.

I only hear his side of the conversation, urgently asking if she remembers seeing Spanky this afternoon.

"You did?" His voice rises, and my heart leaps. "When you were helping bring the flowers in from the truck..."

My eyes widen, and I whisper, "The gate was open..."

"Yeah, we can't find him. Okay." Mav disconnects. "She's coming right over."

"He's chipped..." I try to think as I walk around the room.

"So that's like GPS? Is there an app on your phone? Like Life 360?"

"I wish." Pain pierces the side of my temple. "It just means if he's taken to a shelter, they'll scan it and identify him."

"That's something at least." Maverick puts both hands

on the back of his head. "What the hell? Spanky never runs away."

"Oh, Maverick!" The panic wins, and I sit on the floor right in the middle of the living room crying. "If something happens to him..."

"Nothing's going to happen to him." Mav rushes over to sit on the floor beside me, and his voice is fierce as he pulls me into a hug. "What was the name of that punk with the plastic nut?"

"The guy from the dog show?" I jerk back, eyes wide. "You think he had something to do with this?"

"Gina? Are you okay?" The front door flies open, and Haddy rushes in with Gavin holding baby Lucy right behind her. "Did you find him? What can we do?"

"No... I don't know..." My throat aches, and I can't stop the tears flooding my cheeks.

"We'll span out over the neighborhood," Gavin says. "Did you call Owen and Heather? They can help us."

"Good idea!" Mav whips out his phone, tapping fast.

"This was not the call I expected to get." Haddy holds my arm as I slowly get up off the floor. "I thought you'd call about the flowers."

Nodding, I sniff, wiping my cheeks. "They're really beautiful... Thank you..." But I can't be happy right now. "We've got to find Spanky."

Her lips press together, and she takes my hand. "Come on. Let's go."

We run out into the yard, and immediately start jogging our usual dog-walking route around the neighborhood. Adrenaline drives me, and I strain my eyes, looking up and down the sidewalks, looking into backyards as I call his name.

Haddy does the same on the opposite side of the street.

It's all wrong. Spanky doesn't run away. He's playful and impish, but he likes being with us. He doesn't want to leave home.

We've circled all our routes, and when we meet up again at the house, Owen is there with Heather and Maddie.

He walks straight to me, pulling me into his arms. "We're going to find him."

"Daddy, can't Ladybird help us?" Maddie tugs on her dad's arm. "You told me she can find anything. She's a bloodhound!"

My eyes widen, and I step back, meeting Owen's equally wide eyes. "Of course!" We practically shout.

If anyone can find Spanky, it's his best girl. Holding hands, Owen and I jog the short distance to his house.

"I haven't even checked on Ladybird since I got back," he says. "Heather had dinner ready, and I was catching up with Maddie..."

"It's okay!" I don't know why he's apologizing to me.

I follow him through the house, out to the back patio where I notice Ladybird's cage is set up with her big cedar-filled cushion and a few chew toys.

Owen stops so fast, I literally run into him with a soft *oof!*

"Sorry," he whispers, turning around to catch me, then he nods his head towards the pen. "Look."

My brow furrows, and I look around his arm to see...

"Spanky!" I cry, rushing to the cage, where Ladybird is lying on her pillow with my rascally dog perched right beside her as if he's on guard.

"What are you doing here?" Dropping to my knees, I reach inside to pet his head. "Don't you know we've been looking everywhere for you?"

He licks the tears off my cheeks, and I laugh, leaning

forward to hug him. Still, he shows no signs of leaving his lady-friend's side.

"I can't say I blame him." Owen's voice is low, and I look over my shoulder to see him watching me, a possessive light in his eyes.

It tightens my core, and I pet my dog once more before standing. "Do you think he followed you home?"

"I didn't notice if he did, but I was thinking about you the whole way." He reaches out to slide a finger along the side of my face, moving my hair behind my ear.

My eyes flutter closed, and I almost lean into his touch. I want to reach up and kiss him, but it hasn't been eight hours yet. I have to be strong. He has to learn he can't treat me that way and get off so easily... even if my silly dog is weakening my resolve.

Blinking down, I shake my head. "I guess I'd better go and get some dinner myself. It's late."

The side of his mouth lifts with the hint of a smile, and I'm pretty sure he's onto me. "It's not so late."

"Still, I'm sure you'd like to visit with Maddie."

"We had a pretty good visit over dinner. It's her bedtime now."

I start to go, but I hesitate. "Is it okay if Spanky spends the night?"

"I'll bring him home when I walk over in the morning."

"Well... goodnight, then."

"Goodnight, Gina." His voice is low, and when I blink up at him, a sly grin is on his lips.

I swallow the desire in my throat before walking back inside the house where Haddy and the rest of our search party are gathered.

"Don't tell me," my cousin says, grabbing my hands.

"Yep, he's in there with Ladybird."

"Spanky, you stinker!" she calls over my shoulder, and I laugh, looping my arm in hers.

"At least we know where he is. I've never been so scared in my life."

"Spanky's in the cage with Ladybird!" Maddie skips up and takes my free hand, her voice raised. "We were running all over the place looking for him, and he was here the whole time!"

"Can you believe him?" I bend down to give her a hug. "He's such a stinker."

Her nose wrinkles. "It's like he doesn't want her to be here without him."

"It is like that." And I think of someone else who feels the same way. Someone six-foot-two with ridiculously sexy blue eyes. "We're going to let them have a sleepover, since they're missing each other so much."

Maddie's eyes widen. "Can dogs get married, Miss Gina?"

"I don't see why not." I take a knee, tilting my head to the side. "By the way, I've been wondering... why do you call Haddy *Aunt Haddy* and me *Miss Gina*?"

She puts her hand on my shoulder. "Uncle Gavin plays on the team with Daddy, so she's like my aunt, but if you were with my Daddy, you wouldn't be my aunt. You'd be like..."

Her voice trails off, getting quieter, and I bite my bottom lip, glancing up at the adults, who are suddenly acting very distracted by their phones, the piece of paper on the counter, baby Lucy, who is starting to fuss.

"I understand." Our eyes meet, and I give her a warm smile before pulling her into a hug, whispering in her ear, "I understand completely."

"Well, we'd better get our little nugget home," Haddy says brightly. "Glad that mystery had a happy ending!"

Gavin only chuckles, giving me a wink as he follows his wife, carrying his little girl.

"Here's to many more happy endings," Heather adds.

"Yeah, I'd better get back and make some dinner." Mav steps in the direction Haddy and her little family just went, doing finger guns. "See you bright and early, Sly."

My eyes return to Maddie's, and I give her one more squeeze. "We'll practice walking Peepee again tomorrow after school. You're going to walk her in the Pucks and Pups show, okay?"

She nods rapidly, whispering excitedly, "Okay!"

Our eyes meet, and we share a moment before I rise to follow my cousins.

"I'm coming with you." I do a little wave to the room. "Thank you all for helping me find my dog."

"Next time, we'll check Ladybird's cage first!" Maddie skips along beside me, holding my hand.

"Night, Heather," I call over my shoulder.

Maddie stops to hold the door, and I look back once more to see Owen standing with his hand on his daughter's shoulder, his eyes on me.

MAVERICK WHIPPED up a batch of "kitchen sink" quesadillas when we got home, and as we munched, we chatted about Spanky and LB. He agreed that *Snooperdoodle* was far superior to *Bloodhoodle*, or the much, *much* worse *Bloodpoo*, which he said made him barf in his mouth.

I told him with a smile, Haddy did the same thing!

He assiduously avoided any questions about what

happened with Owen, which I appreciated, but he also retired quickly to his suite letting me know he'd be sleeping with his AirPods in all night.

I shook my head, but I didn't reply. Instead, I quickly cleaned up our plates, washed up the one dirty pan, and slowly climbed the stairs to my bedroom.

Now, the fresh scent of roses mixed with the earthy scent of hyacinths greets me from the hall, and my room is like a magical garden when I enter it.

I sit on my bed, looking around at all the gorgeous blooms highlighted by the soft yellow light of my cube lamp. I pick up my phone and take a quick photo, texting it to my cousin.

GINA

You really outdid yourself here.

HADDY

All I did was put them on the shelves. Owen did all the work.

Inhaling softly, I close my eyes, letting his grand gesture soothe the anger in my chest. I think about everything he said... *I love you, Gina Grace. I can't live without you. I'm a jealous motherfucker when it comes to you...*

I'm lost in the memory of his sapphire blue eyes, full lips, dark hair, when my phone buzzes in my hand.

HADDY

Did you forgive him?

My thumbs twitch. I'm about to reply to her when another text lights up my phone.

OWEN

Just catching up on my messages… Sorry
for the delay—I was in a bad place and
needed to get my head straight.

My heart beats faster, and I press my lips together. Lying back on my bed, I tap a quick reply.

GINA

I think you've apologized enough for one
weekend.

OWEN

But you never said if you accepted.

Holding my phone, I look at the clock. It's after eleven, and the red roses he gave me are opening in the crystal vase where I put them. *These say I love you…*

My phone buzzes again.

OWEN

John received Kendall's message. He'd like
to see her now if she's still waiting for him.

Energy squeezes my chest, and I roll onto my stomach tapping out a quick reply.

GINA

She's still waiting.

Gray dots float and disappear. Then they reappear… then they're gone.

I set my phone aside, resting my cheek on my hand as I wait for his answer. My eyes close, and I imagine him going home to Eureka, talking to his dad about me. I wonder what they said.

I don't realize I've fallen asleep until a warm hand touches my arm, and I open my eyes.

28

OWEN

The sound of a Shania Twain song punctuated by long, low dog howls draws me to the back patio where I find my daughter sitting outside the cage in her PJs holding a small speaker in her hand.

Inside, Ladybird is lifting her head and howling along to her favorite song. At least I think it's her favorite. She sure seems to enjoy howling in time to it.

Spanky simply watches her, as if that racket is the most beautiful sound he's ever heard. I get it. I'm entranced by everything Gina does. She's smart, thoughtful, caring, beautiful, sexy...

My dick tightens just thinking the words. Watching her leave, it was hard not to follow her out the door. It was hard not to pull her into my arms and hold her, never letting her go.

I want her here with me, joining my family, my life. I want her in my bed.

Speaking of bed, I clear those lusty thoughts away and focus on the task at hand.

"Bedtime, Maddie," I call to my daughter. "Come on—you've got school tomorrow, and the neighbors need to sleep."

Standing, she crawls into the cage to pet and hug both of the dogs before crawling out again and taking my hand.

"They're doggie besties," she says, looking back at them.

I smile, giving her hand a gentle squeeze. "Aunt Heather said you made a new friend at school today. What's her name?"

"Charlotte!" she cries, and her walking turns into happy skipping. "She loves hockey just like me, and she was so excited when I told her my dad plays for the Champions!"

"Maybe she can go to a game with you sometime."

"Yeah!" She pumps her arms as I turn the blankets back on her bed.

We decorated her room the same way as her room in Eureka to help her feel at home. Tiny fairies are scattered all over the wallpaper, flying on little wings and holding star-tipped wands. Her bed has a sheer mosquito net hanging from a circle attached to the ceiling.

I move it aside so I can sit beside her, leaning against a pillow. She snuggles into my side holding Zander, and I open the book she's chosen for us tonight. Of course, it's a Junie B. Jones title.

"My name is Junie B. Jones," I begin. "The *B* stands for Beatrice. Except I don't like Beatrice..."

The chapter is filled with a lot of little-girl antics that make my daughter laugh—and me as well. When we reach the end, her eyes are closing, and I put the book on her side table.

Placing my hand on her head, I kiss her crown. "I'm glad you like it here, and you're having fun and making friends. I miss you when I'm on the road, but I think about you all the time."

"It's okay, Daddy." She pats my arm. "You're busy beating all those other teams and doing hat tricks."

"It's true." Her little-girl innocence makes me smile, but I have something else on my mind. "What do you think about Miss Gina?"

"She's my best new friend. She teaches me all about dogs and how to walk with Peepee, and she even said I could walk in the dog show... after you said it was okay."

She's getting so excited, I'm almost sorry I asked. At the same time, I'm deeply satisfied by her reply.

"I love her, too," I say. "Is that okay?"

Her small lips press and twist before breaking into a big smile. "Yes!" she nods emphatically. "She makes you smile... just like that." Maddie points her small finger at my face, and I realize I *am* smiling. "Maybe she could come here and stay with us, and you could share your room with her like LB does with Spanky."

My brows rise. "How would you feel about *that*?"

"I like it." She presses her lips together, nodding. "Then I'd have a mommy here on Earth like all my friends do, and not just one up in heaven."

My throat aches, and I know that feeling. I had it myself when I was her age, a little boy without a mom. I remember how happy I was when Dad told me Britt was going to join our family, and knowing my daughter feels similarly is a huge weight off my chest.

Leaning down, I give her another hug. "I love you, Shortcake."

She squeezes me back, whispering, "I love you, too, Daddy."

GINA

She's still waiting.

I START to reply to her text, then I shove my phone into my pocket and walk out of my bedroom. I make a brief stop by Maddie's room to be sure she's asleep, then I go downstairs to Heather's room to let her know I'm going out for a bit.

She looks up from the book she's reading to give me a wink. "Don't feel like you have to come home tonight, Bubba."

A hissing noise slides through my lips, but I let it go, shaking my head. The anticipation surging in my veins cancels out any minor irritation.

That little blue pouch is still in my pocket, and I'm glad I was able to have that conversation with Maddie tonight. Knowing she's onboard makes all of this so much better.

Waiting was the right thing to do. The timing wasn't right earlier. I needed to talk to my daughter, and it was clear Gina wasn't going to forgive me that easily. I deserved it, which is why I suggested she cut my hair.

It melted the walls. It brought us closer. It showed her how much I need her, and I love having her fingers in my hair. I love having her touch me, take care of me... even if it was fucking torture not to be able to hold her, kiss her, tell her all the things on my mind.

Then our dogs solidified everything. Those crazy canines have known since the day they met this family belongs together.

Gina likes to say dogs are smarter than people. I'm not sure I agree with that, but they do seem to pick up on things quicker.

Now I'm standing on the sidewalk in front of her house. Looking up, I see the light is on in her room, and I jog up the steps, entering the code on the lock and slipping off my boots inside the door.

Soft, yellow light comes from a glowing cube in the corner, and the flowers surrounding her form a fragrant garden. She's the enchanting creature in the center, holding my heart, my soul, my future, everything in the palm of that slim hand tucked beneath her cheek.

Stepping closer, I notice her eyes are closed. I take a knee, and I see she's asleep.

For a moment, I drink her in. She's so beautiful, her soft hair curling on her cheek. I'm torn between needing to touch her and wanting to let her rest.

With a soft inhale, she moves, blinking her eyes open, and when she sees me, she jumps awake, then her face relaxes with a smile.

Reaching up to me, she whispers, "You came."

"You were waiting." I lean down, capturing her soft lips with mine.

Her hands rise, fingers threading in the sides of my hair, and I place both my hands on each side of her pillow. She reaches higher, wrapping her arms around my neck, and I move my hand behind her head, lifting her so I can kiss her deeper.

I'm lost in the minty taste of her lips, the feel of her warm breath against my cheek, her cherry scent, her soft body in my arms.

I ache to possess her, but I manage to pull back so I can say all the things I couldn't say before.

I help her move to a sitting position with her back against the pillows, and I'm on one knee at her bedside, holding her hand in mine.

With her other hand, she reaches out to comb my hair behind my ear. "What is it?"

I lift my chin, meeting her eyes. "I need to tell you the truth."

Her brow quirks, but she nods. "Okay."

"The truth is I love you, but not only that... I want you with everything I have, with all my soul. I was afraid at first, but I'm not afraid now. Now I know what I want. I want you. I was jealous because I'll do everything in my power to protect and keep what's mine."

As I speak her expression changes from confused to smiling to blinking fast as she reaches for me. "What are you saying?"

"I'm saying you're my home, Gina. You're comfort and love and everything I want in my life. As I flew back from Eureka, I did a lot of things, but the most important thing I did was call your dad."

Her pretty green eyes widen. "You called *my* dad? Why?"

"I wanted to apologize to him for not being able to ask him in person."

Her full lips part. "Ask him... what?"

I slide my hand down the side of her cheek to her neck, placing my thumb on that small cleft in her chin. "If it was okay to make you my wife. He said he'd give me a pass this one time, but if I ever did anything to hurt you, he'd find me."

"Owen..." Tears are in her eyes, but she's smiling so big my throat aches.

I reach into my pocket and take out the blue pouch, then I take out the ring.

"Will you marry me, Gina Grace? I love you... and just like your devoted dog, I need to be beside you always. I burn for you. I want you to be my wife, my life partner, my soul mate. It's always been you."

She nods rapidly, faster with every word as tears spill onto her cheeks. "Yes, Owen, yes." Reaching forward, she puts her hands on my shoulders. "I love you!"

I take her left hand in mine and slide the ring onto her third finger. It's a round diamond set in platinum with seven small diamonds on each side arranged to look like paw prints.

"Haddy helped me with the size. I tried to find something that captured your personality. This seemed perfect."

"Oh my gosh!" She holds it up, turning her hand side to side. "I adore it—it has paw prints!"

"Maddie also gave me the thumbs up to ask you…"

"You asked *Maddie*?" Her forehead crinkles. "When?"

"Tonight, when I was putting her to bed." I rise off my knee to sit beside her on the bed. "I wanted to tell you all of this earlier, when I got back into town, but I think you were still mad at me."

"I'm not mad now." She scoots closer, pulling her body flush with mine. "I'm so happy."

My hands slide from her waist, under the hem of her shirt. I place my palms flat against the warm skin of her bare back, moving them higher as I lift it over her head.

"I've missed you." Dipping my chin, I kiss the top of her shoulder, the side of her neck. "It's so hard to be away from you. I'm like Spanky. I need to be with my woman."

Her nose wrinkles as she lifts the bottom of my shirt. "I thought you hated a cage."

"It's not a cage if you're with the person you love." I whip the garment over my head, then lean forward to pull her lips with mine. "Didn't you say cages were safe spaces?"

"Mm-hmm..." She nods, chasing my kisses with her own. "Are you saying you'd live in a cage with me?"

"Yes." I seal my mouth to hers, swiping my tongue inside to curl with hers, moving her body onto my lap in a straddle, and she exhales a soft noise that registers straight to my hardening cock.

Flexing my arms around her back, I hold her bare chest against mine, loving the feel of her softness against my strength.

I look around the room. "We've got to pack you up."

"What are you saying?" The words slip from her lips on a sigh, and she presses her lips to my shoulder.

I quickly lean down to kiss her. "You're moving into my house. I want you in my bed. Every night."

"What about Maddie?" Her lips are like brands against my skin.

"It was her idea."

She stretches higher in my arms, placing her hands on my neck as she traces her lips along my jaw. "I'll move in with you when we're married."

I dip my chin, capturing her mouth again with mine. "Are you afraid I won't go through with it? You're wrong. I'm ready to marry you right now. Right here."

"No..." Her mouth is on my shoulder, and I feel the light sting of her teeth as she places her lips on my skin and sucks.

I exhale a groan, knowing it's going to leave a mark. My cock is hard, and I grip her ass in my hands, sliding her body forward and back to ease the ache. Her mouth breaks away with a moan.

"Why not, then?" My hands trace her sides, lifting her breasts and sliding my thumbs over her taut nipples.

"I can't leave Maverick here alone." Her fingers thread in

my hair as I bend down to kiss and pull one between my lips before moving to the other. "He'll be so sad," she sighs.

"He'll manage." I lower her onto the mattress on her back, kissing my way lower to her navel. "He's a big boy."

"We can spend the night together, but I can't move out." Her hips lift as I pull her PJ pants down the length of her thighs.

"Sure, you can." Hooking my fingers in the sides of her underwear, I have them gone just as fast. "I'll show you how easy it is."

Covering her pussy with my mouth, I sweep my tongue inside to circle her clit firmly. Her hips rise, and exhales a loud moan. My palms hold her soft ass, and I feast on her as her fingers curl into my hair.

"Owen..." It's an urgent cry, and she rocks her hips in time with the movement of my tongue.

Faster and faster. Her fingers flex and tighten, pulling my face closer. Her moans turn to chants. She's softly swearing in a way that makes me crazy. It's like we're sharing a dirty secret about how much she wants to fuck me.

I circle again and again until she breaks with a loud sound, shuddering against my face in quick, jerky movements.

"Oh, God, stop," she laughs, doing her best to roll away from me. "I'm too sensitive."

I have her firmly in my grasp, and I kiss the side of her hip, making my way higher to her belly, then her waist.

Placing my hands on each side of her in the bed, I hover over her body, looking down at her flushed and beautiful. "I need to fuck you now, my beautiful wife."

A lazy smile curls her sexy lips. "You say that like it's already happened."

I lean down to kiss her. "In my mind, it happened ages

ago. Somewhere around the first time you looked up at me with those bright eyes. The first time I heard you laugh. The first time you hugged my daughter."

She exhales a sigh, and I kiss her again, rising onto my knees. I unbutton my jeans, sliding them down my hips, ready to plunge into her sweet, slippery depths.

I lift a leg to remove them when her cool fingers curl around my hot erection. My forehead tightens, and I can't move as she pulls my tip into her mouth.

"Gina..." I place my palm gently against the side of her cheek, doing my best to hold on as my vision tunnels.

Round, green eyes blink up at me, her lips surrounding my dick, and her head bobs as she pulls me deeper, all the way to the back of her throat.

"Jesus..." I groan, my fingers curling in her hair. "That feels so good."

My hips rock forward, and I can't fight the insane pleasure radiating through my body. Both my hands are in her hair, and I drop my head back, letting her own me.

Her palms are on my bare ass, and her fingers curl, fingernails cutting into my flesh as she pulls me closer, deeper.

Orgasm races through my pelvis, into my thighs. I want to stop this. I want to come inside her beautiful body, but I can't fight it. It's too much.

Pleasure drives me forward. Her eagerness drives me mad. I sweep her hair back, looking down as she sucks my tip, pumping my shaft with her hand. Then her fingernails tickle my balls, and I break.

"Fuck..." I groan, unable to move as my dick jerks and pulses.

She holds my ass, and I feel her swallow again and again. My eyes squeeze shut, and I'm out of my body, flying through the stars as orgasm shakes me, pulling my muscles forward.

I'm still coming, and she's not letting me go. My hands smooth her hair, her soft skin, until I slowly regain control.

The temporary blindness leaves my eyes, and I exhale a shuddering breath. "Fuck, Gina... damn, that was good."

She smiles, rising higher to kiss my stomach. She pauses at my chest, tracing her tongue around a tight nipple, and I groan, cupping her face in my hands. Leaning down, I kiss the side of her neck, her ear.

She straightens, looking into my eyes. "John and Kendall have nothing on Owen and Gina."

I place my forehead against hers, chuckling with my eyes closed. "From now on, it's only Owen and Gina."

"Aw..." She makes a pretend pout. "I kind of like our alter-egos."

My thumbs slide gently across the tops of her cheeks. "Whatever you want, my beautiful girl. Just as long as everyone knows, Gina belongs to Owen."

"And Owen is Gina's."

"Forever."

29

GINA

"That's great, Saxon. Just hold the leash up, but don't jerk it. Cheese knows what to do. He's done this a hundred times."

I'm standing back with my arms crossed, watching the Beagle's gait and our stocky defenseman leading him around the rink. It's our one and only rehearsal before the Pucks and Pups charity show next week.

We were able to talk to all the guys about it and even recruit some of my dog show pals at our Friendsgiving dinner to help prepare.

Haddy's been working overtime, and she really seems to enjoy being busy. Lisa is a pro as always, along with Carla, who handles the foster dogs.

"This is such a great idea." Carla leans into my ear, whispering as I watch them. "I wouldn't be surprised if we don't have all the foster dogs placed by the end of the night."

"I wouldn't be surprised if you get a waiting list of people wanting more." I wave as Sax goes to his spot in the lineup. "Great job Sax and Cheese!"

"That dog's name is *Cheese*?" Haddy laughs, jogging up to me. "Sorry, I'm late. I had to feed Lucy and pass her off to her daddy."

"His name is actually *Say it with Cheese*, but Mav's right. What dog is going to come to that?"

"Well, 'Sax and Cheese' is hilarious," she replies, bumping my hip.

I look up to see who's next, and my chest squeezes when I see my gorgeous fiancé standing at the starting line, holding the leash for Ladybird.

"Ready, Owen?" Even I can hear the change in my voice when I tell him what to do. It's way less business and way more swoon.

In addition to catching up *horizontally*, we've been spending a lot of time working on the right speed for LB's gait. Turns out, it's a jog. Good thing Owen Stone is in great shape physically. (Internal *rawr*.)

When he gets the cue, he lifts the leash and takes off, looking like a professional dog handler. Ladybird actually seems to remember all the things we've been drilling for the past few weeks. She lifts her legs, trotting alongside her owner like she's been doing it as long as Spanky has.

She's not completely up to AKC standards, but for the purposes of our charity show and the people who'll be watching, she could be a purebred show dog.

I watch them make the large oval, around the tables, past the ribbons, and slow to a halt in front of Carla and me. I look over at my friend, and her eyes are bright, her lips parted.

Owen is sex on a stick. His long hair hangs in shiny

waves off his face, and the T-shirt he's wearing is losing its battle to contain his muscles.

His chest rises and falls as he catches his breath, and a proud smile curls those full, sexy lips, revealing a deep dimple in the side of his cheek.

Don't forget his straight white teeth, a rarity in this sport, and the possessive glint in his sapphire-blue eyes when he looks at me.

"That was perfect," I say, smiling up at him, a little breathless myself.

"Really?" His brow quirks, almost like he's surprised. "You don't think I need to do it again?"

"I wouldn't mind seeing it again." Carla grabs my arm, and I laugh, giving her a nudge with my elbow.

"Easy, girl. He's mine."

She shakes her head. "I only meant, if you'd *like* to go again, that would be okay. It's hard to believe you've never done this before. You seem so... skilled."

"Is it my turn, Mama G?" Maddie yells from across the arena where she stands at the starting line with Princess Petunia on a leash.

A big smile splits my cheeks at the sight of them. "It sure is, sweetie. Show me what you've got!"

My helper says their names, and Maddie's posture straightens. She lifts her chin, and the little dog at her side trots in perfect time with her steps.

Maddie knows the exact speed for the toy poodle, and Peepee's fluffy cinnamon legs flurry as she scampers around the ring like she was born to do it.

"Look at her go," Lisa says at my side. "I think that little girl's a natural handler."

"They're so cute," Haddy coos. "Who knew my little Patsy could walk that way?"

"I did," I say with a shrug. "Lisa judges toy divisions all the time."

"Is she a winner, Lisa?" Haddy leans forward, and my friend gives her a thumbs up.

"They're going to be the finale," I explain, examining the list. "The crowd will love seeing the two of them after all the big guys. Mav, you're up!"

"I think the crowd's going to love seeing all the guys," Carla says under her breath as my cousin steps up to the line, holding Spanky's leash.

"Yeah, he has that effect on everyone," I tease. "Ready?"

They give the signal, and Mav does a flawless impersonation of the John Michael Higgins character from the movie *Best in Show*. His arm is extended, his pinky raised, and his hips swish side to side.

"He's so funny!" Maddie bounces on her toes, clapping.

"Well, darn," Carla groans beside me. "All the hot ones are gay."

"Oh, no!" I hold my nose, snorting a laugh. "Mav's totally straight."

"A little too straight if you ask me." Haddy rolls her eyes.

"Oh, is he an *eff*-boy?" Her lip wrinkles, and she lowers her voice so Maddie doesn't hear.

"No, not that!" My cousin shakes her head. "He's actually very respectful of women. He's just... a lot of man."

"I don't mind a lot of man." Carla's eyebrow arches, and I just shake my head.

Even pretending to be gay, Mav has the ladies falling at his feet.

Donovan, on the other hand, looked fantastic earlier, walking with my favorite borzoi Haze. I'm pretty sure the fellow he brought with him to Owen's housewarming party and who also joined us at Friendsgiving might be someone special. I hope so. He's such a nice man.

Mav finishes with a flourish, doing a dramatic bow right in front of us while Spanky stacks beside him like a pro.

"Very impressive," I say, checking off the last name on the list. "Now bring on the show."

SHOW DAY IS as hectic as a real Continental Dog Show.

The hockey rink has been transformed into an enormous venue with thick velvet curtains, podiums for the dogs to stand on while they're being evaluated, and smooth turf for the handlers to walk the dogs around the perimeter.

Backstage, the foster dogs are jumping and barking, while the show dogs are waiting, sitting or standing, calmly looking around like it's just another day at the office.

Haddy runs around making sure the guys have their numbers, and I walk through the crowd of six-foot-something men in designer suits holding dogs on leashes like I've died and gone to dog-lady heaven.

The truth is, I only have eyes for one sexy handler, and he's on one knee beside his daughter, helping her straighten her dress and giving her what appears to be a pep-talk.

"You've practiced so much with Mama G, just relax and let your muscle memory do the work." His voice is low, and I *love* the way they call me Mama G now.

I didn't even have to ask them. It's like Maddie had that nickname locked and loaded and was just waiting for her cue to start using it.

"Everything okay over here?" I pause as Owen rises to give me a quick kiss on the lips, sending sparkles through my chest.

"We've got a case of nerves." He tilts his head in his daughter's direction.

"Oh no..." I look down to see Maddie sitting on the turf in her raw silk gown, holding Peepee on her lap.

"It's okay, Peep," she tells the little dog. "Everybody gets scared walking out in front of a big crowd for the first time."

I'm in a beige skirt and blazer, but I take a knee beside her. "You doing okay, honey?"

"I'm okay," she nods, holding Peepee up to show me. "She's worried about walking in front of all those people for the first time. She's afraid she might trip and fall and show her underwear and be super embarrassed."

"I see..." I don't point out her dog isn't wearing underwear. "You know what I like to do after a big show?" She shakes her head, and I reach out to hold her hand. "I like to go home and get in my comfy clothes and have a facial."

"With real cucumbers on your eyes?" Her eyes widen.

"Always, and we can make pigs in blankets and watch a funny Christmas movie."

"Like *Elf*?" She's on her feet now, putting her hand on my shoulder.

"Whichever funny movie you choose." I straighten, taking her hand in mine. "We've just got to get this walk done, and then it's party time. Okay?"

"Okay!" She bends down to pet the toy poodle. "Ready to walk, Peep?"

The little dog hops around, doing her squeak-barks. She's such a cute pooch. I'm smiling down at them when a large hand covers my shoulder, pulling me against his rock-hard chest for a hug.

"Is it wrong that I want to sneak you behind that curtain and show my appreciation right now?" Owen's low voice in my ear makes my core clench.

He leans down to kiss the side of my neck, and the scuff of his beard flushes my entire body.

"Just doing my job." I lift my face to give him a quick kiss. "I've got to check on the others. You all set here?"

"All set." His pretty eyes meet mine, and they're so full of love.

My thumb automatically goes to the shining engagement ring on my finger, and I'm so happy.

It all came true. My vision, Heather's reading. Hope has found me. There's no more fear. We've won, and we've healed each other's hearts in the process.

Haddy is calling for the guys to line up in order, starting with Donovan and Haze. They're the leaders, all polished and shiny.

They're followed by Saxon and Cheese, Hancock and a small foster dog named Rory, Akers with another foster dog, all the way down to Owen with Ladybird. Mav is the last player to go, walking Spanky, and Maddie will be the fun finale walking with Peepee.

"I think it's really cool that we were able to get actual AKC judges to come out for this," Lisa says as I help her straighten the numbers on the guys' upper arms. "It's like the dogs are winning legitimate awards."

"I can't believe they agreed to do it for free," I quip.

The music begins, and the color commentator opens by thanking everyone for attending the first Pucks and Pups charity dog show. I walk down the lineup giving the guys and the dogs one final inspection before I'll sneak out and sit in the stands to watch.

"Are you going to stay with me?" Maddie looks up at me when I reach her.

"Yeah, MG," Mav teases. "You can't leave us hanging back here."

"I can't?" I pretend to argue, and Maddie's brown eyes widen. "I'm teasing. Of course, I'll stay if you want me to."

Her little body visibly relaxes, and I put my hand on her back, rubbing it in a circle. She puts her arm around my waist, resting her head on my hip, and we step forward as each pair exits through the curtain to do their promenade.

Out in the arena, we hear the crowds cheering and blowing air horns.

"Sounds like they're having a good time," Owen says, leaning closer to me. "I hadn't considered the possibility of falling and showing everyone my underwear before now."

A laugh snorts through my nose, and I rest my head against his broad chest. "That would be some trick."

We take another step, and it's his turn to go. Our eyes meet, and he takes a deep breath, eyes wide.

"Just pretend you're on razor thin ice skates facing off against a six-foot-four, three-hundred-pound enforcer," I tease.

"Now that I can do." He does a finger gun at me, and I shake my head.

The announcer calls his name, and they step through the curtain. Maddie and I hold hands as we peek out to see her dad jogging Ladybird around the rink.

Fans are on their feet, screaming and clapping as they pass, and all the other teammates are in their places, smiling and holding their show poses.

Lisa stands in the center with two other judges I know from the circuit. They're making notes and leaning in to speak in each other's ears.

"He did great," I say, looking down at Maddie.

Just then, a loud *AHH!* yells from behind us. We jump, turning around to see Mav on his butt on the turf holding his leg and rocking back and forth.

"Maverick!" We run over to where he's groaning. "What happened? Are you okay?"

"I was playing with Spanky, and my foot got caught in a fold in the carpet. I think I broke my ankle."

"What!" My eyes widen. "No! You can't... not during hockey season!"

"I don't know..." He looks down, still grimacing. "It might not be broken, but I definitely can't walk on it. You'll have to show Spanky."

"Me?" I straighten, looking from him to my dog, standing and waiting. "I'm not a hockey player. The crowd is waiting to see *you*! You're the star!"

"We don't have a choice, Gigi. You have to do it."

"We'll just tell them you're injured. Spanky doesn't have to be in the show."

"Yes, he does," Mav argues. "Just look at his face. He's so eager."

"He always looks like that," I argue. "He probably spotted somebody wearing a towel."

"No, no! You have to walk him, Mama G," Maddie holds my arm in both her hands, shaking it. "Spanky wants to walk like Ladybird did. They're besties."

"And you gave him his special trim just for the occasion." Mav meets my eyes, pleading. "Don't let our boy down."

"Good grief, Maverick," I grumble, but he's already up, standing on one foot and pinning his number on my sleeve. "I haven't practiced."

"You've walked in a bazillion dog shows. Just get out there and give 'em the ole razzle dazzle."

"I'm not a stripper," I mutter, shaking my head. "Come on, Spanks, let's do this."

Smoothing my hands down my skirt, I move my hair behind my shoulders. It's true, Spanky's continental pom poms have grown out beautifully, and I spent last night giving him the perfect trim. Thankfully Ladybird didn't "help" this time.

He's flawless as the announcer reads the unexpected change in the lineup, and we start to walk. I brace for the disappointment in the crowd, but instead, I'm happily surprised by all the cheers and air horns.

The noise is a little overwhelming because of the size of the crowd, but my heart rises, and I can't help a smile surrounded by so much support as we walk the perimeter.

Spanky is undeterred by the noise. He does his very best gait, and we pass the judging table, garnering a few nods, then take our place beside Owen and Ladybird at the end of the row.

The crowd dies down, and the judges confer in the center of the space.

"Good work," Owen stage-whispers. "You didn't fall and show your underwear."

"I'm not wearing any," I whisper back, and he freezes.

A naughty grin spreads across his lips. "Why didn't you tell me sooner?"

I shake my head. "It wasn't for that. I didn't want VPL." His nose wrinkles, and I translate. "Visible panty line."

The announcer calls Maddie's name as the very special finale, and the crowd is on their feet cheering, whistling, clapping, and making all the noise as Maddie walks out with Peepee.

They're absolutely adorable. Maddie holds her head high, and Princess Petunia does the same as they walk all around the stadium. If she's still nervous, I can't tell at all.

My cheeks hurt from smiling, and my eyes mist with unshed tears. "I'm so proud of her."

Owen reaches over to cover my hand with his, giving it a squeeze. "Thank you for including her in this."

"Of course!" I blink up at him. "I could never leave her out."

She finishes her walk, coming to stand on the other side of me, and the little dog assumes her perfect stack, looking up at the stands like she's so proud as well.

The judges make their way down the line, observing and occasionally stepping forward to check a dog's muzzle or feel its shoulders.

Haddy and I decided to award five prizes, first and second place pedigreed, first and second place non-pedigreed, and Best in Show. I'm already doing the math in my head, picking out who should win the awards. Spanky is a shoo-in to win something, even if he is my dog.

I'm just not sure how much sentiment will play into their decisions for the foster dogs, and I don't know what they might base their decision on when it comes to the show dogs. All of them are first place winners, with Spanky being the only one who's never had a Best in Show.

The announcer comes on the mic to let us know it's time for the awards.

"We have a surprise for all you dog lovers out there," he says. "Since this event is being overseen and certified by American Kennel Club judges, the results will go on the record as official wins for these special dogs."

My eyebrows rise, and I look up at Owen. "I've never heard of such a thing."

"I think it's nice." He shrugs, but something about the way he says it, the look in his eyes makes me suspicious.

"What do you know?" I ask, looking around until I spot Haddy standing with the judges, making a note in the official book.

"It looks like they're ready to call it," he dodges, putting his arm around me, and pulling me close to his side.

I frown, looking from him to them and back. "We really should be standing with our dogs."

"Our dogs are standing with each other." He nods at the two of them standing side by side.

Maddie walks over to my other side and puts her arm around my waist, resting her head against my side like she's started doing more and more frequently.

I like it a lot, and I put my arm around her, holding her close as well.

The male judge I've only worked with a few times walks down the line, motioning to the foster dogs. "I'd like to see the Chiweenie and the Shihtzuranian, please."

Hancock and Akers step out with their dogs, and a ripple of laughter rolls across the crowd at the sight of the two big guys walking tiny pooches. I confess, that was my goal.

The female judge walks over to our side, slowly making her way down the row. "I'd like to see the toy poodle, the borzoi, and the standard poodle.

I squeeze Maddie's hand as we take our dogs forward. I'm pretty sure I know how this is going to go when the judge gives us the motion to gait. We all circle the center table, and they call it.

"That's the order: first, second, Best in Show!"

The entire arena is on their feet, cheering and blowing airhorns, and for a moment, I'm confused.

"What just happened?" I stop, looking all around as Heather, Haddy, Owen, and Maverick all come running into the center of the ring to surround me.

"You won Best in Show!" Haddy puts her hands on my shoulders, looking me straight in the eyes. "You did it!"

"I don't understand…" I also don't understand why my eyes are filling with tears.

"Spanky's Best in Show!" Mav scoops me around the waist, lifting me off my feet and doing a little spin. "You won!"

"I thought you broke your ankle?" I frown, pushing out of his arms. "You faked it… That's why you made me stay backstage!"

"You're supposed to scream with joy," he replies. "I know you know how the movie ends."

"You won, Mama G!" Small arms go around my waist, giving me a squeeze.

It makes me laugh. "Were you in on this, too? Were you even nervous?"

"Congrats, babe." Owen puts his arms around me, leaning down to kiss my temple. "I'm sorry LB screwed it up for you last time, but I'm glad we were able to make it right."

My forehead wrinkles, and I swallow hard as tears leak out of my eyes. "You all planned this for me?"

"I made a few calls." Haddy shrugs like it's all so obvious. "I asked how we could get Spanky a Best in Show honor for real. He might be a rascal, but he deserves it. And so do you."

"Y'all!" My nose is hot, and I can't stop the tears filling my eyes. "What am I going to do with all of you?"

"Oh, you know," Mav pokes my side. "Just keep being awesome and supplying us with pets."

The group closes around us, and I can't remember when I've been happier, more at home, and so surrounded by family. I guess it was the last time I was in Newhope, at Cooters & Shooters, watching my sweet cousin marry the man of her dreams.

Looking up at Owen, I smile so big. His face breaks with a smile, and he leans down to kiss me. I guess we're next.

30

OWEN

"They thought Ladybird was a show dog," Haddy complains, leaning on the table in Gina's house reading through the judges' notes. "That's why they didn't pick her for the non-pedigreed group."

"It's really okay," I tell her, holding a box of Gina's things.

I've finally convinced her Maverick will be just fine living in this big house all by himself—her words. She's trying to find him a dog to keep him company, and I'm moving all her things out today before she has a chance to change her mind.

"I was just glad I jogged her all the way to our spot without falling," I add with a laugh.

Haddy's lips poke out with a frown. "But Ladybird did a great job, and she worked so hard. She deserved to be recognized."

I chuckle, reaching out to shake her shoulder. "We had fun. We raised a bunch of money for the children's hospital. That was the point."

"I can't believe I'm helping you move all this stuff out," Mav grumbles, stomping down the stairs. "At the end of the day, it means I'm stuck here all alone."

"You could always recruit another roommate," I suggest.

Gina stops in the middle of carrying her box down the stairs. Her shoulders drop, and I know what's coming.

"Maverick!" Her face is full of consternation, and my eyes narrow.

It's taken me weeks of convincing her he'll be fine. He's almost thirty. Still, she worries about him. Then she tells me I don't understand. They all grew up together in Newhope, in each other's houses all the time, walking to school together, sneaking off to hockey games together...

Apparently, Mav's mother didn't know he played hockey. She wanted him to play a "safe sport" like golf—even though his dad was a star wide receiver for New York.

Eureka's got nothing on Newhope.

"Come on, Gina," I say firmly, turning to the door where a very pretty petite blonde is standing, holding up her hand as if she'll knock.

"Hello?" Her voice is high, but full.

It reminds me of one of those Broadway singers I've heard interviewed before, like it sounds delicate, but you know she can belt out a song on cue. Auntie Monay taught me how to spot this.

"Hi, there." I step forward still holding the box of Gina's things.

"I'm sorry..." She frowns, looking from the box up to me. "I was trying to find Hayden Bradford? This is the last address I have for her... I'm so sorry if she moved, and I didn't know—"

"Dove?" Mav trots down the stairs to stand beside me.

His entire demeanor has changed. Gone is the poor-me

routine, and now he's the hockey star who's on billboards all over town. He gives her his megawatt smile, complete with dimple, and I roll my eyes.

"Oh, hi, Mav." The woman waves her hand, seeming not at all impressed by his smile or his swagger. "Thank goodness you're here. I thought this was going to get *really* embarrassing for a minute."

My brow shoots up. I've watched that smile send panties flying from coast to coast, but not today.

"What are you doing here?" His voice is quiet, almost like he's in church.

My brow furrows, and I can't help thinking... *Who is this person?*

Dove steps through the doorway, looking all around. "Is Haddy here?"

Haddy comes around the corner, and as soon as their eyes meet, everything changes. The two women go off like bottle rockets. They wave their hands over their heads, squealing and running to each other. When they meet, they hug and jump up and down laughing.

"Oh my gosh!" Dove cries, falling back with a loud cackle. "That was the scariest moment of my *life!*"

"You are so crazy!" Haddy holds Dove's arms. "You're the only person I know who would travel from Louisiana to LA and barge into a house hoping for the best."

Dove lifts her chin, closing her eyes, and adopting a super-exaggerated southern accent. "I always rely on the kindness of strangers."

Haddy laughs, pulling her in for another hug. "I'm so happy to see you! How long has it been? What are you doing here?"

"Well, I'll tell you." She puts her hand on Haddy's arm, and they walk to the living room. "I'm right at the end of my thesis, and I need to do a semester studying with the foremost scholar in Armillaria root rot."

"Dr. Smithfield," Haddy says, nodding. "He's the best mycologist in the nation."

My eyes have been on Maverick this whole time, watching the hearts in his eyes get bigger and bigger. I'm pretty sure I hear him sigh as the two women discuss mycology and fungi and the life cycle of the North American peach tree.

I get it. It's fun listening to beautiful, smart women saying words I don't understand like it's the most normal thing in the world.

Actually, now that I think about it, my stepmom Britt was a forensic photographer. She was my first introduction to the fact that women can be beautiful and smart and really, really interested in science. It's fucking cool.

"Maverick!" Haddy calls to him from where the two of them are sitting on the couch. "Dove can stay here with you next semester!" She bounces around to clutch her friend's hands. "The entire upstairs is empty, and Mav will be gone all the time playing hockey. I'm right across the street, and Gina's right down the block. It's perfect! Problem solved!"

"Oh..." Dove gives my smitten teammate a worried look. "Only if it's not too much trouble. I don't want Mav to feel inhibited with me in the house. I won't narc you out, Mav. You can go on living your life like I'm not even here."

"No... You won't... I won't..." Mav shakes his head like he's waking up from a dream. "I mean, yeah, absolutely you can stay here."

I'm trying to figure out if I'm the only one who sees how he's reacting to all of this.

"Oh my gosh, Gina!" Dove's eyes widen as my girl comes down the stairs again.

"Dove?" Gina's voice rises. "What the heck are you doing here?"

Dove hops off the couch, and Gina shoves the box she's holding into Mav's hands.

They meet in a hug, laughing and leaning side to side, similar to the greeting she gave Haddy.

"You are just as beautiful as you ever were," Gina laughs.

"Shut up," Dove cries. "Just look at your gorgeous hair! I want to shave it all off and put it on my head."

They laugh more, and I can tell this is a good, old friend. If I weren't holding a box, I'd have my arms crossed smiling and watching the floor show.

"I'm only here for the weekend," Dove explains. "Then I've got to get back to the peach farm for Christmas. Mom and Dad would pitch a fit if I missed any of the festivities."

They walk back to join Haddy, and the three of them excitedly make plans for next semester. I look at Mav still watching with a look of wondrous confusion on his face.

I can't resist teasing him. "Pretty girl."

"Oh..." Mav straightens, clearing his throat and doing his best swagger. "Yeah, we've known Dove forever. She did pageant stuff with Haddy, and then her mom met my mom and it was all over."

"How so?"

"We'd go to the peach festival in Louisiana every June, then they'd come and visit us in Newhope every summer. We'd hang out at the beach and stuff. That kind of thing."

"You hook up with her?"

"No." He gives me a brief, irritated look before snatching the box he was carrying off the floor. "We're moving Gina today, right?"

"Are we? I thought you had objections."

"Dude. Don't try to pin it on me if you're having second

thoughts." He gives me the eye, and I lift my chin with a laugh.

"I couldn't be more sure if I tried. Just keep walking, pal."

Later that night, when all of my fiancée's things are moved into my house and we've had dinner and we've put my daughter to bed and we're sweaty and sated and holding each other in our arms, I lean down to kiss the top of her shoulder.

"I think your cousin has a thing for Dove Rhodes." My voice is low, and Gina tucks her chin before looking up at me with a smug grin.

"I've been saying that for years. Don't tell Mav we're onto him. He'll deny it til the cows come home."

A grin spreads across my cheeks, and I kiss her nose. "As long as it means you're here with me, he can deny it all he wants."

She gives me an adorable grin, her lips tilting to the side. "I still need to find him a dog. Maybe a goldendoodle. They're better indoor dogs than retrievers, and it's totally Mav's type."

"I want you to come home with me for Christmas." I lift my hand, smoothing it down her cheek and resting my thumb on her chin. "I know that's asking a lot, but I want you to meet my family. They're going to love you."

"Okay." Her nose wrinkles with her smile. "I guess it's only fair since you met all my family at Haddy's wedding."

She's so adorable. I pull her close, tracing the path of her freckles with my lips down to her cheeks.

For so long, I thought I'd never feel this way again. I thought if I loved someone with my whole heart this way, I was betraying what had gone before. I didn't know love could be a safe place, and as much as I want to protect Gina, her love protects me as well.

My daughter is safe and happy. The circle is forming. It's not a cage, it's a home, a shelter where we're all secure and free.

We're like the foster dogs Gina is always so proud of placing. We chose each other. It's how we're meant to be through time, through magic, forever.

EPILOGUE

GINA

"It's just a good thing I didn't know cynology was a field of study," Britt says, looking from me to the group of ladies sitting out on the back deck with us at Owen's parents' home. "I might never have married Aiden!"

"That's not how it works, Birgitte," her mother argues. "The universe put you and Aiden together on the day your father died. He's said many times he was there, and his heart connected with yours in that moment."

"Well, that can't be right," Britt counters. "Aiden married Owen's mother after all."

"And we know how that turned out." Gwen crosses her arms, smugly satisfied. "Aiden Stone should have trusted his instincts."

Britt leans forward to place her hand over mine. "Don't mind her, Gina. Mom and Aiden have bickered as long as I've known them."

I can't stop a smile curling my lips. It's a beautiful, cool

Christmas eve. Strings of lights are draped overhead, and a fire pit is in the center of this circle of women who have taken me in as one of their own.

Owen introduced me to all of them, but it's a lot of names to remember. What I do know is his dad has two brothers, and they all married Britt's best friends. I also know Heather is just like her mystical grandmother.

The moment I met Gwen, she scooped my hands into both of hers and looked deep into my eyes. I laughed nervously until she announced my aura was perfectly aligned with her grandson's, and we would have a long and happy life together.

"I could've told you that, Grammy G," Owen said, leaning down to kiss her cheek.

She caught his chin in her fingers, examining his teeth. "I see my spell is still strong."

Maddie is in heaven being the only grandchild. She skips around eating all the cookies and collecting early Christmas presents.

I happily watch her, remembering how much I loved growing up with all my family close. Every year, when Haddy would travel with her parents from LA to Newhope for Christmas, it felt like all was right with the world.

I have the same feeling sitting here now, holding Owen's mother's hand, listening to his grandmother talking about magic and fate and destiny.

Lifting my chin, I look up to where Owen is inside with his best friend Ryan, his father, and all three of his uncles standing around the bar. They're laughing and talking, and I notice his uncle Alex pouring tumblers of their family's signature bourbon.

By contrast, we're sharing glasses of Owen's aunt Piper's special "home brew." She said it's actually her mother's special moonshine recipe. She also told me her mother was a doomsday prepper for a while, and she had all types of ways to survive underground for long periods of time.

"Piper Stone, you know very well why your mother did all that prepping," Owen's grandmother Patricia fusses.

Piper is engrossed in a conversation with Owen's aunt Cass and his cousin Penelope, and she just waves at her mother-in-law. I'd like to know more about the real reason for her mother's prepping, but they leave me hanging on that one.

Maddie walks out to join us rubbing her eyes before climbing into my lap and putting her head on my shoulder.

"Are you tired, Shortcake?"

She shakes her head, poking out her lips. "I miss Spanky and Ladybird."

"Oh..." I rub small circles on her back. "You know Miss Carla is taking good care of them, right?"

She nods against my shoulder. "But LB won't get to sing Merry Christmas with me."

My lips press together in a grin. "I bet we can call in the morning and sing, and as long as they're together, they don't mind skipping the cross-country flight."

"I think it's time for bed." Britt stands, extending her hand to her granddaughter. "You're spending Christmas night with me and Pop. Let's hurry and get to sleep so Santa can bring you all your presents."

"Okay!" Maddie hops off my lap quickly, taking her grandmother's hand and walking with her into the house.

Britt looks back and gives me a wink. "Have a good night, Gina. I'm so happy you're joining our family."

"Me too," I say, watching her slip through the sliding doors.

"My granddaughter tells me your spirit animal is a dog." Gwen puts her hand in the crook of my arm.

"It's true." Heather walks up to hold my other arm as we enter the house. "She saw it on a psilocybin trip."

Gwen leans closer, her upper lip curled. "Did you barf?"

"I did the first time, but not this last time."

"Good." She nods. "Now tell me about the dog. A dog is a very good spirit animal. It means you're surrounded by protective love. It also represents loyalty."

"It was a Bichon Frisé."

"Very good," Gwen pats my arm. "A companionable, good-natured breed."

"It really is." I smile. "My mom said the dog that helped her go into labor when she was overdue with me looked like a Bichon."

"It's a full circle. A very good sign."

"What's a very good sign?" Owen joins us, smiling down as he takes me from his mystical gran.

"All of this, dear." Gwen holds up her hands, and he leans down to kiss her cheek. "It was all destined to be, the two of you finding your way to each other, led by your faithful dogs. Now I have to go. Bender's probably waiting up for me."

"Tell him I said Merry Christmas," Alex calls from the kitchen.

She waves, making her way to the door, and I lean my head against Owen as he pulls my back to his chest. I wonder what she would say about her grandson's psilocybin trip.

That one would probably blow her mind.

"Merry Christmas, Gina." His dad steps over, leaning down to give me a hug. "I'm really glad to meet you. You sure had this one all shook up."

"Thank you, sir," I say, feeling a bit shy. "The feeling is mutual."

Owen's dad is very handsome. He looks a lot like his son, only with the fine lines around his eyes and sprinkles of gray at his temples. He's not like my sheriff-dad, who is boisterous and huge, but I think they'd be good friends. My dad has a big personality, but I've never met a person who didn't like him.

After saying our goodnights, we walk down a short gravel path to an adorable little cottage with flower boxes on the windows.

Inside, it has a one-bedroom suite on the first floor off the kitchen, and another bedroom with a small bathroom is up a narrow flight of stairs.

Owen told me it's where his aunt Piper lived with his friend Ryan before she married his uncle Adam, and they all moved into his home.

"It's funny to stay here as an adult," he says, leading me to the first-floor suite. "Growing up, it was always Ryan's house."

"Eureka reminds me so much of Newhope," I sigh as he sits on the edge of the bed, pulling me between his legs. "All we needed was a dash of magic."

"From what I've seen and heard, you had your own kind of magic."

"We had hot peppers and *big* personalities," I laugh, threading my fingers in the sides of his hair.

"Are you sorry to be here instead of there?" His brow furrows, and I smooth the lines away with my fingertips, shaking my head no.

"We'll be with them next year, and we've got plenty of time to go back and forth."

His warm hands find the skin beneath my shirt, and he

slides them higher. "Speaking of back and forth..." He lifts the garment over my head, leaving me in only my lace bra. "How would you like to go back and forth on my dick?"

I lean forward, snorting a laugh. "That was terrible!"

"I think it was pretty good," he shrugs, laughing. "We don't have to worry about keeping it down with Maddie at her grandparents."

"No, we don't." I pull the hem of his shirt up, helping him lift it over his head, putting his gorgeous chest and broad, muscled shoulders on full display.

Exhaling a hum, I lean forward to trace my lips across his warm skin, inhaling the scent of soap and cedar. I open my mouth, and salt touches my tongue. His hand slides under the hem of my skirt, and I moan as his fingers fumble inside my panties to stroke and tease me.

"Owen..." I gasp, putting my arms around his neck, and moving closer so I can seal my mouth to his.

Lips part, tongues curl, and heat floods my body. He stands, turning me to face a small desk against the wall. He unfastens my bra, and my breasts spill out. He gathers them in both hands, lifting them as his thumbs slide over my tightened nipples, as he kisses the side of my neck.

His lips travel to my ear as he kisses the shell before giving me a low order. "Lean forward..." the scruff of his beard sends shivers through my body. "...and don't let go."

"Oh, God..." I do as he says, gripping the sides of the desk as he lifts the back of my skirt over my lower back and takes a knee.

They almost buckle when he jerks my panties down and off before burying his face between my thighs. His tongue goes straight to my clit, circling and massaging, up and down, again and again.

Whimpers slip through my lips, and I hold onto the

solid wood. My lips part, and my eyes flutter closed as orgasm surges through my core. I do my best not to let go, but my arms shake. The tightening pleasure curls in my thighs with every stroke of his tongue.

I'm right there, right on the edge. Shuddering moans grind in my throat, and I'm just about to break when he stops.

"Owen!" I cry. "Don't stop now!"

He huffs a laugh, kissing my shoulder as he shoves his pants down. "I said don't let go."

My body trembles when he slides the tip of his hard cock against my body, up and down my slippery core before finding the place and thrusting fully inside me.

He pushes me forward onto the desk, rocking his hips hard and fast as his hand slides around the front of my body.

"We're going to come together," he says at the back of my ear.

Two thick fingers take over where his tongue had been, circling my clit as he fucks me hard and fast doggy style. My hand slaps the top of the desk, and I push my hips back against him, needing more, deeper, faster.

"Yes..." he groans. "Right there."

We're feverish and desperate. His fingers don't stop, and he groans at the back of my neck where my skin is so sensitive.

I'm on my tiptoes, rising higher with every hard thrust, and with a strangled voice, he groans, "Come, Gina."

"Almost..." I gasp, eyes squeezed shut as my muscles tighten more with every stroke.

I hold my breath, arching my back, and when I feel the bite of his teeth against my shoulder, I cry out.

My body shudders, and I collapse forward. He catches me, holding me as we bow forward.

His stomach shudders at my back, and his groans are deep and sexy. We're breathless, clinging to each other as we come back from that gorgeous place.

We're still catching our breath as he steps back. He bends down and lifts me into his arms, carrying me to the bed. Leaving me a moment, he steps over to the small bathroom and returns with a warm washcloth to clean us both. Then he climbs in behind me, holding my back firmly against his chest in strong arms.

His lips press to my shoulder, then he kisses my neck, moving his nose into the side of my hair and inhaling deeply. "However long it took, despite what I went through, having you was worth it all, Gina Grace."

My eyes close, and I wrap my arms over his, smiling as I think about how we got to this place. "Dogs are the best."

His chest vibrates with a gentle laugh, and I close my eyes wrapped in love, shelter, and home.

"I THINK we might have to add snuggling by the fire with s'mores to our list of favorite things." I'm holding Maddie's hand as she sits on her dad's lap beside me.

She spent the morning opening presents around the Christmas tree while we all watched. Then we had a big Christmas dinner with the family—after which we called and "sang" Merry Christmas with Ladybird.

I had a fun group text with my cousins, and they sent pictures of baby Lucy having her first Christmas in Newhope. Gavin's family was there as well, and I laughed at the photo of the dynamic duo showing off their matching mouthguards. My heart was warm and only a little nostalgic. It looked like a fun time was had by all.

Now we're lounging on Owen's parents' back deck, wrapped in blankets under the twinkle lights, watching the flames flicker in the fire pit. Britt is at the picnic table behind us arranging graham crackers and Hershey's chocolate bars to receive the marshmallows Aiden is roasting for her.

"We can put it right after facials with real cucumbers and pigs in blankets," I continue.

Maddie nods rapidly, a smear of chocolate on her cheek. "S'mores are more delicious than cucumbers."

"It's true," I laugh, remembering the night after the dog show, her in her little robe with her turban on her head, eating cucumbers while we watched *Elf*. "And to think some people just use them to depuff their eyes."

She studies the graham cracker in her hand thoughtfully. "I saw my mommy in heaven last night."

It's like a record scratch. My eyes meet Owen's, and I sit forward, catching her gaze. "What did you say, honey?"

She nods, her little brow furrowed. "My angel mom came to see me last night after Santa Claus left."

"Are you sure you weren't having a dream?" Owen puts his hand on her shoulder, and she shakes her head no.

"She was dressed in white, and she was all glowy like the fairy in that movie Aunt Haddy made me watch with all the roller skates."

Owen and I exchange a glance. I know she's talking about the old movie *Xanadu*, which Haddy thinks should be a rite of passage for all seven- to nine-year-old girls. I think it has some adult language in it...

I'm still holding her hand, and I give her an encouraging smile. "What happened?"

Maddie tilts her head, still studying her s'more. "She told me not to be scared, because I was scared at first. Then she told me to look at the ceiling, so I did. She moved her hands like this..." Maddie moves her hands in a circle. "And you were there and you were there..." She points to her dad and me. "And she took my hand and put it in yours. Then she took your hands and put them together so we were all holding hands. Then she smiled and waved goodbye."

I look at Owen with wide eyes. My stomach twists, but he's smiling.

A calm expression is on his face, and he pulls his daughter close. "She was telling you that Mama G will always take care of you and love you the way I will. She wants us to be a family."

"She does?" Maddie's eyes are wide.

"Yep." My eyes heat, and I swallow the thickness in my throat. "It's true, honey, and I will."

My voice wavers, and Owen sits forward, putting his arm around my shoulders, drawing me closer to join their hug.

Then I notice additional hands on our backs, and I look up to see Aiden and Britt have joined us. It's the final sign, the dog biscuit on top, completing the circle. A home created not by fate, but by love.

Thank you for reading *Cage*!
Please use the QR code below to download your **Free Bonus Scene.**

Up next is ***Flow***, Maverick & Dove's roommates-to-lovers, fake dating hockey romance.
Hockey star Maverick Bradford has been in love with STEM

girlie Dove Rhodes since they were teenagers. For one semester, she'll be his roommate while she finishes her degree at CalTech. He's ready to shoot his shot. He's not ready for her to suggest they pretend to be in love...

Order your copy today on Amazon or whoever books are sold. Also available on duet audio.

NEW TO THE FAMILY?

PINCH is Gavin & Haddy's enemies-to-lovers, accidental pregnancy hockey romance. It kicks off the New Bradfords series with quirky characters, found family, hilarious doggy antics, angst, and *all the spice* you crave.

Keep turning for a short preview, or order your copy today on Amazon or wherever books are sold. Also available on duet audio.

Learn about all of my books on TiaLouise.com/Books, including a **downloadable Reading Guide.**

Scan for CAGE Bonus Scene.

PINCH

BY TIA LOUISE

Lane "Gavin" Knight is the hottest new defenseman for the LA Champions **hockey team.**

He's my cousin **Maverick's best friend,** and by trick of fate, **my new roommate.**

But just because he caught me when I fell off the "Welcome Back" parade float in my International Princess crown doesn't mean he's a hero.

I know him better than that.

Hayden "Haddy" Bradford is the most beautiful woman I've ever seen.

She's a princess, **a brilliant scientist...** And **she hates me.**

Until a purple-drink-fueled Halloween hook-up changes both of our lives.

It's something I've wanted a long time, but I never dreamed I'd have it with her.

Still, I'm the master of high-risk, high-reward plays, and I'll

do what it takes to show her I'm not the man she thinks
I am.

(*Pinch* is a hockey romance with enemies to lovers, roommates to lovers, a cocky bad-boy Hero, a sassy
STEM/pageant-princess FMC, an accidental pregnancy,
foster dogs, family, and loads of spicy fun. No cheating, no
cliffhanger, and no third-act breakup.)

1

———

Haddy

"Who says you can't be a beauty queen *and* a scientist?" My best friend, roommate, and first cousin Gigi Bradford slides her brush through the silky coat of a tall dog with a long nose secured in a large, empty tub.

As soon as the envelope appeared in our mailbox, I snatched it out and ran to her small grooming studio in our converted she-shed behind our rented house in Los Feliz.

I didn't want to open it alone, which is silly, I know. It's just a check in an amount that will cover my entire tuition, room, and board for my next semester of graduate school. Still, my fingers tremble as I carefully unfold the green paper and read the dollar amount.

A letter with a golden-embossed "Congratulations, Princess!" printed across the top is also enclosed.

"It's kind of embarrassing." My voice lowers as I recall Dr. Warwick's face when I told him why I wouldn't be returning as his graduate assistant in the fall.

Winning International Princess Woman will allow me to focus on my lab work without the extra strain of grading papers and proctoring exams.

"Why are you embarrassed?" Gigi's nose wrinkles. "It's simple genetics, same as in the dog world."

"Don't say it…"

"You're just like your mother."

"You said it." I fall back against the porcelain-tiled countertop.

My cousin pauses, cutting her green eyes at me. "More like Princess Drama Queen."

"You can't be a princess and a queen. It's redundant."

"Whatever. Your mom is a meteorologist, which is why you love science, and your grandmother was Miss Georgia World. You're a natural for the nerdy International Princess Woman. It's in your blood."

"So you're saying I'm bred for it?"

"Exactly!" Gina shakes her head talking in a baby voice as she rubs both of her hands on the golden dog's muzzle. "Those silly scientists should understand. It's in your DNA. Yes, it is!"

It's annoying, but as a dog breeder, groomer, trainer, and judge in championship dog shows, it's how my cousin views the world.

I have a pedigree. My family excels in science *and* pageants with ridiculous names that pay a lot of money.

I study the large check. "For a program that awards millions in scholarships every year, I don't understand why they have to have the word *princess* in the title. It's demeaning. They should just call it 'International Scholarship Woman.'"

"But they give you a crown?" She tilts her head, glancing up at me.

"Yes."

"And you wear it at events along with an evening gown and a sash."

I exhale a heavy sigh. I can't argue. Such commitments do come with the title.

"Some women like to be princesses." Gina straightens, picking up a pair of sharp scissors.

"My professors are so confused." I fold the check and slip it into my pocket. It's too big for mobile deposit, so I'll have to make a special trip to the bank. "Calling me a princess only makes it weirder."

Gigi pushes a lock of strawberry-blonde hair behind her ear and leans closer to trim the dog's whiskers. "Your dad is the one who should be confused. He has enough money to cover all their bills and yours. You don't have to keep doing these pageants if they embarrass you."

"No." I shake my head determinedly. "I'm paying my own way. If I keep taking money from them, I'll always be a spoiled nepo-baby. No one will ever take me seriously."

Gigi's lips twist. "I'm pretty sure your mom married Uncle Hen because of that same independent streak. She understands you better than you think."

The woman smiling back at me from the cover of the pageant brochure has perfectly coiffed, wavy blonde hair, and she's wearing a white, strapless dress with a red and white striped sash that reads *International Princess Woman*. It's basically how I look at events, only my hair is dark brown and long waves, which makes my blue eyes more noticeable.

"It doesn't matter." I shake it off. "Winning this means I'll be able to finish my research without having to worry about money. I'll happily pivot, hold, smile, and wave all day for that privilege."

"Don't forget you're riding on the *Welcome Back* float in the parade tomorrow." The screen door slams as our other cousin and third roommate Maverick Murphy enters the room. "We're rolling out at 10 a.m. sharp."

Gigi puts the scissors aside and unhooks the dog's leash. "We're just happy to be your ladies in waiting. Aren't we, Haze?"

"That dog's name is *Haze*?" Mav's dark brows furrow. "He's not even purple."

"*Her* name is Some Like it Hot Hazel, but I call her *Haze* for short."

"What the fuck?" He goes to the cabinet and opens the door, digging around. "What dog is going to come to *Some Like it Hot Hazel*? 'Here, Some Like it Hot Hazel!'" He pretends to call the dog, who doesn't even move. "See? Dog breeders are nuts."

"She's got better hair than I do." I walk over to slide my hand through her silky coat.

"She's an Afghan Borzoi. She'll be on the float with us tomorrow." Gigi helps the large dog out of the grooming pen then goes to our cousin. "Why are you digging in my supplies?"

"I need to borrow your good tweezers." Mav takes out the stainless-steel tool. "I've got something stuck in my blade."

"Maverick, no." Gigi reaches over his shoulder in an attempt to grab it. "I can't afford to have you break those. They cost two hundred dollars!"

"I can afford to replace them." He dodges her arms.

Gigi is five-eight like me, but Mav is six-two and wily. I shake my head at them wrestling like they're still kids as I head for the door.

Maverick makes enough money as the star right winger for the LA Champions to buy twenty sets of tweezers. He doesn't have to live with us. He just likes the company—and driving us crazy.

"I've got to finish grading papers. See y'all in the morning."

"Wave pretty," Maverick calls after me, and I wave my middle finger at him over my head. "That's my Princess. I'm so proud."

"Just like your mom," I yell back.

Mav's mother, our aunt Dylan, actually cried when she discovered that after years of trying to guide him into the "safe sport" of golf, her only son is the best hockey player in the southern region.

There was a lot of interest in him when he became a free agent, and he chose LA because we were here. He was only supposed to stay with us until he found his own place, then he never left.

We have an adorable two-story bungalow with four bedrooms and two bathrooms in the best part of LA, and not far from Caltech, where I attend school.

We weren't looking for a third roommate, but with the cost of everything these days, we were glad to have another person to share expenses.

He was more than happy to stay, especially since we all grew up like siblings. Say what he wants, Mav's a total family guy and an excellent chef, which Gina and I are not. So, perks!

"I'll bring the purple drink!" Gigi shouts after me, and I snort a laugh.

Purple drink is a New Orleans beverage made of purple Kool-Aid and Everclear. It's been in our family since before we were born, so of course, we ran off with the recipe as soon as we turned twenty-one.

"Purple drink before ten in the morning?" I turn, pushing the door open with my butt.

"Our mammas raised us right!" she replies with a wink.

If we're going to start the day with purple drink tomorrow, I definitely have to lock up in my bedroom tonight. It's possible I could be out for two days, and these finals won't grade themselves.

"WHY IS IT SO COLD?" I stand at the back of the line of cars with Maverick's coat around my shoulders. "October is supposed to be one of the best times to visit LA!"

"Talk to your mom," Gina quips.

"She'll just blame global climate change."

Maverick shoves a red Solo cup into my hand. "More purple drink. It'll warm you up."

"Hold my cup a second." I smooth my dark hair behind my shoulders before placing the crown on my head. "Help me pin this, Geeg."

"Hold Haze's leash." She passes the sparkling strap to me before taking the hairpins.

Under Mav's bright purple and black team jacket I'm wearing a sequined white dress with black accents to match the Champions' jerseys.

My *International Princess Woman* sash is in place, and a helper waits with the oversized bouquet of white and black roses I'll carry in the parade.

"Where do they get black roses?" Gina squints at the bouquet. "Will you be able to hold those *and* the safety bar?"

"Of course." I take the Solo cup from Mav. "This isn't my first rodeo."

Or pageant parade.

"Hurry up—it's almost time." He nods at my cup.

I take a big gulp, pulling my chin back as I swallow. "How much Everclear did you put in this, Gigi? You're not supposed to be able to taste it."

"Mav made it. I had a doggy emergency last night."

My blue eyes widen at Mav. A maniacal grin is on his face, and he nods, sticking out his tongue. "Extra strength, Princess!"

He takes another big gulp, but my stomach drops. "Maverick…"

I'm about to fuss at him, about how as a representative of the International Princess Woman Scholarship Program, I can't be drunk on a float, when a lady on a bullhorn orders all riders to take their place.

I'm already feeling the effects of too much grain alcohol when I take my first step up the short flight of stairs to the platform that will carry us through the crowd of fans lining the streets.

"Why didn't you warn me?" I hiss as I stow Mav's jacket behind the decorated podium I'll hold as I wave. "What's a doggy emergency anyway?"

Gigi arranges my skirt then positions Hazel and her own show dog, a white standard Poodle she calls Spanky (short for Spank My Bottom) at her side.

"One of the breeders had a breakdown. It might've been related to her messy divorce." Gigi makes a worried face. "By the way, we're fostering a dog for the next few weeks."

Before I can argue that *we said no more fostering dogs*, the attendant shoves the massive bouquet of roses into my arms.

"Hold these over your shoulder..." He proceeds to push my hair behind my back again. "Then hold this strap around your wrist."

"I need something sturdier than a strap." I'm still speaking as the guy walks to the edge and hops off the float. "Wait! I'm in three-inch heels!"

Not to mention I've had two cups of extra-strength purple drink.

The guy doesn't look back as he blends into the crowd of organizers preparing to roll.

Gigi steps closer. "Grab my arm if you get wobbly."

"And throw these flowers everywhere? They're heavy!" For a reason called *purple drink* mixed with the lingering, horrifying memory of dog vomit from our last foster pet, I want to sit down right here and cross my arms. "Who is this foster dog, anyway?"

"Oh, she's the cutest little thing!" Gigi smiles enraptured. "She's a little teacup poodle named Princess Petunia. You'll love her. She's practically made to be your pet!"

"I don't want a pet. Where is she now?"

"At the house." Gigi's eyes narrow. "Are you okay? You're swaying, and we haven't started moving yet."

She's right. I didn't eat breakfast, and it feels like the float is already rolling.

I'm in trouble.

"Hey, ladies!" Maverick waves at us from where he stands at the side of the float. "I want y'all to meet my new teammate. He's going to be staying at the house a few days while he finds his own place."

"Maverick!" Gigi's voice is loud and cross. "We didn't discuss this first!"

"You're one to talk." I'm still cross about our surprise

foster-dog. "If this new dog barfs in my bed like the last one—"

"You're going to love her," Gigi interrupts me.

Our cousin waves over a big guy with shaggy brown hair, then holds out a red Solo cup to him as he hustles up to give Mav a bro-hug.

"That's my man!" Maverick is still yelling, pointing at the guy whose back is turned.

The lady is on the bullhorn again, giving us all the ten-second warning.

Doing my best to shake off this buzz, I roll my shoulders back and adjust my posture. The float does a sharp lurch forward, and I wobble on my heels, jerking hard on the strap.

"Whoa..." It's a low yell, and Gina grabs my hand.

"Are you okay?"

"Yo, Princess, Maid Marian, over here!" Mav is yelling, and now his arm is looped around the new teammate's shoulders. "I present to you Gavin Knight of the dynamite, unstoppable Gav and Mav hockey duo!"

The tall fellow lifts his square chin, and ice-blue eyes blink up to mine. When they clash, cold water surges through my bloodstream followed quickly by fire.

He's standing there, all six-foot-two, broad shoulders, rounded biceps, square jaw with that dimple right in the middle of his cheek. Full lips part over straight white teeth, and my stomach dips.

I'm frozen as my mind tumbles back to my college days in Chapel Hill, North Carolina, my roommate Karen crying her eyes out on the sofa because the man she loved, the man she trusted, her first college boyfriend, was sleeping with every girl in the Tri-Delta sorority house.

I don't know when he started going by Gavin, but *Lane* Knight is the most notorious playboy I've ever met. He has the body of a god and the heart of a villain.

"No!" My voice is sharp, and I release the strap, taking a step in the direction of my cousin. "Not him!"

I guess purple drink makes me think I'm going to do something right here in the middle of a parade in my dress, crown, and three-inch heels.

The float starts to roll, and the words morph into a scream as I throw white and black roses into the air.

Spanky lunges forward, dragging Gina with him, as if he'll rescue me, but it's too late. Nothing is going to stop me as I fly through the air.

Nothing except the rock-hard chest of the world's biggest jerk, who I vowed to my college roommate I'd never speak to again.

With an *oof!* I land, Cinderella-style in his arms.

He has the nerve to catch me.

"Well, hello, Hayden." His chin dips, and he grins at me like the player he is. "Nice of you to drop in. I hear we're going to be roommates."

"Put me down." I struggle to get out of his strong arms.

He doesn't let me go. Instead, his eyes narrow. "I guess that's your funny way of saying thank you for saving your life."

"You didn't save my life. You only broke my fall." I push his chest, and he relents. "Like you break everything."

I said the last part under my breath, but I can tell he heard me by the way his jaw tightens.

I'm all set to walk away and take my place on the float again, when my heel catches in the hem of my gown, and with a loud rip, the bottom of my skirt disappears along with my appearance in the LA Champions official Welcome Back Parade.

Get PINCH (link) and fall in love with this small-town, brother's best friend, football romance today!

*Available in print, Kindle Unlimited and **on Duet Audio (link)**.*

BOOKS BY TIA LOUISE

ROMANCE IN KINDLE UNLIMITED

THE NEW BRADFORDS
PINCH, 2025*
CAGE, 2026*
FLOW, 2026*
ZONE, 2026*
CLAIM, 2026*
(*Available on Audiobook.)

THE BRADFORD BOYS
The Way We Touch, 2024*
The Way We Play, 2024*
The Way We Score, 2025*
The Way We Collide, 2025*
The Way We Win, 2025*
(*Available on Audiobook.)

THE BE STILL SERIES
*A Little Taste, 2023**
*A Little Twist, 2023**
*A Little Luck, 2023**
*A Little Naughty, 2024**
(*Available on Audiobook.)

THE HAMILTOWN HEAT SERIES
*Fearless, 2022**
*Filthy, 2022**
For Your Eyes Only, 2022
*Forbidden, 2023**
(*Available on Audiobook.)

THE TAKING CHANCES SERIES
*This Much is True**
*Twist of Fate**
*Trouble**
(*Available on Audiobook.)

FIGHT FOR LOVE SERIES
*Wait for Me**
*Boss of Me**
*Here with Me**
*Reckless Kiss**
(*Available on Audiobook.)

BELIEVE IN LOVE SERIES
Make You Mine
*Make Me Yours**
*Stay**
(*Available on Audiobook.)

SOUTHERN HEAT SERIES
When We Touch
When We Kiss

THE ONE TO HOLD SERIES
One to Hold (#1 - Derek & Melissa)*
One to Keep (#2 - Patrick & Elaine)*
One to Protect (#3 - Derek & Melissa)*
One to Love (#4 - Kenny & Slayde)
One to Leave (#5 - Stuart & Mariska)
One to Save (#6 - Derek & Melissa)*
One to Chase (#7 - Marcus & Amy)*
One to Take (#8 - Stuart & Mariska)
(*Available on Audiobook.)

THE DIRTY PLAYERS SERIES
PRINCE (#1)*
PLAYER (#2)*
DEALER (#3)
THIEF (#4)
(*Available on Audiobook.)

THE BRIGHT LIGHTS SERIES
Under the Lights (#1)
Under the Stars (#2)
Hit Girl (#3)

COLLABORATIONS
*The Last Guy**
The Right Stud
Tangled Up
Save Me
(*Available on Audiobook.)

PARANORMAL ROMANCES
One Immortal (vampires)
One Insatiable (shifters)

Books by Tia Louise

ACKNOWLEDGMENTS

So many people played a role in the writing of this book, and I had so much fun including friends in the planning and composition...

Always, always massive thanks to my husband "Mr. TL" for all the things he does, from encouragement to brainstorming to reading the first draft to support when I'm doubting everything... *I love you!*

My amazing PA Kat is The Best. Yes, she's my daughter, but she helps me more than I can ever say. *Thank you, Kat!*

The team who produces my covers and all the fun supporting art, illustrator Laura Moore (@LCMdesignss) and Kari March (cover design); Wander Aguiar (model photographer) and Lori Jackson (cover design). You always make my vision come to life, and *I love you all!*

Jen DeJong is my cheerleader, Leticia Teixeira is my guide when I'm stuck, Patti Rapozo is my sports pro, and Jaime Ryter is my eagle-eyed editor when all is said and done. *My A-Team!*

Huge thanks to my *incredible* betas, Maria Black, Corinne Akers, Amy Reierson, Courtney Anderson, Jennifer Christy, Heather Heaton, and Michelle Mastandrea. *I ADORE you all!*

To my awesome friends Heather S. (psychic sister), Ryan G. (photography), Meredith C. (LA location scout), Kim B. (hockey buddy), Melissa O. and Allyson J. (zany dog tricks). *My rockstars!*

Thanks to my dear Starfish, to my Mermaids, and to my Veeps for keeping me sane and organized and helping me spread the word and all the incredible influencers and book lovers, who I've come to think of as friends.

Last but not least, to my readers everywhere—***thank you*** for reading, sharing, reviewing, making art, and allowing me do what I do.

So much love,

 *Tia*

ABOUT THE AUTHOR

Tia Louise is the *USA Today* and #4 Amazon bestselling author of small-town, single-parent, second-chance, sports, and military romances set at or near the beach.

From Readers' Choice awards, to *USA Today* "Happily Ever After" nods, to winning Favorite Erotica Author and the "Lady Boner Award" (*lol!*), nothing makes her happier than communicating with fellow Mermaids (*fans*) and creating romances that are smart, sassy, and *very sexy*.

Connect with Tia:
  TiaLouise.com (signed copies)
  Instagram, @AuthorTLouise
  TikTok, @TheTiaLouise

GET THREE FREE STORIES!
Scan the QR code below to sign up for my newsletter and never miss a sale or new release by me!